The
Difficult Saint

By Sharan Newman from Tom Doherty Associates

The Difficult Saint

SHARAN NEWMAN

A TOM DOHERTY ASSOCIATES BOOK
NEW YORK

THE DIFFICULT SAINT

Copyright © 1999 by Sharan Newman

A Forge Book
Published by Tom Doherty Associates, LLC
175 Fifth Avenue
New York, NY 10010

Forge® is a registered trademark of Tom Doherty Associates, LLC.

Library of Congress Cataloging-in-Publication Data

Newman, Sharan.
    The difficult saint / Sharan Newman. — 1st. ed.
        p.   cm.
    "A Tom Doherty Associates book."
    ISBN 0-312-86966-5 (acid-free paper)
    I. Title.
PS3564.E926D5   1999
813'.54—dc21   99-26644
                                                     CIP

First Edition: October 1999

Printed in the United States of America

0 9 8 7 6 5 4 3 2 1

For Claire Eddy,
who trusts that I can get it right,
with thanks for sticking with me
through six books.

Acknowledgments

My thanks go to the following people.

Dr. Christoph Cluse, Universität Trier, for inviting me to the Institut für Geschichte der Juden and taking time off from his own work to help me with mine.

Prof. Susan Einbinder, Hebrew Union College, Cincinnati, for advice on the *derash* of Ephraim of Bonn's *Sefer Zekirah*.

Profs. John Van Engen and Michael Signer, Notre Dame University, for organizing the colloquium; *In the Shadow of the Millennium: Jew and Christians in the Twelfth Century*. The papers given there are now available from Notre Dame Press.

Yoram Gordon, for reading the Hebrew for me and translating the quotations.

Prof. Dr. Alfred Haverkamp, Universität Trier, for his warm welcome and for assembling such an impressive collection of material on Jewish History in Europe in such a short time.

Annegret Holtman, Universität Trier, for advice on the Jews of Germany during the Second Crusade and for making me feel at home in a strange town.

Prof. Stephen Jaeger, University of Washington, for checking my attempts at Mittelhochdeutsch and providing me with even better expletives, and also for allowing me to use his translation of Gottfried von Strassbourg at the beginning of Chapter Twelve.

Prof. Jeffrey Russell, University of California at Santa Barbara, for Latin advice and editorial and emotional support—more than I can ever repay.

Susan Shapiro, RN, for telling me what was wrong with Hubert and what to do about it.

Prof. Kenneth Stow, University of Haifa, for guiding me to experts on Ephraim of Bonn.

Prof. Richard Unger, University of British Columbia, for always getting my characters where they should be by the best route.

Prof. Bruce Venarde, University of Pittsburgh, for dropping his own work to do emergency research for me.

Fr. Chrysogonus Waddell, Gethesemani Abbey, for reading the first draft and making sure the monks and nuns obeyed the customs of the time; and also for sending me Bernard of Clairvaux's 1146–47 itinerary. That man traveled more than I do.

Luci Zahray, R.Ph. M.S., toxicologist, for helping out with plant studies and giving me a way to solve the mystery.

As usual, all of these people did their best to help me be as accurate as possible. Any mistakes are solely due to my own inability to transmit the knowlege properly.

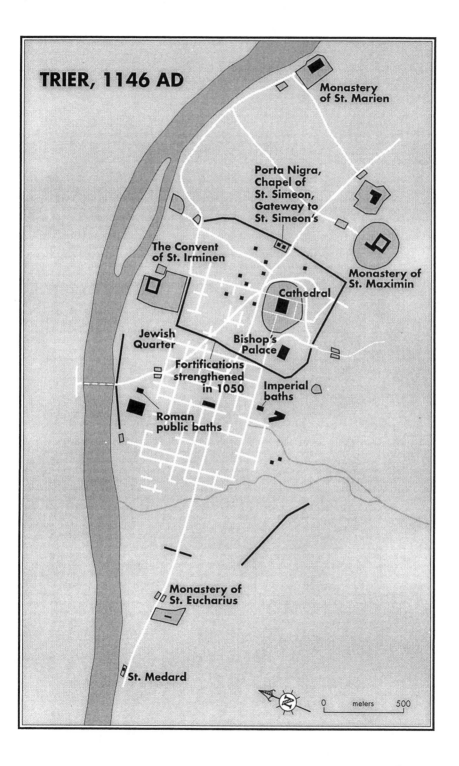

TRIER, 1146 AD

Monastery of St. Marien

Porta Nigra, Chapel of St. Simeon, Gateway to St. Simeon's

The Convent of St. Irminen

Monastery of St. Maximin

Cathedral

Jewish Quarter

Bishop's Palace

Fortifications strengthened in 1050

Imperial baths

Roman public baths

Monastery of St. Eucharius

St. Medard

0   meters   500

One

Paris, the home of Hubert LeVendeur and his family. Quin-
quagesima Monday, 2 ides of February (February 11), 1146;
27 Shevat, 4906. The third birthday of James, son of Catherine and Edgar.

אכתוב ספר וכירה פקודח
מקרת חנורה רעה וצרה שהוקרה יתר פלטה הנשארה מנורה הראשונה
המרה. ברוך ה נאמרה ש קיימנו ללוכרה ברחמיו יוקֿמֿןו במהרה משופכי
דמינו

I shall write a book of remembrance, telling the incidents of
the decree, regarding the evil and adversity which happened
to the few who survived the first bitter decree. "Blessed be
the Lord," we declare, "for having kept us alive to remember
his mercy and take revenge from our bloodshed."

—Rabbi Ephraim of Bonn
Sefer Zekhirah

*H*ubert leaned back in his chair with a worried sigh. "It will mean the ruin of us, you know, total ruin."

His daughter Catherine looked up from her sewing.

"Just because King Louis says he's going on an expedition to the Holy Land, that doesn't mean anyone will follow him," she assured her father. "It's only Edessa that fell, not Jerusalem. I heard that the nobles aren't very enthusiastic about taking their men to fight the Saracens, nor is Abbot Suger."

Hubert wouldn't be comforted.

"In the middle of winter, no one wants to fight," he muttered. "But just wait until spring. The first warm day and they'll all be sharpening their swords, eager for something to conquer."

"I wouldn't worry, Hubert." Catherine's husband, Edgar, spoke from the corner where he had set up his carving apparatus. "There are enough small wars here in France to keep them busy."

Hubert shook his head. "You don't know what it's like, armies swarming across the land, determined to destroy the infidel. I remember . . ."

He was silent a moment. Then he pulled himself up again.

"Bad for trade," he stated. "No goods will get through; it will drive me to poverty. We'll all end up ragged beggars living in the street."

Catherine set the sewing down and went over to her father. She put her arms around him, knowing that it wasn't the loss of trade that he feared, but a repeat of the massacres of 1096, in which he had lost his mother and sisters and, for a long time, his faith.

"It won't happen again," she whispered. "The king has shown

no animosity toward the Jews. There are even those who say he's overindulgent to them."

She wanted to remind her father that in the eyes of the world he was a Christian, as she and Edgar were in fact. But she only hugged him more tightly. Though it grieved her, Catherine understood how ashamed Hubert was of allowing himself to be rescued from the soldiers, baptized and raised as a Christian. Now it was too late for him to return publicly to the faith of his ancestors. He had married a Christian woman, had three children and now, grandchildren, whose lives would be forever altered if the truth were known.

Hubert accepted the embrace but not the solace.

"It's not the king I fear, but the soldiers, the townspeople—the faceless, furious mob that a moment ago had been people I knew, some even my friends." He shook his head.

"Hubert!" Edgar's voice was sharp. "That was fifty years ago. People know better now. It won't happen again. We have more immediate matters to worry about."

Catherine threw her husband an angry glance. However, the words caused Hubert to shake himself, take a deep breath and gently release the arms clasped around his shoulders.

"Quite right, Edgar," he said. "Trouble will find us soon enough without our going in search of it. What particular matters were you thinking of?"

Edgar put down the pincers he had been using to lay gold wire onto the lid of a wooden box.

"The one that just rode past the window." He grimaced. "I saw him through the gap in the shutter."

His words were almost drowned out by a heavy pounding at the outer gate.

"Who is it?" Catherine asked anxiously. The previous conversation had made her nervous. "Where are the children?"

"All upstairs," Edgar answered. "They're in no danger. But I can't believe that bastard has returned. What can he want with us now?"

"Which bastard?" Hubert asked.

Catherine shivered, although the fire was radiant. In the seven years she had known Edgar they had encountered a number of bastards.

There was a stomping of boots in the corridor and a moment later the visitor was announced.

"Sir Jehan de Blois." Ullo, the page, barely had time to get the words out before he was pushed aside.

The man scowling at them from the doorway was of middle height and lean with a face lined by years of fighting and travel in all weather.

Hubert leaped to his feet.

"Agnes?" he asked. "Is she all right?"

The visitor's scowl deepened.

"Your daughter is in excellent health, Master Hubert," he said. "No thanks to you. She has sent me to remind you of your duty to her; it's been forgotten long enough."

"Don't you speak to my father in that way, Jehan." Catherine couldn't allow the slur to go unanswered. "It's Agnes who has denied us. She exiled herself to Blois."

The knight refused to look at her. He concentrated on Hubert alone.

"The Lady Agnes sent me with a message for you. She wishes you to know that her grandfather, Lord Garnegaud, has arranged a marriage for her," Jehan began stiffly.

"Oh, no! Not to you!" Catherine couldn't contain her wail of dismay.

She was immediatly stabbed by Jehan's look of fury and despair.

"Oh," she said more softly. "Not to you."

"If she's worried about her dowry," Hubert said, "I can assure you that there will be no problem about it. There's land from her mother that was marked for her and I'll provide whatever else is needed."

Jehan repressed a sigh at the interruptions. Catherine almost felt pity for him. She knew how long he had loved Agnes, almost as long as he had hated Catherine. Now he had to help arrange to give Agnes to another.

"May I continue?" the knight asked.

Hubert nodded.

"Her request is indeed that you provide the dowry required as well as the jewelry her mother left behind when she entered the convent," Jehan said.

"Of course," Hubert answered. "Although Catherine should be allowed to decide on the allotment of the jewelry, as well. When will the wedding be and to whom?"

"She is marrying a Lord Gerhardt of Trier." Jehan swallowed. "His fief is, I understand, not far from that city."

"Trier? But that's in Germany!" Hubert said. "So far away! And Agnes has no German. What could Garnegaud be thinking of?"

"He didn't tell me." Jehan stared over Hubert's head. It was obvious that he wanted to be away from there.

"No, of course not." Hubert was deep in thought. "The dowry was mainly land from her mother's dower and that's in Blois. Does she want me to give her the value in money or to retain the income from the property?"

Jehan sighed. "I have no information on that. However, if you wish to question her yourself, she will receive you this evening."

"She's in Paris?" Hubert exclaimed. "And she didn't come to us?"

Hubert swallowed the pain. He should have expected this. He knew why his youngest child refused to visit him, why she had allowed herself to be betrothed without his consent.

The fact that Hubert had been born a Jew had been a secret, known only to his wife and later, his brother, Eliazar, who had long thought Hubert had been killed with the rest of the family. When Catherine discovered the relationship she had been able to accept it, partly because she found she liked her Jewish relatives and partly because of the attitude of her teachers, Abelard and Heloise. They had kept her from absorbing the contempt for the Jews felt by most Christians.

A few years earlier Agnes had discovered the secret and been both horrified and repulsed. She had told no one, as far as Hubert knew, but the knowledge of his apostasy and Agnes's belief that this was part of what had driven her mother into madness and the care of the nuns had combined to destroy all the love and respect she felt for him. Of course she would refuse to come to his home.

Edgar hadn't moved from his corner. He knew Jehan well of old, mostly as the man holding the other end of the knife threatening him. Jehan seemed to have an uncanny talent for choosing to be on the opposite side of those Edgar supported. And Jehan had no scruples about crushing anyone in his way. The less Edgar had to do with him, the better he liked it.

Still, Jehan was waiting for some reply. Hubert seemed lost in thought and Edgar could tell that Catherine was about to say something that would only antagonize their visitor further.

"If you tell us where she is, Jehan," he said quietly, "then you'll have fulfilled your task and can leave."

Edgar tensed as Jehan examined him, grimy in his old work clothes. The man's eyes widened as he noted the smooth leather-covered stump where Edgar's left hand had been. They flicked back to Edgar's face.

"She's at the convent of Monmartre," he told them. "She'll expect you this evening between Vespers and Compline."

"Tell her we'll come or send word," Edgar told him.

Jehan nodded, then turned and left. He neither bowed nor took formal leave. They heard his voice in the corridor, cursing someone. Then the outside door slammed shut; the knocker clanked in reproach.

A moment later the curtain to the hall was slowly pushed aside.

"Now what do you want—" Catherine began. Then she saw who it was. "Oh, Solomon, you picked the worst time to arrive!"

Solomon ben Jacob was the only Jewish member of the family Hubert had left in Paris. Two years earlier Hubert's brother and business partner, Eliazar, had petitioned the Jewish community at Troyes to move there and had been accepted. The move had been forced by an anonymous accusation against the two men that threatened to expose their relationship. Solomon, nephew to both Hubert and Eliazar, now alternated between the two towns when he wasn't on a trading journey.

He was also Catherine and Edgar's best friend. They normally greeted him with more enthusiasm.

"Your sister is being married in Trier? But that's wonderful!" he exclaimed when they had told him why Jehan had been in the house. "What are you all so sour about?"

"She's only asked for her dowry. She hasn't even invited us to attend the wedding," Catherine said. "Not that I could, with the children and all."

But her face showed that it hurt her.

"That really is unreasonable of her," Solomon said. "Why should she cut you off just because you aren't ashamed of being related to me? If I don't mind, why should she?"

But his face showed that he knew why very well.

"Since we're not likely to have anything more to do with her, I don't see why you're pleased about the marriage," Hubert said.

"Because of the place, of course." Solomon sat himself on a low stool by the fire and looked around expectantly. "Where's the pitcher?"

"Oh, I'm sorry." Catherine was brought back to her duty as hostess. "I'll get it. Wine or beer?"

"Beer, for now," Solomon answered. "But when I get to Trier I want wine. Don't you see, Hubert? With your daughter living there, we could have a chance to get into the wine trade on the Moselle. We do well enough with Burgundy, but we might add a whole new region if we could buy that far east and even make a deal to export Burgundian wine to Denmark and the north countries."

Hubert stroked his chin. "But Agnes won't help. She's ashamed of my being a merchant even without the fact of my Jewish birth. And what of the *kehillot* at Trier? We can't steal business from fellow Jews."

"No, but we could arrange for them to expand their trade into Burgundy and Champagne," Solomon argued. "It would be advantageous for everyone. And if you appeared there, what could Agnes do?"

"It's a pointless argument, Solomon," Hubert said. "If you want to do business in Trier, then go. But there's nothing to be gained from Agnes's being there, too. I won't put her in a position where she has to either denounce me or pretend to give me welcome."

"I agree," Catherine said. She sniffed and tried to hold back the tears.

Edgar got up and went to Catherine, putting his arm around her shoulders. Catherine brushed her cheek against the empty space where his hand should have been. He pulled away a fraction. She sighed. Two years now since the hand had been lost and he still needed her to remind him that his touch didn't upset her. Why couldn't he believe that she loved him no matter what life did to his body?

She looked at him and he smiled.

"Um . . . Catherine." Solomon's voice brought her back with a start. "No woman should look at her husband like that. It makes other people discontented."

Edgar laughed. "If you stayed in one place long enough, Solomon, you might have a wife, too."

"Ah, but what kind could I hope for?" Solomon laughed. "With my luck she might be just like Agnes."

Hubert had been paying no attention to the conversation. His thoughts were jumbled and his throat tight from the pain of his daughter's rejection. He picked up the beer pitcher and shook it. Empty. He glared at Solomon.

"This will wait until tomorrow," Hubert stated. "We'll send word to Agnes that we'll see her in the morning instead of tonight. I need to sleep on this news. And to think that just a few moments ago I had nothing more to worry about than war and impoverishment. I should have rejoiced."

Solomon left soon after and Catherine and Edgar went upstairs to check on the children and prepare for bed. In the alcove James was sound asleep, a toy horse clutched in his fist. Next to him lay Margaret, Edgar's half sister, one arm thrown protectively over her nephew. Edana, the daughter conceived in the midst of war in England, was in the trundle bed beneath. She was now a year and a half old and would be promoted to sleeping with the others as soon as she stopped wetting.

Edgar drew open the curtain hiding their bed. He had brought up a pan of coals to warm the sheets before they got in, but he was hoping Catherine would help him heat them further.

Catherine took her time undressing and rebraiding her hair. Edgar could tell she needed to talk.

"There's nothing you can do for your sister now," he said gently. "Not unless you renounce the rest of us."

"I know that." Catherine slipped into the bed and rolled toward the wall to make room for him.

Edgar dropped his *brais* on the floor and climbed in. She rolled back against him, her head on his chest.

"It just seems so odd that Agnes would want to go so far and marry a stranger," she continued. "It's not as if she were a princess or a great lady who needed to seal an alliance with her body. She could have chosen someone she already knew."

"Like you did?" Edgar smiled.

"Well, since the first time we met you threw yourself at me and knocked me to the ground, I wouldn't recommend it."

"There was a body falling on you," Edgar reminded her. "I was trying to save you from being hurt."

"That's what you say now." She idly spun circles around his navel with her finger. "I think you just wanted to get on top of me."

The circles spiraled down his belly, and Catherine found something rising to greet her.

"How nice." She smiled contentedly. "Some things never change."

Edgar reached up and closed the bed curtain.

At the abbey of Clairvaux in Champagne there was also worry about the king's plan to wage war in the Holy Land. Abbot Bernard considered it only proper that Louis should go. The king still hadn't done penance for his sin of burning a church full of people at Vitry during his war with Thibault, Count of Champagne. Saving a city for God would be the least he could do after committing such an enormity. But Bernard was not as enthusiastic over the rumors that Queen Eleanor had decided to accompany her husband.

As usual, it had been laid on the abbot to bring the people of Christendom together for this great expedition.

Both his former acolyte, now Pope Eugenius III, and King Louis had begged him to preach. Only his influence, they insisted, would convince both the lords and the people to give their support to the endeavor.

Bernard sat in the speaking room, surrounded by monastic secretaries and piles of parchment and writing tablets. He was a man of middle height, thin and pale from ascetic fasts. Yet there was nothing weak about his spirit. All the energy he might have spent as a warrior, lord and husband he had channeled into his quest for God and the service of the faith.

The abbot looked up from the letter he was reading.

"Nicholas," he said.

The clerk was beside him in an instant.

"Are the encyclicals ready to be sent out?" Bernard asked. "Have you finished copying the letters for me to sign?"

"All complete, my lord abbot," Nicholas answered. He was an energetic young man, with sharp eyes and an air of competence.

"Have them ready for me after morning work," Bernard told him. "Have you ordered that crosses be made to give out to the pilgrims?"

"Yes, lord, the cellerar has arranged for the nuns of Jully to cut them for you."

Nicholas bowed, waiting for another command to perform perfectly.

Bernard only nodded. "Excellent, as always, my son. Now, I should like to retire to my cell for a time to meditate alone. Thank you for your assistance."

The monks bowed and left. Nicholas remained a moment.

"Is there nothing more I can do for you, my lord?"

The abbot shook his head. He eyes had already closed as he prepared to pray. They opened again.

"Yes, Nicholas," he said quietly. "Please close the door when you go."

Nicholas returned to the scriptorium, where a dozen men were making copies of the abbot's writings.

"Brother Geoffrey," he said, looking over the monk's shoulder. "I believe the ablative form is called for in this sentence."

Geoffrey looked up. Nicholas could tell he was almost biting his tongue in half in the effort not to make a sharp retort.

"The accusative would be more appropriate, in my estimation," Geoffrey said finally. "But I shall, of course, change it according to your wishes."

"Not mine!" Nicholas held up both hands in denial. "Abbot Bernard's. All I do is at his command."

Geoffrey returned to his work. Once he was certain that Nicholas was out of the room, he allowed himself to mutter his disbelief. The monk next to him nudged him.

"Don't worry, Geoffrey," he said. "The abbot is too trusting of his friends, but one day even he'll see the truth about Nicholas."

"And until then?" Geoffrey scowled.

"Do what I do." The monk smiled. "Offer up time spent with him as a penance."

Geoffrey considered. "Yes, I suppose I could also pray that he receives a martyr's death, as such a saint deserves."

He went back to his work in a much more cheerful frame of mind.

Jehan returned to the convent to tell Agnes that her family would call upon her. She met him in the portress's hall. As always, her frail blond beauty took his breath away. He never understood how she could be sister to Catherine, who was dark and headstrong. Jehan had long suspected that Catherine was some sort of demon insinuated upon Hubert as a false daughter in order to destroy the world. She seemed very talented at destroying his.

"I don't know why you insist on seeing your family," he complained to Agnes. "They haven't changed at all. I saw that Jew when I left, coming in as if he had a right to be there."

Agnes cringed.

"That's why I won't have them interfering in my life," she said. "I only want what's mine by right. Afterwards I plan to get as far away from them as possible so they can't shame me before my husband's family."

It was Jehan's turn to cringe.

Agnes noticed. She put her hand on his arm.

"I'm sorry, Jehan," she whispered as the portress looked on, guarding against any improprieties. "And I'm very proud of you for planning to join the soldiers of Christ and find glory in the Holy Land."

"Yes," Jehan answered, mindful of the woman listening. "It is, of course, the closest a man like me can come to the religious life."

His expression suggested that it was a lot closer than he had ever intended.

"I plan to come to Vézelay." Agnes tried to cheer him. "To see you receive the cross from the hands of Abbot Bernard, himself."

"The day will be that much brighter because of your presence," he answered, his voice toneless.

When he had left and Agnes was alone in the guest house, she sank down onto the bed. After a moment, she pulled herself onto her knees, reached out and slid the curtains shut. Then she allowed herself to lie flat, her face in the pillows, crying silently but thoroughly.

The winter rain streamed down on the house, causing sudden eruptions of steam in the hearth. It was barely past midday but gloomy and dark out. Catherine, Solomon and Edgar sat on pillows by the fire, baby Edana asleep on Catherine's lap. James, his brown curls perpetually tangled, was being chased around the hall by twelve-year-old Margaret. Edgar and Catherine had brought her back from Scotland with them after her mother died. Her long red braids had come undone and, as she passed Solomon, he would make a feint at catching the loose hair. She would get close enough to make him think he could grab her and then slip away laughing.

Hubert sat on the one comfortable chair next to the fire and watched them with a lump in his throat.

This is how it should always be, he thought. Why do moments like these never last?

As James went flying past, Edgar reached out with his good hand and caught him, tumbling him onto the pillows.

"Aren't you ready to take your nap yet, young man?" he asked.

"No, Papa." James grinned. "First I kill the dragon."

He got up again at once and began racing the circuit of the room again, yelling battle cries.

"I almost think he does see a dragon," Catherine said.

"At his age, I always did." Edgar smiled.

Catherine gave him a sideways glance. Having met Edgar's uncle Æthelræd, she was half inclined to believe he had. She decided to change the subject.

"Shall we all go to visit Agnes this evening?" she asked. "Perhaps seeing the children will soften her heart."

"Or convince her never to have any of her own," Solomon suggested as James careened into him. "I'm not your dragon, Sir James!"

James, switching roles, roared at him.

Edgar watched them. "I think James and Edana can remain here," he decided. "I don't remember Agnes as being that fond of small children, do you?"

Catherine was embarrassed to realize that she didn't know.

"It's been so long," she said. "I don't know my own sister anymore."

She bit her lip in worry.

"What am I going to wear?"

Catherine settled for a proper matronly *bliaut* of green and blue embroidered with spring flowers at the collar and hem. With some effort, she had managed to get all of her hair braided and covered so that no stray curls emerged from under the scarf. That didn't keep her from being ridiculously nervous as they were ushered into Agnes's presence in the convent visitor's room.

Agnes looked at them all as if meeting strangers. Then her eyes widened as she saw Edgar's left arm.

"Saint Ambrose's three-tailed whip!" she exclaimed. "What happened to you?"

She stopped. "I mean . . ." she started again.

"It's all right, Agnes," Edgar said. "I got between a man with a sword and his victim. That's all."

"I . . . I see." Agnes couldn't keep her eyes from the emptiness at the end of the arm.

"Is that what you called us here for?" Catherine asked, ever protective of Edgar's feelings. "If so, we can leave at once."

"Catherine!" Hubert's voice was sharp. "This is as hard for her as it is for us. Agnes, I'm very happy to see you again. You are more beautiful than ever, just like your mother."

He paused at her expression. He shouldn't have mentioned Madeleine.

Agnes took a deep breath. "Perhaps we could all start again," she said. "Father, Sister, I wanted you to rejoice with me at my contract of marriage. I ask nothing from you but the dowry and property that is rightfully mine."

She was daring them to object.

Hubert nodded slowly. "I trust that your grandfather investigated this man before he allowed you to agree to the contract."

"Of course," Agnes answered. "Grandfather is old, but as sharp as ever. Sharper. This time he made sure that Gerhardt's family was also above reproach."

"Agnes!" Catherine shouted. "How can you hurt our father so!"

She wished she were still young enough to pull Agnes's hair and rub her face in the mud.

Agnes faced her, fury barely in check. "I see that you at least, are just the same, beloved sister."

Catherine heard the scorn in Agnes's voice. She pressed her lips together to keep from answering in anger.

"I was once just that, Agnes," she said softly. "Just as you were to me."

Her sister blinked hard for a moment, but no tears escaped.

"That was long ago," Agnes stated. "Now we have only duty holding us to each other. I am here to ask if you'll fulfill yours."

Hubert answered for all of them.

"You are welcome to all we have, Agnes, to impress your new husband. I'll send a troop of men to guard you and find waiting women. We wish you well in your new life."

Agnes's expression didn't change. She might have been carved from the wall she stood before.

"Very well," she answered. "That's all I need from you. You may go."

"Agnes, please!" Catherine stepped toward her.

"Don't touch me!" Agnes was on the edge of screaming. "All of you. Don't try to pacify me. There's nothing you can do. All I want is my share of Mother's jewels and never to see any of you again."

"Of course, child," Hubert said. "If you insist. But you must understand . . ."

"I do, Father, all too well." Agnes turned away from him. "You chose those infidels instead of me, instead of my poor mother and instead of Our Lord. I refuse to be damned along with you. There's nothing more to say."

She fumbled with the latch on the door and swore under her breath. Then the door opened and she was gone.

Edgar, Catherine and Hubert looked at one another.

"That didn't go very well, did it?" Edgar said.

Hubert's face was grey. "My beautiful, golden child. What have I done to you?"

Catherine put her hand on his shoulder. "We are all to blame," she said. "I could have helped her understand when she found out you and Eliazar were brothers. Even earlier, I ignored her for my books. I should have helped her more when Mother began to fail. But it's too late for regret."

Hubert sighed. "My poor Agnes; I only wish I could win back her love."

"Father," Catherine said. "She's made it clear. She doesn't want our love. She doesn't want us at all."

In her room, Agnes sat and unfolded a square piece of vellum. She touched the wax seal, feeling the pattern beneath her fingers. It was her betrothal contract, her last chance for the security she craved.

Happiness was more than she expected.

The castle of Gerhardt of Trier was perched north of the city high above the east bank of the Moselle River. It had been rebuilt in stone by his father only ten years before. The walls were still raw from the quarry and the ruts made in the earth from dragging the the blocks up the hill were still deep in the road. Below, the slope was covered in vines all the way down to the river path. Grapes were his family's gold. They owed the land and military service to the archbishop, but the vines had been theirs since the time of Constantine and Gerhardt was as proud of the wine from them as any other craftsman of his work. As he should be; the wine was among the best in the region. Gerhardt oversaw its production personally. He was the one who decided the days for picking and pressing and when the barreling should end. It was a long family tradition.

This day he was being unpleasantly reminded of another long family tradition.

"How could you do this without asking me!" he wailed at his brother, Hermann.

"We did ask you," Hermann said patiently, glancing around at the rest of the family, consisting of their sister, Maria, her husband, Folmar, and Peter, Gerhardt's thirteen-year-old son.

"He did, Father," Peter confirmed. "I said I wanted a new mother and you said you hadn't time to find me one and so Uncle Hermann said . . ."

Gerhardt put his hands over his ears.

"I know what Hermann said." He glared at them all. "But I can't believe he would act on it. I don't want another wife. I can't marry again."

"But, Gerhardt, you signed the contract!" Maria was shocked. "You can't change your mind now!"

"But I never made up my mind!" Gerhardt uncovered his ears only to tug at his long, blond hair. "How could I have signed a contract?"

Hermann coughed. "Well, do you remember when I gave you those documents having to do with the purchase of the property in Köln?"

"The houses I bought from the monks of Regensberg." Gerhardt nodded. "Of course. You and Folmar handled that well, Brother."

"Yes, thank you." Hermann smiled tightly. "The fourth one, and I told you quite clearly, was the contract of betrothal to Agnes de Bois Vert, of Blois."

Gerhardt sat stunned. He hadn't been paying much attention at the time. There were so many other things to do. Could he have signed himself, body and soul, to some woman from France? He shivered. It was possible. And it was impossible. He rounded on his brother-in-law, who had stayed silent up to now.

"Folmar, how could you agree to this?" he asked. "You know well that I can't remarry now!"

Folmar gave a gesture of helplessness. "I wasn't consulted, Gerhardt."

Gerhardt raised his eyes to heaven, but no advice came from that direction. So he pounded the wall with his fist.

"There is no way I will marry this woman!" he shouted.

Maria took his hand and gently examined his fingers to see if any were broken.

"*Wie gehabet ir dich so?*" she asked her brother. "From all accounts this Agnes is beautiful, docile and pious. She comes with a fine dowry and an excellent lineage on her mother's side. Her father is a wealthy merchant of Paris—very wealthy. I don't believe there is any thing you can find fault with in our selection, Gerhardt. It's not as if our family were that well born."

"It's not that." Gerhardt knew he couldn't give them the real reason for his intransigence. They'd never accept it. "I don't want to remarry. I'm happy as I am. I have a fine son. There's nothing more I need, least of all a French bride. You have to cancel the contract."

Hermann pursed his lips. "We can't do that, Brother," he said. "We swore oaths before witnesses and you signed the contract. By now the girl's most likely ordered new robes and begun packing. No, if you don't want to marry, you're going to have to tell Agnes yourself, and take the consequences."

Gerhardt groaned. They found his misery baffling and a bit amusing. Even Peter, his own child! They all thought that once he saw she was a perfectly nice young woman, he would accept his fate and go happily into wedlock.

But Gerhardt knew that to do so would be to send himself straight to hell. And, if he revealed his reasons, he feared that the fires would reach him long before he died.

Two

A field outside Vézelay. Sunday, pridie kalends April
(March 31), 1146; 15 Nisan, 4906. Easter Sunday, the first
day of Passover.

*Anno Verbi incarnati millesimo centesimo quadragesimo sexto, glo-
riosus rex Francorum et dux Aquitanorum Ludovicus, regis filius
Ludovici, cum esset viginti quinque annorum, ut dignus esset
Christo, Vezeliaco in Pascha baiulando crucem suam, agressus est
eum sequi.*

In the year of the Incarnation of the Word 1146, the glorious
king of the Franks and duke of Aquitaine, Louis, son of King
Louis, in his twenty-fifth year, in order that he might be wor-
thy of Christ, at Vézelay on Easter resolved to follow him by
carrying the burden of his cross.

—Odo of Deuil
Book I
De profectione Ludovici VII in orientem

*T*he crowd in the field was so thick that Catherine couldn't see the men standing on the platform. Someone jostled her and she would have fallen if there had been space. As it was, she was pushed back into Edgar's arms.

"I'm glad now that we left the children with Willa and Margaret at the inn," he said, setting her upright with his good hand.

"I suppose they're too little to remember anyway," Catherine agreed. "I only wanted them to be able to tell their children that they had heard the preaching of Bernard of Clairvaux."

"We may be too far back to hear it ourselves," Edgar said. "In this mob, there's no hope of getting closer."

Catherine looked up at the platform tower at the north edge of the field. It had been built hastily when it was realized that the number of pilgrims come to take the cross was far more than would fit safely in the cathedral. Edgar shook his head when he saw the rickety structure, muttering that he hoped Saint Mary Magdalene, the patron of Vézelay, was guarding those present for it would be a miracle if anything built so roughly on that damp and sloping earth survived.

Catherine felt out of place among the mass of the faithful. She and Edgar had no intention of pledging themselves to a pilgrimage. They had already taken one to Compostela and received the miracle of James when they had almost given up ever having a living child. It would be hubris to ask God for more. But the excitement of the moment had drawn them to come and cheer those who did take the cross.

All pilgrimages were dangerous, of course. It was traditional to prepare for them as if one would never return. But this journey was even more likely to result in martyrdom for it was to be one of battle. The fall of the Christian town of Rohes, once called Edessa, to the Saracens the year before had stirred the young king to raise an army to free it.

Edgar noticed how many men of fighting age stood around him. He could feel their tension, almost see their visions of conquest and glory. He forced down the bile that rose in his throat. He told himself he had never been much of a warrior in any case. Now there was no chance of it. A soldier with one hand was as useless as a three-legged horse.

Sometimes he felt that his life had been a series of sudden changes. Meeting Catherine had taken him from the path his father had set him on toward a bishopric in Scotland. He had hoped that this would leave him free to work at carving and metalwork, something a nobleman should never do. Then, one stroke of a sword and he had been forced to begin again, teaching himself to work with only his right hand. His anger at the loss still bubbled close to the surface.

His bitter reflections were interrupted as he and Catherine were pushed forward by the throng around them. The abbot of Clairvaux, accompanied by the king, the bishop of Liège and other dignitaries, had climbed to the tower and begun to speak.

Catherine stood on tiptoe and squinted in an effort to make out the abbot's face clearly. She hadn't seen him since the day at Sens when Bernard had spoken out against her teacher, Peter Abelard. It had been hard for her to feel kindly toward the man, even though it was generally agreed that he was a living saint. But when she learned that Abelard and Bernard had been reconciled just before Abelard's death, she had decided she could do no less than forgive as well.

The faces of the people around her were upturned to catch the words like rain on dry earth. But she could hear nothing. The abbot's arms spread out, inviting all to join the king in his pilgrimage. Then he stopped and waited.

The response was instantaneous.

"Give us crosses!" the crowd roared. "Crosses!"

They surged toward the platform, causing some alarm among those perched on it. It swung wildly and one corner suddenly collapsed. The crowd gasped in horror as the abbot disappeared, leaving the king hanging from the railing, the floor sloping away from him. He was able to pull himself up as retainers rushed to shove the populace away and rescue the abbot.

"Dear Virgin, save them!" Catherine cried, echoing the shouts of the others.

Everyone held their breath until the head of Abbot Bernard appeared and he waved to show that he was unharmed.

Catherine exhaled in relief and joined the rejoicing.

"I thought he would be crushed!" she exclaimed to Edgar. "It's a miracle he wasn't."

"It's a miracle that thing didn't fall apart sooner," Edgar answered. "And look, those idiots are putting it together again so that Bernard can finish his sermon. Only a fool would go back up there!"

"Or a man of faith," Catherine reminded him.

Edgar gave her a look of exasperation. "*Carissima*, faith in God's providence is one thing. I have none in the skill of those carpenters."

Nevertheless, within a few moments, the platform had been repaired and Bernard and Louis climbed the ladder to resume.

The crowd chose to see this as an omen of success in the retaking of the city, and the level of fervor increased tenfold.

After he finished speaking, the abbot reached into a bag at his feet and began to distribute the cloth crosses to the men and women who pressed forward to receive them. Soon he began scattering them like seed upon the people below until the bag was empty. Still more people reached out to him. Bernard looked about for help and, getting none, took off his cowl and tore it to make more crosses for the faithful.

Despite himself, Edgar was carried along by the enthusiasm of the others. For a moment, it seemed to him that there was something he could do, that he mustn't be left behind. He started toward the platform.

"Edgar?" Catherine was left behind and tried to shove her way through, terrified of losing him in the throng. "Edgar!"

He didn't hear her. Someone knocked her aside and she fell in the muddy grass. Still the people moved forward, stepping over and then on her every time she tried to get up.

"Edgar!" she screamed again.

She felt someone grab her about the waist from behind and lift her to her feet.

"Thank you," she gasped. "I thought they would trample . . ." Her eyes grew wide as she saw the face of her rescuer.

"Jehan! I thought you'd be in the front of that mob!"

The man had recognized her, as well, and gave her a look that said he would have stomped on her, himself, if he had known who she was.

"I received my cross last night from the abbot personally," he answered proudly.

"Is my sister here with you?" Catherine asked. Perhaps here, amidst the fervor of the faithful, the two of them might find some reconciliation.

Jehan's face grew bleak. "I haven't seen her yet today. As she promised, she was here last night to see me accept my cross but then she vanished. I don't know where she is."

"But she must be here someplace!" Catherine automatically looked around, although it was impossible to see more than an arm's length and she was in danger of falling again as people pushed around her. "Help me search for her!"

Jehan didn't bother to answer. He simply gave her another look of disgust and vanished back into the crowd.

Catherine pushed against the mass of people, squeezing between bodies until she reached a less-populated area. Then she took a deep breath, shaken as much by the sight of Jehan in a pilgrim's cross as by nearly being crushed in the wild rush of the people to receive their badges.

Jehan. Solidier, knight, warrior. Implacable enemy. He had been on the fringes of her family for years, first as the friend of her uncle Roger, then as messenger for her father and grandfather and then as guard to Agnes. Through a number of ill-fated events Jehan managed to blame Catherine for every piece of misfortune he had ever had, not least that he had no chance of ever marrying Agnes.

She tried to find the charity to pity him. After a moment she shook her head. She wasn't a good enough Christian for that.

She climbed a bit up the opposite side of the field, trying to spot

Edgar's blond head above the others. It was hopeless. What could have possessed him to leave her like that? She could only hope he would find her later.

The tumult was far too great to find anyone. Catherine decided that the only sensible thing to do was to find a soft place to sit and eat the bread and cheese she had cached in her sleeve that morning. She found a mossy spot under a tree and settled, shaking the crumbs from the cloth as she munched. Sooner or later, someone would find her.

In another part of the field, Solomon watched the escalating madness with growing horror. He was uneasy among large numbers of Christians at the best of times and was only here because his uncle Eliazar had asked him to observe and report back to him. As more and more of the pilgrims came past him, faces effulgent with the vision of salvation and crosses pinned to their tunics, Solomon's disquiet became physical.

"Wait until they find that a piece of cloth won't stop an arrow," he muttered to his friend.

The man standing next to him smiled. It might have seemed odd that a cleric would respond so mildly to a slur on his faith, but Astrolabe came from an unconventional family and he had known Solomon a long time.

"I'm sure most of them will realize that and find some mail and a shield to add to their protection," he told Solomon. "People are looking at you, by the way."

An old woman was certainly staring at him. She caught Solomon's eye.

"What's wrong with you," she shouted. "A big, strong boy like you not going with the king! What's the matter? Think you have no sins to repent of?"

Solomon backed away from her. "If I thought I could free the Holy Land, I assure you, *bonne feme*, I would leave tonight."

She started to say more to him, but Astrolabe pulled his friend away.

"Don't even suggest it," Solomon snapped. "I won't put one of those things on, not even to save my life."

"I don't expect you to, but others will wonder." Astrolabe

grinned at a sudden idea. "I know. If anyone else asks why you're not taking the cross, I can tell them you have an serious infirmity that keeps you from fighting."

"Circumcision?" Solomon asked.

This time his friend laughed aloud. "Not at all. The fatal disease of levity," he said. "It will be the death of you, yet."

Solomon shook his head. "I don't take this lightly, I assure you. All I can think is, how long will it be before someone decides it would be easier to attack the Jews in France instead of going all the way to the Holy Land for Saracens?"

"That won't happen this time, Solomon," Astrolabe assured him. "Abbot Bernard wouldn't allow it. He was very clear about who the enemy is and he didn't mention Jews."

Solomon gave him a look of disgust. "He didn't have to, Astrolabe. What has been the text of the sermons for the past week? The death of your god at the hands of the Jews. Do you think none of these people listened to that?"

The other man's laughter stopped cold. "I'm not so naive as that, Solomon," he admitted. "I know that many of these people see no difference between the Jews in their midst and the Pharisees of old Jerusalem. Logic has no place in their world. My father learned that all too well."

"And I don't believe he ever changed his beliefs either," Solomon replied softly.

"No, he reconciled with Bernard but felt himself answerable to God alone," Astrolabe agreed. "Very well, point taken. I promise not to suggest it again."

"Thank you, now if you could only get my cousin Catherine to stop trying to get my soul into her heaven, I'd be much obliged."

"A woman taught by both my father and mother, are you mad?" Astrolabe gasped in mock horror. "I'd sooner try to convince a band of Saracens racing toward me with swords."

"In that case, why don't we go back to the inn and have some beer before that mob drinks the village dry?"

Astrolabe thought that a fine idea and the two men went back up the hill in complete accord. Behind them people stood proudly clutching their cloth crosses, aware only of the glory to come when they marched triumphantly through the Holy Land.

Edgar came to his senses again quickly with the first person who bumped against him and then noticed his missing hand. The sneers of strangers was something he would never become used to. They all assumed that he was a thief who had been justly punished.

"Out of the way, you stinking *mesfetor!*" The new soldier of Christ shoved Edgar aside. "Clear a path for honest men."

"*Mesel!*" Edgar shoved back. "Who do you think you are?"

The man spun around to retort and Edgar realized that he was in the middle of a well-armed circle of people who had just been exhorted strongly to kill the infidel. Perhaps he should have simply stood aside.

"What did you steal?" a woman jeered. "The church plate? Why couldn't you work like the rest of us?"

Edgar ignored her. The circle closed in. He swung at the first man that came for him. Someone picked up a rock.

"Hold! Hold there!" The voice came from above. It was that of someone used to being obeyed. "What's this? Attacking fellow Christians? Shame on you all!"

For a moment it crossed everyone's mind that the voice came from Heaven. There was a sigh of relief as they realized it was a man on a black war horse. This did not slow their obedience. Men on horseback wielded justice that was more sure and certain than divine retribution.

As the crowd fell away, Edgar looked up at his rescuer. The sun in his eyes made it hard to make out his features. Then the man leaned down, offering him a hand up.

"Walter of Grancy!" Edgar exclaimed in delight. "Saint Alban's persecuted priest! I am glad to see you!"

Walter, as tall as Edgar and twice as thick, easily lifted his friend up behind him on the horse. Edgar noticed that Walter, too, wore a cross.

"I'm going for the soul of my Alys," Walter said. "If I couldn't save her life, at least I can help make her place in Heaven more secure."

"A noble reason," Edgar said warmly. He and Catherine had helped Walter find the one who had killed Alys six years before and they had become friends.

"Don't give me my palm and crown, yet." Walter laughed. "I'll enjoy bashing a few Saracen heads. I'll need to, just to keep me in a charitable mood toward my fellow pilgrims, especially that one."

He indicated another mounted man not far away. Edgar's jaw dropped.

"Raynald of Tonnerre!" he gasped. "I can't believe it. But he's a murderer!"

Walter shrugged. "All the more reason to go to the Holy Land. How else could anyone expiate such a crime?"

Edgar could think of a number of ways, including the one his own father was enduring now, that of becoming a lay brother and working at the most menial tasks under the stern eyes of an English abbot. In comparison, dying in battle was infinitely preferable.

"Still," he said aloud. "I imagine that it's the only way that would be acceptable to Raynald and his father. Is Count William going as well?"

"No, just both his sons," Walter told him. "Now, how did you come to be at the center of a mob of angry peasants?"

Edgar explained, now ashamed of his momentary ardor. "Catherine, who didn't you . . . ?" he finished, then looked around. "Catherine! Walter, I thought she was right behind me. Saint Ethelwold's mighty organ! I've lost her. How could I be such an idiot?"

"I'm sure she'll tell you." Walter laughed. "Well, where was she when you last saw her? As I remember, we need only look for a spot where everyone seems to be tripping over something."

"Yes, that would be Catherine," Edgar said, not laughing. "But in this chaos how can we tell? Oh, *leoffest*, I hope your name saint is watching out for you."

Catherine had actually got well out of the pathway for once. However, she was soon joined by a collection of beggars who saw that she had more food than she needed.

"Please, kind lady," a woman pleaded. "For Christ's pity, help me feed my child."

Catherine gave her half the cheese.

"I've had nothing since Thursday." A man whose body was covered with open sores edged closer. "And no one will give me a place to rest."

Catherine tossed her bread to him and prayed he would go away.

Another woman only stared at her with eyes much too large for her thin face. Beneath her rags, Catherine saw that she was close to the end of her pregnancy, if she survived that long. She handed over the remainder of the cheese and her linen scarf.

That left only one man, who had seated himself next to her. He was as thin as the others and pale as a prisoner.

"I'm sorry," Catherine said. "I have no more food to give. I thought that here, of all places, there would be alms enough."

"There are never alms enough, good lady," the man looked at her with compassion.

There was something about him that made Catherine embarrassed that she had offered him charity. His clothes were as ragged as any of the poor but he had an air of calm, even contentment, that she had rarely seen in any human outside of the cloister.

"But we give so much," she said. "One would think that there should be no one hungry, except when all are."

"When the vessels of the Mass are bedecked in gold and jewels and women wear *bliaux* of silk trimmed with fur, then the poor will be with us," he said sadly. "But it need not be so."

Catherine looked guiltily at her clothes, then remembered that she was wearing wool and linen. But the man saw her expression and smiled.

She looked at him suspiciously. "Are you a follower of Arnold of Brescia or a Patarene?" she asked. "Would you have all people hold property in common, with no kings or lords?"

"Perhaps I'm nothing more than a monk who believes we should all live as monks." He was laughing at her, she could tell, although his face remained kind.

"If you're a monk, then why have you no tonsure?" she countered. "And, if we were all cloistered and celibate it would be but a short time before there was no one left on earth. Then where would we be?"

"In heaven, my lady," he stood. "Of course. May the Lord be with you."

"And with you," she responded automatically.

After he had gone, she sat for some time, going over the conversation in her mind.

"*He's a heretic,*" one side assured her.

"*But he said nothing counter to the Faith,*" Catherine answered.

"*Saying that all men should live as monks? That property should belong to everyone? That's not heresy?*" The voices were shocked.

"*Many of the fathers of the Church said the same,*" Catherine reasoned.

"Catherine! Thank God!"

Catherine looked up with a start. Edgar jumped down and took her in his arms.

"I was so worried," he said, holding her tightly. "I thought you'd been crushed. Instead I find you sitting alone, talking to yourself."

"Well, you abandoned me in the crowd," she explained. "Do you want me to talk to strangers? Where did you go?" She looked up then and recognized the man on the horse. "Walter! How wonderful to see you again. Will you dine with us tonight?"

Walter grinned and nodded.

Edgar stepped back but kept hold of Catherine's hand.

"You are all right, aren't you?" he asked. "I'm so sorry. I should have watched out for you."

Catherine brushed his cheek with her hand. "I'm fine," she said. "I was only afraid for you."

He pulled her close again. "The worst thing that could happen to me," he said, "would be losing you."

Above them, Walter turned his face away. He knew exactly what Edgar meant.

In the moment Catherine forgot all about the man who was not a beggar.

Their room at the inn was only a curtain across one end of a loft that didn't deaden the noise from below in the least. However, it was private. When Catherine and Edgar went up they found that Solomon had returned some time before, bringing Astrolabe, who had not procured a bed with the other clerics. They were playing some sort of clapping game with the children that even Willa, the young servant who took care of the little ones, was enjoying.

Catherine scooped up her baby daughter. She had been away from her all day and that was too long, although she had to admit that the freedom weaning had given her was nice.

"Edana, *ma douce*, have you been good today?"

Edana giggled something unintelligible. Catherine looked to James for a translation.

"She says she was very good, Mama," James told her, "but that's not true. She chewed on the soldiers Papa made for me. They're all wet and bitten now."

"Edana!" Catherine wasn't as upset as her son would have liked. "Well, she is getting her back teeth. I should have left a strip of leather for her. Papa will fix the soldiers or make you more. You know that, James."

The little boy pouted but didn't complain any more.

Solomon sat next to Margaret, who leaned on his shoulder. She was his special pet and they were devoted to each other. Catherine knew that her cousin had promised Margaret's mother, Adalisa, to care for the child always and the affection he had for her made Catherine sure he would keep that vow. Edgar assumed that it was because Solomon hadn't been able to save Adalisa from her attackers, but Catherine always wondered if there wasn't more to it. She also wondered what Solomon would do in a few years, when it was time for Margaret to marry.

She sat on the blankets and studied them all. This disparate collection of people was the whole world to her. Despite everything, she couldn't understand how Agnes could leave her family and home for a strange land. Catherine couldn't imagine even a day away from those she loved.

There were rumors that King Louis's mother was going with him, as well as his wife. Perhaps Queen Adelhaide could understand Catherine's feelings, even if Louis was not only all grown up but an anointed ruler. If Queen Eleanor went on the expedition, as well, would she take her daughter, Marie? After so many barren years, how could she leave her only child behind?

Then again, how could she take that child into such danger?

Catherine smoothed Edana's dark curls. Despite the uproar below them, the child was soon fast asleep. Catherine kissed her.

Why were there never any clear answers any more? Everything had been so simple once and she had been as certain as that strange man in the field this afternoon. Now every decision came with a doubt. She prayed all the time, but if the saints were guiding her steps, they were being deeply obscure about it.

At another inn, Agnes ate in a private room with the men from Blois who had taken the cross and the women who had come to support them. Jehan was attentive as usual.

"Your grandfather sent word with his men that we are to accompany you back to Paris and then to Trier," he told her. "We have close to a year before the expedition can leave. I'm at your service until then."

"Grandfather is most generous to take such care of me," Agnes said.

She ate in silence until Jehan spoke again.

"Did you know your sister and that crippled husband of hers are here?" he asked.

Agnes dropped her spoon into the soup.

"Whatever for?" she asked. "Are they following me?"

Jehan shrugged. "I have no idea. Perhaps they're going to Jerusalem to ask God to give that English *mesel* a new hand."

Agnes retrieved her spoon and tried to concentrate on her dinner. Seeing Edgar's handless arm had been a shock to her. That sort of thing happened to warriors and thieves. In some part she felt it was a just punishment for making Catherine change her mind about staying in the convent. He had stolen her from God and also deprived the family of all the prayers she would have said for them. Catherine's return to the world had driven their mother mad. It had uncovered all the secrets of their father's past that should have stayed buried.

It was all Edgar's fault.

And yet, she remembered how Catherine had defended him, how he had stood always close enough to her to touch, if she needed him. Agnes found she couldn't swallow the thick soup because of the lump in her throat. In her heart, she wanted to love and be loved like that.

And all she had was Jehan.

At the edge of the field, now empty but for a few cooking fires and the detritus of thousands, sat a group of people huddled near their small fire. They chewed bravely on dry bread that they had soaked in beer until it was almost edible. Among them was the man who had spoken to Catherine that afternoon.

"Lanval." His wife's voice quavered with worry. "You weren't out preaching today, were you? I thought we agreed only to approach those who seemed open to our belief and speak with them privately."

"That's all I did, my dear Denise," Lanval assured her. "I only looked for those who didn't appear to be in some state of holy frenzy and greeted them in a friendly manner."

"I saw you talking with some woman," one of the others charged. "From her expression, you were doing more than greeting."

Lanval gave his friend a disgusted glance. "I admit, I was intrigued by her. She gave all the food she had brought to the beggars, and even some of her clothing."

"So you were praising her for her generosity?" Denise's tone told the others that she doubted this.

"No, I confess that I was berating her for having so much that she could give and not suffer for it." Lanval hung his head.

"I knew it," Denise said. "My darling, you mustn't take such risks, not yet. Do you want to be condemned before you're even heard?"

Lanval was not completely convinced. "If we're never heard, then our cause will die and the world will continue in its squalor. Would you have me watch souls damn themselves and say nothing?"

"No, Lanval," Denise said tenderly. "I would have you wait until we reach Köln and are among others who share the faith. Then we can preach in a voice so loud, all of Christendom will hear us."

"Amen," the others chorused.

They finished their bread, banked the fire and rolled up in their thin cloaks for the night.

Vézelay sheltered many sorts of pilgrims and, to some, it didn't matter if Edessa were free or not, for the Apocalypse would soon level all cities and only the chosen would survive.

Three

Troyes, Champagne, the home of Eliazar, Catherine's uncle.
Thursday, 2 nones April (April 4), 1146; 19 Nisan, 4906.
The feast of Saint Ambrose, who forebade the pope to rebuild a synogogue the people of Rome had burnt; the fifth
day of Passover.

*1146: Ex libris Sibillinis ad votum interpretatis regi Franciae ituro
Iherusolimam magnificam falso promuntur.*

1146: Success was falsely promised by the books of the Sibil-
lines for the journey of the French king, as he had vowed,
to Jerusalem.

—*Lamberti Parvi Annales A*

*H*ubert's brother, Eliazar, looked across the small table at his wife, Johanna. The candlelight was gentle on her face, the lines smoothed. He could almost imagine her the shy yet hopeful girl he had married so many years before. So many years.

The two of them sat alone, eating their unleavened bread and chicken. They should have had children and grandchildren around them, but the Holy One, blessed be He, had not seen fit to grant them any. Instead they had been given their nephew, Solomon, to raise when his father had been lost and his mother died. He had given them all the joy that a son would have and also all the worry.

Johanna smiled at her husband. She knew that was what he was fretting about.

"Solomon is a good boy," she said. "He knows better than to start trouble when he's among the Christians."

Eliazar grunted. "He won't start it, but he won't run from it, either."

"True." Johanna took the bowls and got up to take them to the kitchen. They had no servant tonight. Then she stopped and hesitated before speaking.

"But my dearest, don't you wish more of us were like him?" she said. "Don't you hate having to rely for our safety on the strength of a prince or a bishop who might turn on us at any moment?"

"Of course I do!" Eliazar's stool tipped over as he stood. "But we must, just like the priests and the peasants do, or be constantly vulnerable to attack. Solomon should have lived in the days of the Maccabees when we could form an army and drive out the infidels. But those days are gone and . . ."

"And his courage endangers us all," Johanna finished. "I know and I fear for him every moment. But I'm proud of him, too."

"So am I," Eliazar admitted. He looked around the room as if seeing it for the first time. "It's lonely here."

It was lonely and so quiet that the creaking of the hinges of the front door caused them both to jump.

"Aunt Johanna? Uncle?"

The subject of their discussion entered the room. Solomon's face fell when he saw that they had finished their meal.

"My dear boy," Johanna exclaimed. "You startled me! We didn't think you'd be here before Friday. Don't look so glum. I'll find you food. Lord knows what *treyf* you've been eating among the Edomites."

Solomon gave her a lopsided smile.

"It's better that you don't think about it, Aunt."

Johanna hurried to the kitchen, shaking her head and muttering that she must have done something wrong in the raising of him.

With a sigh of exhaustion, Solomon plopped himself on a cushion on the floor.

"Did she make cinnamon wine sauce?" he asked.

"She did," Eliazar told him.

His nephew sighed contentedly and let his head fall back against the wall. His eyes closed.

Eliazar waited a moment.

"We do have beds, you know," he said mildly.

Solomon sat upright again. "And it will be a rare treat to sleep in one, but I intend to eat first. Aunt Johanna can make matzoh taste like manna."

"Solomon, what's wrong?" Eliazar cut through the platitudes.

His nephew had a look about him that Eliazar had never seen before. Solomon had always had a streak of intolerance for the world he lived in, but this was more like contempt.

"I've never seen it so bad out there," Solomon told him. "Bernard of Clairvaux could convince a Saracen to take arms against his own brother. These people listen to him and go off with their hearts full of the wrongs done, not just to the Church or the Christians in the Holy Land, but to the body of their savior over a thousand years ago. And you know who they blame for that."

Eliazar glanced toward the kitchen and lowered his voice.

"Have there been any incidents?"

"Not yet, but I believe it's only a matter of time before someone decides the Jews should be killed or at least baptized before the soldiers take the long journey to the Holy Land."

Eliazar closed his eyes. He had been in Paris when word had come that his mother and sisters and, he believed, his baby brother had been slaughtered by the fanatics on their way to Jerusalem in 1096. If the soldiers were to start purging the towns of Jews, he knew he would rather die with his people than receive such news again.

"Solomon." He swallowed to keep his voice from shaking. "Don't go back out there. Stay in the community. Count Thibault and Bishop Henri won't let anyone hurt us. Out among madmen, who knows what could happen?"

"Uncle! You're letting your fear create demons," Solomon answered. "I can take care of myself. And I refuse to hide behind a bishop's wall. In any case, most of the time no one knows what I am. It's not as if I have some badge on my chest proclaiming, 'Here comes a Jew.' "

"That doesn't comfort me," Eliazar said.

Solomon got up, and put his arms around his uncle. "I know what you fear most and I can promise you that I'll never convert, not for anyone, not with a knife at my throat. I may not be a good Jew who knows the Talmud by heart, but I'm a determined one."

"I know that, Solomon," Eliazar whispered. "May I be forgiven, but for you what I truly fear most is *qiddush ha-Shem*."

"Do you know, I'd never considered it." Solomon sounded surprised. "I'd rather go down fighting than make a sacrifice of myself. But, if it came to that, wouldn't you rather I died by my own hand in sanctification of the Holy Name, than submit to baptism?"

"I hope so," Eliazar answered. "But you're all we have. I don't know if I could be as pure in my faith as Abraham was to give Isaac."

Solomon gave him a firm pat on the back. "Then let's assume the question will never arise. Now, where is my dinner?"

Eliazar tried to put the worry from his mind, but it lay there all night and woke with him the following day. He was willing to be martyred for the faith, if necessary. But at times like these he would rather hide with those he loved until the danger passed than court martyrdom. He hoped that the Lord would forgive him for it, but dying was the very last thing he wanted to do, and he wanted to put it off a good many more years.

Agnes had returned to Paris along with the faithful Jehan, as well as the guards and waiting women sent from Blois. Now that she had her entourage, Agnes started preparing for the journey in earnest.

Catherine and Edgar brought their family back, satisfied with their view of great events and settled back into normal life.

A few days later, Walter of Grancy arrived at their door. Catherine greeted him with delight but also surprise.

"What brings you to Paris?" she asked. "I thought you had gone back to Grancy until the mustering."

"Actually," he told her, "I was wondering if your sister needed someone to watch out for her on the road to Trier."

"I don't know," Catherine answered. "We can ask. But why would you want to take such trouble?"

"It will be months before the king is ready to set out," Walter explained. "But I'm prepared now. I've donated most of my land to Saint Peter through the monks of Cluny. I've settled my debts. I suppose I could begin the journey on my own, but I'd rather be part of Louis's army. However, I have nothing to do until then. So, if you need someone to accompany your sister to Germany, I'm happy to offer myself as escort. I spent some years in the service of the duke of Burgundy and the old emperor and I speak the language."

Hubert was pleased with the offer, since Walter was not only well born, but huge, strong and skilled at fighting. Unlike Jehan, no one had ever bested him in a tournament. Having him at one's side was almost as good as traveling with a whole troop of retainers. But Hubert knew that the final decision must rest with Agnes.

"I understand," Walter said. "I'll go at once to ask her."

"Tell her I will pay your expenses," Hubert said. "You and I will settle that. It's not for her to worry about."

Walter was known to the nuns and admitted without question. Agnes knew him by reputation and seemed pleased to meet him. She said at once that she would be happy for his company on the road.

It did occur to him that she might not know of his friendship with Catherine and Edgar. He felt it only right to tell her. She received the news calmly enough, with only one reservation.

"Does that affect your loyalty to me?" Agnes asked.

"In no way," Walter promised.

"Then we shan't discuss it again." Agnes closed the subject decidedly.

Walter was intrigued by Agnes's decision to marry so far away. Before he left, he had to ask her why.

"My grandfather knew Lord Gerhardt's uncle, back when they both fought at Antioch. He thinks it will be an advantageous alliance," she answered.

It didn't satisfy Walter.

"But the language will be difficult for you," he told her. "The Germans have different customs than ours and, what's more, they put something in their beer that makes it bitter. But most of all, if you need help, you'll have no kin around to stand up for you."

Agnes's lips tightened. "I'm not afraid of that," she said. "Nor of the language. If Edgar can learn French, I can certainly learn German."

"I'm sure you can," Walter said. "But to be so far from family makes life doubly hard. I have no one and yet it pains me to be leaving my home, even for the Holy Land."

Agnes appeared insulted.

"My reasons aren't your concern," she said. "And I can't possibly get too far from my family. Once the arrangements here are made, I'll be happy never to see them again."

Walter shook his head. Her words made no sense to him. "That reminds me," he added. "I have a message from your sister. She wants to know when you wish to meet to divide your mother's jewelry."

"Tell Catherine to come tomorrow so that we can make a list," Agnes said. "I want to get this over with."

Edgar was waiting outside when Walter left the convent.

"She's beautiful," Walter said, to no one in particular. "But not at all like Catherine."

"She's as arrogant as Matilda Empress," Edgar said. "And yet Catherine still loves her."

"Odd," Walter commented. "Your wife never struck me as one

who misjudges the nature of people. Perhaps her sister is not as haughty as she appears."

Edgar didn't want to argue with Walter so he said no more. The two men strolled across the bridge to the Île, stopping to look at some cloth samples and to listen a moment to a preacher who stood on a wooden box between two stalls.

"Brothers! Heed me!" the man exhorted. "The day of Judgement is near! Mankind wallows in greed and blasphemy. Heretics and infidels walk freely through our lands. The holy city of Rome has become Sodom. The time for the cleansing is coming. Will you be among the saved?"

Walter shook his head. "I'd like them to preach something more definite. Those signs have been around for a long time. Now, if there were an earthquake or the sun dripping blood, then I'd know that the Apocalypse was at hand."

"There are some that say that the fall of Edessa is a sign," Edgar commented, his mouth full of the hot *gauffre* he had just bought. The honey on the pastry burned his tongue.

"Not good enough," Walter answered. "A pestilence, now, I'd believe that, or a rain of frogs."

"You're a hard man to please, Walter," Edgar said panting to cool his mouth. "And dangerous. The person who insists upon a sign of doom is most likely to receive one."

"Move away from me, then." Walter laughed. "The lightning will probably strike any time now."

They meandered back across the Île de la Cité, stopping at a tavern Edgar knew well from his student days and finally arrived back home as twilight was fading.

Hubert greeted them with a grunt of annoyance.

"You reek of beer," he told them.

"We filled a jug for you." Edgar held it out.

"Oh. In that case." Hubert took the clay bottle and drank deeply from it. He wiped his mouth. "Thank you. I needed something."

"What's wrong, Sir?" Walter asked.

Hubert gestured to a pile of writing tablets on the table before him. Lists and numbers were scrawled over every clear space.

"Agnes couldn't have picked a worse time to be married," he said. "Especially so far away. Look at these prices! Everything needed for a journey is being bought up by the pilgrims. And everything I sell is being condemned as frivolous luxury. I had a man today tell me I should give him a bolt of my best Scottish wool because he was off to die for my sins! I told him I'd do my own penances and he'd best look to his own sins. He can die in clothes he can afford."

Edgar fought back the urge to laugh. It wasn't funny. He sometimes forgot that their livelihood depended on trade. His own father had thought it shameful but Edgar had come to the conclusion that it was no worse than depending on the kindness of kings or the loyalty of peasants, and more reliable. Usually.

"Will there be a problem getting everything Agnes needs?" he asked Hubert.

"There's always a problem." Hubert took another draught of beer. "But I think I can manage, if she makes no more extravagant demands. At least you and Catherine made no nonsense about pearl earrings and gold-plated wedding coffers."

"Gold-plated?" Edgar was interested at once. "Does she want a design on one? Precious stones added? I might have time before she goes."

"No, you won't." Catherine's voice came from the doorway. "You promised to finish the gold pyx for Mother Heloise. I would very much like to visit her this summer. She's never seen the children."

"Oh, yes." Edgar grimaced. "It's ready, all but the handles. Those will take a few more days. I don't have any solder made. I'd prefer to deliver it to the nuns myself, so I see no reason why we can't plan on a few days at the Paraclete, if they can accommodate us all."

"I wish I could go that far with you, to pray at Alys's grave," Walter said softly. "It's been some time since I was last there, although I send the nuns ten chickens every month to remember her in their prayers."

Hubert tried to remember who Alys had been. Walter's sister? No. Something Catherine had told him. Of course, the poor woman who had been beaten to death.

"I'm sorry, Walter, I'd forgotten." Catherine was ashamed of herself. "How could I! I know the sisters would never forget to pray for Alys, even if you sent them nothing."

It hurt her to see how Walter still grieved for the one woman he had loved. Alys had been married to someone richer and of a higher rank than Walter but her husband hadn't cared for her at all. And she had died without ever knowing that she mattered to anyone or what it felt like to be loved.

And what of Agnes? Could she be going into just such a trap? What did anyone know of this man she was going to marry?

Catherine forced down her fears and handed Walter a cloth. He wiped his eyes and gave it back.

"They say God knows best, but I expect him to do some explaining when I face him," Walter muttered and sniffed deeply.

"I think we're the ones who'll have to explain ourselves," she told him. "But I do hope a few things will be justified. I've listened to the masters lecture and I've read the fathers of the Church, but none of them have really explained to me why there is such suffering in the world. How could we have sinned so badly?"

Walter shrugged, embarrassed. His theology was much more basic than Catherine's. God was his Lord and must be obeyed. As with an earthly lord, Walter felt that God might sometimes make a mistake. That made no difference to obedience, however. Walter owed unquestioning service to his lord, right or wrong, and expected a reward for his loyalty. Instead of booty, his prize from God was to be eternal happiness in Heaven. He only hoped that would include being with Alys again.

Catherine realized that she had taken Walter far beyond his depth. She smiled an apology and turned the conversation to the weather.

"They say the summer will be hotter than usual." She led them into the hall where the table had been set up and a soup of egg, barley and fresh greens was being poured into bowls. There was some rye bread from last week's baking to dip in it.

Margaret and the children were already seated. That is, Margaret was seated with Edana wriggling on her lap, and James was crawling under the table, chasing his new puppy, Dragon.

"I hope you don't mind the children," Edgar said. "We don't make them eat upstairs unless Hubert is entertaining other merchants or noble guests. Oh, sorry. I don't mean that you're not . . ."

Walter laughed. "You know me better than that. I'm flattered to be allowed to join your family meal."

"Wait until you've survived one," Catherine said, as she re-trieved her son with one hand and the puppy with the other and bade them be still for the blessing.

That was the last moment of quiet for the rest of the evening.

Agnes was alone in the room assigned to her in the convent guest house. Most women visiting Paris had relatives or friends who took them in. The guest house was normally only for the families of the nuns. It was plain: a bed, a small table, a brazier if the night were frosty, a few hooks and a cross on the wall.

Agnes had brought her own mirror.

She stared into it now, her image wavering in the uneven silver and the flame of the oil lamp.

They all hated her. She knew that. Much as she despised Cath-erine for accepting her Jewish ancestry, much as she was revolted by her father's apostasy, it still bothered her that they now disliked her so much.

If only they had begged her forgiveness. She'd have given it gladly. Perhaps her poor mother could even have been brought home again. If Hubert denied his parentage and became a good Christian, Madeleine might regain her senses and everything at home could be as it had been when Agnes was a child.

Agnes suppressed such an impossible hope. She must deal with what was. They were afraid of her, too. Of what she could do to them. That made Agnes most angry. How dare they think she would betray her family! Everyone knew that was worse than any crime. The Savior had said that one must leave father and mother to follow him, but there had been nothing in the commandment about giving them over to the authorities.

Catherine wasn't the only one who had studied religion.

The face that looked back at Agnes was distorted more by anger than by the faults in the mirror. She schooled it to an impassive expression.

It was essential that she be able to hide her feelings, her fears. No one must ever guess that her heart contradicted her words.

There was a knock at the door. Agnes went to open it, expecting to see one of the sisters.

"How did you get in here?" she gasped.

Jehan pushed his way in before she could slam the door.

"Don't scream," he begged. "It would cause scandal for both of us."

"Are you planning on doing something that would make me want to scream?" Agnes said coldly.

"No, I swear," Jehan answered. "Please, I bribed the portress, told her I was your brother. She didn't believe me, but she took my coin."

"Wonderful. Now she believes I'm entertaining a lover. How long do you think she'll keep silent? What if Lord Gerhardt learns of this? He might consider that enough to break our contract."

Agnes moved as far away from him as possible, close to the narrow window that overlooked the street. There were people walking by if she needed assistance. Jehan guessed her thoughts.

"Agnes!" Jehan fell to his knees. "You know I would never do anything to dishonor you! I only want you to give me your blessing before I leave for the Holy Land."

"You couldn't ask for that in public?" Agnes's voice could have withered oak. "Why do you think I went to Vézelay? You have it already. Now go."

"Please, my adored one!" Jehan's posture would have astonished Catherine, who had never seen him do anything but sneer.

Agnes sighed. "Jehan, you know that I have only feelings of friendship for you and those are rapidly fading."

"What if I gain a castle at Antioch?" Jehan pleaded. "Would you come then and be its lady?"

"No," she answered. "I'm officially betrothed. I've agreed to the marriage in front of witnesses and I have no intention of breaking my vow. Please, please, Jehan, get up. Don't I have enough grief in my life without the burden of your affection?"

The soldier stayed on his knees, head bowed.

"I wanted to heal the pain your family has caused you," he whispered. "Whatever it is."

Despite her resolve, Agnes pitied him. She stretched out her hand, then pulled it back. She didn't dare give him any encouragement.

"Please go," she said instead. "I wish you well on your pilgrimage. May you gain glory, a fine castle and a beautiful bride. I can give you nothing, not even hope."

Jehan threw back his head. Agnes was afraid for a moment that he would howl like a wounded wolf. But he simply got to his feet, gave her a look that would haunt her for weeks and then a warning that would haunt her even longer.

"There will come a day, Agnes," he told her, "when you'll wish you'd been kinder to me tonight."

Agnes barred the door behind him. She spent the rest of the night on her knees, praying for guidance.

Catherine was braiding her hair for bed.

"Edgar, do you think the trestle table will support Walter?" she asked. "Perhaps we should have given him a more solid place to sleep."

"If it doesn't, we'll hear the swearing from here," he answered. "Hurry up. I'm cold."

She smiled.

"You know," she said as she took a maddeningly long time to tie her sleeping cap, "Agnes and I always slept in our shifts when we were girls. Now I wear just a cap. Doesn't that seem strange?"

"Are you coming to bed or am I coming out to get you?" Edgar tried to look threatening. Catherine laughed.

"Since I'm cold, as well, I'll come to you," she said and blew out the candle.

Sometime later Catherine snuggled against her husband.

"Are you asleep, yet?" she asked.

"Mmmf," he answered.

"Good. We never have time to talk. I'm worried about Agnes. I don't think she has any idea of what it will be like for her in Trier. What if this Gerhardt is cruel to her?"

Edgar put out his left hand to cover her mouth. When the stump hit her face, he was jolted to wakefulness by the realization.

"*Carissima!*" he cried. "I'm sorry. Did I hurt you?"

"Of course not," she lied, hoping her lip wouldn't swell. "I gather that you'd rather discuss this in the morning?"

"No." He yawned. "I'm awake now. But I don't see what we can do. Agnes has made her choice."

"I know," Catherine said, drawing his arm close around her. "I was just remembering how hard it was on our journey in England when I realized that I was responsible for James and Margaret, too. Without enough English, I never really understood what was happening. I felt so helpless. Germany might be the same for Agnes. And if Gerhardt isn't kind . . ."

"It won't be like England," Edgar reminded her. "For one thing, there's no war there, as far as I know. She'll have maids and retainers to care for her. And Walter won't leave her unless he's sure she'll be safe."

"I suppose," Catherine was getting sleepy now. "I just don't want Agnes hurt. Whatever she thinks of me, she's still my little sister. I feel responsible for her."

"Then why don't you pray for her." Edgar yawned. "Silently. Now, go to sleep, *carissima*. I love you."

He rolled over onto his side. Catherine adjusted her body to fit against his, draping her arm across his chest.

"I love you, too," she murmured. "Good night."

In her narrow bed at the convent Agnes lay awake through the night, all alone.

Gerhardt von Trier gazed down at his budding vines and across the Moselle. He had given up arguing with his family about the marriage. But they hadn't given up on him. The constant reproaches were wearing him down. When his own son begged him for a new mother, it was difficult to deny him. Perhaps there was a way to please everyone and still keep his vow.

He was tempted to simply run away before the girl arrived. He could deed the land to Peter with Hermann as guardian until his son was of age, then let them sort it out with this French bride. But Gerhardt came from a long line of warriors. Like Agnes, he had vague connections in the distant past to some intimate of Charlemagne. It had been drilled into him early that his heritage made it impossible for him to act the coward.

He wished his parents had been goatherders.

There was too much else to do for him to have to be troubled with this, Gerhardt thought. Bishop Albero was being ridiculous in his demands on the countryside. Gerhardt had consulted with his neighbors on this. For once they were all in agreement. Even the burghers in the town, even the Jews were in accord. The bishop was taxing everyone into poverty and for what? Was he building a great cathedral? No. The one that the Emperor Constantine had built was still in use. What did he need the money for, except to gouge as much as he could from his lands? He wouldn't even pay to have the city walls repaired. The burghers had been forced to do it themselves. And they had to pay to defend the city in Albero's constant feud with Graf Heinrich of Luxemburg. Gerhardt wanted that resolved soon. It was unnerving to be no more than an arrow's flight from an enemy.

"Ah, there you are, Brother! I should have known." Hermann had climbed the spiral staircase to the tower looking out across the river. "Not much to see today, through the rain."

"I wasn't looking at today," Gerhardt said.

"Ah yes, always planning ahead to the harvest." Hermann was desperate to cheer up his melancholy brother. "A good hot summer and we'll have the best crop yet. We'll show that Hubert LeVendeur a wine that he'll beg to be allowed to sell in Paris."

"Hubert who?" Gerhardt asked. "Oh yes, the French woman's father. When are they expected?"

"Mid-May, when the roads are dryer and the rivers calmer," Hermann answered, peering at him closely. "You are finally reconciled to this marriage, aren't you? We only arranged it for you and your son, you know. Peter needs a kind stepmother."

Gerhardt raised his eyebrows. "You were only thinking of Peter?"

"And you, Brother," Hermann said. "You need more children. All my attempts at securing a proper alliance for myself have failed. My pittance of land isn't attractive to anyone. If Peter dies without issue, then what will happen to all that our family has preserved for the past four hundred years?"

"Our sister may have children," Gerhardt suggested.

"Maria has been married five years now. She'd have to dispose of that idiot mule of a husband before we'd have a chance at a nephew." Hermann didn't seem adverse to the idea.

"Yes, we didn't do well with that match," Gerhardt said. "She does seem fond of Folmar however. And he's been a great help to me in matters of buying and selling. You'd have had to go to Köln if he hadn't offered to take care of the tranfer of the houses there to us. He an excellent man at bargaining."

"Perhaps his mother betrayed his father with a Jew." Hermann laughed.

"That's absurd." Gerhardt dismissed the idea.

Both men were silent as the rain fell and leaked through the places where the wooden roof had warped. Hermann stared out the window, watching the land slowly vanish into the rain. He fancied he could hear the river rushing far below, flowing to the Rhine and then the North Sea, carrying their wines and bringing back fur, amber and gold. Hermann didn't think a talent for trade made Folmar attractive at all. But he was Maria's husband and they were stuck with him, even if he couldn't supply her with children.

Therefore Hermann was convinced that Gerhardt had no choice but to marry again. There had to be a sure inheritance. Hermann wouldn't let this land leave the family. His brother must be made to understand.

Hermann's frustration boiled up as he thought of this. He had to show Gerhardt how important this was.

"Hermann! You don't need to pound on the table for me to know what you're thinking." Gerhardt sighed. "I've been thinking, too. You're right. I must consider the family. I signed the contract, even though I didn't realize it at the time. If the girl is half what you say she is, I'll do my duty and marry her."

"You will?" Hermann dragged Gerhardt off his stool and held him in a bear hug. "I knew you'd finally see reason! Maria will be so relieved. She's already hired the entertainers!"

He couldn't see his brother's face at that moment. If he had, he would have known that it was too soon to rejoice. Gerhardt's expression was one of desperate panic.

Four

Paris. Wednesday, 4 ides of April (April 10), 1146; 25 Nisan, 4906. Feast of Saint Ezekiel, Jewish prophet, celebrated because he foresaw the birth of Christ.

Inter haec Radolfus monachus, vir quidem religionis habitum religionisque severitatem sollerter imitans, sed litterarum noticia sobrie imbutus, est partes Gallias quae Rhemum attingunt ingreditur multaque populorum milia ex Aggripina, Maguntia, Warmatia, Spira, Argentina, aliique vincis civtatibus, oppidis sue vicus ad accipiendam crucem accendit.

Meanwhile, the monk, Radulf, a man who wore the habit of religion and imitated the strictness of religion, but was only slightly literate, entered those parts of Gaul along the Rhine and inflamed many of the inhabitants of Cologne, Mainz, Worms, Speyer, Strasbourg and other neighboring cities, towns and villages to accept the cross.

—Otto of Freising
Gesta Friderici I imperatoris
Book I, xxxviii

*W*hy did you bring them with you?" Agnes asked Catherine, regarding the squirming bundle in her arms with distaste.

"The children should get to know you," Catherine answered calmly, taking off her wool cloak. "And Margaret wanted to meet you. She's Edgar's sister, but she's French as well, and ought to spend more time with people of her own class. Don't be afraid, *ma douz*," she added to Margaret, "my sister won't hurt you."

The girl held out her hand to Agnes with a shy bob of her head.

"You don't look like Catherine," she observed. "Are you half sisters, like I am to Edgar?"

"No," Agnes answered. "We're just different."

Agnes seemed interested in neither Margaret nor the younger children. James was fortunately worn out from the walk across the city but Edana had been carried and was eager to get down and play.

"Are the rushes clean?" Catherine asked. "I have a blanket but since she started walking, she won't stay on it."

Agnes looked from her to the wriggling baby. She shook her head in amazement.

"The nuns are most careful about sweeping," she told Catherine. "Who would have thought it? My scholar sister, with her hands always stained with ink and her head a maze of philosophy, reduced to being little more than a nursemaid to her own children."

Catherine was stung. "They have a nurse. I just left her at home. And I still read and go to the lectures of the masters when I can. In four years James will be sent for fostering. I want as much of him as possible before he goes away. I'm not sorry, Agnes. I know you wish I'd stayed at the Paraclete and taken my vows, but this is what I think was intended for me. I have a good life."

Agnes's expression indicated disbelief. She motioned for them to sit and gave them dried fruit and nuts from a dish the nuns had left for guests. James went to sleep on the blanket as Edana explored the room.

"Why did you come?" Agnes asked.

"Mother's jewelry," Catherine reminded her. "You may have all of it if you like. There's a gold cross I would like to save for Edana that belonged to our grandmother, but I have no need of the rest."

"You'll need some to make a decent impression among Father's friends," Agnes insisted. "You can't have people mistaking you for one of the servants."

"Perhaps you would prefer it if they did," Catherine suggested sharply. She needed all her patience to deal with her children. There wasn't much left for Agnes.

"I can't tell you how glad I am to be going where no one knows you." Agnes stood as if to go. "You seem to take such joy in giving me shame."

"Catherine would never shame anyone with her manners!" Margaret exclaimed. "You should have seen the dress she wore to our castle. And the jewels. She looked as fine as a queen! Mother was very impressed."

Catherine smiled. "Thank you, Margaret. I'm doing better than when we were young, Agnes. I cover my hair most of the time, I remember to use my napkin at table and I don't argue theology however much I'm provoked. At least not often."

Agnes looked doubtful, but returned to the box Catherine had brought. She glanced at a movement from the corner. "Should your daughter be eating that?"

She gestured to where Edana was investigating a piece of metal she had uncovered from among the rushes and herbs.

Catherine jumped up to grab the thing from the child before she cut herself.

"No, no!" she said. "Not in the mouth!"

She examined what Edana had found. "I thought you said the nuns cleaned here. What is it?"

It was a roughly square piece of metal, about half the size of her palm. There was a sharp edge to it and holes at two of the corners.

Margaret peered at it from her seat.

"It looks like it fell off a leather tunic," she guessed. "From a soldier's gear?"

"I suppose," Catherine said. "It reminds me of something else. I'll take it to Edgar. He'll know."

She started to tie it up in her sleeve but Agnes leaped from her stool and snatched it from her.

"It's not yours," she insisted. "You can't just take things."

"But it's just a bit of detritus left on the floor," Catherine said. "Some visitor must have dropped it. It's not as if it were a ruby."

"That's not the point." Agnes was firm. "I'll give it to the nuns. The owner may return for it."

Catherine nodded. "Of course," she said as soothingly as she could. "You never know. It may be have been a very strategically placed bit of metal. From over the heart, for instance."

Agnes's hand shook as she tied the metal into her own sleeve. Her reaction surprised Catherine, but this was just one of many things she didn't understand about her sister.

Catherine picked up James, who flopped over her shoulder sound asleep. Margaret retrieved Edana from the corner, where she was still investigating.

"If you'll make a list of the jewelry you've taken," Catherine told Agnes, "I'll send one of Father's men to bring back what's left. I think we should be going now. You know that you're welcome to stay with us. Margaret has our old room, but she can share or come down and sleep with us."

"I'll never return until you totally disassociate yourself from those Jews," Agnes answered. "Whatever their blood ties to us, there should be no spiritual ones and certainly no friendship. You may not care about the state of your soul, but I won't risk damnation along with you."

"I have no fear for my soul," Catherine answered proudly. "At least not from the arguments of the Jews. I love our cousin and won't give up seeing him, just as I'll never stop praying for him to wake to the true faith. Just as I pray for you to wake again to your family's love." Her voice softened. "To my love, Agnes. You'll always be dear to me. You're my only sister."

Agnes bit her lip and looked away. "I can't risk my soul for sentiment," she said.

Catherine had meant to sweep out with a dignified swish of her garments but that was hard to do while burdened with an unconscious three-year-old and one's cloak still hanging on a peg on the wall. So she contented herself with keeping back a sharp reply and bundling everyone up as quickly as she could.

Eventually they were sorted out and left for the walk back to the Greve, the merchants' quarter on the north bank of the Seine. The trip back took longer than the one there, for Catherine felt burdened by Agnes's animosity as much as by the weight of her son.

As they were heading down the rue de la Lanterne, toward the Grand Pont, Catherine noticed a disturbance to their right. She tried to look around James's head to see what it was.

"There's a crowd around the synogogue," Margaret said. "What could they want?"

"I don't know," Catherine said, although she feared that she did. "I think we should hurry past, don't you?"

She could hear the angry shouting as they went by and then the sound of rocks thrown against wooden shutters. Her first thought was to get her children to safety. The second was relief that Solomon and Uncle Eliazar were in Troyes far away from danger.

But if this were happening in sensible Paris and weeks after Eastertide, what might be going on in other places? Could her father's family be truly secure anywhere?

They pushed their way across the bridge, fighting the people who had heard the commotion and come to investigate. It wasn't until they were on their own street, with the gate in sight, that Catherine slowed down. She could hear Margaret panting behind her.

"Father! Edgar!" she called as they entered the house. "There's a mob attacking the *juiverie!*"

No one answered. The house was silent.

"Samonie! Willa!" Catherine called again for the servants. Still no answer.

"Where could they all have gone?" Margaret asked. "None of the boys are here, either."

Catherine bit her lip in worry. It was unheard of for the house to be left empty. She set James on a pile of cushions on the floor and went to investigate.

"Margaret, mind the baby and don't go upstairs until I see what's wrong."

"I will," Margaret answered. "I mean, I won't."

The quaver in her voice told Catherine how frightened she was.

"Stulta!" she said to herself. *"Margaret's been through so much already. We brought her here to escape all that. You can't expect her to be brave all the time."*

"Perhaps she'd be happier someplace secure, like a convent."

Catherine swore as she continued up the stairs. She had no time now to start one of her internal arguments.

"Samonie!" She called her maid. "Ullo! Hugh! Martin! Anyone?"

All the rooms on the upper floors were empty. Catherine came down again, assured herself that Margaret was coping and went out to the kitchen. There was no one there, either. An iron kettle hung from a hook over the fire, which had recently been stoked. They hadn't been gone long.

She looked out the back window. The fruit trees were beginning to bud. The creek was still high from winter rain and had flooded the garden. In the summer it would be paradise. Now it just seemed forlorn and definitely uninhabited.

She returned to the hall.

"I don't know where they've gone," she told Margaret. "But there's no point in rushing out to hunt for them since we have no idea where to start. We'll just stay here and wait. Someone should return soon."

It went against every natural inclination for Catherine to remain. In the old days she would have run back at once to find out what was going on at the synagogue. But now, life was different. She sat next to James and laid her hand on his brown curls. He shifted in his sleep. Margaret had put Edana on a chamber pot and was encouraging her to make use of it. The child wasn't happy with the idea. She preferred leaving presents in the soft rushes to depositing them in cold pottery.

Catherine sighed. Yes, things were very different now. And so she would wait. But not patiently.

∽

It was nearly dark before they heard steps in the entry. Catherine had taken everyone into the kitchen, where she was tending the fire and chopping dried herbs to mix with honey and vinegar for a meat sauce.

"I'm not going to go out there," she told Margaret. "They can look for us for a change."

But she dropped the knife and went running when Edgar shouted.

"Catherine! Hurry! He's hurt!"

Catherine stopped short at the doorway. Edgar was bleeding from a cut on his cheek, but Hubert was hanging unconscious between Ullo and Hugh, the boys straining to keep him upright until they could lay him on a bed.

"Margaret, get the sauce I was making and some old bread," Catherine ordered. "Ullo, put my father next to the hearth. Edgar, I'll help you set up the bed. Has anyone called for a doctor?"

"Mother and Willa went," Hugh panted. "We met them coming through the market."

Margaret came back with the bowl. Catherine spread a mattress on the trestle bed she and Edgar had assembled, giving the girl directions at the same time.

"Crumble the bread into the sauce until you have a paste. No, it doesn't matter if it's moldy. Those aren't the right herbs but honey and vinegar should be enough." She finished with the mattress. "There, now you boys can lower him onto it. Ullo, run to the storage chest for a blanket. Hugh, down to the creek for water."

She leaned over to examine Hubert. His skin was pale and his breathing shallow. She felt all over his head through the thick grey hair, but found no wound.

"What's wrong with him?" she demanded. "What happened, Edgar? Oh, *carissime!* Are you all right?"

Edgar knelt next to her, wiping the blood from his cheek with his left arm.

"Isaac the draper came to us, saying that there was a mob outside the synagogue. He wanted your father to help," Edgar began.

"So, of course, you went," Catherine said. "You didn't think of sending to the palace for the guards."

"We wanted to see how bad it was first." Edgar winced as Catherine wiped his cut with a clean cloth and then spread the paste over it.

"It will dry soon and keep out putrefaction," she told him. "Don't touch it. I knew something was happening; we went near there on our way back from seeing Agnes. What started it?"

"I'm not sure," Edgar said. "It began in a tavern, most likely. From what I could get, someone said that a lot more people could join the king's pilgrimage if they had the money of the Jews. Then someone else said it wasn't right that Jews should profit from the misfortunes of the King of Jerusalem. Someone else mentioned Judas and the crucifixion. Then one idea stood upon another until there was a crowd bent on storming the synagogue and stealing all the gold and jewels kept there—"

"But, Edgar, there's nothing at the synagogue but the books they use in their service," Catherine interrupted.

"That's what Abraham the vintner tried to tell them, when they demanded gold," Edgar said. "And then your father arrived. He pushed through to Abraham's side and shouted that the people must be mad to attack their neighbors. It wasn't the right thing to say."

They both looked at Hubert.

"Someone yelled that he was no better than a Jew, himself," Edgar continued. "I thought Hubert was going to say something really dangerous then, so I tried to get to him to stop him. That's when they started throwing things. You'd be amazed at the hard objects that just lie about in the street for any fool to use as a weapon. I think I was hit by a ragged-edged bone."

"And Father?"

Edgar shook his head. "I don't know. I didn't see what happened. I was between him and the crowd so I don't think he was hit. He just suddenly slumped against the wall. It was shortly after that the king's guards appeared and broke things up. The boys and I thought it would be best to bring Hubert home, but it took some time to carry him through the streets."

"And no one offered to help you?" Catherine's lips tightened.

"We were nearly here when we saw Samonie and sent her for Master Clement," Edgar finished. He didn't want to discuss the time they had had getting Hubert back, nor the things the kindly inhab-itants of Paris had yelled at them.

Catherine leaned over her father. He was breathing, but his skin was clammy and grey.

"There seems to be no sign of a blow, but he's so still. I don't know what to do." Catherine swallowed her tears. "Why doesn't the doctor come?"

It seemed forever before Samonie returned with the doctor, al-though it was really but a few moments before the man arrived. In the meantime all Catherine could think of was to keep her father warm and to put herbal compresses on his feet to draw out whatever evil was keeping him from waking.

The serving woman had dragged the doctor from his meal and insisted that he accompany her. He didn't try to hide his irritation when he came in.

"She told me that Master Hubert was dying," he said. "He'd better be. My wife whipped up egg and quince jam to pour over lamb tonight. Do you know what that tastes like cold?

"Oh, my!" he said when he saw Hubert. He was instantly serious. "How long has he been like this?"

"Perhaps an hour," Edgar told him. "There was a crowd, shouting and pelting us with street refuse, but I don't think he was hit."

"Nor do I." The doctor took off his cloak and tunic and rolled up his sleeves. He listened to Hubert's breathing and his heart. "When was he last bled?" he asked.

"I don't know," Catherine said.

"Idiot! I told him the last time we met that a man in his fifties has to take care of himself." The doctor turned to Edgar. "I'll need a urine specimen. However, I believe that he has allowed his humors to become decidedly imbalanced and the excitment today simply pushed them too far. As you can see, he's cold and moist, when he should be warm and dry."

"What can we do?" Catherine begged. "Will he waken?"

The man pursed his lips. "I think so, but he must be bled as soon as he does. At least you've kept him warm. Take the poultice off his feet and apply one to his head. When he does wake, give him a broth made of partridge, with fennel, marjoram and leeks. I'll be back tomorrow."

"Partridge!" Edgar said, when the man had left. "Where can we find partridge this time of year?"

"Veal will do," Catherine answered. "It just has to have warm and dry properties. Ullo, run down to the butcher and see if you can get a soup bone."

She closed her eyes but the tears spilled out anyway.

"Edgar, what shall we do if he doesn't wake?"

Edgar held her close. "For now, why don't we just pray that he does."

The Cistercian monastery of Clairvaux was unadorned—no bell tower, no elaborate paintings or carving. Everything in it was for utility only and not for the edification or comfort of the inhabitants. But, looking out over the fields that the monks and lay brothers had cleared, where grain and vines ripened and wild flowers bloomed, Astrolabe was struck by the beauty of the place.

He had been kept waiting some time in the porter's lodge. This didn't surprise him. There were far more important people here to see the abbot. Also, since he had refused to tell Bernard's protective secretary, Nicholas, the reason for his visit, there was no way for anyone to gauge its importance. And somehow Astrolabe suspected that Nicholas had no interest in letting him approach his master.

He tried not to be bothered by this. Ever since he'd been old enough to understand who his parents were, he'd had to live with the fact that his father's enemies and even some of his friends could not forgive Astrolabe for existing. The son of Abelard and Heloise took on the weight of their transgression simply by continuing to live. To their credit, neither of his parents had ever shown him anything but love, the few times he had seen them. His mother still seemed to treasure his visits. It was the rest of the world that made the situation difficult.

The monk who had just entered the room, Geoffrey, was one of the difficulties. A former student of Abelard's, he was now a staunch supporter of Bernard of Clairvaux. And, in castigating his former teacher, he had also conceived a strong dislike for Astrolabe as well.

So, when Geoffrey beckoned him to follow, Astrolabe half suspected that he was being shown the door.

Instead he was conducted into the abbot's refectory in the guest house where Abbot Bernard, himself, soon joined him for the meal of bread and soup. No one spoke to him or to each other, although the abbot nodded his greeting. The only sound was that of the lector reading a passage from a life of Saint Anthony. As he listened, Astrolabe reflected that compared to what that hermit saint had eaten, bread and thin soup was a feast.

After the meal the abbot rose and beckoned Astrolabe to follow him. They went to a room in the guest quarters where Bernard motioned for Astrolabe to seat himself.

Astrolabe handed Bernard the letter his mother had entrusted him with. The abbot broke the seal and read it quickly then gave Astrolabe a wry smile.

"I would have known you, even without the letter from your mother," he said. "You have her eyes, but in all other respects, the features are your father's."

"So I've been told." Astrolabe squirmed uncomfortably under the abbot's gaze.

"And inside?" Bernard regarded him with curiosity.

"I'm not the scholar my father was," Astrolabe answered. "Nor do I have his need to understand the mind of the Creator. But I loved and admired him very much and am not ashamed to be thought like him."

"As is only proper," Bernard answered. "Now, what is the message your mother sent you to tell me? Her letter only says the matter is urgent."

"Others may have already told you of this," Astrolabe began uneasily, "but she wanted to be certain you were aware of the growing menace in Lotharingia and the Rhineland."

"Menace?" Bernard seemed surprised. "What sort? Heretics again?"

"No, my lord abbot." Astrolabe shifted from foot to foot. "It has come to my mother's attention that a man claiming to be a monk has been preaching the upcoming expedition to the Holy Land and, in the course of his preaching, has been inciting the people to attack the Jews living among them."

Bernard was instantly attentive. "That's impossible!" he said. "I sent a letter to all the bishops forbidding anyone to molest the Jews. We want no repetition of the shameful episodes of 1096."

"I am aware of that," Astrolabe said. "But it seems that this brother Radulf is not. They say he is preaching in your name."

"No!"

The abbot stood suddenly, his right hand in a fist. Astrolabe took a step back.

"Mother had it from witnesses," he told Bernard. "Merchants coming back from Metz. They had heard Radulf and feared the damage he might do."

The abbot forced himself to be calm.

"My missives may not have reached the bishops of Lotharingia and Germany, yet," he said. "But, in any case, I'm sure that the lords of the land will remember that they owe protection to their Jews."

"Yes, my lord abbot," Astrolabe answered. "Shall I then return to the Paraclete and tell my mother that her worries are groundless? That you assure her no one will dare to attack the Jews against your instructions?"

Bernard regarded him sharply. "Perhaps there is something of your father in you, after all. I can tell from your tone that you doubt the ability of the bishops."

"No, Lord Abbot," Astrolabe said quickly. "But there is nothing so dangerous or deadly as evil rumor, and Mother and I fear that this is what this monk is spreading."

Bernard considered this for a moment, then nodded agreement.

"I'll have the matter looked into," he promised. "And, now, there was something more in your mother's letter."

Astrolabe looked at the floor and sighed deeply. He loved his mother and knew she wanted the best for him, but to ask this man of all people to help him! What was she thinking of?

The abbot smiled. "I presume that you know what she has asked of me?"

"I'm afraid so," Astrolabe answered. "She's worried because she has nothing to leave me. She wants to see that I have a living. She already asked the abbot of Cluny about it, but he had nothing. I've tried to tell her that I survive quite well. I teach a little and write letters and documents for those who need them. I have no real need of a benefice."

"I'm glad to hear it, my son." Bernard held up his hand to give a farewell benediction. "For I'm afraid I have none to give. But I shall keep you in mind, should something appear."

Astrolabe tried to make his grimace a grateful smile.

"Thank you, my lord abbot." He bowed and left.

Alone, Bernard carefully folded the letter from Heloise. A beautiful woman, he recalled, filled with a passion that was now being put to the service of God. Perhaps he could find a way to help her son. And as for this renegade self-proclaimed monk . . .

"Porter!" he called. "Run fetch brother Nicholas. I need him to send another letter to the bishops of Germany! At once!"

"I think he's waking."

"Hush! don't startle him!"

Hubert heard the voices but couldn't seem to wake up enough to answer. He felt cold. With a great effort, he made a noise.

"Ghharrr."

"Father?" Catherine leaned over him. "Father, what happened? Are you all right?"

"Give him some wine; his throat's parched," Edgar said.

"Broth." Catherine was firm.

Hubert wished they'd stop arguing and give him something. The feeling was coming back to his limbs now. Nothing hurt. He was just tired, as if he'd been running for hours without a rest. He felt a spoon between his lips. He opened and swallowed.

"More," he grunted.

Soon he felt able to sit up enough to drink without spilling half the broth down his jaw and into his shift.

"We could find no wound," Edgar told him. "Were you hit?"

Hubert tried to remember. "No, I don't think so. I just felt suddenly dizzy and cold and too weak to stand. Then I woke up here."

Catherine bit her lip. "We'll have the doctor back," she told him. "He thinks your humors just became imbalanced. You need to remember to be bled once a month."

"Nonsense!" Hubert said. "That's only for clerks and monks who pray and fast all day. I'm fine. Probably just something I ate. I feel better already."

He moved to get up but three pairs of arms stopped him.

"Rest for now, Hubert," Edgar entreated over Hubert's protest. "You fightened us. We want you to regain your strength. I won't let you up unless you can promise that this won't happen again. Can you?"

Grudgingly, Hubert admitted that he couldn't, since he had no idea why he had collapsed like that. It frightened him, too, all the more because he had been having odd feelings for some time: a tingling in his hands and feet, slight dizziness and the sensation that his heart was slowing down, even as he urged it on. He had told no one and, looking at the worried faces around him, vowed not to mention it ever.

"Very well," he said. "You may baby me for tonight but I have work to do tomorrow. When Agnes has left with all her trappings and boxes, then I promise to take a long rest, perhaps go see Eliazar for the rest of the summer. Is that agreeable to you?"

Catherine scowled but nodded.

"You'd think we were trying to punish you," she complained.

"I won't be treated like a sick old man," Hubert responded mildly. "When I am one, I'll tell you. I promise."

All the same, he allowed Ullo and Hugh to help him up to his bed and, after drinking a bowl of hot wine and herbs, fell back to sleep for the night.

Edgar could tell how shaken Catherine was by the incident.

"Don't worry, *leoffest,*" he murmured as he held her that night. "He's not that old. It may have just been the shock of seeing the anger of the crowd added to the memory of what happened to him as a child."

"Perhaps." Catherine's voice was distant. "But his symptoms are so strange. It's not like any sickness I know. It's more as if he had been struck down."

"Catherine," Edgar reminded her. "The day was clear. Are you saying God sent a bolt of lightning to punish him for protecting the Jews?"

"No, God wouldn't do that," Catherine said. "At least, I don't think so. I was thinking of a person. We never found out who denounced him to the bishop two years ago."

Edgar didn't like the direction this was taking.

"You think someone cursed him?" he asked. "That's nonsense."

"Why?" Catherine asked. She shivered in his arms. "There are those who use evil forces to do evil. You know that."

"Well, I've heard that," Edgar said cautiously. "But I've never seen it. I don't think anyone does such things anymore. Not seriously. Remember our friend John's story about the old priest who tried to do magic. None of the charms worked. This is the twelfth century, Catherine. We study the world with logic. The time of curses actually working is over."

Catherine was doubtful. "What about miracles?"

"Well, you know that most scholars say that the time when God manifests himself in miracles is also over," Edgar hedged. "But then, there's James. I believe he lives only because of our pilgrimage. So I think that there are still minor miracles."

"Then it's possible that there are still minor curses, too," Catherine stated and rolled over, pressing her back against Edgar's stomach. "Good night, carissime."

Edgar lay awake for a long time, wondering just who Catherine had in mind as the perpetrator and, if she were right, what they could do to defeat him.

Agnes finished going through the jewelry and laid the pieces she had rejected back in the casket, each wrapped in felt to keep it from chipping or tarnishing. She had left more than she had originally intended. Perhaps Catherine's daughter would need them one day. With a cripple for a father, she couldn't expect much.

Agnes had never trusted Edgar. If he hadn't made Catherine fall in love with him she would have gone back to the convent. Then she could have spent her life in prayer as their mother had desired. Father and Mother should have forced Catherine to return, Agnes thought angrily. Everything started going wrong when she left the Paraclete. It had to be a punishment.

She sniffed and wiped the tears on her sleeve. But if the sin were Catherine's, why was it that the doom fell on the other members of the family? Uncle Roger, dead. Mother, lost in her own delusions, so far gone that she needed constant watching. Thank God the nuns had been willing to take her in. Even Edgar's mutilation was part of it, although Agnes felt he deserved that. Why did nothing horrible ever happen to Catherine?

Wearily, Agnes knelt before the cross on the wall over her bed, praying for comprehension.

"If I just understood, Lord," she begged. "Then I could accept. It can't be that she's right. She abandoned You for a mere man, and a foreigner, at that. She consorts with Jews. You can't condone such behavior!"

The room was silent. Agnes gazed at the cross, almost hoping to see the answer written on the wood.

"Lord?" she asked. "Please, tell me why. Or at least send a sign that I'm doing right in going so far away. Let me know that my new life will be a happy one. Sweet Jesus, Blessed Virgin, I'm so afraid."

Silence.

So. Even God was angry with her. Agnes hurt too much for tears but there was a hot lump in her throat that made her lips tremble and her jaw tighten. She pulled off her *bliaut* and dropped it on the floor. Something clanked. She picked the overdress up again and unknotted the sleeve. As she fumbled with the material, she felt a sharp pain in her finger. She pulled it out, bleeding.

Sucking the cut clean, she felt more carefully with the other hand until she found the bit of metal Edana had uncovered amid the rushes.

"Poor Jehan," she whispered. "I hope this didn't come from the space over your heart. You must stay safe. I wish I could care for you as you want me to. After all, no one else loves me. Not even God."

Five

The castle of Lord Gerhardt, near Trier. Saturday, 12 kalends May (April 20), 1146; 5 Iyyar, 4906. Feast of Saint Marcellin, bishop of Embrun, protector of his people. The oil from the lamp by his grave cures any malady.

Audivimus et gaudemus, ut in vobis ferveat zealus Dei: sed oportet omnino temperamentum sceintæ non deesse. Non sunt persequendi Judæi, non sunt trucidandi sed nec effugandi quidem.

We have heard and rejoiced that the zeal for God burns within you: but one ought in no way to wander from the moderate path of wisdom. The Jews are not to be persecuted, nor are they to be killed nor even driven out.

—Bernard of Clairvaux
Letter 363
To the people of Eastern
Francia, both clerical and lay

Gerhardt was kneeling next to a row of budding vines. The day was misty and his clothes and face already had a thin coating of mud. For the first time since he had agreed to go through with the marriage the Frenchwoman, Gerhardt was at peace.

"Look here, son." He lifted the new leaves to show Peter the minute green globes just starting to grow beneath them. "This is our treasure, as fine as gold. And it's our duty to see that it continues to thrive. No overseer or steward will ever care for our vines as we can."

Peter put a finger out and brushed it against the baby grapes. "I understand, Father," he said. "You don't need to worry. I love our land as much as you do. I won't let anyone take it from us, nor will I trade it for wealth or power."

Gerhardt leaned back on his heels and clapped his son on the back in hearty approval.

"Excellent *mîn Liebelin!*" he cried. "Then I have no fear for the future any more."

Peter stood, brushing at the mud on his knees, but he only succeeded in smearing it more deeply into his woolen pants. He looked at his father with some concern.

"Why should you fear the future?" he asked. "It will be a long time before I become lord here, and now that you're marrying, I may have many brothers to take over if I should fail."

"You won't fail," Gerhardt said firmly. "And I wouldn't count on brothers to take the burden from you. I'm not all that young anymore. Why, I have to rub a salve on my joints every night just to keep them from creaking. You'd better make up your mind that this will be in your keeping one day."

Peter seemed confused. "If you say so, Father. I just wanted you to know that what we have is more important to me than the idea that I should have it all. As long as someone of our blood is lord, I don't care if it's a younger brother."

Gerhardt laughed at this, causing the boy to blush. "Peter, I haven't even seen the lady yet, and you have us already parents many times over! One should prepare for the future but not to that extreme. Come now. Let's check on the progress of last year's harvest."

As he watched Peter walking in front of him, so confident and trusting, Gerhardt cursed himself again for the weakness that had made him give in to the family. There had to be a way, somehow, for him to escape the consequences of his promise to marry.

The two of them headed for the barn housing the great oaken barrels of new wine. As they headed up the path they were stopped by a shout from Hermann.

"Gerhardt! Come quickly! Something terrible has happened!"

Gerhardt broke into a run, his mind full of unnamed fears. He reached the porter's hut outside the castle, where Hermann was kneeling next to a body. Two of the field workers stood uneasily at one side.

"What is it?" Gerhardt panted. "Who's been hurt?"

"More than hurt," Hermann said. "Dead. These two men found him caught in the river among some roots along the bank. I think he was a messenger. He was carrying this wrapped in oilcloth and tied by a cord around his thigh."

He rose from the body, holding a piece of folded vellum in his hand. There was a red ribbon and a grey wax seal attached to it.

Gerhardt looked from the man to the seal, not sure which to examine first.

"There's nothing on the outside to tell who the message is for," Hermann told him. "And nothing on the body to identify him. I don't recognize the seal. Should we open it? Perhaps that will explain who he was and where he was going."

Gerhardt took a good look at the body. No one he knew, thank God. But he could tell at once that the man hadn't drowned. There was a gaping slit in his neck.

"He hasn't been in the water long," one of the men observed. "The body isn't bloated. He must have been killed near here and recently. Shall I get the baliff?"

Gerhardt nodded.

"Yes, and warn the other villagers not to go out alone or unarmed until we discover what happened."

He turned to Hermann.

"Was there anything else on him, a ring or token to show where he came from?"

Hermann shook his head. "Whoever killed him must have stolen his purse and jewelry. I think we'll have to open the letter."

"Give it to me," Gerhardt said. "I'll see to it. Oskar, Gerd, fetch the priest and have some of the men take the body to the chapel. Whoever he was, he should have a Christian burial. Peter, come up to the keep with us. I want you where I know you're safe."

The rough vellum was still dry enough to crackle in his hand. The sound to Gerhardt was like that of flames in sunburned brushwood. He shuddered. He hoped the sender had been careful not to write anything equally incendiary. How could he manage to find a way to open the letter without others near? He had a cold fear that the man had been coming to see him.

"Where do you suppose he was going?" Peter asked, looking curiously at the letter.

"Any number of places," Gerhardt answered. "We're on a well-traveled thoroughfare. But, I imagine this will tell us."

They reached the courtyard within the stone walls.

"Hermann," Gerhardt said. "Would you take Peter to his aunt Maria and tell her what has happened? See if she has any material for a shroud."

Hermann looked as if he would protest. He was as curious as Gerhardt about the contents of the message. However, he was being careful with his elder brother these days. He nodded.

Gerhardt went into the keep and up to his sleeping chamber. Sitting on a folding stool by the window, he held the seal up to the light.

The journey had caused it to crack and chip but the mark was still clear enough. It was a cross with each arm of equal length placed inside a circle.

Gerhardt bit his lip. That was harmless enough to those unaware of the sign. He slid his knife under the wax and opened the letter.

When he saw what was inside, he started and drew his breath in sharply.

On the paper was a crude drawing of a man dressed for the chase. But he carried no weapon. His hands, enormous hands, were raised palm out as if to surrender or to pray. Gerhardt took his knife and scraped at the vellum until all trace of the picture had vanished. Then he crumpled it with shaking hands.

The messenger *had* been trying to reach him. But what had the message been?

Gerhardt drummed his fingers nervously on the windowsill. His confederates wouldn't have been careless enough to write a message that anyone might understand. So the real message must have been lost with the poor murdered courier. Unless someone had made him talk before they slit his throat. The thought sent chills down his body and made him rub his own throat as if the knife were poised to slice.

Now he had much more to worry about than ridding himself of this unwanted bride. If his secret were discovered before he was ready there was a good chance that he might lose his whole family and everything they possessed.

Who could have needed to reach him so badly that they would risk that?

It was the first sunny day of spring in Paris. Along with every other woman on the street, Catherine had thrown open the windows and hung all the bedding out to air. Letting in the light seemed to banish the shadows of winter. As Catherine surveyed the rooms in the sunshine, she realized that it also showed all the grime. There were streaks of soot on the walls and ceilings from oil lamps and candles. The floor, where the rushes had been swept up, showed stains she preferred not to think about but which probably came from both Edana and the puppy.

Why had she thought that leaving the convent would free her from manual labor?

Samonie, who had once been her personal maid and was now the housekeeper, and her three children, Willa, Hugh and Martin, had grown to be of great use in the household. Still, there was too much for them to do alone and, for many reasons, Hubert prefered not to have too many outsiders introduced to the vagaries of his family.

So Catherine was faced with more than directing the spring cleaning.

"I hope that Agnes has people to do this for her," Catherine grunted as she dragged another mattress to the window. "She's grown too fine, I'm sure, to be seen with feathers in her hair."

"From what I know of her," Samonie commented as she dumped soapy water on the wood floor. "She could do this without causing feathers to fly."

Gloomily, Catherine agreed. "Agnes was always better than I at housework."

Samonie stopped her floor scrubbing to wipe the sweat from her forehead. She called out to her younger son as he raced passed the doorway.

"Martin! Come help Lady Catherine heft the bedding!" To Catherine she added, "You're worried about Agnes, aren't you?"

"She might have told us when she left," Catherine said as Martin tried to grab enough of the mattress to lift. "Instead of letting us learn it from neighbors. And, of course, I don't expect her to send word when she arrives safely. Not the way she feels about us."

"Lord Walter will let you know," Samonie assured her.

"Dear Walter!" Catherine smiled as she resumed her struggle with the bedding. "I wish Agnes had met someone like him long ago. But it's too late now, with him going off to the the Holy Land and her entering this marriage."

She mused on this as she whacked the dust from the wall hangings and took down all the bed curtains to go to the laundress. Why couldn't fate have arranged things better? Catherine knew that human lives were ordained to follow a certain path but if free will were to mean anything, there must be a way to direct the path to another end.

If only she were wise enough to know the right time and the right thing to do!

"Catherine! It's finished! Come and see!"

Edgar's voice was rich with delight. Catherine dropped the tapestry beater and ran to look. He hadn't let anyone inspect the pyx for the Paraclete while he was working on it and she had been afraid it was because he didn't want them to see his failure. It had taken him months of preparation before he even started on it. It had been necessary to devise a whole range of gripping tools to take the place of his missing hand. The echoes of his swearing during that process still rang through the house and the children had acquired a full vocabulary of English obscenity in the process.

The box he showed them was good sized, large enough to hold enough hosts for both the nuns and the townspeople who came to Mass. Edgar had shaped it like a covered trencher, only in silver over cedar. The hinges of the lid were gold and the lid itself had scenes from the events of Holy Week etched into the metal with gold wire halos around the heads of Christ and the Virgin.

"Oh, Edgar!" Catherine breathed. "It's beautiful! The best thing you've ever done."

"Saint Cecelia's botched beheading!" Hubert exclaimed as he entered. "It's a wonder, son. A master silversmith couldn't have done better."

Edgar looked from one to the other. He was suspicious of so much praise. Especially when he could see every flaw.

"Don't you think the joinings are a bit rough?" he asked.

"No, I don't," Hubert said, "or else I'd say so. You've been with me enough times to the fairs to know that I can tell the difference between good craft and bad. And I don't buy apprentice-quality goods. The sisters of the Paraclete will be honored by such a gift."

Catherine only nodded. There was nothing she could add. Approval from her father meant more to Edgar than anything she might say about his work. He had long felt that Hubert was merely tolerating him for Catherine's sake. At the beginning, it had been true, but Catherine felt that in the past years the two men had come to respect and even like each other. At least, she hoped so.

"I want Mother Heloise to see it right away," she said. "When can we leave?"

Hubert gave it some thought. "I have some things to finish here, but we could go by the end of next week," he told them. "I have to stop to do business in Provins, but you could go on. You could stay at the convent through Ascension Thursday and then meet me at Eliazar's home in Troyes."

"Do you think it's wise for us to meet there openly?" Edgar asked.

Hubert was taken aback. "Why not? Are you suddenly ashamed of my brother?"

"No, of course not, but I am wary where my children are concerned," Edgar answered. "Solomon told us that the situation in Champagne was calm for now, but who knows what will happen? Haven't we all heard rumors about that monk preaching against the Jews in Lotharingia and Germany? How long before the sentiment spreads?"

Hubert turned bright red with anger. "You forget yourself, young man! How dare you suggest that I'd let my family go anywhere there might be danger! Especially after what you exposed them to in England!"

"Father!" Catherine caught at his arm. "Calm down! Think of your health! Edgar is worried *because* of what happened in England. He doesn't want to risk our being separated in the middle of someone else's war again."

Edgar rose from his workbench in alarm at Hubert's reaction. "Yes, of course," he soothed. "Of course. You're quite right. I'm sure that nothing will happen in Troyes. Everything will be fine, Hubert. Now, just have some cool beer and rest yourself."

"Stop cosseting me!" Hubert sputtered. "I'm not a dotard to be humored. And I'm not going to collapse in a fit of apoplexy if I'm crossed."

He waved away the bowl of beer that Catherine was trying to give him. It spilt down the front of her gown. She looked from the stain to her father in resignation. That finally calmed him down. If Catherine were so worried about his health that she refused to become angry with him, she must think him very ill indeed.

"I apologize, *ma douz*," he said. "But I feel fine. Go change into something dry and we'll discuss this rationally."

"There's no need for futher talk, Hubert," Edgar said. "I know you love the children as much as we do. If you say it's safe for them to be in the Jewish quarter of Troyes, then we need no other assurance."

Mollified, Hubert allowed Edgar to pour him another bowl of beer while Catherine went up to change and to tell the others of the upcoming journey.

The two men drank in silence. Hubert held his bowl in both hands and let the sweet herbs and alcohol cool his choler. He noted the ease with which Edgar managed the large bowl with only one hand. He'd never realized before how much bigger Edgar's hands . . . hand, that is, was than his. His fingers were long and graceful, like a king's. Like the nobleman Edgar had been born.

"Damn it all!" Hubert thought.

"It is fine workmanship," he said aloud, gesturing at the pyx.

"Thank you," Edgar answered.

Both men felt that cautious peace had been restored.

Agnes had taken riverboats as far as she could, but they had finally had to use land routes. The women with her had enjoyed the journey so far, flirting openly with the men hired to guard them and dropping more subtle hints to Jehan and Walter, neither of whom showed any interest.

As the centerpiece in this tableau, Agnes felt it necessary to maintain a certain aloofness. She was, after all, about to be married to a lord. And, she told herself, she might as well get used to being lonely. But it was difficult to endure both Jehan's reproachful stare and the other women's enjoyment of the trip.

Walter of Grancy spent much of his time riding near her. Agnes knew that he was also constantly alert for danger about them. She was reminded of the times in her childhood when her uncle, Roger, would take her from Paris to Saint Denis. She had always felt so safe. But Roger had been dead a long time now and she was no longer a child to be protected from fear.

Agnes looked at Walter, solid as a fortress. She gave a long sigh that loosened the tightness in her shoulders. Perhaps for a few more days she could pretend she was a little child again.

Walter noticed her watching him. He smiled.

"Are you tired, Agnes?" he asked. "We can rest a while here if you like, but it's not far to the village of Jarny. We can pass the night there and make Metz by tomorrow night. From there we can take the river again, all the way to Trier."

"So soon?" The closer they got, the more unsure Agnes became. She had to collect herself. "Tired? No, not at all," she said. "The journey has been most pleasant and easy, thanks to your care. I'm surprised that it's passed so quickly."

Walter bowed quite elegantly for a man on horseback.

"I assure you, it's my pleasure to be of assistance to you and your family. I owe a great deal to your sister and her husband."

"Really?" Agnes stiffened.

"If not for them, I might still be living under the accusation of murder," he explained. "It was Catherine who discovered the real miscreant."

"Really?" Agnes said in a different tone. "Catherine does insist on following things through. Her curiosity has always been her misfortune."

"It was great good fortune to me," Walter said. "Although she certainly suffered in the course of it. And she and Edgar only just married, too. Yes, an easy trip in spring in the company of a beautiful woman is the least I could do to repay their kindness."

He laughed and she joined in a bit shakily. It was a shock to her to think that Catherine's endless prying into things not her concern could actually have been helpful to anyone.

Her second thought was almost as shocking. She found it very gratifying to realize that Walter thought she was beautiful.

As Walter had predicted, they reached Metz late the following afternoon. All during their trip, the crosses worn by Jehan and Walter had been greeted with respect and admiration. But in Metz they were only two of hundreds of soldiers with crosses. It seemed to Agnes that every man of fighting age was planning to join the pilgrimage.

The reason for this was made clear when they arrived at the hostel at the convent of Saint Pierre les Nonnains.

"The representative of Abbot Bernard is here," Jehan informed them, after talking with one of the clerics. "He read the abbot's encyclical yesterday in the town square and it was all they could do to keep the whole of Metz from taking the cross."

"Do you think the abbot himself will preach soon?" Agnes asked. "I didn't hear him at Vézelay."

"I don't know. He seems to be everywhere at once these days," Jehan said. "They say he may go to Germany to try to convince the emperor to join King Louis. And then there's this news from the Rhineland."

"And what is this news?" Walter asked impatiently.

"Oh, something about the Jews again." Jehan grimaced. "Some of them have been attacked and now they're whining to their bishops to protect them. As if those *mavaises bestes* deserved protection."

"Jehan!" Walter said in surprise. "Of course they do! The fathers of the Church all say so, as does Abbot Bernard. How will they ever be converted to the true faith if they're persecuted and killed?"

"They only way those stubborn bastards will ever come to the faith is at the point of a sword," Jehan told him.

Agnes began to feel uneasy with the conversation.

"I don't like them, either, Jehan," she said. "But I don't think anyone was ever converted in their hearts through intimidation."

Jehan gave her a startled glance, as if a favorite hunting dog had suddenly tried to bite him.

"Also," Walter added, "the bishops swore an oath to protect the Jews under them. Breaking it would imperil their immortal souls."

"Yes, of course." Jehan seized at this solution. "One must never break a sacred oath, however foolish."

He turned to Agnes for her reaction, but she wasn't paying attention to either of them. One of the guards had helped her down and she was busy directing the unloading of her baggage while she waited for the portress to admit her and the other ladies.

Walter shook his head in sympathy.

"Turn your mind to Heaven, Jehan, as I do," he said. "Or you'll find no peace anywhere on Earth."

"I have no hope of either Heaven or happiness." Jehan's voice was bleak.

Walter leaned over and gave him a pat that nearly unseated him.

"In that case, we might as well see to the women and then go drown ourselves in the first tavern we can find."

Jehan brightened slightly. "That's the best idea I've heard since this journey began."

Agnes didn't notice them leave. There was too much to be done. It was the private belief of her maids that she would run a household better than the kings did their armies. She oversaw everything and missed nothing. While she was, they admitted, fair in her demands, there was no warmth in her manner. Her prospective husband was the subject of sincere pity.

Agnes gave no sign that she knew or cared what they thought. She gave the directions for the temporary storage of her goods and then allowed the portress to lead her to greet the abbess before re-tiring to her room.

The maids stopped for a moment after she had gone.

"Do you think she even confides in a priest?" Laudine asked asked.

"Hmmph! That one wouldn't tell her secrets to the Virgin her-self," Lisette stated.

A third woman bent over and began gathering up bundles of clothing and toiletries that would be needed that night.

"She's a close one," the woman agreed. "But I'd think she must be lonely as Eve without another woman to share her troubles with."

The others considered that horrible fate and continued their work in a spirit of thankfulness.

Once he had made his own arrangements for the night and seen Jehan tucked in with a skin of wine, Walter decided to explore the town. Metz was in imperial territory and had recently been granted the freedom to answer only to Emperor Conrad III instead of a local lord. A ruler had been selected from the local noblemen but not on any inherited or territorial principle. It sounded to Walter something like the anarchy that was currently prevailing in Italy and he was curious about how the locals were faring under such a system.

He strolled through the streets with the confidence of a man who wore both sword and knife and knew that only a lunatic would dare bother him. The shops were all busy, the shutters open wide to catch the spring air and tables set up in the streets so that there was only a narrow path for people to walk through. Walter bumped and apologized his way along, stopping now and then to buy a sausage or a bowl of beer.

He was just turning around, the sausage half-eaten, when he came face-to-face with a man who seemed very familiar.

"Pardon," the man said as he made to pass him.

"Of course," Walter answered, swallowing the rest of the sausage. "Don't I know you?"

The man smiled as if used to the question. "I think not," he answered. "You may have once met my father. If your accent is any guide, you're from south of Dijon, right?"

"Grancy," Walter said. "I've some land there."

The man nodded. "Well I don't think we've—wait," he looked at Walter again. "You weren't at Sens, were you, when my father was condemned by the bishops?"

"That's it!" Walter was delighted to have an answer to the puzzle. "You're Abelard's son, the one with the funny name."

"Astrolabe," he answered and smiled. "I remember now. You were friends with that poor woman who died at my mother's convent. Catherine LeVendeur was very concerned about her."

"I saw Catherine and Edgar only recently in Paris!" Walter felt he had discovered a lost relative. "You know about his accident, don't you?"

They both started down the road again, stomping unconcernedly through the refuse that ran down the ditch in the middle. Walter explained to Astrolabe why he was in Metz.

"It's good of you to go to that trouble," Astrolabe said. "It will make Catherine easier in her mind to know you're watching over her sister."

"Now, are you attached to the church here?" Walter asked.

Astrolabe seemed embarrassed. "No. Actually, well, actually, I'm here at the request of Abbot Bernard. I know it's odd, considering his relations with my father, but I happened to be at Clairvaux when he needed someone to carry his letters this way and I offered. My mother feels that I need to have a benefice, or a position tutoring or as a clerk. The abbot may be willing to help."

"What does he think of this news that the Jews are being attacked again?" Walter asked.

"I'm not sure he believes it yet," Astrolabe said. "He's sent letters everywhere telling people to leave the Jews in peace. It's incredible to him that he would be ignored."

"I heard that one of his own monks was leading the persecutions."

"That's only rumor."

"But it concerns you?" Walter read Astolabe's expression.

"Yes." Astrolabe stopped walking and rubbed his forehead. "I agree with my father and Abbot Bernard that Jews should be brought to Christ through logic and divine grace, not coercion. And I have friends among them whom I would not see hurt."

"Yes," Walter said. "So do I."

They continued their perambulation into the wider area in front of the church of Notre Dame de la Ronde. There Astrolabe took leave of Walter.

Walter started to say good-bye, then bit his lip, as if trying to come to a decision. He decided quickly. He had to ask.

"Astrolabe, does your mother know that you're in the service of the man who condemned your father?"

Astrolabe chuckled. "It was her idea for me to come to him for assistance. If I didn't know her nature better, I would have thought she was trying to induce Abbot Bernard to show remorse and make some restitution for his act."

"Has he shown any?" Walter's eyes were wide at the concept.

"None at all." Astrolabe grinned now. "He hasn't mentioned the council once. He treats me with exactly the same Christian kindness he shows to everyone."

"Oh." Walter was somehow disappointed.

"Everyone who agrees with him, that is," Astrolabe added over his shoulder as he walked away.

Walter turned this over in his mind all the way back to the hostel.

"Are we finally ready to go?" Hubert asked. "Why does it take so long to prepare for a journey? Your mother always did it easily in a day."

"Father," Catherine said in exasperation, as she dealt with a crying daughter and servants asking five questions at once. "When the whole household went any place, you left long before the rest of the family. Mother had more help and more experience and it was still chaos until the door shut behind us."

Hubert looked puzzled. "I don't remember it like that. Well, never mind. When can we leave, then?"

"As soon as Edgar returns," Catherine told him. "Everything is packed or stored except his tools. At the last minute he decided he needed a knife sharpened or something. Yes, James, you can ride with Grandfather. No, the puppy will be happier here. He'll be waiting for you when we return. It will only be a few weeks. Edana, be quiet! Wood Bunny is already in the bag hanging from my saddle. You can't get him now."

The child's screams rose to shrieks. Hubert covered his ears.

"Which bag is it?" he shouted. "I'll find the damn rabbit!"

Catherine was furious. Where was Edgar? What had possessed him to run off on some *fatuus* errand? If she weren't so tired, she'd go in search of him and give him grief all the way home, like a wife from the *jongleur* stories.

But, when he finally arrived, contrite and out of breath, she forgave him, as he knew she would. He had brought everyone sweet *pagnon*, made with honey and just the right size to fit into Edana's mouth and stop her wailing for the rabbit Edgar had carved for her.

"Where have you been?" she was human enough to ask. "It's nearly None and we've all been waiting for you."

"I know," Edgar answered. "I'm sorry. I was talking with the silversmith. His son is studying in Köln right now and Samuel is worried that the family has had no news of him since before septuagesima."

"Did you reassure him?" Catherine asked. "Letters often go astray. Half the messages we sent Father from Scotland never reached him."

Edgar busied himself with helping Hubert put back all the things from Edana's bag so they could leave. Everyone else was mounted and ready. He then handed James up to Hubert, helped Catherine onto her horse and, finally, inserted his arm into the loop hanging from his saddle that allowed him to mount with only one hand. He was still clumsy at it and the adults all found something else to look at until he had finished.

They made their way single file through the city, to the Roman road that led east, past the new monastery of the Knights Templar and into the forest. Hubert didn't like taking the roads as there was constant danger of attack from outlaws in the forest. But it was easier than sailing the Seine upstream. He planned to sell the horses in Troyes and bring them all home by boat. They would all stay with Eliazar until summer, when the river was slow and docile.

Once they had entered the shade of the woods, everyone grew quiet. The children went to sleep, even Margaret, leaning against Edgar's back. Catherine found herself remembering her first trip to Provins for the fair. She'd been hardly older that James and it took the combined efforts of her father, Eliazar and Solomon to keep her from falling off or onto something or wandering away and getting lost.

Very different was the journey to the Paraclete, when she had been fifteen. She had believed then that she would never come this way again, but remain in the convent all her life. At the time, there was no greater joy imaginable than to be the bride of Christ.

Catherine gave a rueful snort at the child she had been. Dearly as she loved her savior, she knew she loved Edgar more. Sacrilegious it might be, but there was no remedy for it.

The thought gave Catherine a slight qualm. She had sent word to Mother Heloise that they were coming but had received no answer. It suddenly occurred to her that, returning with a growing family and small but definite entourage, the nuns might not be inclined to welcome her at all.

Six

Lord Gerhardt's castle, Trier. Friday, 5 nones May (May 3), 1146; 19 Iyyar, 4906. Commemoration of the finding of the True Cross by Saint Helena, of which a piece the size of a thumb was brought to Trier, along with nails from the cross, the Crown of Thorns and bits of clothing worn by Jesus.

Treviris alma per hunc major, tibi Roma Quirites
Transmisit cives, fecit et esse tuos.
Hucque caput mundi veniens, hic esse cor orbis
Non negat, et nomen Roma secunda tuum.

Kind Trier, greater through this man [Albero] Rome sent you noble citizens and made them yours. The capital of the whole world, all who come here do not deny that this is the heart of the globe, its name "second Rome."

—The Life of Archbishop Albero
Metric version

$\mathcal{M}$aria, is there somewhere we can speak in private?" Hermann stopped his sister as she was going out to the herb garden.

"If it's about Gerhardt again," she answered, pulling away from his grasp, "there isn't anything more to say. We've done all we can. He's agreed to marry the girl. It's really too much to expect him to be cheerful about it, I suppose. Perhaps when he meets her."

"No, it's not about Gerhardt this time," Hermann said. "At least, not exactly."

Maria sighed. "Very well. Come help me thin the mint and you can tell me what's worrying you now."

The sharp scent of the herb rose around them as Hermann and Maria knelt in the enclosed garden. Around them were wattle fences and on the other side a great elm tree shaded the area, allowing the mint to run wild. Maria inhaled deeply. It made a change from the tang of fermenting wine.

Hermann tugged nervously at a plant. He tossed it over his shoulder. Maria glared at him.

"What do you think I brought the basket for?" she asked, pointing to it.

"*Ez ist mir leit*, I was thinking of something else." Hermann dropped a muddy bunch of mint into it. "Now, it's about that messenger that was found at the edge of the river."

"I thought the matter had been refered to Bishop Albero," Maria spoke without interest. "We prayed for the poor man. What more is there to do?"

"Find out what he was doing on our land," Hermann answered. "He wasn't here by chance. I'm sure of it. Gerhardt knows more than he told us or the bishop. I don't believe the message in the letter that was found was washed out by the water or that the seal had been obliterated. It wasn't when I gave it to Gerhardt."

"Are you saying that our brother lied?" Maria's eyebrows rose. Hermann's jaw set stubbornly. It was a look Maria knew well from their nursery days.

"I know what I saw," he said. "The vellum was dry and the seal unbroken when Gerhardt took it. And why did he feel the need to open it alone? He's hiding something from us. Something he's ashamed of, I fear."

Maria wanted to laugh at him, or become angry, but she could do neither. Even before this marriage issue had come up, Gerhardt had been behaving strangely. All those trips to Köln. The visitors who only stayed a night and left before dawn. Hermann wasn't imagining things. Something was wrong and it hurt her deeply that Gerhardt didn't trust her enough to tell her what it was.

"You don't think he's plotting against the bishop . . . or the emperor?" Her voice shook at the thought.

"I don't know!" Hermann's voice rose and he immediatly looked around to see if anyone had heard. "He's never acted treasonous before. Why should he? What have either of them done to him?"

"But then what else could it be?" Maria yanked at the mint and a whole chain of it came away in her hand. She stared at it for a long moment. "He wouldn't risk having the land confiscated. He loves nothing more. And yet . . ."

"And yet." Hermann shivered as the tree above them sent a splash of water down his neck.

He got to his feet and took the basket.

"We must get him to confide in us," he said. "Whatever is wrong, he mustn't keep it from the rest of the family. We never had secrets from each other before. Perhaps he just has a concubine in Köln and is embarrassed to admit it."

The thought cheered him, but Maria was doubtful. She wished Hermann hadn't unsettled her with his worries. Still, if the problem were no more than a woman, the coming of this French bride might solve everything.

The two of them returned to the keep. On the quivering branch of the elm tree, young Peter watched them until they went inside. Then he slid down. His aunt and uncle had given him much to ponder.

∞

Catherine enjoyed traveling to the fairs, especially in spring. There
was always something new to see and interesting people to meet. She
was never worried about trade or the eternal feuds among the ven-
dors. With her father's guards always near, she didn't concern herself
with the thought of robbers. And now, with James wanting to try
everything and Edana shrieking in delight at the jugglers or in terror
at the captive bear, it was as if she were a child again, herself.

"Mama! Want ball!" Edana nearly fell out of her arms as the
child tried to snatch the ball out of the air as it spun by. The juggler
laughed, put the balls back in his sack and took out a wooden doll
on a stick. When a string was pulled, the doll danced.

"Mama!" Edana cried again. "Want doll."

"Only a halfpenny of Paris." The man smiled.

"Edana, your father makes you all the dolls you'll ever need."
Catherine tried to reason with her, then realized anew that at a year
and a half, her daughter wasn't interested in reason.

"I don't have any pennies," she told the man. "Let me ask my
husband."

She looked around for Edgar, who had taken Margaret and James
with Hubert to look at the horses. The juggler seemed happy to
follow her until she found money. To keep Edana interested, he
made the doll wiggle in his hand and then climb up his arm and
onto his shoulder, well out of her reach.

"I know they were here a moment ago," Catherine said as she
bumped into a woman who was holding up a length of cloth to
examine it in the sunlight. "Sorry."

The woman paid her no attention. The juggler stayed on their
heels. Catherine stopped and, hardening her heart to Edana's pleas,
decided that she wasn't going to spend the rest of the morning hunting for pennies to get everything the child took a fancy to.

"I'm sorry," she told the juggler. "I don't see my husband, and
my daughter really doesn't need another toy. You'll do better continuing your trade somewhere else."

The man's face turned from geniality to anger.

"Then why waste my time dragging me from my corner!" he
yelled at her. "I've lost my place now and maybe the day's profit!
Damn you and all your kind!"

Catherine was shocked at the intensity of his anger. He had seemed so friendly only a moment before. She backed away from him, her arms wrapped protectively about her child.

"I am sorry," she said.

He gave her a sneer, wheeled about and marched off. Catherine watched him go. His behavior was confusing. It had only been a few minutes. He would hardly lose a day's worth of sales in that time. Why reproach her with such venom?

She tried to shrug it off but the fair had been spoiled now. The laughter seemed fake and the goods tawdry. All she wanted was to find Edgar and feel safe again.

She didn't see the juggler as he reversed his parti-colored cloak so that only the dull brown lining showed. He removed his hat with the silver bells and put on a cap of soft leather. Then he followed her.

By the time Catherine saw James balanced on his father's shoulders she felt a bit silly for her uneasiness. The juggler may have counted on her money. Perhaps the takings had been poor so far. With so many people thinking about a journey to the Holy Land or fearing the loss of someone they loved there, they might not be throwing coin to frivolous entertainers. No wonder he was angry.

"We were waiting for you," Edgar said. "James wants a sausage and I want some beer."

"Both sound good to me." Catherine handed Edana over to Margaret and shook her tired arms. The child was getting too heavy to carry all the time.

"Are you all right?" Edgar always sensed when she was upset.

"It's nothing," she said. "An argument with a man selling toys."

"You didn't get her any?" Edgar was firm.

"No penny," Catherine told him. "What did you do?"

"Your father bought a horse from Spain," Edgar told her. "He knows a man in Paris who will pay well for it. I negotiated with a cooper for wine barrels to be sent to Eliazar in Troyes. Not a very exciting day."

"In the past few years, we've had enough excitement," Catherine said. "I'm happy for a long spate of ordinary life."

"With you, it will never be ordinary," Edgar grinned in a way that still made her stomach tighten. "Come along. I'm starving."

They gathered up the family and went in search of the sausage seller.

Behind them, the juggler watched and waited.

The evening was warm as summer and the tent they had brought was more comfortable than the inns that normally provided for the traders. The children went to sleep early, wrapped in feather quilts. Hubert had gone to drink and trade stories with some merchants who had just returned from the Balkans with a supply of amber.

"I hope he gets some," Edgar commented. "I'd like to try carving amber."

"I'd like a brooch of a piece set in gold," Catherine said. "Could you make me one?"

"Could I set my own price?" He smiled wickedly.

Catherine checked the sleeping children. "Would you like payment in advance?" she asked, holding her hand out to him.

"How did you know what I was going to demand?" He took her hand and let himself be drawn into the tent.

Sometime later Hubert was walking a little unsteadily back to the tent. One of the Easterm traders was with him, still trying to convince him that the coming war would only improve trade.

"I tell you, the soldiers will return with a taste for perfume from Constantinople and Baghdad. They'll want silks and Indian spices. Why shouldn't you be ready to supply them?" He belched and pounded his stomach.

Hubert shook his head. "There's no profit in death, Alexis," he answered. "Those that return may have acquired rich tastes but that doesn't mean they'll be able to afford them. Half the pilgrims have sold everything they own just to make the journey. No, I'll stick to wine and goods for the monasteries. Whatever happens, they'll always need more and eventually, they pay."

Alexis belched again. "I can see you haven't had dealings with Peter of Cluny. He's mortgaged and borrowed most of his property to rebuild his church. You should hear him go on about the Jews. They say he's trying to get King Louis to make them bear the cost of retaking Edessa."

"Not really?" Hubert was shocked almost sober. "I know that

interest has been suspended on Jewish loans but nothing more. You don't think the king will do it?"

"No, everyone knows he's a Jew lover," Alexis said. "They pay him tribute. Cluny is in Burgundy, not France, so Louis gets nothing from Peter."

Hubert hoped this was true. He and Eliazar had tried to avoid moneylending but lately it had become more difficult. He had many Jewish friends who were being slowly pushed into usury as Christians became more adept at trade. His guilt at being one of those Christian merchants, at least in the eyes of the world, was growing each year. It turned his stomach to have to agree when fellow traders complained about how the Jews were stealing business from them as well as seducing their wives, daughters and occasionally, horses.

Alexis went on. "But, even with the king's protection, they know which way the wind blows." He tapped the side of his nose. "Notice how few of them dared show their faces here this year? Who would buy from them?"

Hubert had noticed. He had been given several commissions from friends too cautious to appear openly in the climate of hate that was gathering. He was relieved when Alexis reached his tent and he could stumble back to his own in peace.

He untied the tent flap and crawled in, loosening his belt before lying down. It was only then that he realized that it was lighter than usual. He felt for a purse that should be hanging there. All he felt was the leather tie. It had been cut cleanly and the purse lifted without him ever feeling it.

"*Enondu!*" he shouted. "I've been robbed!"

Around him, the family awoke with a start. Edana began to cry. "Father?" Catherine said sleepily. "What's wrong?"

"Some *cavete* bastard stole my purse while I was drinking!" Hubert roared. "Call out the guard! I want him captured!"

He backed out of the tent, still shouting.

Edgar sat up. "What are you doing, Hubert?"

"I'm going to find the thief before he can spend all my money." Hubert grunted as he tightened his belt again.

"Father!" Catherine called from the tent. She was wrapped in a blanket and her braids had come undone. "Edgar will come with you. He's dressing now. How much was in the purse?"

She caught Hubert in midrage and made him stop and think.

"Not much, really," he admitted in a lower voice. "Only a few sou. I used most of what I had to buy the horse this afternoon. But that doesn't matter."

"Was there anything else?" Catherine asked.

"No, just a bit of parchment, a note." He stopped. "A note Eliazar had given me with specifications for a candelabra that the count wanted made."

Hubert bit his lip. "It was in French," he added, "but the letters were Hebrew."

Catherine considered this. "The thief probably wouldn't know one letter from another," she told him. "He'll likely just toss it away. And even if he took it to someone, how could he explain where he had found it?"

Hubert was calm now.

"Yes, I suppose you're right," he said. "But it does mean that it wouldn't be wise to go after this *putier*. I might have to identify the contents and I don't want anyone asking how it is that I can read Hebrew."

"But everyone knows you and Eliazar are partners," Edgar said as he hesitated before putting on his boots.

Hubert sighed. "No, not since that business two years ago. Everyone thinks I've cut off all ties with him. And I don't know any Christian merchants who carry messages in Hebrew."

"Father!" Catherine was confused. "Why didn't you tell us about Eliazar? What about Solomon? No, come back in first. We mustn't wake the whole fair."

Hubert saw the sense of this and returned to the tent. He hoped that Edana's crying had masked his shouts. He patted the baby's head.

"I was ashamed to tell you," he admitted. "Eliazar and I both felt things were becoming too dangerous for us but to abandon my own brother to our enemies—! The shame is horrible. As for Solomon, he travels among Christians so much that no one seems to notice him any more."

Catherine kissed his cheek.

"Uncle Eliazar understands how you feel and I agree," she said. "Things are unsettled enough now without adding the fear of discovery. It would go harder on you than him if your relationship were known. And it might well hurt all of us, including my brother and his family even though they know nothing of your past."

"Yes, you're right." Hubert didn't sound happy about it. "But that means that the man who stole my purse will never pay for it."

"Of course he will," Catherine said, as she settled back next to Edgar. "God will see to him."

It was just as well she couldn't see Hubert's face in the dark. His expression said all too clearly what he thought of leaving the punishment to God.

Outside the circle of trader tents, outside the walls of the town, almost to the edge of the dark woods, there was another encampment. No one here could afford a tent although some had fashioned a cover with sticks and ragged cloth. The fire was small and only hot enough to warm the barley broth out of its congealed state. They had set no guard for there was nothing to steal but their lives and they had long since commended those to Fate.

Yet one man sat with his back to the dying coals keeping some sort of watch. His head was thrown back, his eyes on the stars, but he was alert for any noise. So, when the juggler arrived, he was not caught unprepared.

"Matfras." He greeted the juggler. "I thought you had left us. What kept you so late?"

Matfras squatted next to him and tried to coax some warmth from the dregs of the fire to his chilled hands.

"I fell into a vat," he answered. "Head first, I'm glad to say."

"The day went badly?"

"Not so much as a crust," Matfras spat. "Too many other jugglers, one who does knives and gourds at the same time. No one wants my toys. It was late in the day before I had any luck at all and then only enough to slake my thirst."

The man waited.

"But I did come across something I thought you should see," Matfras added.

"Yes." He had known that when Matfras arrived.

The juggler took a piece of parchment from his sleeve and unfolded it.

"I showed it to a monk and he could make nothing of it," he told the watcher. "I think it's magic, a spell of some sort. Could you use it?"

He held out the paper with Eliazar's hasty scrawl across it. The watcher pressed it to his forehead, eyes closed.

"Yes," he said at last. "It is a very powerful charm. The ink was made from the charred bones of heretics mixed with the blood of Saracens. But it has no value unless one can pronounce the words and knows the right time to say them."

"But you do," Matfras said eagerly. "What will you give me for it?"

The watcher smiled.

"Life everlasting," he whispered as his knife entered the juggler's heart.

It was Sunday morning. Catherine and her family packed their belongings and prepared to set out for the Paraclete. A body that had once been a juggler from the south was now hidden under a lilac tree in full bloom. His bones would not be found until autumn. And the boat that carried Agnes down the Moselle to her new home docked at the city of Trier in time for her to attend Mass.

"It's not so different from the cities I know," she said bravely as Walter handed her onto the riverbank. "Really, it's much smaller than Paris. I'm told that the nuns at Saint Irminen will shelter me until Lord Gerhardt comes. Can you find out where that is?"

One of the boatmen had overheard her.

"You can see it from here, my lady." He pointed. "Up there, just inside the city walls."

Agnes looked. The convent was substantial, with an air of wealth and tradition. Surely there would be someone there who could instruct her as to local customs. She didn't want to offend unintentionally before she learned the ways of her new home.

As they walked through the city to the convent, Agnes tried not to stare. She knew that Trier had once been a great capital. Constantine the Great had ruled here before he built his namesake city. The cathedral still held the Holy Tunic, the robe Christ had worn and the Roman soldiers cast lots for. Constantine's mother, Saint Helena, had brought it from Jerusalem and, when Constantine had departed, the tunic had remained. Pilgrims came all through the year to see it.

There were other signs of the emperor's presence; the enormous church he had built, along with a sense of order in the way the streets and marketplace were laid out that was nothing like the haphazard design of Paris. The Roman patterns had not been obliterated here. It was a prosperous place, as well. She could tell that from the clothing of the citizens, their fine glass and metal brooches and gold earrings.

Agnes willed herself to appear regal, even haughty. Instinctively she knew she mustn't show how daunted she was.

She tightened her hold on Walter's arm. He looked down at her with concern.

"Perhaps we should have ridden," she told him.

"We can still, if you like," he told her. "I didn't realize that the streets would be so wide. I thought it would be easier to walk."

"No, we're almost there." Agnes realized that they had passed through the marketplace and were approaching the gate to the convent. "While my women and I are being settled, would you find someone to take a message to Lord Gerhardt to tell him that I have arrived?"

"Of course," Walter answered. "I shall go myself and then return to tell you what this husband of yours is like."

For the first time in weeks, Agnes smiled.

"Thank you, Walter," she said as the gate opened.

Gerhardt's land wasn't very far from Trier, only just past the monastery of Saint Marien, but it took Walter the better part of the afternoon to reach it for the road wound through the vineyards as though it had been cut from land too rocky to plant. Even in Burgundy, Walter had never seen so many vines. They stretched as far up the hillside as he could see and down to the river. He wondered where they grew grain or if they did. Wine was all very well, but he wouldn't like to rely on trade to provide himself with bread.

He approved of the new castle, though. It was set high above the river with a clear view in three directions and the mountain at the rear. With a water supply inside, it could be defended against any invader.

Before leaving with a local man to guide him, Walter had taken time to change into a black velvet *chainse* and put a fine wool tunic over it with his pilgrim's cross as the only ornament. He was well aware that he looked imposing as he gave his name to the guard at the gate.

"Lord Walter of Grancy, in Burgundy," he announced. "Come to deliver a message to Lord Gerhardt that he has long been expecting."

He was admitted at once and shown into an anteroom off the great hall, which was being set up for the evening meal. A servant brought him some cheese and a cup of wine. Walter settled down to wait, but only a moment later a man burst in on him.

"*Wie nû?*" he demanded. "What's happened?"

Walter stared at him in astonishment. The man was wearing leather *brais* and a short tunic. A conical straw hat hung from a string around his neck. His hands were grimy and his shoes covered in mud.

"Saint Menas's sacred spring!" Walter said. "Who the devil are you?"

"I'm Lord Gerhardt," the man answered.

He followed Walter's gaze to his filthy attire.

"I understood that the message was urgent," he explained.

"No," Walter said. "Just expected. A least I assumed so. I've come to announce the arrival of the Lady Agnes de Bois Vert at Trier."

Gerhardt seemed confused. "Yes?"

Walter stood. "You are planning to marry her, aren't you?"

"Oh my God! Agnes!" Gerhardt breathed. "She's here already? Oh dear, let me fetch my sister. She'll know what to do."

He started to go, then turned back.

"I apologize for my appearance," he said. "I thought you were . . . well. I'll send my sister and go change. Should we give you a bed tonight?"

Walter shook his head but Gerhardt had already gone. Through the curtain he could hear the lord of the castle shouting orders at the servants. The loudest was to find his sister and bring her at once.

Interesting, Walter thought. Not at all what he'd expected. It boded ill for poor Agnes if her intended husband couldn't even remember her name. He returned to the cheese and wished he had been brought a pitcher of wine along with the cup.

As if his need had been anticipated a boy entered, carrying a clay pitcher. He set it on the table next to Walter and then looked around, puzzled.

"I thought they said that my new stepmother had arrived," he said. "I'm Peter, Gerhardt's son."

He gave Walter his hand with a slight bow. Walter took it.

"Are you really going to free Edessa?" Peter asked, pointing to the cross.

"As soon as King Louis raises the rest of his army," Walter told him. "But if he takes his time about it, I may go alone."

Peter regarded the man before him, too big to fit comfortably in the folding chair he had been given. The sword at Walter's side was almost as tall as Peter himself.

"I would very much like to go with you," he said. "Do you need a squire?"

Walter chuckled. "I have one waiting for me back in Burgundy, but I'll remember your offer if he turns coward. Would you like to examine the sword?"

Peter had not taken his eyes off it. Walter unbuckled it and handed it to him, scabbard and all.

"Have you fought many battles with this?" Peter asked. He longed to try it on, but could tell that the sword would drag along behind if it didn't topple him over.

"None at all," Walter said. "This was forged especially for this journey. I have a friend who trades in Spain and he found a sword-smith who is superior to any master I've ever known. It's strong and light and impervious to rust, they say."

"What is its name?" Peter asked.

"You know," Walter said, after thinking, "it never occured to me to give it one. Perhaps when I first use the blade, a name will come to me."

"Yes." Peter considered that. "I suppose one shouldn't name something until you know what it can do."

At that moment the curtain drew aside and Maria entered, followed by her husband, Folmar, and Hermann. All were dressed formally, if with a certain dishevelment indicative of haste.

"Lord Walter." Maria bowed to him and introduced herself. "Welcome to our home. We understand that your German is excellent. Does that mean the Lady Agnes also speaks it?"

Walter stood and bowed.

"I'm most happy to be here," he said. "Unfortunately, she hasn't been taught the language, but she has been studying since the betrothal was signed and I'm sure she'll soon be able to speak with you. One of the maids she brought is fluent in both French and German and can be trusted to keep the meaning whole."

"Where is she at the moment?" Maria asked.

Walter explained. "She would be most happy if Lord Gerhardt himself came to welcome her. Tomorrow perhaps?"

He caught the look the three exchanged. What was happening here? This was all wrong. If the wedding were set for Ascension Sunday, then they should have known she'd arrive by now. It was barely two weeks away. Walter vowed that he would not leave Agnes among them until he knew she would be safe.

Hermann answered for he three of them. "Of course. We'll all come to greet her. Her coming has been greatly anticipated. My sister has been making preparations since quinquegesima."

Walter wondered if Gerhardt had been told of them.

"You will remain with us for the night?" Maria asked.

"No, I thank you, but I must return before dark to report to Lady Agnes," he answered. "She has had a long journey and is understandably curious about her new family."

"Of course. Please tell her that we are eager to meet her and to give her every comfort and honor," Maria told him. Hermann and Folmar nodded agreement.

"We have a small house in the city," Hermann said. "You're welcome to stay there. We'll arrive by Sext tomorrow to visit our new sister and to entertain her and her party in the evening. I suppose it would be more appropriate if she stayed with the nuns until the wedding, but we have prepared a room for her and her maids if she prefers."

"I'll ask her," Walter promised.

He waited some time more for his host to reappear but there was no sign of Gerhardt, although Ulrich vanished at one point, presumably to hunt for him. Finally, Walter took his leave. The others walked him to the gate. As he left he thought he saw a man in grimy leather and a straw hat emerge from one of the outbuildings.

"I don't like it," Walter muttered to himself as he rode away. "It seems that poor Agnes may have been given to a lunatic."

Seven

The convent of the Paraclete. Monday, 2 nones May (May 6), 1146; 22 Iyyar, 4906. The feast of Saint John at the Latin Gate.

Magisterium habetis in matre quod omnia vobis sufficere . . . que non solum Latine, verum eciam tam Ebraice quam Grece non expers litterature . . .

You have in your mother all the master that you need, who is not only learned in Latin, but also Hebrew and Greek.

—Peter Abelard
Letter Nine
To the nuns of the Paraclete

$\mathcal{A}$bbess Heloise was in her room writing. She had intended to work on her weekly talk to the nuns, this one an explication of a particularly obscure phrase in Isaiah. Instead she found herself opening again the casket containing the letters from her once-husband, Peter Abelard, along with copies of her replies. Peter was dead now. They had sent his body home to her, acknowledging that no one had more right to it. The letters were all she had left, all that proved that his love for her hadn't died when he became a monk. Over and over she read them, even when she vowed not to, for the pain of loss was as great as the joy of memory and both fought to control her soul.

She was so deep in the past that it was some time before she was aware of the commotion outside her door. Several people were talking at once and at least one voice was male. Alarmed, Heloise rose from her stool and went to see what was happening. There was a group over by the guest house. When they saw her, a woman broke from the others and started running toward her.

"Catherine!" Heloise cried.

Catherine hugged her before remembering her manners. Abashed, she knelt for a blessing.

"I wish you a thousand," Heloise said. "From the look of it, you have already been much blessed."

She nodded toward the guest house, where Edgar and Hubert sat on a bench by the door. The nuns were bringing them water to wash with. But it was obvious to Heloise that they were prompted by more than the rules of hospitality. She could see what the real attraction was.

"Want up!" Edana only had to ask once. There were forty pairs of arms willing to hold her.

"Oh, Mother." Catherine laughed. "I mustn't let them give Edana everything she wants. She's spoiled enough already! What she needs is a dose of Sister Bertrada's discipline."

"Sister Bertrada uses her cane more for support than to ferule the novices these days," Heloise said. "You've been away a long time."

Catherine bent her head. "I'm sorry, Mother. We were in Spain when the news came of Master Abelard's death and then my confinement with James was strict. I had lost so many before him. But I should have come after Edana was born. I've been very remiss. Forgive me."

"Nonsense," Heloise told her. "I wasn't chastising you, simply stating a fact. You are all more than welcome any time."

"Thank you, Mother, I know that." Catherine paused. "It's partly why I've come. But we can discuss that later. I want you to meet the children. They aren't perfect but they're ours and I'm terribly attached to them."

"As it should be." Heloise walked with her to the guest house. "It seems strange to me now that I could have left my poor Astrolabe for his aunt to raise. How young I was then! Sometimes I wonder what would have happened if I had stayed with him in Le Pallet and never returned to Paris."

She dismissed the thought as soon as it had been spoken. "Our Lord knew best, of course," she added. "This was where He wanted me to be all along."

"Do you think, Mother, that I was never meant to take the veil?" Catherine asked.

"The mind of God isn't open to me, Catherine." Heloise smiled. "But I suspect that you too have followed His design.

"Now," she added in a much different voice, "this boy, with his mother's curls and his father's eyes, would you be James, sir?"

James stared up at her, transfixed by her enormous brown eyes. For the first time in his young life, he was speechless. Edgar came to his rescue.

"James has come specifically to present you and the sisters with a gift, haven't you?"

James nodded. Edgar handed him the box. He held it up.

"Father made this for you," he said with some prompting. "It's a pyx and I helped."

Heloise opened the box and admired the craftsmanship, all the more because Edgar had accomplished it with only one hand.

"When I begin to lament the work to be done here and feel I can never finish, I shall look at this and remember what can be done with faith and perseverance," she told him.

"Not to mention the patience of those around the artisan," Hubert added. "To endure his swearing while he worked."

Edgar joined the laughter. He wasn't comfortable with praise or with notice of his missing hand. Enough that he had to live with it.

They were given dinner in the guest house, with Abbess Heloise and several of the other nuns present. Sister Melisande, the infirmarian who had taught Catherine about medicine, was called halfway through the meal to attend to Sister Bertrada.

"Is she very ill?" Catherine asked. Bertrada had been the bane of her life, but now that she was free of the nun's sharp tongue and hard cane, she was more charitable.

"Bertrada is dying," Heloise said simply. "She's been failing for some time. The pain in her joints is extreme, so that every step is agony for her. But she still attends the singing of the Office. We've made a room for her next to the chapel so she won't have far to go, but each day it's harder and now she has no appetite. I don't think it will be long before she's released from her bodily prison at last. If you can bear it, Catherine, I think she'd like to see you."

"Me?" Catherine was astonished. "But I was such a disappointment to her."

"Why ever do you think that?" Heloise said. "She told me many a time that you were the brightest, clumsiest girl she'd ever taught and that one day you would fly from us because our walls were too narrow for your spirit."

"Not my spirit, Mother," Catherine said sadly. "The soul feels neither walls nor bars. It was my perverse will that sent me back into the world. Is it wrong to have found such happiness there?"

"I would reassure you, *ma douz.*" Heloise patted her cheek. "But

I truly don't know. I can only believe, as I said before, that we are following the path we were meant to be on."

"Well, I do wish I could see a little farther down it." Catherine sighed. "Every year, the way seems much more twisting, with side roads that become deer trails that lead nowhere. And now, I'm responsible for so much more than my own life."

"So am I, Catherine." Heloise echoed her sigh. "It makes me wonder if hermits are so much holy as selfish. Some days a solitary hut in the woods seems like Heaven."

There had been a time when Catherine would have agreed with her wholeheartedly. But her life was so entwined with those of her family that to be pulled from them now would cause her to shrivel and die.

She let her mind wander to Agnes, facing a new country as a stranger with no one tied to her at all. It would have been proper for Catherine to accompany her sister, despite the rift between them. Catherine felt a stab of guilt. With all her heart she wished Agnes well.

Agnes wasn't thinking of Catherine at all. Now that the moment had come to meet her betrothed, she was terrified.

"Do you think this is elegant enough?" she asked her maids. "They're wearing the sleeves longer in Paris, but I haven't seen anyone in *bliauts* of this cut in Trier. What about the jewelry? I don't want Gerhardt to think I came to him in poverty but I don't want to appear too haughty, either."

"I think you should dazzle him with everything you can," Laudine advised. "The diadem of emeralds and gold with the pearl drop in the center of your forehead is splendid and emphasizes your eyes. Do you want some kohl, as well, to darken the lids?"

Agnes dithered about it all day but when Walter and Hermann came to escort her over, she had manufactured an air of calm. The gasp from Walter when he saw her told her she had done well.

"My lady Agnes." He bowed. "May I present Hermann of Hauptmergen, the brother of Lord Gerhardt."

Hermann bowed also, and Agnes extended her hand.

"*Ich grüeze iuch,*" she said carefully. "I am happy to be here at last and hope that we may become friends as well as relations." She looked at Walter, who translated the rest.

"As I told you, she is eager to learn German," he added to Hermann, "but has had little time to do so before the journey."

"I'm sure she will have no trouble. Of course, we will all be delighted to help her." Hermann offered his arm and led Agnes into the spring twilight.

She could feel the eyes on her as she crossed the open marketplace to Gerhardt's town house. She was too nervous about tripping on the cobblestones to look around. Her slippers were soft leather and silk and not intended for outdoor use. She tried to concentrate on the discomfort instead of the way her heart was pounding in her throat.

Walter was amazed at how composed she was. He would much rather face an army of Saracens than enter into marriage with a stranger. He hoped Agnes would allow him to remain until King Louis called him back to join the expedition. After the reception he had received that afternoon, he suspected that she might need a friend as well as a translator.

Walking at her left side, Hermann was enchanted by his choice. Agnes's grandfather's emissary had not lied about her beauty or poise, and her voice was sweet and low as a maiden's should be. How could Gerhardt resist her?

The page opened the doors to the hall where Gerhardt waited, surrounded by fifty friends and relatives all eager to catch his expression on first sight of his bride. One of them watched with greater intensity than the others. What would happen if Gerhardt actually went through with the wedding? Could he be so faithless? And, if he were, then should he be allowed to live?

The object of all this attention was outwardly as still and composed as Agnes pretended to be. But Gerhardt's gut was in knots and his thoughts a jumble of terrors. He tried to take a breath as the door opened but it became a gasp that stuck in his throat so that his first view of Agnes was through a spasm of coughing.

"Aaah!" The assembly exhaled together.

Agnes kept her eyes lowered modestly. She bit her lips to keep them from trembling. What if he were ugly? What if he were cruel?

The procession stopped. She could delay no longer. Agnes faced her betrothed.

She saw a man of about thirty, tall and blond, with light eyes,

the sort that changed color according to his moods. He was handsome in her eyes and his expresion was kind, if sad.

Agnes smiled a genuine smile, not just with her lips, but her
whole being.

Gerhardt smiled back before he could stop himself.

What have you sent me, Lord? he thought in alarm. *What sort of
test is this for me to overcome? She's lovely, all that they told me. How
can I keep my oath with her beside me in my bed?*

He didn't hear the introductions. He was aware of nothing but
her face until Maria nudged him. There was a ribald chuckle from
someone.

"Oh, yes, my sister, Maria," Gerhardt presented her. "And my
son, Peter."

Peter bowed to Agnes and offered his arm.

"Father said I might serve you at dinner tonight," he announced.
"Will you permit it?"

Walter repeated his words in French.

Agnes nodded. "I would be honored," she said.

Forty-nine guests found their places at the tables. One slipped
out unnoticed. This French woman was a danger to them all, he
feared, but mostly to Lord Gerhardt. She had to be removed before
she could lead him to destruction.

Catherine found it easy to slip again into the pattern of life at the
Paraclete. But it was more difficult to explain to Mother Heloise
what she wanted.

"A haven, Mother," Catherine said nervously. "I'm afraid for
the safety of my family. For the past year I've been feeling that people
in Paris were changing, becoming harder, more suspicious. Ugly,
anonymous accusations forced Father to break off his partnership of
twenty-five years with the Jew Eliazar. But it isn't just directed at
him. There's talk of heresy; apostasy everywhere. The parvis of the
church always seems to have at least one person shouting the need
for repentance and reform at the top of his voice. And Edgar . . ."
she faltered.

"Edgar hasn't been accused of heresy, surely!" Heloise exclaimed.

"Not exactly." Catherine avoided looking into Heloise's eyes.
"It's his hand. People see it missing and always assume that he did

something terrible and was punished for it. Mother, he was trying to save a life!"

Heloise was sitting on her bed and Catherine on the stool beside it. At this point, Heloise leaned over and put her arms around Catherine who gave in to the tears she never let Edgar see.

"I can't bear having him hurt like that!" she cried. "Wasn't it enough to be maimed without having to endure the sneers of fools who know nothing about it?"

"It is difficult to bear," Heloise agreed. "My Abelard had to suffer loss and shame as well, although we both deserved it far more than your poor husband. But, my dear, what can I do? I'm far removed from all that now, although not as far as I would like."

Catherine wiped her eyes and nose on her sleeve. "I want to know that if things become too dangerous, we have a place to come to. If my children are threatened; if Edgar is castigated for his missing hand; if Father . . . if anyone accuses him falsely, I beg you to take us under your protection."

"Catherine," Heloise began, "the Paraclete is hardly a fortress."

Catherine sniffed again and then smiled. "Yes, it is, Mother. The walls are of faith and the defenses are piety and prayer. You couldn't fight off an army, but you've already proved you can defeat those who would harm you with whispers and rumors of scandal. I believe you could keep us safe."

Heloise laid her cheek against Catherine's unruly curls. "I cannot allow you to have such confidence in me. But I promise that if you or yours need shelter, I will do everything in my power to see that you are given it."

"That's all I hoped for, Mother, and I thank you." Catherine tilted her head up to kiss the abbess's cheek. "Now, are you certain that Sister Bertrada has asked to see me?"

"Quite certain." Heloise got up. "And doing so is the price I shall extract from you for my promise. Bring your children."

"Mother! Do you want to hasten her death?" Catherine laughed. "Why inflict them on the poor old woman?"

But Heloise was firm and so Catherine prepared Edana and James to visit the nun who had been the terror of her school days. She tried to caution James about making rude personal remarks but feared that she had only suggested some he wouldn't have thought of on his own.

They were ushered into a room that was dark and hot. Even in the spring air a brazier of coals was glowing and Sister Bertrada was wrapped in blankets. Next to the bed was a jar of herbal ointment that gave off a scent that helped to mask the odor of the closed room. Sister Melisande sat nearby. She beckoned Catherine to come closer to the bed.

"She's very weak," the infirmarian whispered. "But I know she'll be glad you came."

Catherine approached the bed, half expecting the old woman to leap from it, swinging her stick. However, Bertrada was long past that. Her hands on the covers were twisted, the knuckles swollen. Her eyes were filmed over but her hearing must have been as sharp as ever for she caught Melisande's whisper and gave a snort.

"I'm not deaf," she said. "And not so weak that I can't at least sit up to see you."

"Bertrada," Melisande cautioned, but she helped her to sit with many pillows to prop her up.

"It's been a long time, Sister, have I changed much?" Catherine had to ask.

Sister Bertrada squinted to see her better. "You've grown," she announced. "For the better, I'd say. You're not so muddy, at least. But if that husband of yours imagines he's tamed you, he'll be sorely disappointed."

"Edgar has no illusions about me," Catherine assured her.

James tugged at her skirts.

"It smells funny in here," he said.

Catherine closed her eyes. "This is my son, James," she admitted. "And his sister, Edana. James, make a proper greeting."

James scowled and then put one hand over his heart and bowed. "May our lord Jesus save and protect you," he recited. "And all in this place."

Bertrada held out her hand to him. James shrank from it as he would a dragon's claw. Catherine held him firmly so the woman could stroke his curls.

"Henri," she murmured. "My beautiful child. And Adele! I knew you would come for me at the end. But where are the others?"

Catherine glanced at Melisande in alarm. What was Bertrada talking about? Edana came closer to the bed, fascinated by the glint of the silver ring embedded in Bertrada's gnarled finger.

"*Bel joiel,*" she observed and reached for it.

Bertrada held up her hand so that Edana could grasp it.

"Adele, *ma douz,*" she said. "I knew you would come back to me."

Then she shook her head slightly and her eyes seemed to clear. She looked at Catherine.

"Never grieve when they go to be fostered," she said. "Send them far from each other and then one, at least, will live to come home. Remember that and learn from my sorrow. Melisande, I'm cold."

Catherine hurried the children out as Melisande wrapped more blankets around Sister Bertrada.

It was like being reborn to leave the stuffy room for the sunshine. Edgar and Hubert were in the garden outside the chapel and Catherine loosed James to run to them.

A few moments later, Melisande came out.

"I'm sorry, Catherine," she said. "I hope you weren't too upset by her speech. I confess that I feared the sight of your little ones would call back the memory of her own. But I think it may have helped her. She's never forgiven herself for keeping them with her. When the spotted fever came, all five of them caught it and died, one after the other, in less than a week."

Catherine was astounded.

"No one ever told me," she said. "I thought Sister Bertrada had always been here."

The infirmarian smiled. "Few of us entered the convent as children. Bertrada helped raise Mother Heloise at Argenteuil and then followed her here. But before that she was the lady of a castle, with children she adored. It comforts me to know she'll be joining them soon."

That evening, Catherine told Edgar of the promise she had received from Heloise to take them in if it were ever necessary. Edgar wasn't pleased.

"Do you think I'm so crippled that I couldn't care for all of you?" he asked.

"Of course not!" It had never occurred to her. She cursed her own stupidity. "But if such a mob as attacked the synogogue of Paris came for us, what could we do?"

"If that happened, we'd hardly have time to escape to Champagne," Edgar pointed out.

Catherine put her arms around his neck. "I'm sorry. I wasn't thinking logically. But lately I feel frightened and I sense cruelty in people I had always believed were kind. I had to know there was some place that was perdurant and safe that would take us in should the storm come."

Edgar kissed her in apology for his outburst, then studied her face.

"Catherine, you aren't pregnant again, are you?" he asked.

"I don't think so," she said. "I would have told you. Why?"

"You become more irrational then," he said. "And that's what your worries are. Nothing new has happened. Wickedness ebbs and flows but it's no stronger lately. It takes little for people to decide to set upon the Jews, or anyone else, for that matter. But these storms end quickly and everything returns to normal. We've seen it before. This will be no different. You've brooded on fear too much."

He held her more tightly. Catherine felt the steady beat of his heart against her cheek. He was right, of course. She let herself become panicky over small things. But Edgar was the balance that always brought her back to the mean. His humours must be in perfect harmony. With all the men in the world she might have been given to it was a miracle that Edgar had found her. How could she have doubted that the hand of God had guided them to each other?

"I'm sorry," she murmured into his throat. "You're right. I do fret about nothing. I should have more faith."

"Good," he answered. "Now that you've settled your spirit about that, can we finally go to bed?"

It should be noted that Catherine's answer to that decidedly lacked reverence.

In Trier, Agnes found herself almost light-headed with relief. These people were not that different from those in Blois. The styles and customs were much the same. Most of the guests were nobles from the surrounding area. A few were clerics from the bishop's court, distinguishable only by their small tonsure. There were even some monks. Walter pointed out the abbot of Saint Maximin, who had nodded to her in a friendly fashion. So far she had made no obvious mistakes. And as for Gerhardt, Agnes felt no fears about him any more. He was all she could have hoped.

Everything was going to be all right.

Smiling, she accepted the cuts of meat that Gerhardt had sent her from his own plate. Peter studied her gravely as he offered the salver. Her smile wavered a little.

"*Vürhete dich niht,*" he whispered.

She didn't understand the words but his tone was encouraging.

Gerhardt watched them together. Obviously his son was taken with Agnes. She did not appear to be the kind of person who would resent a stepson. Of course, that often changed when a woman had children of her own. Thank God, Gerhardt thought, that there was no chance of that. He held out his arm to Peter.

"*Liebelin!*" he called. "If the Lady Agnes has taken all she cares for, would you mind returning the rest to me?"

Peter blushed.

"Forgive me, Father." He returned to his duties. But when he was near enough to Gerhardt he leaned over and whispered. "I like her, Father. She's beautiful. Don't you agree?"

"Oh, yes, very beautiful," Gerhardt said.

At the other end of the table Hermann turned to Maria with a look of satisfaction.

"We did well, didn't we?" he said. "There'll be no more secret visits to Köln now. That one has charm enough to keep any man home."

"She seems to be all they said," Maria admitted. "I only hope Gerhardt is as taken with her as you are. And there's still the problem of the message on the man pulled from the river."

Hermann waved that away. "I made too much of the matter. Perhaps I was mistaken about the condition of the message. It might well have been ruined in the water. Nothing has come of it. I'm sure we'll hear nothing more about it."

Maria answered something, but at that moment the butler signaled for the entertainment to begin and her voice was drowned out by the jingling of bells and the drone of a bow across a rebec as the minestrals gathered to sing the tale of the swan knight and how he fought with Charlemagne to defeat the Saracens.

It was long past dark when the dinner ended, and there were few people in the street as Agnes and her entourage returned to the convent. Between the wine she had consumed and her elation at the reception she had been given, Agnes was nearly floating. Now she looked around eagerly, trying to see more of this place that would be her home.

In the dark she could make out little; the shapes of buildings, trees, a dung-collector making his rounds. They passed a stone gateway that was lit by torches set on either side. Agnes glanced in as a man came out. She gave a squeak of shock. It couldn't be. Oh, Saint Eusebia's lost lips! It was. How dare he come here! And why?

All Agnes's joy evaporated into fear as her cousin Solomon grinned at her and bowed.

Eight

Trier, the gate to the Jewish quarter. The same moment.

ברוך אתה יי אלהינומלך העולם
אשר ברא יין עסיס / ותירוש טוב מעצי גפנים /
והוא ערב לנפשוטוב לאדם / ומשמח לב ומצהיל פנים /
והוא תנחומין לאבלים / ומרי נפש ישכחו רישן /
והוא רפואה לכל שותיו

Blessed art Thou, O Lord, our God, King of the Universe,
who created the *asis* wine and good must from the vines. It is
pleasing to the soul and good for man. It cheers the heart
and makes one glow with joy. It is comfort to those who
mourn and the miserable will forget their poverty; it is a cure
for all who drink it.

—A Karite *yên*
Cairo Geniza

*J*ehan turned to find out what had startled Agnes. His sword was out at once.

"*Bewau!*" he exclaimed. "You filthy infidel! How dare you follow us here!"

Solomon's right hand was already on his left wrist, releasing the sheath that kept his knife hidden. Before he could draw it, Walter stepped in front of Jehan.

"Solomon!" he cried. "Good to see you! I forgot that you must know Agnes, too, since your families did business together. Are you here for the wedding?"

His beaming innocence abashed the others. Jehan and Solomon relaxed their fighting stances. Agnes took Walter's elbow and tried, unsucessfully, to move him on. It was like trying to budge a cliff.

Solomon shook Walter's hand.

"Good to see you," he said heartily. "I'd heard you had left for the Holy Land. And you, as well."

He stared pointedly at Jehan's cross. Jehan snarled at him.

"Why bother, when there's filth to clean up here first."

Walter ignored him. "I'm awaiting the rest of King Louis's army. So I offered to escort Lady Agnes to Trier."

Agnes had had enough of politeness. She circled Walter and faced Solomon.

"If my family sent you here to spoil my wedding, I'll ask for your head as my morning gift," she warned.

Solomon looked her up and down with contempt.

"Why should I care whom you marry?" he asked wearily. "I'm here on business of my own. I knew you were coming, but I certainly didn't wait for you or expect to see you. As it is, I wish you more happiness than you've ever given others and bid you good night." He nodded to Walter and continued on his way.

Shaken, Agnes refused to answer any questions, although Walter had several. He held his tongue, planning to find Solomon later and get the rest of the story from him.

The ladies in Agnes's party had no such delicacy, however. They were barely in their room when Agnes was bombarded with comments about the encounter.

"How did you ever meet such a man?" one asked. "I've seen nothing like him around your grandfather's court."

"Is that why you left Paris?" another one added.

"Does he want you to run away with him?"

Horrified, Agnes could only stutter denials.

"Lisette! Laudine! How could you even think that of me?"

They weren't at all discomfited. "Oh, look!" Laudine crowed. "She's blushing! It must be true."

"You idiots!" Agnes screamed at last. "You are, all of you, totally *mesacointe*. Don't you see what he is?"

"An incredibly handsome man." Lisette grinned. "He looks like a Greek pirate."

Agnes rolled her eyes. "You've been listening to too many poets, Lisette," she sneered. "He's nothing but an errand boy for my father and," she paused for effect, "he's a Jew!"

The women recoiled in pious horror, but Agnes saw all too well that it was tainted with fascination. They had heard the rumors about Jewish men. Was Solomon that good-looking? She tried to go beyond her antipathy and regard him as a woman would. It was difficult. She supposed that his dark curls and green eyes might be attractive to some and he was well formed. But still . . .

"If you must know," she said coldly, "I left Paris because I refused to associate with my father's Jewish 'partners.' I don't want to be contaminated by those people."

Lisette was suitably shamed. "I beg your pardon, Agnes. I didn't know. It was very brave of you to flee from their evil influence."

"Thank you." Agnes inclined her head. "Now help me to prepare for bed."

When her back was turned, Laudine nudged Lisette. "A night with that man might be worth a little damnation." She giggled. "And, who knows, I could be his pathway to salvation."

They both smothered their laughter, but Agnes heard. The joy and relief she had felt that evening seemed long, long ago. Now there was only the terror that all she had fled from would follow her here. In retribution for the maids' unkindness, she curled up in the middle of the bed, forcing the other two to lie on either side of her, facing the cold.

Solomon forced his temper down as he continued to his destination. Agnes was a haughty bitch and there was nothing for it. That she would think he'd come all the way to Trier just to disrupt her plans only proved her arrogance. As if he had nothing better to do!

He adjusted his cloak and smoothed his beard before knocking. They must have been listening for him, for the door was opened at once.

"*Brukhim habaim*, Solomon ben Jacob!"

"*Shalom*, Simon," Solomon greeted his friend. "Mina! I've brought you pepper and cinnamon!"

Simon's wife came running from the hall to kiss Solomon and take the package.

"You never forget, dear friend," she said. "Come in. Let me take your cloak. I'll have the children bring you water to wash. We'll be eating soon."

As the cloak slipped from him, so did Solomon's resentment. It didn't matter what hatred and ignorance lay outside. He was back among his own, within the walls of the Torah, which was the Holy One's promise to His people. In here there was security and peace.

The next morning, Solomon joined in the prayers at the synagogue with the other men. It was the first time in many weeks and it calmed his angry heart. He spent too much time among the Edomites, he realized, even good ones, like Edgar and Catherine. It was easy to forget that there was someplace where he truly belonged.

They came home to find Mina and the three children waiting.

"Hurry, Papa, I'm hungry," the youngest, Asher, whined.

"And what have you been doing to be so hungry?" Mina chided him. "Your father has been to pray for us all and now he must go on a long journey just to pay for the food to put in your belly. Show more respect."

Asher only heard part of her rebuke. "You're going away, Papa?"

Simon lifted his son and kissed him. "Just to England," he explained. "I'll be back by Tisha B'av."

"But that's weeks away," his daughter Rebecca blurted.

Simon looked at his wife. "I'm glad to know that our children consider me important in their lives."

Mina sniffed. "They just know that you spoil them more than I do."

But Simon saw the tears she was forcing back.

"Well," he said with false heartiness. "What do we break our fast with? Ah, bread, sausage and beer, the same as every morning. Aren't we lucky to have so much?"

They ate quickly and then the children scattered to study or do chores. Simon poured a last bowl of beer and took his wife's hand.

"Should I go?" Solomon offered.

"Of course not," she answered. "We said all we needed to last night. And Simon will be lucky if he doesn't return home to find another child on the way."

"My dear," Simon said. "Should you say such things in front of Solomon?"

"I'll say anything I can to convince him to marry and start a family of his own," Mina answered. "You're thirty now, Solomon. What are you waiting for?"

"A nice demure Jewish girl like you, Mina," Solomon laughed. "But they're hard to find."

"You just don't look in the right places," Mina answered. "Nice Jewish girls don't pass the time in Christian taverns."

Still grumbling, she got up and took the last tray out to the pantry. Simon watched her fondly.

"You will be careful in England?" Solomon asked. "There's a lot of ill feeling against us there. This business in Norwich, for instance."

"That was two years ago," Simon answered. "And hardly anyone believed that nonsense about Jews murdering a child for some barbaric ritual. It's too preposterous even for credulous Edomites."

"Perhaps," Solomon told him. "But all this talk of holy war again has stirred people to even more irrational thought than usual.

Remember the tales from the great expedition fifty years ago, when hundreds of idiots let a goose choose the road for them? Remember how many of us were murdered or driven to *qiddush ha-shem* by these fanatics? The community at Metz never recovered from the deaths there."

"I know, here in Trier we still bear the scars of that dark time. But we've learned from the disasters," Simon assured him. "Most Christians were horrified by the atrocities. It won't happen again."

Solomon didn't pursue the subject, for Mina came back to take their bowls and shoo them out so that she could clean. She opened the door to let the foul humors out of the house, and a cold wind entered.

Solomon shivered. All at once the walls he had hoped to hide behind seemed very thin indeed.

Catherine's visit to the Paraclete seemed too short. She knew that Edgar and her father were spending the days arranging for the purchase of articles the convent needed. Hubert planned for them to continue on to Troyes and the yearly fair there but for once, Catherine wasn't excited about attending.

"Now I understand why Solomon resented having me put in his charge," she confessed to Heloise. "I wake up at night shaking from dreams of losing one of the children in that throng. The fair at Troyes is much larger than the one at Provins. And Margaret has become so mature this past year! I see the men watching her and wish they could be struck blind for their thoughts."

They were sitting on the stone wall edging the kitchen garden. The children were helping the lay sisters pull weeds.

Heloise followed Catherine's gaze. Margaret's braids shone like chains of copper as they swung while she worked. Heloise gave a sad smile. "And men would say it's her fault for being young and beautiful. She has blossomed. Have any plans been made for her?"

"That's another reason to go to Troyes," Catherine admitted. "I want to take her to Count Thibault. He doesn't know she exists, but she's his granddaughter."

"What?"

"Edgar's stepmother, Adalisa, was a product of the count's younger days in Blois," Catherine explained. "I believe he acknowledged her as his daughter even though her mother later married someone else. I'm hoping he'll accept Margaret as well. We love her dearly but she deserves a better marriage than we could arrange."

"I don't suppose she has shown any interest in monastic life?" Heloise ventured.

"No, Mother," Catherine said, cringing at what Solomon would say to that. "But if she does, I'll seek your advice at once."

Heloise watched Margaret as she lifted a basket full of weeds, dirt and a grubby Edana. She strained under the weight but made no complaint, until one of the women noticed and relieved her of the living half of the burden. Then Heloise turned back to Catherine.

"Does Margaret know Thibault is her grandfather?" she asked.

"No, I thought it best to talk with him first," Catherine answered. "I haven't mentioned seeing Thibault to Edgar, even. He'd rather forget everything to do with the family in Scotland."

"If you'll accept my advice," Heloise said, "go to Countess Mahaut before you see her husband. She's well aware that Thibault has bastards and she has a kind heart, especially since the liaison happened long before they were married. Her sympathy for the child's situation would guarantee Margaret's acceptance."

"Of course!" Catherine exclaimed. "I should have thought of that. The countess *is* kind. I've seen her give judgement and she's not a person who would punish Margaret for the sins of her grandparents. Thank you, Mother. You've eased my mind on this matter."

"There's another matter?" Heloise's eyebrows raised.

"I'm afraid so." Catherine lowered her voice. "It's about what Sister Bertrada said. Of course both of my children are too young for fostering, but others have told me that it's madness to traipse about in foreign places taking them with us, and yet I can't bear to leave them behind for others to tend. Who loves them more than I do? Who would watch over them as carefully?"

Heloise sighed deeply. She put her hand on Catherine's.

"I have no answer for you in this, my dear," she said. "Whatever you do, someone will question it. That is certain. You can only pray for guidance. If you have faith enough, a way will be shown to you. I know you too well, Catherine. You want definite answers to everything. We always berated you for intellectual pride but the real fault isn't in thinking you know everything but in refusing to accept that some things can't be understood. My poor Abelard taught you too well. He always felt that God gave him reason so that he could use it to understand our maker."

"But isn't that correct?" Catherine asked. She had always believed so.

"I'm not sure anymore," Heloise said gently. "Recently I've been wondering if we weren't given reason so that we could understand each other."

She kissed Catherine's cheek and left her to sit in the sunlit garden and consider the possibility of comprehending her fellow man.

After some thought, Catherine decided it might be easier to comprehend God.

It was early June when the party loaded up again and set out. The day was bright and Catherine's mood joyful again. The nuns had given them hard-cooked eggs and bread for the journey and the children were each sucking a stick of honey and herbs that Sister Melisande assured Catherine would ward off summer agues.

Edgar lifted Catherine onto his horse and then handed the baby up to her.

"Are you sorry to be leaving your sanctuary?" he asked.

She laughed. "Don't worry carissime, I have no regrets over not taking vows. But it has been good to see everyone again. This will always be my second home."

The journey to Troyes was less than three days, even with the pack animals and frequent stops to eat or rest. As they neared the town the traffic became thick and they often had to take to the verge to pass ox carts, laden with grain or wine or even building stones, all on their way to the city.

"Do you think Solomon will be there to greet us?" Margaret asked Catherine as they passed through a village near the city walls.

Catherine had been wondering the same thing.

"I hope so," she answered. "He might have news of Agnes. It's strange to think that she must be married by now."

Hubert overheard them. "She might have at least sent word to us of her safe arrival," he complained.

"Did you really expect her to?"

Hubert shrugged. "Once I'd have said that she wouldn't have crossed Paris without my approval. Perhaps I just long for those days to return."

Catherine agreed that it would be pleasant but she really didn't want her childhood back. Her father had often been gone for months to trade and her mother, she now realized, was slipping into melancholia long before she succumbed to madness. The convent where she lived now wasn't that far from here, but Catherine knew it would only increase Madeleine's confusion to see her daughter again.

No, it was better to live in the present.

They left the packhorses with some of Hubert's associates who were already preparing for the fair, which wouldn't start officially until Saint John's Eve. Then they hurried to the house of Eliazar where they were greeted with cries of delight.

"Oh, look how the children have grown!" Johanna exclaimed. "Edana, sweeting, come to your aunt Johanna."

"Johanna!" Eliazar's angry shout almost caused her to drop the child. He lowered his voice. "What are you thinking of? What if someone overheard them calling you 'Aunt'?"

Johanna went pale. "How stupid of me," she whispered. "Never mind, Edana, we'll find a name we can use."

"How about 'nutrix,'" Catherine suggested. "It means nurse-maid."

"Or even 'nutricula,'" Edgar added.

Johanna didn't care for it. "Nutricula Johanna?"

"'Tricula." Edana laughed.

Johanna hugged her. "Well, that's not quite as bad. Very well, love, come with your 'tricula."

Catherine sighed as they followed her into the dining hall. It was a great sorrow to her to have to pretend that Johanna and Eliazar weren't related to her. If only they would accept baptism.

That thought led to another.

"Is Solomon back, yet?" she asked. Spiritual intransigence was always linked to him in her mind.

"He arrived two days ago," Eliazar said. "He's gone out to meet with some friends who've come up from Arles with several lengths of Egyptian cotton. You should see the dyes! He'll be back tonight."

"Does he have news from Trier?" Hubert asked.

"He says that your daughter made a beautiful bride," Johanna answered. "The procession to the church went all the way through the town and she glittered like a princess. The people there seem very happy with her."

Hubert exhaled. "I'm glad of that, at least."

They didn't see Solomon that night. He came in well after the gate had been locked and was still snoring when Catherine and Margaret left for the bathhouse the next morning.

"I don't understand why I'm to meet the countess," Margaret said through the suds Catherine was pouring over her head. "Is she a friend of yours?"

"Not exactly," Catherine said. "Father has had dealings with her and Count Thibault over the years and they've been good to the family. It's only polite to pay her a visit."

"So we are to be nice to her so she'll buy from your father." Margaret nodded as if she understood all about such things.

"Yes, I suppose so." Catherine was becoming more unsure about her decision. Keeping this from Edgar worried her considerably. But his pride was of the sort that would never ask favors. Margaret deserved a chance.

She scrubbed the girl's head until Margaret squealed in pain. Then they spent another hour combing out the tangles and braiding her hair again. Back at the house, Catherine first assured herself that the men were gone and then dressed herself and Margaret in their best.

"I've sent a messenger to the countess," she told Margaret. "We need to be ready to go with him when he returns."

"What if she has no time for us today?" Margaret fidgeted with the unaccustomed amount of jewelry.

"Then we try again tomorrow," Catherine was firm.

They sat in silence, too fine to do anything but wait.

"Margaret," Catherine began. "You'll be thirteen soon. Have you thought about what you want to do when you're grown?"

"Oh yes," Margaret said with confidence. "I'm going to marry Solomon and go with him to Baghdad and ride a camel."

Catherine's jaw dropped.

"Um, does Solomon know about this?" she managed to ask.

Margaret frowned. "Not exactly. But he said he'd take me with him someday and I know it wouldn't be proper unless he was my husband."

This revelation sent Catherine's thoughts racing in panic down a very different path that she had intended. She vowed to have a serious talk with Solomon about Margaret before the day was out. She tried a different tack.

"Do you know what your mother had planned for you?" she asked.

"She thought I should be a nun." Margaret sighed. "I do love God, of course, but I don't like having to get up in the middle of the night and I don't want to sleep in a narrow bed all alone."

That seemed fairly definite.

"Did she ever suggest that you go back to France for fostering?" Catherine ventured.

Margaret tried to remember. "She did say that she wished I could learn about how other people lived. I know that my father's keep wasn't very . . ."

"Civilized," Catherine supplied. "No, it wasn't, although your mother tried. I believe that she would have wanted you to learn more about the talents a lady should have: music and embroidery and other such things."

Margaret suddenly understood.

"You want to leave me with the countess?" Her voice had an edge of terror.

Catherine took the child in her arms and held her tightly, regardless of their finery.

"Not now, ma douz, not ever if it frightens you so," she soothed. "But we must consider your future, and the patronage of the count of Champagne is a great thing."

Margaret saw the wisdom of this, even if the actuality frightened her. She had barely regained her composure when the messenger arrived, saying that the countess would be pleased for them to come to her at once.

Outside the city, the broad plain on which the fair took place was already dotted with tents and stakes roped off for areas to show cattle, sheep and horses. Hubert, Solomon and Edgar had brought James

along so that he could watch while they inspected the section assigned to them and checked on the goods they had brought. Edana
had been left at home for her new "nurse" to cosset.

James immediately demanded to be put on a horse, where he sat
with legs splayed, waving a stick at unseen opponents.

Hubert watched him with amusement, Edgar with misgiving.

"That's all he ever seems to play: warrior and dragons, or knight
and Saracens," he commented, shaking his head.

"All little boys do," Hubert said.

"And in my family they grew to playing at it in earnest," Edgar
reminded him. "I don't want James to become the kind of man my
brothers are, using their power to murder and rape. These games only
encourage him."

"There are noble knights, you know, who protect others," Hubert reminded him. "Your friend Walter, for example. After all, what
would you have James play at, money changing? He's but three now.
If he goes to my son Guillaume to be trained, he may someday rise
to the level where he'll be a castellan. Let him be for now."

Edgar bit back a sharp reply. Hubert was right. It galled him,
though. Some part of himself wanted James to have his birthright,
even if it was just as the son of a lord's younger son. He tried to
quash these feelings, but they would erupt again when he was least
prepared. Logically, he knew that James was infinitely better off living in Paris as a merchant's grandson than he would ever be in
Scotland amidst the thousand enemies that were also his birthright.

They were distracted by shouting from across the field. Men ran
past them as they hurried to see what was happening. The shouts
grew louder as they neared and they could make out words.

"God's teeth! I say this is my spot! Get off it or I'll have the
count's men throw you off!"

"We've been here for twenty years, Hugues," another voice
yelled back. "You know that well!"

"That sounds like Yehiel!" Hubert said and started running.

"Hubert, wait!" Edgar ran after him. "Remember what happened
last time!"

Hubert kept running and, scooping James up, Edgar raced after
him, afraid that this time Hubert might collapse and not get up
again. The commotion grew as they neared the site.

Yehiel was one of the Jewish traders of Troyes. He was standing with Solomon and a few other Jews at the section that they were marking for their stalls. Facing them was a group of other merchants and some men from the nearby village. Edgar noted that several men on both sides were holding wood and iron tools balanced in their hands like weapons.

"What's wrong with you, Hugues?" Solomon said. "The Jews of Troyes always set up here. It's the custom."

"Not any longer," Hugues announced. "We met last night and decided that you Christ-killers aren't wanted here. We've put up with you long enough. Why should you make a profit from the sale of supplies to pilgrims?"

"Why should you?" Solomon answered. "I thought they were going to fight for the glory of your false God."

"Oh, Solomon, don't!" Edgar warned under his breath.

Hugues stepped forward, his sickle raised.

Yehiel grabbed Solomon's arm before he could draw his knife.

"Are you mad?" he muttered. "Show a weapon and we'll all be dead."

Hubert pushed through the circle of local Christians, panting and gasping.

"Hugues de Chappes!" He faced the leader of the group. "What's happened to you? Last year you were all drinking together. Now you want to ban these men from the fair? Who will you sell your linen to? And where will you buy gold thread?"

"There's enough Christians to sell to." Hugues's face was set in resentment. "And if it means buying from unbelievers, I'll not use gold thread."

There were mutters of agreement from those around him.

Edgar touched Hubert's shoulder.

"You won't convince them with sense," he said. "These men aren't susceptible to logic."

Yehiel moved to stand closer to them.

"I've sent for the count's men," he whispered. "I just pray that they arrive before this comes to blows. Edgar's right, Hubert. You can't talk to them. The tolls on the stalls were raised this year and they need someone to blame."

Hugues heard the last part of this.

"That's right. Why should we pay more? The Jews come here, make profit from our need and leave. They should be fined the extra toll."

"Hugues," Yehiel said in exasperation. "I live two streets over from you. I'm at the market at Saint Jean every Tuesday."

"I thought you said reason wouldn't work," Hubert reminded him.

Yehiel threw up his hands. "It didn't." He gestured at one man who was holding what looked like a piece from a hackling board, sharp spikes running most of the length of it. "They've come to hurt us and won't leave until blood in spilt."

Edgar was acutely aware of James clinging to him, eyes wide with fear.

"Hubert," he said. "We need to get your grandson somewhere safe."

"Enough talk!" Hugues roared suddenly, causing James to shriek in fear. "Start packing up your goods."

Solomon faced him.

"Only the count can force us to leave," he stated. "You have no authority."

Hugues raised the sickle. Solomon crouched to leap at him, drawing the knife.

"Solomon!" Hubert rushed forward to stop them.

Edgar's heart froze. He grabbed at Hubert with his free hand at the same time as Yehiel pulled Solomon back so that the sickle passed through the air where Solomon's head had been and stuck fast in a tree stump.

"Halt in the name of the count!" a voice cried from above them.

The clanking of chain mail and the breath of the horses on their necks was enough to cause most of the men to stop. Hugues struggled to remove the sickle from the stump, but everyone else turned. Only James cried on, impervious to Edgar's attempts to calm him.

The guards moved aside and Henry, son of Count Thibault, rode through. The cross he had taken at Vézelay had been sewn to his tunic and embellished with gold braid.

"Where are the men who have decided who shall attend my father's fair and who shall not?" he boomed.

Those on the edge of the crowd started moving away, but a few at the core stood their ground.

"We want no more dealings with the Jews!" one shouted. "They shouldn't be allowed to take trade from honest Christians."

Henry's eyes lit on the man who had spoken.

"Ah, Ithier!" he said. "Honesty isn't a word I've heard much in connection with you. Weren't you fined last year for putting sand in your salt? I thought you'd been banned altogether."

The man sputtered but backed down. Henry scanned the rest of the group.

"Violence committed at the fairs is judged in the count's court," he reminded them. "All who attend and pay the duty are under his protection. Anyone who wishes to dispute that is welcome to come with me and do so. Or, you can come with me even further and help me to free Edessa from the hands of the Saracens instead of persecuting your fellow traders."

No one was inclined to accept his offers. The group quickly dispersed. Henry waited until all the men had left.

"Thank you, my lord," Yehiel said. "We are grateful for your intervention and wish you much success on your expedition to the Holy Land."

"I'll see that the guards remain for the whole of the fair," Henry told him. "You've been good and loyal subjects and I'll not have you harmed."

Yehiel bowed. "I have just received several casks of wine from Rabbenu Jacob's vineyard at Ramerupt. May I send some to you as a gift, in return for your benevolence."

Henry smiled. "That would be most welcome," he told them.

After he had left, Hubert and Edgar took Solomon home. They made him walk between them and stayed in open spaces as much as possible.

"Did you expect me to stand there and let that imbecile Edomite drive us off?" he grumbled.

"You drew a knife on him," Edgar said.

"And I meant to use it." Solomon took James from Edgar and put the boy on his shoulders. "James isn't the only one who believes in slaying dragons."

Edgar understood and respected his friend for it. But Solomon's pride could lead to destruction. He didn't relax his watchfulness until they were all back at Eliazar's, with the door barred.

It wasn't until he had downed half of a pitcher of beer that he noticed Margaret, still in her finest clothes.

"Is it a feast day?" he asked.

"No, Brother," Margaret said, coming to sit by him. "Catherine and I went to visit with Countess Mahaut today."

Edgar stopped with his bowl halfway to his lips.

"Where's Catherine?"

Margaret caught the tone of anger and was puzzled.

"I think she took James to the kitchen to be washed. Why?"

Edgar stood and went to the kitchen without answering her.

"Catherine," he started.

"Yes, I did," she answered, as she peeled James's muddy tunic and *brais* off him. "And I didn't tell you because you would have tried to forbid it."

"Of course I would!" Edgar raised his voice. "Margaret is my sister and my ward. You have no right making plans for her without consulting me!"

"I know," Catherine admitted. "Now, step in the tub, James. But I did mention it once and you refused to discuss the matter. I don't think you're being rational in this. Margaret has a right to any help her grandfather might be willing to give. It's more than we can do for her."

"So you also told her who he is?" Edgar remembered at the last minute that his sister might be listening and spoke more softly.

"No, I didn't," Catherine said. "Yes, James, I have to wash you everywhere; you have dirt everywhere. But the countess knew at once when I told her who Margaret's mother was. No one had told Thibault that Adalisa had been killed, poor man. She thinks he'll want to meet Margaret. It's not just your decision now, Edgar. The count has a say in it, too."

She was on her knees next to the shallow wooden tub. She looked up at Edgar, half in defiance, but half in fear. He was angry. He had some right to be. She knew what she risked.

"Don't look at me like that," he ordered. "I'm not a monster like my father. I'm not going to beat you."

She bit her lip. "I know that. I'm not afraid of that kind of pain." Catherine hid her face as she scrubbed her son, who was protesting all through the conversation. She knew she was starting to cry and it was a weapon she despised.

But Edgar wasn't ready to give up his anger. He turned without speaking to go back to the hall. As he did, the door to the kitchen swung open and, to their astonishment, Walter burst in.

"Edgar, Catherine," he said without preamble. "You must come back with me at once. Lord Gerhardt is dead and they're saying that Agnes killed him!"

Nine

Troyes, the home of Eliazar. Tuesday, 14 kalends July (June 18), 1146; 5 Tammuz, 4906. Feast of Saint Marina the Disguised, who lived as a monk until her death, without anyone guessing she was a woman.

Sic inclusa . . . sola sedet et taceat ore, ut spiritu loquantur, et credat se non esse solam, quando sola est. Tunc enim cum Christo est, qui non dignatur in turbis esse cum ea.

Let the recluse . . . sit alone and say nothing aloud, but speak with her soul and believe herself not to be alone when she is alone. It is then that she is with Christ, who does not deign to be with her in a crowd.

—Aelred of Rievaux
The Life of a Recluse

I went to Paris first," Walter explained. "They told me where you had gone and so I rushed here. But it's still more than a week since I left Trier. You've got to come back with me. Agnes has no one to speak for her."

Everyone had gathered around him, all shouting questions at once. Finally Hubert ordered silence.

"Johanna, could you bring Walter something to eat and drink?" he asked. "He's clearly traveled without rest. Now, everyone keep still and let the man tell us what happened."

Walter drank deeply from the bowl that Johanna gave him, the beer running down the edges of his beard. He gave it back to her for refilling and began his tale.

"Everything seemed to be fine," he started. "Agnes charmed everyone, even Gerhardt's son. I had taught her a few phrases of German and she pronounced them well. She was eager to learn more and that endeared her to them. There were no clouds at all. She was married Acension Sunday. I thought it all went well. Gerhardt ordered casks of wine brought from his own cellar and the celebration lasted two days. The whole town participated. Agnes was beautiful and charming to everyone. I heard nothing against her the whole time."

He shook his head, still bewildered.

"I went on to Köln to see a friend who had sent word that he wanted to come with me to the Holy Land. When I passed through Trier on my return, I was told that Lord Gerhardt's new bride had poisoned him and that she was being held at the keep until her execution."

"This can't be!" Hubert cried.

"They mean to kill her?" Catherine couldn't believe it either. Walter took another long drink.

"The feeling among the people is that she must have used sorcery or poison, or both, to kill Gerhardt and they're demanding that she be hanged," he told them.

"How dare they!" Hubert was as outraged about this as the accusation itself. "She's not some peasant to be publicly humiliated and left dangling at the crossroads! Solomon, fetch the horses. Johanna, Catherine, pack me some food and clothes. I'm leaving at once. What sort of people has she gone among?"

"Father, wait," Catherine said. "Of course we're going to get her, but we have to know more. What else, Walter? What does Gerhardt's family say? Why do they believe Agnes is guilty?"

Walter noted Edgar's reaction to Catherine's use of "we" but continued his tale.

"I talked with Hermann, Gerhardt's brother. He says that Gerhardt woke in the night, shrieking in agony and died horribly, with convulsions and choking. However, Hermann's not as certain as the townspeople that Agnes is responsible for the death. I don't understand his forbearance. Most men would leap to assume that the alien bride had killed him. But I felt the first day I met them that there was a hidden problem in the family. I should have heeded it. In any case, he's kept her locked up at their castle rather than turn her over to the bishop for trial."

"Couldn't this man have died of illness or eating a bad mushroom accidentally, instead?" Edgar asked. "Poison is a difficult thing to prove, sorcercy even harder."

"Perhaps that's why they're hesitant at the castle to accuse her formally," Walter answered. "I didn't ask why the local people were so certain. All I could think of was reaching you as quickly as possible. Hermann told me that Agnes is the logical person to suspect since she was physically closest to Gerhardt but he won't have her tried until she has an advocate. I think he fears what she might say, but I couldn't begin to guess what that would be. You're the ones to ferret out the truth behind this."

"Could he have poisoned Gerhardt himself?" Catherine asked. "To prevent the possibility of any other heir to the land?"

Walter shook his head. "Gerhardt already has a son who's nearly of age. Peter is now the lord, although Hermann might be able to lay claim to the title on the grounds that he's better able to defend it. But it was Hermann who arranged the marriage. Why would he have done that if he wanted the land for himself? I don't understand this at all. I tried to get him to release Agnes to me, but the best I could do was to make him agree not to let anyone harm her until there was someone there to speak for her."

"She isn't locked in a dungeon, is she?" Catherine couldn't stand the thought of golden Agnes shut up in the dark, no matter how nasty she had been.

"Of course not," Walter said. "They're not barbarians. She's in a small tower room with her maids. The door is barred but I was allowed to see her a moment and she hasn't been hurt. She's only confused and . . . actually—" Walter stopped. He'd only just realized it. "She appeared more angry than frightened."

"That sounds like Agnes," Solomon murmured.

"Mama, what's wrong?" Catherine had almost forgotten James, who had climbed from the bath and stood next to her naked and wet.

"Jesus's sacred milk teeth, James!" she exclaimed. "You'll freeze like that. Margaret, run get his tunic, please. It's on the table next to the tub."

In the meantime she wrapped him in her own tunic, pulled up from the hem like a basket.

"Mama!" James was indignant. "What is it? Where are we going?"

There was silence as everyone stared at him. Finally Hubert cleared his throat.

"I am going to Trier, James, to see to something," he said carefully. "You and your parents are staying here."

"Father!" Catherine wasn't about to let it rest there. "Agnes will need me, whether she'll admit it or not. She must have asked for me, didn't she, Walter?"

"Well," Walter said. "Actually, she didn't ask for any of you by name. She told me to go to her grandfather and have him send an advocate to argue for her."

"That's nonsense," Hubert said. "What good would that do? This isn't a dispute about a piece of land! She needs family members who will vouch for her. It may well be that this Hermann fears the revenge we might take if Agnes were unjustly condemned."

"That's right," Catherine added as she struggled to get James's arms into his tunic. "That's why I should be there, too. All the family must defend her."

"Not without me," Edgar said.

Catherine gaped at him. "Edgar, Agnes is my sister. I must stand with her. You needn't be involved. It's nothing to do with you."

She regretted the words as soon as they were spoken.

Edgar raised his eyebrows and tightened his lips.

"Really?" he said. "And Margaret is my sister. What has her fate to do with you?"

Catherine looked at him, then lifted James and handed him to Hubert.

"Father, will you mind him for a few moments?" she asked. "I think Edgar and I need to talk alone."

Edgar nodded agreement and the two of them left the room.

Walter used the pause to pour another bowl of beer. The others went for bowls of their own.

"Do they throw things at each other?" Walter asked nervously.

"They haven't so far," Solomon answered. "But I've never seen either one of them look at the other like that before. It's best to leave them to it. Now, Hubert, what do you want me to do in aid of this troublesome daughter of yours?"

Edgar led Catherine out to a bench in the back garden. Neither said a word until they were seated next to each other, not touching or looking at each other. The silence became thick around them. At last Catherine could endure it no longer.

"I'm sorry I took Margaret to Countess Mahaut without telling you," she said.

He didn't answer at once and she could feel him struggling with his anger. She knew that it wasn't like hers, a flare and then over, but something slow to kindle and hard to extinguish. But she also knew that he was fair and judged himself as severely as he did others. She waited, holding herself motionless with an effort more tiring than action would have been.

"It was unfair not to give me the chance to decide the matter," he said at last, as if analyzing the argument with each word. "But perhaps, when I refused to discuss it, I wasn't thinking of Margaret's interests as much as my own anger at my father. I left all of that world behind and," he smiled and she closed her eyes in relief, "I didn't want my sister to return to it. But, you're right. The choice should be hers, not ours."

Now Catherine turned to face him, putting a hand to his cheek.

"And so you understand why I must go to Agnes?" she said. "Whatever she has done, she's my sister and I can't abandon her. We know what happens when families turn against themselves."

"I do," he answered. "And that's why *we* must go."

He took her hand in his and kissed the palm.

"Your father will have a great deal to say about it, but he should know by now that he can't defeat the both of us." He put both arms around her and pulled her close.

"What about the children?" Catherine hated to mention it. "It's not a difficult journey, but we don't know what enmity we'll face at the end of it."

Edgar thought a while.

"We can be home by the end of summer," he said. "So the weather shouldn't be a problem. They won't be hurt by the travel. And, perhaps the sight of her poor little niece and nephew will soften the hearts of those judging Agnes."

"Father will certainly object to that," Catherine warned him.

"But we can overcome his objections together." Edgar kissed her. "Can't we?"

They became so involved in their reconciliation that they were unaware of anything else until a suppressed cough brought them back to the present.

Solomon stood at the gateway, shaking his head at them.

"I was sent to see if you had come to blows," he told them. "Now I find you just wanted an excuse to embrace. I'm shocked."

"Not as much as you will be," Edgar rose. "We need to pack up everyone and set out at once."

"All of you?" Solomon was doubtful. "Is that wise?"

"No," Catherine answered. "But that's what we've decided."

"You're mad, you know," he observed.

"Yes, we know." Edgar was complacent.

Solomon shrugged. "It's no worry of mine. I doubt that Agnes will want me to stand up for her. And someone has to stay here for the fair and see that the Edomites don't try anything more. But I'll keep a horse ready, just in case you fall into misfortune and need rescuing yourselves. I'll see to it that your children get home."

"If they're with us," Edgar told him, "they are home."

Peter sat on the slopes of the vineyard, sobbing for his lost father. It still seemed impossible to him that between sunset and dawn his life could have reversed so completely. People were calling him Lord Peter now, expecting him to make decisions. Uncle Hermann tried to keep them from bothering him, but Peter knew he wouldn't be allowed much time to mourn. He was almost fourteen; boys his age fought alongside their kin. Some even led them into the battle.

Peter felt as though he'd already been through a war. If only there had been some warning. Why would Agnes have wanted to kill his father? She seemed happy with him. But Aunt Maria said that she had heard crying on the wedding night. Had his father done something terrible to her? Peter knew what men and women did together; he'd been contemplating trying it himself. Agnes would have been prepared for that, he assumed. So what had gone wrong?

In the town people were calling her a sorceress or worse, saying that she was some river spirit who had enchanted Gerhardt only to destroy him. Peter had heard about that sort of being, too. But he also knew that one could always find them out by the fact that they never stayed to the Elevation of the Host at Mass. Now, Agnes went to Mass every day, if she could. Peter had even seen her take communion. A sorceress's tongue would shrivel and burn at the touch of the body of Our Lord. So Agnes couldn't be a demon. She must have a reason other than pure evil to wish his father dead. But what?

The bells were ringing for Vespers. Peter wiped his eyes and nose and trudged back up to the keep. He wished there were someplace else to go.

His aunt Maria and uncle Folmar were waiting for him, their faces taut with grief.

"Oh, Peter," Maria moaned. "Look at yourself! Covered in mud and the archdeacon coming to dinner tonight."

"I'll wash and change at once, Aunt," Peter replied listlessly.

"But why must we feed the archdeacon? Doesn't he know we're a house in mourning?"

"Of course, my dear," his aunt said. "He hopes to bring consolation."

Peter continued on to the room that had been his father's and was now his. Absently, he sent for wash water. Despite the numbness of desolation, he started to wonder about the archdeacon's visit. Aunt Maria's explanation had been too facile. Was it something to do with Agnes? Perhaps Uncle Hermann wanted the man to use his authority to make Agnes confess. They had tried that once before with a French-speaking priest from Saint Maximin's who had been sent for when Agnes complained that her bodily needs and those of her maid's were being met but their spiritual ones ignored.

Apparently there had been no sudden admission that one of them had slipped poison in Gerhardt's wine cup, for Father Otto had seemed disappointed when he came down from seeing the women.

Peter would have liked to question Agnes himself, but his new position didn't seem to include being allowed to do so. He would have to wait for Walter of Grancy to return with Agnes's family so that the trial could begin.

He finished dressing, carefully smoothing the pressed linen tunic with his damp hands before leaving the room. Aunt Maria was so exacting about his appearance. It was trying. He wondered how much longer he'd have to pay attention to her.

As he went down the stairs the clink of platters and the murmur of polite voices rose to meet him. Even the dogs were behaving. The contrast to the raucus meals with his father was almost more than he could bear.

Peter clenched his teeth and lifted his chin, determined to see this through as Gerhardt would have wished. But all the time his heart cried out for his father to come back.

Even though they had tried to hurry, it was another week before Catherine and Edgar arrived in Metz, where they hoped to buy space on a boat going downriver to Trier. Hubert chafed at each delay, threatening to take a pair of horses and ride off on his own.

"Father, you can't do that," Catherine told him. "I won't let you risk yourself. It will be of no use to Agnes if you fall dead by the roadside in your haste to reach her."

"Stop treating me like an old man!" Hubert shouted at her. "That doctor in Paris is an idiot. There's nothing wrong with me. Nothing except my youngest child being a prisoner alone in a barbaric country, subject to calumny and on trial for her life!"

"Walter says she's not being mistreated," Catherine said. "Lord Gerhardt's family is prepared to follow the law in this and wait until she can be tried according to custom. And we're traveling as swiftly as possible. The children have been good and not held us up at all."

"As if that weren't an altogether greater madness!" Hubert interrupted, glaring at Edgar, who had just come back from arranging for the boat.

"You're right, Hubert," he said. "But it's our madness." He hesitated, licking his lips. "I know that Eliazar and Johanna offered to keep the children with them while we were gone. Perhaps they would have been safer in Troyes, but perhaps not."

Hubert started to give an angry answer, but Catherine interrupted.

"You can't pretend you don't understand, Father," she said. "I know that Abbot Bernard sent letters to try to stop the monk who is preaching destruction of the Jews. But that doesn't mean he'll succeed. And there are those who need no urging. I know the count and the bishop of Troyes will do everything they can to protect their Jews, but it may not be enough. I don't want my children slaughtered or stolen because someone thinks they aren't Christians."

"I'm sorry, Hubert," Edgar said softly. "At least with us, they have nothing to fear from fanatics."

Hubert heard the unspoken statement. As long as he traveled with them, he had nothing to fear, either. They were a good Christian family, all of them. Catherine wore an ivory cross at her neck and his grandchildren were being taught Christian prayers. So no one doubted his orthodoxy. He felt the bile of self-loathing in his throat and swallowed it. He must think only of Agnes, not his own pride.

Edgar continued. "There's a man taking wine barrels down river to Trier to refill. He leaves tomorrow and has room for us all. We can put our baggage in the empty barrels."

"And arrive smelling like a tavern," Hubert grunted.

"Walter will ride ahead to let Agnes know we're coming," Edgar went on, ignoring him. "The river is fairly tranquil now so it should be a calm journey. The boatman says it should only take two days."

Two more days. Catherine's throat constricted. What if Agnes were angry at them for coming, ashamed to be found in such a situation? Even worse, what if there were nothing they could do to help her?

Margaret sensed her fears and came to sit by her, putting her hand in Catherine's. Catherine smiled down at her. Poor Margaret! There hadn't been time to take her to Count Thibault. She had considered asking if the girl might stay under the protection of the countess, but Edgar had forbidden it. It wasn't right to leave her with strangers, he insisted, not after all she had been through. Catherine reluctantly agreed. There would be time when this was settled to introduce her to her grandfather.

Hubert stood up suddenly.

"Tomorrow," he said. "Good work, Edgar. That's the best we could have hoped for. But if I sit here until then, I'll start raving. I'm going out. I need to walk."

"Let me come with you, Father," Catherine said. "I'm restless, too."

He hesitated, then gave in.

"Very well, if you must," he said.

Catherine laced up her street shoes. Edgar had reminded her earlier that there might be some in Metz who knew Hubert as a man often in the company of Jews. The scene in Paris had frightened her. If he were alone and challenged, her father might well proclaim his Jewish birth. If she were there, she could prevent that.

At least she hoped she could.

The afternoon was warm, the sun heating the cobblestones of the street and glinting off copper pots hanging from a stand in the square. Children ran past them, some rolling a hoop, others intent on a game of hunting, riding on worn broomsticks and brandishing toy bows. Women sat by open windows with their spindles and chatted with friends passing by. The normality of the scene calmed Catherine's spirit. She took her father's arm.

"Remember how you used to take us on feast days to see the

tumblers in front of Notre Dame?" she asked. "Agnes still doesn't know how the man was able to find a whole egg behind her ear."

"And you wanted him to repeat the trick until you figured it out." Hubert laughed. "Even as a child you refused to believe that it was magic."

"No, I thought it was, but I believed I could learn how to do it, too," Catherine said. "I broke so many eggs trying that Mother finally forbid the cook to let me have any."

As soon as she mentioned her mother, Catherine knew she had broken the mood. Hubert grimaced.

"She was very tolerant of you." He sighed. "Your cleverness pleased her. She had visions of seeing you become an abbess one day."

They walked in silence for a few moments, each thinking about the way their lives had altered from expectations. A wooden ball rolled into Catherine's foot and she kicked it back toward the little girl who had lost it. She thought of Edana. No, it grieved her that her refusal to enter religious life might have led to her mother's derangement, but she had chosen the right path.

"Father, don't dwell on it," she said. "You did the best you knew how. You gave all of us anything we ever wanted. And I know how much you give the nuns for Mother's care. We can't change anything."

"I know that." Hubert wasn't comforted. "But perhaps I can redress the harm I did to Agnes, even if she never forgives me."

There was a way, Catherine knew. If Hubert honestly in his soul accepted Christianity and told Agnes of the sincerity of his faith, then she would have to forgive him and accept him again. But for that to happen would need a real miracle. And right now, her prayers were so occupied with sparing her sister's life that it seemed impolite to bother God for anything more.

Walter had only rested a night before heading back to Trier. Even though he trusted Hermann not to harm Agnes, he was uneasy about what was happening among the rest of the people at the castle and in the town. Accusations of sorcery were hard to prove, but people were more inclined to believe them if the accused were a stranger.

He was also worried about Jehan. The knight had literally set up camp at the edge of Gerhardt's land. He brought gifts of food or flowers for Agnes and was loud in protesting her innocence, offering to prove it in combat at any time. Walter had been unable to make him see that his devotion could only hurt Agnes. Soon people would suspect that the two had conspired to murder Gerhardt, if the rumors weren't flying already. If the true culprit weren't discovered, there would be little hope for either of them to prove innocence.

Walter urged his horse to a faster pace. It seemed that, instead of fighting the servants of Satan in the Holy Land, he first would have to confront evil much closer to home.

He was even more aware of it as soon as he arrived in Trier. He was surprised to find that even his pilgrim's cross and his imposing presence weren't enough to get him a room at one of the inns. He finally ended up again at the monastery of Saint Maximin, which refused shelter to no one.

After seeing that his worn horse was being cared for and changing into a clean tunic, Walter set out on foot for the castle. After some thought he took both his sword and crossbow. He doubted that anyone would try to attack him but wanted it made clear that anyone who tried to harm Agnes would have to climb over him to do so.

The first person he encountered was the last one he wanted to see.

"Walter!" Jehan greeted him from his tent by the gate. "Have you seen Lord Garnegaud? Is he sending help for Agnes? When will they be here?"

"God save you, Jehan," Walter greeted him. "I didn't see Agnes's grandfather. I went to her father, instead. They should be here within the week."

Jehan's dismay was palpable.

"Her father? What were you thinking of? How could you go to those people?" he shouted. "Agnes would rather die than have them come to her aid."

"If you'll forgive me, Jehan," Walter said as he opened the gate, "I'll ask Lady Agnes myself if that is her choice. Because it may well be the only one she has."

"You've doomed her, Walter!" Jehan wailed at his back. "They'll hang her and it will be on your soul!"

Walter continued up the hill, giving no sign that he had heard.

If Jehan didn't realize how much his own actions were damning Agnes, then his judgement on Hubert wasn't to be considered.

At first Agnes had simply been in a state of shock, then confusion. This couldn't be happening to her. Wasn't it bad enough that she had been so humiliated by Gerhardt on their wedding night? She had endured that without saying anything to anyone. Each night she had begged him to reconsider his behavior. She couldn't make him understand that eventually someone else would find out and they would both be shamed. But she hadn't reproached him before his family. She knew where her duty lay and she was prepared to bear her suffering in silence.

And then, horribly, he was dead. There on the floor, first thrashing about and shrieking at things only he could see and then going limp in her arms as she screamed in terror.

How could anyone believe that she would poison him and then be there to watch such agony?

But someone must, or they would have set her free.

They thought they were being kind to her. She was put in a comfortable room, allowed her clothes, needlework and the company of her maids. They simply refused to let her go or to tell her what was happening outside.

She had rejoiced when Walter arrived from Köln, believing that he would soon put all to rights. But then he rode away again, with only a quick word of encouragement and the promise that he would not let her be harmed.

And now she was left here with Laudine and Lisette.

After the first week, she began to wish that Hermann had shackled her in a windowless dungeon rather than make her suffer through another minute with them. The dread she had felt at the thought of being imprisoned for murder was replaced by the fear that her punishment might be to live the rest of her life with these two.

"You used all the blue!" Laudine whined as she sifted through the thread. "You always take the color I want."

"You always want the color I have," Lisette retorted. "Why can't you think up a design of your own instead of copying me all the time?"

"Who would want to copy the insipid things you make?" Laudine raised her embroidery hoop and brought it down on Lisette's fingers. Lisette screamed with rage.

A moment later there was a knock on the door. Agnes lowered her hands from her ears to gesture for Laudine to open it.

Two guards stood there. Behind them was Lady Maria, with a basket of new thread.

"I understand you are running out of materials," she said softly. "I thought I would bring more to keep you occupied."

Agnes rose to take the basket. She hadn't understood the words but the meaning was clear. *"Danc,"* she said. "Is there anyone in the castle who speaks French? Frankish?" she added in desperation.

Maria shook her head. Agnes's shoulders drooped. She had to find a way to get rid of her maids. Was it possible that they were hoping she'd confess to the poisoning just to be free of their constant whining?

The door shut and she threw the basket at Lisette and Laudine.

"How could you behave so badly?" she said. "Lady Maria must believe we have brawling cats in here with us."

The two women stared at her in astonishment.

"You killed your husband and forced us to be locked up with you," Laudine answered. "And you reprimand *our* behavior? How dare you!"

"We came with you on the promise that good husbands would be found for us here," Lisette added. "Now we're captives in a strange country. And, even when we get home, what can we hope for, with people suspecting us, too? You're a haughty, ungrateful *mordrisseuse* and I wish you were hanged already!"

Agnes could only gape in disbelief as Lisette burst into tears.

"Look what you've done." Laudine put her arms around Lisette. "Calm yourself, *bele seur*. I've been praying to Saint Perpetua that we'll soon be released. She'll help us."

Agnes could stand it no longer.

"I did not kill Lord Gerhardt," she stated in fury. "And you might find someone better to pray to, if you want to go home. Saint Perpetua wasn't set free; she was martyred on a gladiator's sword."

The looks they gave her told her that they didn't believe her on either count. Agnes turned her back on them and retreated to the window in the far corner of the room. For the first time, she began to despair.

"It doesn't matter if I'm proved innocent or not," she sniffed. "By the time any rescue comes, I shall be drooling with idiocy. Another day with those two should be enough. Dear sweet Virgin Mother, comfort me! I've fallen into Hell."

Ten

Trier. Tuesday, 6 kalends July (June 26), 1146; 10 Tammuz, 4906. Feast of Saint Maxence, soldier, who was converted when his sword froze in midair as he tried to decapitate a monk.

Cotidie morimur, cotidie commutamur et tamen aeternos esse nos credimus.

Each day we die, each day we are changed and still we believe ourselves to be eternal.

—Jerome
Letter LX
To Heliodorus on the death of his nephew

$\mathcal{T}$he boat trip had been lively. Edgar had finally tied one end of a rope around his waist and the other around James to keep the boy from tumbling into the river, or at least to pull him out when he did. That and keeping Edana from following him managed to distract Catherine from what might be awaiting them in Trier. But as the walls of the city appeared on the right, harsh among the burgeoning vines, she was struck with fear.

"Is Agnes in there?" she asked. The stones seemed so forbidding.

"No," Hubert answered. "Gerhardt's castle is farther downriver, Walter says. But we'll have to land on this side of the city."

He pointed to a line of wooden posts coming up on the right bank.

"The boatman is taking the casks only this far," he said. "We'll have to walk the rest of the way, unless I can get a mule to carry Catherine and the children as well as one for the baggage."

"Believe me," Catherine said. "After two days on this boat, all of us will be glad to walk."

With the help of the boatman, they were able to find an ostler who let them have a mule at a reasonable price and they loaded it with their belongings. He also gave them directions to the *porta media*, the southern gate into Trier and advice about where to stay.

"I'd stop the night with the monks of Saint Eucharius, just outside the gate," he said. "And wait until morning to enter the town."

"We're supposed to meet a friend who will be at Saint Maximin," Edgar told him. "Is your monastery near there?"

"Nah, Saint Maximin is north of Trier." The man grunted as he started to unload the barrels. "You'll not make it tonight, not with babies and all. You on some sort of pilgrimage? Can't think why you'd travel with children if they weren't sick."

"It's a family penance." Edgar sighed.

He picked up his daughter and deposited her on the back of the mule, between the parcels. They bade the boatman farewell and set out on the last part of the journey. Tomorrow they would meet Walter at Saint Maximin and reach poor Agnes at last.

The monks greeted them kindly and provided plain, but adequate, shelter. That night Catherine couldn't settle in her bed. Edgar and Hubert had been sent to sleep in a room with other men, but she was the only woman visitor. So she and the children had a room to themselves. It was lonely. Long after they had gone to sleep she lay awake listening to the sounds of night, punctuated by the footsteps of the monks as they rose and hurried to chant the night office.

She wanted to get up and go to the chapel, where she could join the prayers, even though she would have to remain hidden from the monks. But she daren't risk the panic if one of the children, even Margaret, woke to find her gone. So she lay through the hours staring at the darkness above until the light grew enough to make out the thatch ceiling. This last night was the worst, for tomorrow she would be thrust into a strange world where, once again, she couldn't speak the language and didn't know the customs. Even more, she would have to face the stranger her sister had become.

In the soul-searching that only comes in the silence of the hour before dawn, Catherine wondered if it were just possible that Agnes could have changed so much that she might be capable of murdering her husband.

When they reached the marketplace of Trier the next morning, Catherine and Edgar realized at once that they would hardly be noticed among all the other travelers and traders. This was a wine city, as well as the seat of an archbishop. Foreigners were common and a merchant arriving from France, even accompanied by his family, aroused no one's interest. On the journey they had heard that trade had fallen in the past few years, due to the feud between the archbishop and Graf Heinrich and a famine in the lowlands. But the marketplace still seemed busy to Catherine's eyes. Perhaps the fine summer weather had brought people in from nearby villages.

Now Catherine walked with the men beside the mule, which still carried their bags and Edana. James rode proudly on Hubert's shoulders, kicking occasionally to point out something that excited him. Margaret clung to her brother's arm, fearing to be lost in the throng.

They passed a stone column surmounted by a granite cross that seemed to be a meeting point. Several people were sitting at its base, chatting with each other all the while looking around as if expecting someone. Hubert stopped and pointed it out to them.

"If any of you should ever become separated from the rest of us, go here and wait," he said. "James do you understand?"

James kicked acknowledgment.

As they started up again, Hubert was suddenly accosted by a woman who threw her arms about him, kissing him on both cheeks. She was trailed by three children, all of whom seemed delighted to see him.

"Hubert!' she cried. *"Wîs willekomen!"*

The rest of her greeting was in a mix of Hebrew and German. Catherine stared in growing dread. She had heard about merchants who had wives in many towns but it had never before occured to her that her own father would do such a thing.

"Edgar!" She nudged him. *"Who* is that woman?"

"How should I know?" Edgar snapped. The woman's familiarity worried him, too. He wondered if this was why Hubert had been reluctant to take Agnes to Trier for her marriage.

Hubert sensed their consternation. He looked from one to the other and began to laugh.

"Edgar! Catherine! I want you to meet Mina, the wife of Simon, a learned man and a shrewd wine trader. They live here."

"How . . . nice," Catherine said, forcing a smile.

"Simon is a good friend of Solomon's," Hubert added.

Edgar recovered more quickly than Catherine. "Does she know anything about what has happened to Agnes?"

"Enondu!" Hubert exclaimed. "How could I have forgotten?"

He turned back to Mina and spoke in a low voice for a moment.

Her face grew serious as she listened. She shook her head and gave a short answer. Hubert closed his eyes and Mina took his hand, patting it in consolation.

"What's wrong?" Catherine's heart froze.

Hubert came to her at once.

"Agnes is still in the castle," he said. "Mina tells me they recently sent her maids back to a nearby convent so she's all alone there. But there's been no trial and no rumor of her having been harmed."

"Yet," Catherine added without thinking.

"Yet," Hubert echoed.

He said something more to Mina, who then took Catherine's hands in hers and gave them a comforting squeeze.

"*Todah robah.*" Hubert thanked her and they hurried on. "We must find Walter at once" he muttered. "How could they lock her up alone with no one who can speak to her, or for her!"

As they approached the *Porta Nigra*, the northern city gate next to the bishop's palace, Catherine looked back. Mina was still there, now talking to another woman. She pointed at Hubert and her friend stared after them shaking her head.

Catherine felt a chill run up her spine. Had it been her imagination or had she seen the other woman's fingers flickering in the sign to ward off evil?

How many people in Trier believed Agnes to be an enchantress?

Agnes paced back and forth across her room. The sunlight poured in through the glass window, one of two in the keep. Gerhardt had been delighted with them but Agnes prefered the convenience of shutters. The only way to open this window was to break the glass, and so the room was unbearably hot.

Agnes had been rather proud of the way she had managed to rid herself of the bickering Lisette and Laudine without offending them. She had begged that they not be forced to endure her incarceration as they had been accused of nothing. Hermann consuulted with Maria and they agreed that the women should remain with the nuns until they were questioned by those investigating Gerhardt's death. Hermann promised that then they could return to their homes. Agnes had been so obviously relieved when they left that Maria had felt the first twinge of doubt about her guilt. It was such an unselfish act.

But in the days afterward, Agnes had begun to wonder if she had been so clever after all. With the constant irritation of the other ladies, she hadn't had time to dwell overmuch on her predicament. Now, there was nothing else to think about.

As she paced she retraced all the events of the night that Gerhardt had died. She had hidden her outrage at him well enough in the short time they had been married, she thought, trying to behave as a happy bride should. He was eager to please her when they were in public. He showed her all over his land, teaching her more about grapes and wine making than she had ever wanted to know. She smiled and pretended great interest. They drank from the same cup at meals and he gave her the choicest bits from his plate. That alone should have caused people to doubt that she would knowingly poison his food. But more worrying, if someone else had done so, how could he have been poisoned and she remain well?

It made sense to her that people would think she had bewitched him and killed him with a potion. It was the only solution she had come up with so far for his death. She had hardly been apart from him in the brief weeks of their marriage. Someone must have clouded her mind and administered the poison without her seeing. How else could he have been killed?

Therefore, the only answer Agnes could come up with was that someone else in this keep was practicing sorcery. And how could she get anyone to believe that?

Just as she was thinking this, Agnes noticed a thin wisp of smoke rising from the rushes on the floor where the sunshine hit it.

"They heard my very thoughts! Sweet baby Jesus, save me!" she cried. "Protect me from the demons!"

As she prayed, she stomped on the dry rushes and scattered them out of the sunlight. In a moment, the fire was out. The sun beat in upon a scorch mark on the wooden floor. Agnes stared at it. It seemed to her to be in the form of a profile. There was a chin and nose and some sort of crown or helmet. But it didn't appear to be anyone she knew. Was it the face of the demon?

Hurriedly, she went to the basket by her bed and strewed fresh herbs all over the mark. Then, just to be sure, she emptied a flask of holy water on the spot.

"There," she said and crossed herself. "That should do it."

Still, as she resumed her pacing, she carefully avoided treading on the covered face.

Peter saw them as they came up the river path. At first he thought they might be pilgrims, but then he recognized Walter of Grancy, riding his war horse with a little boy seated in front of him. There was a lady in fine silks riding a mule, holding a younger child and two men and a young woman walking beside them.

So this was Agnes's family. He squinted to make them out better. Strange, none of them really looked like her. He wondered how they were connected to her and what they would do to free her.

He ran to tell Uncle Hermann.

Hermann had already seen them from his vantage point at the guardpost over the gate. These people weren't what he had expected, either. Where were the retainers? The pack animals with beds and supplies? Why was no one but Walter armed? Agnes had brought a respectable dowry with her. Had it impoverished the family to raise it?

Most important, how did they intend to convince him to release Agnes?

As he came down the ladder into the bailey, he was accosted by his sister and her husband.

"Are they coming? What are they like? How many men at arms did they bring? Is it my job to feed them all?" Maria pelted him with her questions.

"Yes. You'll see. I wouldn't worry about it," Hermann answered. "Gerd! Raise the gate!"

Maria found it difficult to contain her surprise and disdain at the group before her. Fortunately, her training held and she took a moment to study them before making any remark that could not be withdrawn.

They were dusty from the road, but the clothes were of linen and silk, if she were any judge. The men wore velvet tunics and the jewels in the brooches glittered. The woman was wearing earrings of

pearls the size of wine grapes and even the children were quite elegantly turned out.

Perhaps they had left the servants behind in Trier.

Walter dismounted and saluted them.

"My lords Peter, Hermann, Folmar, Lady Maria." He bowed to
each in turn. "May I present to you Hubert LeVendeur, father of
Lady Agnes. With him are his daughter, Lady Catherine, her husband, Lord Edgar of Wedderlie and the Lady Margaret of Wedderlie."

Hubert pulled himself up to look as stern and avenging as possible without offending. The others just tried to look sufficiently
noble.

"Tell them, Walter, that we have come to prove and give surety
that my child did not harm her husband and that this accusation
against her is vile calumny," he said.

Walter did.

Hermann seemed confused. "How will you do that?" he asked.
"You weren't here. You can't even speak German. I thought you'd
come to plead that she be sent to a convent or to make restitution
for the death of my brother. That's the best you can do, for all your
protestations."

Hubert brushed off his objections.

"I intend to find out what happened," he stated. "My daughter
is no murderer. I have with me a letter from Count Thibault of
Champagne and his brother-in-law, Bishop Henri of Troyes to your
archbishop that attests to my years of service to them, requesting
that I be given every aid in establishing the truth in this matter."

"You've already contacted Archbishop Albero?"

Hermann and Maria exchanged glances. Catherine thought she
saw a flash of fear in them.

"It isn't necessary to involve the archbishop in this unless you
wish to subject Agnes to the humiliation of a trial," Hermann said
quickly. "I'm sure you don't want that. It's best to handle such things
privately."

"We'll do whatever is necessary," Hubert said. "Now, I want to
see Agnes. If she has been mistreated, I'll ask the archbishop to take
her under his protection and have you fined."

"Walter," Hermann answered. "Tell him that if they will all
make themselves comfortable inside, I'll have food and wine brought

to them. And," he added, "I'll inform the prisoner that she is to be brought down so that they may see that we've done nothing to harm her."

"No!" Hubert stepped in front of Walter. "I want to see her alone. And I want to see where she is being held."

He looked straight at Hermann, not waiting for the end of the translation. Hermann bit his lip a moment, then nodded.

"Follow me," he said.

The window in Agnes's room faced east so that all she could see from it was the sun and rows of vines as they marched to the top of the hill behind the castle. So she had no warning that her would-be rescuers had arrived. She was seated at a table, trying to see into the small mirror she had propped up. It bothered her that all this worry had ruined her skin. She had felt a sore on her chin and was sure it was growing.

At the sound of footsteps and the creaking of the door, she spun around so quickly that the mirror fell on the floor with a clang. Agnes stood as the door opened, ready to face whatever came and praying that her complexion was up to the task.

The door opened and a man entered. The door was shut behind him and the bar in the hallway dropped with a thud, locking him in.

At first she could only look at him, wondering how he could possibly be there. Then the weeks of fear and loneliness broke through and, with a cry, Agnes threw herself into her father's arms.

"Oh Papa, Papa!" she wept. "Take me home!"

Hubert held her tightly, one hand caressing her hair.

"My baby! My dear golden child!" He choked on his own tears. "Forgive me for letting you come to this terrible place alone. We've come to make them set you free. I swear to you, *ma douz*, I will not leave here without you."

The first shock over, Agnes began to collect herself. She pulled away and looked up into his face.

" 'We've come'?" she said. "Who is with you, Father? Did Grandfather send men to prove my innocence in combat? Jehan wants to, but I won't let him. Tell me you have the best warriors in his household. Please tell me that."

"Walter is here," Hubert hedged. "I thought he had told you that he came to me instead of going all the way to Blois. He'll fight for you, if necessary."

"What do you mean, 'if necessary'?" Agnes stepped back from him. "How else can I be freed? Do you expect me to undergo the ordeal?"

"Of course not! Oh, Agnes, I'd never let you do that." Hubert tried to hug her again, but she moved away. "I'll hold the hot iron myself first," he declared. "We hoped that the real murderer would have been found by now. But, if not, we intend to find that person and leave no doubt in anyone's mind that you are innocent."

Agnes was growing more and more suspicious.

"Oh no! You brought Catherine, didn't you?" she accused him. "You think that she'll trip over a vial of poison or find some confession written in Latin and, *harou*, the true culprit will be found. Oh, Father, how could you?"

"Agnes, that wasn't my intention," Hubert pleaded. "All we could think of was you. She only wants to stand with you, to help somehow."

Agnes clenched her hands, her jaw, her whole body. Hubert moved back toward the door. Agnes took a deep breath and forced her fingers apart.

"Father." She kept her voice steady. "I don't want Catherine's help. With her training in logic and theology, she'd probably manage to prove I was guilty after all and have me at the stake, watching the flames rising around me, by the end of the day. Send her home. Now, before something even worse happens."

She paused as she thought of what something worse might be.

"You didn't bring that . . . man, did you?" Now her voice trembled. "That Jew."

Hubert looked at her with shame, for her or for himself, he wasn't sure.

"No, Solomon is in Troyes," he said.

"Thank God for that, at least." Agnes rubbed her forehead then stopped, remembering the state of her face.

Something seemed to go out of her then. She went over to her bed and sat down, her arms limp, her shoulders sagging. She looked up at her father, all emotion gone.

"It doesn't matter," she said. "They're going to kill me, whatever you do. Hermann and Maria don't want to, but they'll hand me over to the hangman because that's the only way for order to prevail. They have no one but me to blame for Gerhardt's death. And someone must be punished. Oh, Saint Peter in chains, I'm so tired! Go away, Father. I want to sleep."

She lay down and closed her eyes. Hubert watched this sudden change with consternation.

"Agnes?"

No answer.

He started to leave, if only for the moment, then something she had said hit him.

"Agnes?" he asked again. "Why don't Hermann and Maria want you punished, if they think you poisoned their brother? Agnes? Answer me."

She didn't open her eyes. "I don't know," she said dully. "I think they want me to confess and repent first, so that they can send me to a convent and spare themselves having my death on their souls. But I won't because I didn't. Now let me be."

Hubert bent over and kissed her cheek, but she didn't respond.

"Very well, my sweet," he whispered. "But we aren't going to abandon you and you aren't going to die. I'll return soon."

After he had gone, Agnes rolled over on her her stomach and buried her face in the bolster, so that no one could hear her cry.

Peter didn't know what to think about these new visitors. The man and the young girl were northern pale as he was, but the older man and the woman were darker, like the traders from Aquitaine and Sicily. Yet they seemed to be one family. And they had brought children, just as if they were coming for a festival! No one had told him the French had such strange customs.

Another thing that amazed him was that the girl spoke a language that sounded almost like German. She had said something in it to her brother. He had watched her during the conversation Walter had translated and he was almost sure that she had understood before the words were turned into French.

This Margaret also had the most beautiful auburn hair he had ever seen and eyes that sparkled blue in the sunlight and turned grey in shadows.

She was sitting in shadows now, trying to be unnoticed in a corner. But Peter was drawn to her. Even in the dark she shone in his eyes. He sat next to her.

"I'm Peter," he said, pointing to himself. "I'm the lord here, now, I guess."

She smiled. "Margaret." She pointed to herself, as well. *"Ic beo Edgares sweostra."*

He blinked. "You understand me?" he asked.

She didn't. But her words had been close enough for him, even though he hadn't been able to make out what she had said to her brother. He wondered where they were from and why they were part of this tragedy.

"Peter!" Aunt Maria was shocked. "What are you doing there with the Lady Margaret?"

"Just talking," Peter answered.

"Really? I had no idea you were accomplished in languages," she said. "Come away at once. Do you want her to enchant you as that woman did your father?"

Peter looked at Margaret, staring up at him with innocence in her beautiful eyes. He suspected that she might have enchanted him already.

Hubert returned then, with Hermann and Walter. He was speaking so quickly that he barely gave Walter time to translate. Peter hurried over to them. He wanted to hear everything now and not wait until one of his relatives told him only as much as they thought he should know.

Hermann was answering Hubert's angry questions.

"We do believe her to be guilty," he insisted. "There's no way anyone else could have given him poison. But we haven't found what she used and she refuses to confess. We would rather not resort to trial by combat or ordeal. But if you can't make her admit to it and you won't make any sort of restitution, then there's nothing else to do."

"Have you even looked for another murderer?" Hubert shouted. "The man was lord here, wasn't he? Such a man always has enemies!"

"Not in his own bedroom!" Hermann shouted back.

They both grew louder and louder as if, by yelling, they could somehow bypass the inconvenience of having to converse through Walter.

"He was poisoned, not stabbed," Hubert insisted. "He could have been given it anywhere!"

Hermann hesitated. That had been the niggling doubt in his own mind.

"Then tell me how, and where!" he answered. "And by whom and I'll give you back your daughter and her dowry and send you all away gladly. But if you can't then, I swear, I will give her to the archbishop and his court for justice."

"Father!" Catherine grabbed Hubert's arm, lest he say something that would doom Agnes.

"Give us the freedom to question anyone here," Hubert answered. "And we'll find out what really happened. If not, then you can keep Agnes's dowery and I swear she shall be locked up in any convent you choose, to do penance for the rest of her life."

"That's not enough for what she did," Hermann said.

"Uncle Hermann!" Peter interrupted. "You forget that I am now lord here. It is my father's death and I have the right to decide what should be done to investigate it."

Hermann gaped at him as if a sheep had just spoken.

"Of—of course, Peter," he said. "Forgive me. I was only trying to spare you pain."

"It's too late for that," Peter answered. He lifted his chin and faced Hubert.

"I accept your terms," he said. "I shall send word that all who are under my care must give you every courtesy and answer truthfully any question put to them. But you are not to interfere with their work or intimidate them in any way."

Both Hermann and Maria started to object but Peter silenced them with a gesture that Catherine thought was positively imperial.

"Thank you, my lord," Hubert said.

"One thing more," Peter told him. "This can't go on forever. If you have found nothing by Michaelmass, then my stepmother will be judged according to our laws. And, if it is proved that she used any form of magic or poison to harm my father, then she must die. Do you understand?"

Catherine tried to speak again, but Hubert hushed her.

"My child is a devout Christian and has had no traffic with demons," he said. "I accept your terms."

"Then you may go." Peter waved again. This time the movement was spoilt slightly by the way his eyes moved to see if Margaret were watching.

When they had gathered up their entourage, James ruining the exit by screaming because they wouldn't let him see the dungeon, Catherine let out everything she had kept pent up during Hubert's bargaining.

"Father!" she exclaimed. "How can we possibly find out who killed Lord Gerhardt? We know none of these people, nor can we speak to them without an interpreter. What if one of his family poisoned him? What if the death was accidental? Perhaps he drank one of Agnes's face lotions by mistake."

Edgar intervened. "Catherine, no man would mistake one of those concoctions for something potable. What I fear is that there may be those who wish to draw us all into the trap along with Agnes. I worry that the protection of the archbishop may not be enough. Hermann's expression when you mentioned Albero was hardly respectful."

"I noticed that, too," Walter said. "It may be just as well not to use those letters, yet, Hubert. It's possible that Gerhardt was no friend of Archbishop Albero."

"You're all in the right," Hubert admitted. "I might have simply arranged with the family for Agnes to atone, given all I own for her freedom and taken her home with us. But then she would always be a murderer in the eyes of the world. There must be a way we can prove her innocence, even if the true villain is never known."

"I wish Solomon were here to help." Catherine sighed. "He's naturally distrustful of everyone."

Hubert nodded glumly, then brightened.

"I have an even better idea," he said. "Walter, can you find rooms for us, perhaps for some time? Edgar, Catherine, take the children and go with him. I'm going to talk to Mina."

There was almost as much dismay inside the castle as out.

"What were you thinking of?" Maria demanded. "You gave those people the right to wander freely through our land and accost anyone they like."

Peter bit his lip. Now that Margaret had left, he was feeling much younger and less certain.

"If my stepmother didn't kill my father, then she should go free," he said finally. "What if someone else poisoned him after all?"

"But who, Peter?" Hermann asked. "How?"

"I don't know," Peter answered. "I've been trying to think ever since it happened. There were so many people coming and going then, so many banquets. And not everyone who came was a friend. You all know that."

They did, but they were surprised that Peter had noticed. Maria's husband, Folmar, gaped at him in wonder.

"So you are making Agnes's family find the murderer for us?" he asked. "But what if we're right and she is guilty?"

"Then they'll have to believe it, too," Peter said. "But perhaps we can at least find out why she did it. She might tell one of them something. Don't you think I'm right?"

Hermann put an arm around him.

"Nephew, you are now lord here, in fact and in name," he said. "What you decide is what we will do. At least we won't offend Count Thibault by behaving too rashly toward one under his protection. And, in any case, we still have the woman locked up here. If no other suspect appears, we can always have her hanged as planned."

Eleven

Trien. Thursday, 4 kalends July (June 28), 1146; 12 Tammuz, 4906. The vigil of the passion of Saints Peter and Paul.

Comes vero per exploratores ejus praesentiens adventum archiepiscopi, in fugam conversus, nocte illa in villam episcopi Witelich se recepit: equos et homines reficere volens, et nihil reperiens, villam totam concremavit.

The count [of Namur] through his spies, was forewarned of the coming of the Archbishop [Albero] who had turned about in retreat. That night in the episcopal town of Witelich, the count met him. Horses and men wished for revenge, and nothing was spared; the town was completely destroyed.

—Baldric
The Life of Albero

Of course there's been gossip," Mina told them. "The town's been full of speculation about Lord Gerhardt's death, but nothing that I could swear has any truth behind it."

She looked apologetically at the faces across from her. Edgar, Catherine and Hubert each showed their disappointment.

"Not everyone thinks your daughter is a sorceress," Mina added. "But you'll have a difficult time trying to make anyone believe she didn't poison Gerhardt."

"I know," Hubert said glumly. "She's a stranger. It's easy to think the worst of her."

Catherine leaned forward. "But that's why no one seems to have tried to find another explanation. Gerhardt was a fairly powerful man. He must have made enemies."

"Not so many as you would think," Mina told her. "He treated his people well enough, didn't cheat in his dealings with the town, gave generously to the church, at least until recently. He was even tolerent toward us."

"A veritable saint," Edgar murmured.

Hubert gave him a sour glance.

"Even saints have those who dislike them," he insisted.

Catherine agreed. "If Gerhardt was that honest, it's all the more likely that he offended others. Especially those he traded with. In Simon's dealings, did he know of anyone who was resentful because Gerhardt wouldn't agree to a questionable sale?"

Mina thought. "You mean like buying horses that were stolen?"

"Yes, exactly!" Hubert said eagerly.

"No," Mina said. "Never. He managed to stay on good terms

with both sides of the war between the Graf Heinrich and Archbishop Albero. We think that's why his alms lately have been made
directly to the poor instead of through the monasteries. He didn't
want gifts to Saint Maximin to be considered an insult to the archbishop, since the graf is advocate for the monastery. And yet he took
the side of the town against Albero's demands."

"The archbishop?" Catherine remembered the reaction of Hermann and Maria to his name. "What was he demanding?"

"What they always want," she said wearily. "Higher tolls, more
tithes, a bigger share of everything we have. But, of course, his war
with Graf Heinrich is our worst worry."

"What is this war?" Edgar asked. "We heard nothing of it until
we were almost here."

He and Catherine had returned from England two years before
after being caught and almost killed in that civil war. He wasn't
pleased to discover that they might have fallen into another.

"It's been going on for years," Mina said. "I don't understand
completely what it's about. Something to do with jurisdiction over
lands and the abbey of Saint Maximin. Graf Heinrich's army invaded
a few years ago and destroyed villages all around, although Trier
escaped. Both the Christian and Jewish burghers are caught between
the hammer and the anvil here. Neither lord is better for us than
the other so we aren't concerned about who prevails but the uncertainty and the sudden attacks are intolerable."

"Could Gerhardt have been planning to announce for one or
the other?" Edgar asked.

"I don't know," Mina answered. "There's been no talk of it. He
was really more one of us than a nobleman. His greatest wealth was
the vines, and matters affecting trade were more important to him
than the great battles of the burgraves."

"There must be someone who didn't like him," Catherine insisted. "No one is that wonderful."

Mina shook her head. "If there is, I never heard of it. But I'll
keep asking among my friends."

Edgar had been gnawing on the other side of the problem.

"What I still don't understand," he said. "Is why everyone immediately assumed Gerhardt was murdered. I know what Hermann

told us, but there are a thousand ways he might have eaten something evil or he might have had a cancer or other illness and not known it."

"That bothers me, too," Catherine agreed. "Someone near him must at least guess that there was a reason for him to be killed or they wouldn't have jumped to that conclusion so quickly. We have to discover what it was."

"But how?" Hubert moaned.

Catherine thought a while. Then she lifted her head, jaw set, as if preparing for a fight.

"I have to make Agnes tell me what happened," she announced. "All of it. No, there are things she wouldn't tell you, Father. She may not want to tell me. But we have to learn what Gerhardt was like in private and she's the one who must know best."

"Catherine, you're the last person she'd confess such things to," Hubert said.

"I'm her sister," Catherine maintained. "I just have to get her to remember that. There was a time when we told each other everything. Things we would never tell anyone else."

The others were doubtful.

"That time is gone," Edgar said gently. "Like Jehan, she blames you for the way her life has changed, even more than she blames your father."

Catherine bit her lips. She wasn't convinced, but she couldn't think of an argument.

"Perhaps, you could talk to her maids, first," Mina suggested. "They're still at Saint Irminen with the nuns."

"No one told us that," Hubert said, hope starting to grow in him. "Yes, Catherine, you go to them. If anyone knows what happened between Gerhardt and Agnes, it's the women who dressed her and kept her company."

Catherine saw the sense in that. "If nothing else, they might give me enough information to make Agnes believe I already know everything. But if she did confide in them, why didn't they say something when she was first accused?"

What if they're protecting her? Catherine thought.

Once again, she was confronted with the possibility that Agnes was guilty. She shut the idea out of her mind. That was a solution she refused to face.

Outside Trier a ragged group had found shelter in a cave hollowed out of the hillside. There weren't as many of them as had been at Vézelay. The trip had been hard on the faith and only the true believers remained. Or so they thought.

Denise watched the communal dinner pot as she waited for her husband and Astolfo to return. Of them all, she was the one most certain of the truth of their beliefs.

She had first heard them a year before on the night when she and her husband took in a wandering preacher who had come all the way from Lombardy to Nantes, speading the word. What he told them made so much more sense than the sermons of their local priest, even though he was a good man who seemed as troubled as Denise by his inability to answer her questions.

But Astolfo understood her doubts. The real problem, he explained, was that God never intended Man to stay on the earth so long. Ever since the birth of Christ, people had been free to return to our natural state, but our carnal nature kept us from doing so. It was only by renouncing the temptations of the flesh that we could reach heaven.

Evil was in the world because the world was evil in itself. All that was corporeal had been created by God's first son, Lucifer. Our souls were angelic spirits, trapped in flesh. The world was full of suffering not because God didn't care. It was because mankind had embraced the lowest part of itself. Christ, a perfect spirit who only appeared in the form of a man, had come to free us to return to Heaven. We need only renounce the dross and allow our souls to shine forth as we escape the prison of our bodies.

To Denise and her husband, Lanval, this interpretation of the chaos around them came as a revelation. Of course there was war, famine and poverty. Of course the strong preyed on the weak. God couldn't protect them. He was waging war, Himself, against the darkness, against the snares the devil set for us. The only way to be saved was to return to the ways of the first followers of Christ. But, because we have gone so much farther into iniquity since then, it is necessary to make a greater renunciation. We must, like the first Christians, abandon all possessions. But we must also give up carnal desires. The truly perfect ones of the faith abstained not only from sexual relations but from eating anything created by reproduction.

When Denise protested that they rarely had meat anyway but without eggs or cheese they couldn't survive, Astolfo had smiled and assured her that no one was expected to become perfect all at once. Only a few were able to achieve that, but all could aspire.

There was more to learn, much more. Denise had told Father Milun about Astolfo's words and he'd been very interested. She smiled now as she stirred the thin vegetable broth they would share that night. Father Milun was snoring on his pallet inside the cave at this moment. He had left his parish and come with them when the bishop had forbidden him to learn any more about this foreign heresy. And, while some had grown weary along the way and turned back, others had joined them. The man they met outside Provins, Andreas, was the strongest of converts. He was so eager to spread the news that they had to physically keep him from preaching at every crossroad. It was hard to convince him that it would do no one any good if he were to be martyred now, or worse, jeered at as a madman. They had to work quietly until they were strong enough to burst forth and save all of Christendom.

But Astolfo had assured them that there were many more of his order in Köln who would take them in and that they would find friends along the way. He had sent a message to one of them near here who had been generous before. When the group had arrived he had taken Lanval and gone to find this benefactor, promising that they would return soon with food and clothing and perhaps even passage on a boat that would carry them to the end of their journey.

Denise sighed. It would be good to have a home again.

Catherine's request to be allowed to speak with Lisette and Laudine had been rebuffed by the portress at first. Walter had had to demand that they be taken to the abbess before she was admitted and then only into the small gatehouse.

"Will you be able to reach them on your own?" Walter asked her. "This is as far as I can go."

"I know that." Catherine smiled. "It's amazing that the portress let you this far. It must be the cross you're wearing. If the abbess will see me and if her Latin is at all competent, I'll simply keep arguing until she concedes my right to question these women."

Walter grimaced. "Good luck to you. I'd rather face Greek fire than an angry abbess."

"Believe me, Walter, they're not nearly as terrifying as a novice mistress." Catherine reached up and gave his cheek a pat of reassurance. "She can flay me with her tongue, but there'll be no lasting hurt. You should go now. I'm sure Father and Edgar would appreciate your help."

Left alone, Catherine waited for the door to open, more nervous than she had admitted. She was worried that the abbess would refuse to see her at all. So, she was surprised when the portess returned, leading two women who clearly had not taken the veil.

The two regarded her with contempt, even though Catherine had dressed most carefully in the same clothing she had worn to visit Countess Mahaut.

"You must be the sister." The woman who had spoken was the epitome of the heroine of the *jongleur's* songs, with a round face, receding chin and wide hazel eyes.

The other was also attractive, although her nose was a bit sharp and her blue eyes too small.

"I'm Catherine, daughter of Hubert LeVendeur and wife to Edgar of Wedderlie."

The women did not appear to be impressed. The first one spoke again. "I'm Laudine, daughter of Reginald of Chateauroux and this is Lisette. Her mother is Hersende, lady of Aubigny."

Catherine refused to be drawn into a duel of lineage.

"I didn't realize that you were still in Trier," she told them.

"They say we can't leave until it's proven that we didn't help Agnes poison Gerhardt," Lisette told her. "If that stupid *jael* would confess that she did it alone, we could go home. Can you help us?"

"Hush!" Laudine told her. "After what Agnes said about her, do you think she'd be of any use?"

"What do you mean?" Catherine said.

"You ran away from the convent to marry," Laudine said. "And you're a Jew lover. You'd rather consort with Jews than your own sister or your mother's family. You should hear the things your grandfather says about you and your father."

Catherine would rather not. She'd always been fond of her bombastic grandfather even though he'd made it clear that he felt female relations were useful only for the alliances they made.

"I want to find the truth," she said quietly. "I don't believe Agnes killed her husband, but if it should happen that she did and you had no part in it, then I'd fight to free you."

Lisette looked from her to Laudine.

"I don't know that we can believe you," she said.

Catherine put her hand to the cross at her neck.

"I swear by the body of Our Lord Jesus and by the tears of his mother that if you are innocent, I will do every thing I can to see that you are sent home safely."

The two maids whispered behind their hands, looking from each other to Catherine, who was still holding her cross. Edgar had made it for her, and touching it gave her some of his calmness and strength.

Finally, Laudine slapped Lisette's hand down and they turned back.

"Very well," Laudine said. "What do you want to know?"

"Let's sit down," Catherine suggested. "This may take some time."

Edgar and Margaret didn't like waiting. Catherine and Walter had gone off to the convent. Hubert was talking to the other Jewish traders, so someone had to tend to the little ones.

But James and Edana didn't like waiting, either.

"Papa!" James whined. "I want to go out and play."

"Play, Papa!" Edana echoed.

Margaret didn't say anything. She felt she was too old to whine. But Edgar saw in her eyes that she was also tired of being cooped up indoors.

"Well, perhaps it would be a good idea to explore the town," he said. "I have a few coins of Trier. We could get some bread and sausage and eat it by the river. Do you want to watch the boats, *deorling?*" he asked Edana.

"She says 'yes,' " James answered for her.

The summer sun was hot on the cobblestones in the square when they arrived. Most people were taking an afternoon rest having arisen with the dawn, hours before. Edgar found a stall open in the shadow of the bishop's palace. He bought cold sausage and hard bread and then got a pitcher of beer to soften it in.

The brewess looked at him without interest but, as they left, they heard a shout. As they turned to look, a rotten turnip hit Margaret in the chest. Another grazed Edgar's shoulder, where Edana was perched. He set her down and started angrily toward the boys, who prepared to throw another volley.

As they aimed again, one boy caught sight of Edgar's left arm. His eyes moved from the empty space to the fury in Edgar's eyes. The boy stopped and pointed.

"Sî verwâzet unde verfluochet!" he shrieked. *"Franzeis Tiuvel!"*

The other boys took up the cry in tones that ranged from terror to glee. Edgar bent to pick up a stone to drive them off. As he lifted it, a man came out of one of the buildings on the square. Edgar looked back at Margaret, who was holding each child by the hand. He called to her in English.

"Take them away! Now! I'll follow you, but you have to get yourselves to safety!"

Still holding the stone, Edgar watched the man approach the boys. They all talked at once, pointing toward him. The man looked him up and down, then his eyes flicked to where Margaret was trying to keep James from running to defend his father.

Edgar yelled again. "Margaret, hurry away from here! Wait for Walter and tell him where I am."

The man listened in puzzlement. Then he shouted at the boys. All Edgar could make out was *"Engelisch! Niht Franzeis!"*

It was the first time in many years that Edgar was glad he was English instead of French. The boys dropped their turnips and ran off. The man waited until they were out of sight. Then he came back to Edgar and offered his hand.

Edgar let go of the stone.

"You're a long way from home." The man greeted him in accented English. "We don't get many men from the North this far into Germany."

"I didn't expect to find anyone here who even knew the language." Edgar evaded the implied question. "You must be a merchant. What do you trade in?"

"Whatever I can sell at a profit," the man answered, equally evasive. "I have a home in Norwich, as well as Trier. Those your children?" He nodded toward Margaret and the children. "Odd to bring them so far."

"We have family here," Edgar explained. "Thank you for driving off those young barbarians. Is that the usual welcome given to travelers?"

"Not at all," the man said. "We're glad of the business you bring, especially these past few years with the archbishop's war. No, the boys had some fool idea that you were in league with a sorceress."

Edgar forced a laugh.

"If I were, I wouldn't be stuck here child-minding," he said. "Now, I promised my son we'd go watch the boats. Thank you again."

"It's my duty to help fellow merchants." The man bowed. "Perhaps someday you can rescue me."

Catherine was growing weary of listening to the litany of injustices that had been heaped upon Lisette and Laudine. Agnes had been distant with them, even though they were as well born as she. Gerhardt had promised to find suitable husbands for them and had rudely died, instead. The colors of the German embroidery threads were wrong. The food gave them gas. The two entered into a fierce debate about the quality of the wine that excluded Catherine altogether. It was only by the threat of leaving them in the convent to find their own way home that they were brought to answering Catherine's questions.

"What was your opinion of Gerhardt?" she asked. "Was he kind to his servants, his family?"

"Oh, tremendously!" Laudine said. "He gave both of us gifts and put us at the high table with his closest retainers."

"I saw a serving boy drop a whole platter of meat pies and Gerhardt didn't beat or kick him," Lisette added. "Not even once. He just laughed and let the dogs go for them. Imagine the waste!"

"You could tell that everyone loved him," Laudine added. "He was wonderfully handsome. I don't know why Agnes was so unhappy with him."

"Was she?" Catherine jumped on this. "How could you tell?"

"The morning after the wedding it was obvious that she'd been crying." Lisette leaned forward and lowered her voice. "But Gerhardt treated her kindly. He never shamed her in public about it."

"About what?"

"Why, that she wasn't a virgin, of course," Lisette said. "There was no blood on her shift or the sheets. We saw them the morning after the wedding. I don't know why she wasn't prepared. There are several easy methods to fool a man about that."

"Really?" Catherine almost let herself be diverted, but Laudine interrupted.

"That wasn't it, you goose," she said. "I think he never got far enough into her to find out."

"Really!" Catherine could only repeat.

"I'm sure of it," Laudine nodded sagely. "The man ate only bread and herbs. He wouldn't even have fish. They filled his plate but he gave all the meat to others. He thought no one noticed, but I did. Every day was a fast day for him. I think he was doing penance for something and it weakened him so that he was limp as a wet rag. Poor Agnes!" She giggled.

"That would hardly be reason enough to kill a man," Catherine said, thankful that Edgar never refused meat.

"Well, we don't know what other forms the penance took, do we?" Laudine smiled.

Catherine could tell that their speculations on that were of no more use than hers. She tried another approach.

"What about the rest of the family?" she asked. "What did you think of them?"

"The boy is sweet," Lisette said. "He'll make a fine man soon."

"But not soon enough," Laudine added sourly.

"What about the brother and sister?"

Lisette pursed her lips. "The brother isn't much to look at. His nose is too big and his hair is so thin the top of his head is blistering from the sun."

"Yes, but, what about his relationship with Gerhardt?" Catherine pushed. "Did you see signs of envy or resentment?"

Lisette and Laudine looked at each other, they simultaneously shook their heads.

"Of course, no one in the family of a lord would last long if they showed every jealous thought," Lisette said, "but the two men seemed to be friends. Gerhardt was very generous to him, I think."

"And the sister, Maria?"

"She runs the household well," Laudine conceded. "No one dares disobey her. But I don't think she'd have minded turning the duty over to Agnes. Anyway, if she did, that would be reason to remove Agnes, not her brother. Gerhardt appeared to dote on her and she on him. He was always very attentive to her."

Was there no flaw in the man? Catherine was mystified. There had to be someone who disliked him.

"What about the other one," she said. "What is his name? The sister's husband."

For a moment they looked blank. Then Laudine remembered.

"Oh, Folmar," she said. "He's a complete cipher to me; hardly ever speaks, just follows his wife around like a lap dog. Does whatever she commands."

"His behavior is very distasteful," Lisette agreed. "I want a husband with some backbone."

"Did Folmar make advances to you?" Catherine asked.

Lisette grimaced. "Not one," she said in disgust. "What kind of men do they grow here? Don't look to that one for your murderer; he wouldn't piss without permission."

"This is ridiculous!" Catherine burst out. "There must be someone among his servants or neighbors or relations who bore Gerhardt a grudge."

"Well, if there was, we never met him." Laudine closed the conversation by standing. "That leaves only Agnes, as we said all along. Now, don't forget that you promised to help us get out of here. Come, Lisette."

It was several minutes after they left before Catherine could trust herself to call for the portress to let her out. She was boiling over with anger that she dared not release upon the poor woman. The maids' story was so embroidered with a sense of personal insult that is would take forever to sift out the truth.

There was only one thing to do. If Agnes were to be saved, then Catherine had to make her sister tell her everything that happened, no matter how much it might shame her.

Lanval and Astolfo ran through the fields, slipping on loose stones, falling, clambering up again, oblivious of the scrapes and mud they had collected.

"What shall we do now?" Lanval panted.

"Get to the others and hurry away from here," Astolfo answered between skids.

They reached the cave at last. Denise stared at them in alarm. "What happened?" she asked. "Did you see our patron? Was he gone? Has someone set their dogs on you?"

Lanval leaned against the mouth of the cave, panting. Astolfo bent over, hands on his knees, gasping. As soon as he could, he blurted out the news.

"Our patron. The *perfectus!* He's dead!"

Denise gaped at them, not believing. Father Milun let out a wail and began reciting a *nostre pere*.

"Was he discovered?" Denise managed to ask. "Did they burn him?"

Astolfo shook his head. "I don't think anyone knew he was one of us. They say his new wife poisoned him."

"Wife!" Denise was even more confused. "But how could that be?"

She went over to her husband and held onto him, assuring herself that he was unharmed, then repeated the question.

"We couldn't find out more about that," Astolfo said. "But I did learn that Paganus has been waylaid and murdered, as well."

"May his soul be allowed to return to God," Father Milun said. "And the message he carried?"

"I couldn't ask without causing suspicion. I hope it was lost," Astolfo said. "But there was nothing written on it that names us."

He looked around. "Where's Andreas?"

"He went into Trier," Denise said. "Just after you left."

"You shouldn't have allowed that," Astolfo chided. "His enthusiasm is dangerous."

"He promised that he wouldn't preach," Denise said. "But he's the only one of us with enough German to bargain. And the soles of my shoes are thinner than this broth."

"But he knew we were going for alms," said Lanval. "And the baliff at the castle did give us both blankets and bread, for the soul of the dead lord."

He showed them the parcel slung on his back.

Denise inspected it. "But nothing to repair our shoes with. Andreas's boots are nothing but holes."

"The apostles went barefoot," Astolfo began, but Denise interrupted.

"But we don't," she said. "None of us are perfect, yet. I've walked for months and am grateful that Andreas is willing to use one of his few coins to get leather to protect my tired feet."

Lanval agreed. "It was a kind thing to do, but still foolish. Especially now that both Paganus and Lord Gerhardt have died unexpectedly."

"You don't think there's any connection, do you?" Denise's eyes grew large with fear.

Astolfo started gathering up their belongings. "What I think is that the sooner we arrive in Köln, the better. There's something amiss in this land. Perhaps there's a demon prowling the countryside, sent by Lucifer to destroy us, or perhaps it's only the usual wickedness. But we're not safe. Eat the broth and bread. We leave as soon as Andreas returns."

At that moment Andreas, who had joined the group the morning after leaving the body of a *jongleur* in the woods near Provins, was sitting outside the cathedral, waiting for one of the canons to return with the answer to his question.

He stretched out in the sun and yawned. The *fluc des fols* that he was traveling were becoming tedious, especially in their refusal to provide meat or fornicate. But traveling with them as a pilgrim had been useful. And it was possible that he could get a reward for denouncing them.

But not yet.

If there were really a whole nest of heretics in Köln, then it could be much more profitable to discover the names of the leaders, their so-called bishops, and then come to the authorities with proof of the apostasy.

He wondered who the important leader was that they were supposed to be meeting here. Astolfo and Lanval didn't trust him enough to let him go with them, but Andreas knew he'd find out soon enough and that would be just another bit of gold to add to his purse.

With visions of wealth swimming before him, Andreas nearly missed the canon's return. The man was bending over him with an expression of distasteful duty.

"Archdeacon Bolso will see you," he said. "But you'll need to give him solid facts before he'll believe this tale of yours."

Andreas rose with one graceful movement. He bowed to the canon.

"I assure you," he promised. "The archdeacon will not be disappointed."

He fingered the leather bag around his neck and felt the reassuring crackle of the parchment he had stolen from the juggler. A curse written in the devil's own tongue, that's what the priest in Metz had said. With this curse, Andreas intended to lay the foundations for his fortune.

Catherine was still fuming when she returned to their lodgings. There was no one there but Hubert, who had spent the day in the Jewish quarter.

"Where are Edgar and the children?" she asked.

"They were gone when I got here," Hubert answered. "Don't worry. It will be light for hours, yet. Did the maids tell you anything?"

"They told me so much I'll be all night sorting the few grains from the *miuds* of chaff they tried to feed me." Catherine sat at the table and rubbed her temples. "All I could get from them was that everyone loved Gerhardt and that the wedding night was unsatisfactory."

"In what way?" Hubert asked in alarm.

"They don't know," Catherine answered. "But that didn't stop them from telling me. Father, we must find a way to make Agnes talk to us."

Hubert slumped down in his chair. "I don't see how. I thought for a moment that she had returned to us, but she drew away as soon as I told her you had come with me."

He leaned his head back, eyes closed. For the first time Catherine realized that he was growing old. Even his collapse in Paris hadn't frightened her as much as this posture of despair.

"Where's Walter?" she asked. "I thought he was going to find you as soon as he left me at the convent."

Hubert opened his eyes and sat up. "I haven't seen him all day."

"Do you think he could be with Edgar?" Catherine said. The thought was comforting. Walter would never let them come to harm.

Hubert returned to his gloom and so Catherine went back outside to watch for the others. It seemed forever before she heard James's voice, high and excited, urging his father to go faster "or the dragon will get away."

She hurried down to greet them and take the sleeping Edana from Margaret.

"I was worried," she told Edgar.

"Yes, I feared you would be." He kissed her and James leaned down from his perch to pat her head. "I'm sorry. I didn't notice how low the sun was getting. And I thought it best to stay away from the town for a while."

"Why? What happened?"

Edgar told her about the boys with the turnips and the strange man who spoke English.

"There's more happening here than the death of a local nobleman," he ended. "People wouldn't have leaped to accuse Agnes of sorcery if there hadn't been rumors of it beforehand. I think we need to discover the truth behind those rumors. Then we might have a hope of freeing your sister."

They had gone inside and settled when Edgar looked around.

"Why isn't Walter back, yet?" he asked. "I thought he was only going up to the castle to take Agnes some thread."

"He went back up there?" Catherine exclaimed. "When?"

"This morning, after he left you," Edgar answered. "He said he'd return after None."

"We haven't seen him," Hubert said.

"Well," Catherine said. "At least we know that wherever he is, he can take care of himself."

"All the same," she added, "I wish he were here to take care of us."

Twelve

Outside the castle. Saturday, 3 kalends July (June 29), 1146; 13 Tammuz, 4906. Feast of the martyrdom of Saint Peter, crucified upside down and Saint Paul, beheaded, one of the perks of being a Roman citizen. His head bounced three times before coming to rest and at each spot a spring gushed forth.

Swaz er getet, swaz er gesprach,
daz duhte und waz ouch alse guot
daz ime diu werlt holden muot
und inneclichez herze truc.

Whatever he did, whatever he said
It all seemed so good—and was
That all the world loved him
and held him in heartfelt affection.

—Gottfried von Strassboug
Tristan

*W*alter's head ached as if he had drunk a tun of red wine
the night before. He didn't remember drinking, but then he wouldn't.
He certainly didn't remember falling asleep under a tree on the side
of the road.

Gingerly, he felt his head. In the heat, he hadn't worn his hau-
berk. He hadn't thought he needed mail in this area. Almost a fatal
mistake. His fingers touched a tender place and came away sticky
with drying blood.

He tried to sit up, but that brought such a rush of nausea that
he dropped back immediately. The sun shone on his half-open eyes,
making the world around gleam piercingly. He closed his eyes and
groaned.

"Don't try to move."

Walter froze. Was there a knife pointed at his heart? The voice
didn't sound threatening. It sounded almost . . . motherly. Walter
tried opening his eyes again slowly and turning his head toward the
sound. Yes, it was a woman in ragged clothes.

"Where do you come from?" she asked. "Do you understand me?"

"Yes, of course," he answered. He realized with a shock that she
was speaking French although with a strong Breton accent. Where
was he? What had happened to him? How long had he been uncon-
cious?

The woman held a rough bark cup to his lips. Walter tried to
drink the water but most of it spilled into his beard.

"My name is Denise," the woman told him. "Do you remember
who you are? What happened? Did your horse throw you? Were you
attacked?"

Walter moved his head and instantly regretted it. He gagged and then threw up. When he had finished, Denise wiped his mouth and hair with the hem of her skirt.

"I'm Walter of Grancy," he managed to answer. "I don't know what happened. I remember being on my way to the castle of Lord Gerhardt, but that's all. What day is it?"

"Saturday," she answered. "Yesterday was the feast of Saint Emilion. But if you were going to see Lord Gerhardt, you're too late. He's dead."

"I know that. I was visiting someone else." Walter felt around. "I had some lengths of thread for a lady. I must be going at once. They'll be wondering where I am."

With a great effort and help from Denise he was able to sit up, leaning against a tree. He then looked around and realized that something was missing.

"My horse!" he cried. "Oh, Saint Vincent's guardian ravens, where is my horse? If that horse is lost, I'm ruined. He's worth half my fief! I'll never be able to find another as fine in time to leave for the Holy Land with King Louis."

"I'm sorry," Denise said. "We found only you. I didn't see a horse. Did you, Father Milun?"

Now Walter realized that there were more people around him also ragged, thin and pale.

"I didn't see a horse," Father Milun said. "Perhaps he ran off. The others have gone to the village to find help for you. Do you have friends at the castle? We want to help you but we must be on our way."

"My friends are in Trier," Walter said. "Is this village far? I need to find someone to send word to them that I'm alive."

He tried to stand but was stopped by the queasiness. He let his weight fall against the tree.

"Lanval and Astolfo will be back soon," Denise told him. "They'll bring someone with a litter for you. Lie down again. Here, use my scarf for your head."

"Thank you, Lady," Walter answered. "I shall see that you get a much finer one in thanks for your kindness."

Denise blushed at being addressed so formally.

"You needn't do that. This will wash easily in the river," she said. "And we cannot wait any longer."

"Ah yes, you must be on a pilgrimage to be so far from home," Walter said. "You didn't say where you were going."

"It's not important; we seek no special shrine." Denise arranged the scarf to shield Walter's face from the sun. "Aren't all pilgrimages really journeys of the spirit more than the flesh?"

Walter didn't understand this. "I thought we were supposed to visit the places where the saints live so to better venerate them and so they can better hear our prayers."

"The saints are in Heaven," Denise told him firmly. "One can pray to them anywhere and they will hear."

"Well, yes." Walter's head ached far too much for this conversation. "But I was always told that they pay more attention to the places where their bones lie. You remind me of another woman who talks as you do. I can rarely understand her, either."

Denise laughed and Walter let his eyes fall shut again. These people seemed odd, but harmless. If they had wanted to rob him, they would have done it while he was unconscious. He wondered what had happened to him. He hoped the others weren't too worried.

In Trier, Walter's friends were not terribly worried about him at all, although Catherine did have a qualm about it when he didn't return by morning.

"He left his sword and crossbow behind." She pointed to where they lay in the corner. "How could he defend himself if robbers attacked?"

"If there were fewer than ten of them, I would lay odds on Walter with bare fists." Edgar smiled. "He may have simply stayed at the castle longer than he expected and decided to remain for the night."

"I suppose so." Catherine returned to the chore of mending Edana's little tunic. She seemed to tear it almost every day. "It would have been foolish to send word in that case."

There was a silence.

"Mina wants to know if we'd like to come to Sabbath dinner," Hubert announced abruptly. "Since Simon is still in England, she's lonely for company. And she's a wonderful cook."

Edgar frowned. "I don't like making a habit of joining in the Jewish rituals," he said. "With Johanna and Eliazar it's fine because people are used to seeing us with them. But what will the towns-people think here? They have a bad enough opinion of us already."

"Many of the merchants of Trier share meals with their Jewish friends," Hubert said. "No one will think twice. It's no different from Paris."

"Yes it is, Hubert." Edgar was firm. "We're foreigners. We can't behave as we do in Paris. We've already been called sorcerers; shall we also be considered Judaizers?"

"He's right, Father," Catherine said softly. "We have to consider Agnes."

Hubert was about to argue but at that moment there was a pounding on the door.

Catherine stuck herself with the needle. *"Jesu!"* she cried.

Hubert got up and started to open the door. Then, mindful of Edgar's warning, he called out first, demanding to know who was there.

At first there was silence. Then a small voice answered in French.

"Only I, Milun. I have a message for Hubert LeVendeur."

"He doesn't sound dangerous," Edgar said. All the same, he lifted Walter's sword. It surprised him how light it seemed. His right arm must have grown stronger since his accident.

When he saw the man, he nearly laughed at his fear. The Breton was slight and shaking in terror at the sight of the men. Milun stepped back as Hubert's bulk loomed over him.

"What do you want?" Hubert demanded.

"I come from Walter of Grancy." Milun licked his lips. "He's hurt and needs you to come and bring a horse. We tried to get him to ride in a litter but he wouldn't have it."

"Hurt?" Hubert repeated. "How? Is it bad?"

"Hardly, Father, if he insists on riding," Catherine said.

"We found him unconscious this morning," Milun said, looking at her with reproach. "He's awake now, but there's an ugly wound on his head. He should be carried but he's too fine a knight to be seen alive on a litter."

Catherine put down the sewing at once and went into the next room for her medicine box.

"You and Edgar go to him," Hubert told her when she returned.

"Margaret and I will stay with the little ones. I'm expecting visitors this afternoon."

Catherine didn't think to ask who the visitors might be. She was only concerned with finding out what had happened to Walter. Who would have the temerity to attack him? They would have to be both stupid and impious to try to harm a knight wearing the cross of a pilgrim.

They found Walter under the tree but now he was surrounded by people. There were the men from the village with their litter, making loud complaint about Walter's refusal of their service. Denise, Astolfo and Lanval were waiting and, surprisingly, so was Lord Hermann. All of them were arguing loudly. Catherine realized that Walter must really be hurt, for normally his voice would have ended any debate. She pushed through the throng and knelt beside him.

"Forgive me, Walter," she said as she got out a salve for the cut. "We didn't think to send anyone to search for you when you didn't return. That's a nasty wound. How were you attacked?"

"I don't know," Walter said weakly. "The last thing I remember is riding along the road, enjoying the sun. I saw no one. Can you get those people to be quiet? My head hurts confoundedly."

"I'll try, just hold still so I can bandage this," Catherine said. "Why haven't you been tended to, yet?"

"The people who found me have barely enough cloth to cover their bodies," Walter explained. "I wouldn't let them tear it for me. I'm not bleeding much."

Catherine had no words to answer that so she kissed his forehead next to the gash and then returned to her work.

When they had understood that there was a wounded man outside the village, someone had been sent to tell those at the castle. They remembered the body found in the river and wanted to be sure of protection in case of brigands or another attack by Graf Heinrich.

Peter had wanted to go at once. He admired Walter greatly. It was with difficulty that Hermann convinced him to stay behind and then only by reminding him of his duty to protect those within the keep.

Hermann had reached Walter only moments before Catherine and Edgar arrived. When he had discovered that the victim was the only person who knew both languages he had been forced to send to Saint Maximin for a monk who spoke French. Now he knelt on Walter's other side and watched Catherine.

"Did the pilgrims see anything?" he asked.

Walter turned his head to answer, causing Catherine to use an expletive she had picked up in England.

"Walter, either talk without moving or tell him to wait until I'm finished," she ordered.

Hermann understone the tone, if not the words and moved away, waiting impatiently for the monk to arrive.

Edgar was speaking with Lanval and Denise.

"Have we met before?" he asked them. "I've seen you somewhere."

"Perhaps on the road," Lanval answered. "We've been traveling since early spring."

Catherine looked up from her work. "I remember," she said with a smile. "I spoke with you at Vézelay. You're the man who believes we should all live like monks."

Lanval smiled nervously.

"Now, as to Walter." Edgar returned to the matter at hand. "So you say there was no one about when you found him?"

"No one at all," Denise said. "Just the poor man. We thought he was sleeping at first, until we saw the blood."

"Odd that his purse hasn't been touched," Edgar commented.

"We're not thieves, sir!" Lanval drew himself up proudly.

"I meant no slander," Edgar said. "But don't you think it strange that he would be set upon and then nothing taken from him? I don't suppose he could have hit his head on a low branch instead?"

The idea seemed preposterous, even to him, but how else could a grown man be knocked from a horse with only a head wound? Edgar had a thought.

"Where exactly was he lying?" he asked them.

Denise pointed to a crushed patch of weeds at the roadside. Edgar then walked back down the road, turned and started toward them. He stopped just beyond the place Denise had indicated and looked up. A short distance away on the opposite side of the road there was a tall oak tree, lush with leaves. The branches were low enough that a man could climb it.

A man with two hands, that is.

At times like these Edgar could almost feel his lost fingers stretching out. Would he ever get used to this?

"Lanval, could you get up that tree?" he asked.

"Of course," the man told him.

"Then climb up far enough to be able to sight someone coming down the road. I want to see if you'd be visible."

Lanval nodded and went to the tree, swinging himself up easily. Edgar followed.

"Also look for any sign that someone else has been there. Broken branches, scrapes in the bark, a piece of torn *brais*."

He then went back to the center of the road and watched Lanval's progress. When the man called out that he had found a solid resting place with a clear view, Edgar and Denise scanned carefully.

"I can't find him at all," Edgar said.

"I think I can make out his boot." Denise squinted. "But I couldn't if I didn't know he was there."

Edgar called up to him. "How much space is there free above you? Could you swing your arm?"

"A little farther down I could," Lanval shouted back. "But then there's nothing to shield me."

"Still, if he moved quickly," Edgar muttered to himself. "It could have been done that way. Now, if only I could find the stone."

"What stone?" Denise asked.

"From the sling," Edgar explained. "How else could one topple a man from a horse? There are no branches overhanging the road. Walter certainly hasn't been jousting and that's not an arrow wound."

He got down on his knees to hunt, wincing as he put weight on the stump. Denise got down to help. Edgar went on muttering.

"Now, if it struck with that much force, it must have bounced back the way it came, but in what direction? Damn!"

He straightened. "Catherine are you almost finished there? I need you to do some geometry."

In the end, it wasn't geometry but luck that helped them. The stone wasn't from that part of the road. It was a bit of quartz that had been chipped to form a rough edge.

Catherine felt it digging into her hand while hunting and, as she recoiled, noticed first the sharpness and then the stain of dried blood on the pink rock. She picked it up and waved in triumph.

"Of course, finding this only suggests that Walter was hit by a sling; it doesn't prove it," Edgar said when she handed it to him proudly. "We still don't know who attacked him or why."

"Even if his purse was untouched, the horse is reason enough," Catherine said. "We should ask Lord Hermann to put the word out for people to beware of anyone trying to sell a warhorse. Unless another *miles* did this the thief would be easily marked. A townsman or peasant could hardly own such an animal."

"Yes, Hermann might do it if we can explain the problem to him," Edgar agreed. "Catherine, I think we should stay home in Paris after this. I'm tired of trying to make myself understood."

"Excuse me," a soft voice interrupted in accented French.

The both stopped and turned toward the speaker.

He was an elderly man with the look of tired patience that practicing charity towards one's fellow man for many years in a monastery gives. He cleared his throat nervously.

"My lord Hermann said to me that I did—no, should—help you." His forehead creased with the effort to get the words right. "I am named Berengar."

"Thank you," Edgar said. "We're extremely relieved to find someone who can translate for us."

Berengar eyes widened in panic. Edgar realized that he hadn't understood all of what he'd said.

"Nonne habes latinam?" he asked.

The monk's jaw dropped as if his dog had just spoken.

"Sic aut non?" Catherine said. She was getting impatient.

"Why, yes," Berengar said at last in flowing Latin. "It's much easier for me than French but how do you . . . ?"

"Never mind for now," Edgar said. "Just explain in German to Lord Hermann, if you would, how we think Walter was attacked."

He showed Berengar the stone and the tree and the monk grew very excited. He went to Hermann immediately and told him.

When he had heard the story, Hermann nodded agreement.

"I think we ought to find out where that madman who's been camping at our gate was last night," he said.

"Jehan?" Catherine said when she understood. "He is mad, but why would he hurt Walter? They're friends."

"I, myself, overheard them arguing just a few days ago," Hermann insisted. "I believe the madman is jealous of poor Walter."

"Jealous? Because of my sister?" Catherine couldn't credit that. "Walter is going to the Holy Land. He isn't interested in a wife, even if Agnes were freed."

Hermann shrugged. "The madman wears a cross, too. But he doesn't behave like a pilgrim."

"I don't think we need to worry about Jehan for now. A sling isn't his kind of weapon," Edgar said. "It's more probable that someone was waiting for Walter, just to be sure he didn't do anything that might prove Agnes innocent. After all, he's the only one of use with your language."

Berengar translated. Hermann answered angrily, gave an order to the men with the litter, then mounted his horse and rode back toward the castle.

"He says that he has given you every consideration," the monk told them. "He promised that you wouldn't be hindered or harmed in your investigations and you offend him greatly by your insinuations."

"But we weren't accusing him!" Edgar began.

Catherine stopped him. "I can see how he might think we were," she said. "It may be that he knows of someone talented in the use of a sling."

"That's true," Edgar said. "Berengar, do you know whom he might have been thinking of?"

Berengar raised his hands imploringly.

"I spend my day in the scriptorium," he explained. "I know little of the world outside the cloister. I swear!"

"Can you at least arrange for Lord Hermann to receive us again?" Edgar asked. "Apologize for us. Say that our worry for Lady Agnes causes us to leap when we should stand still. We are fearful among strangers, but he has already been most generous to us and we're grateful. We'll meet with him in town or at the castle. We must find out what happened on the day Lord Gerhardt died. We need to know more about him as a man."

"And ask if I can see my sister," Catherine added. "Please. She's all alone there."

Reluctantly, Berengar agreed to help.

The men with the litter were still trying to load Walter onto it with no success.

"I'm not letting you bounce me anywhere!" he roared at them. He finally managed to stand, with the help of the tree. Upright, he was much more daunting than he had been supine. The men backed off.

"So, how do you think you'll get back to Trier?" Catherine demanded.

Walter scowled. "I'd sooner ride that mule of yours that be carried by anyone. I'll wait here while you go get it."

"You'll ride on a mule?" That was so unlike him that Catherine grew worried about the damage to his mind. Walter saw her expression.

"Sorry," he said. "This has been an Egyptian day for me from the moment I tried to open my eyes."

"I know, Walter," Edgar said. "Here, I brought a skin of wine. You have that while we go back to town and get the mule."

"Bring my crossbow, too," Walter shouted after them. "In case I see the bastard who made off with my horse."

The ride home cooled Hermann down somewhat. It had startled him to find that Agnes's sister and her husband were literate. Long ago there had been talk of making him a cleric, since he was the younger son, but Hermann had shown no aptitude for letters. He was better at fighting, and his father had agreed that it didn't hurt to have two sons able to defend their small holding.

But he had grown up with a respect for those who could read the Church fathers in their own language. His doubts about Agnes's guilt increased.

She had only been imprisoned because there had been no one else to blame. Hermann knew that, and he didn't want to turn her over to be punished unless he was sure in his heart that she was the one who had poisoned Gerhardt. But he couldn't release her, either, not at this point. There had to be proof, either rational or divine.

He only hoped that Agnes's family could provide it. All he wanted was to be free of doubt.

Hermann bit his lip. He was lying to himself. What he really wanted, more than anything, was to have his brother back.

Maria was waiting for him when he arrived.

"Is Walter very badly hurt?" she asked. "What shall we do without him?"

"I believe he'll recover," Hermann said. "And the abbot has sent a monk to talk to the French for us. Tell Folmar to send some men out to hunt for a warhorse without an owner. Walter's is missing."

"Hermann, my husband isn't a servant here," Maria chided.

"No, they do useful work," her brother snapped. "Why didn't we notice before you were bethrothed that the man has no spine?"

"Hermann, *du bist vil alwaere!* Folmar has many fine qualities!"

"I'm sure," he said wearily. "Someday you must show me a list of them, but for now just see to it that the search is begun."

After she had gone he ordered wine and sausage, threw his riding gloves in a corner and seated himself by an open window, looking out across the river to the lands of Graf Heinrich. They looked so peaceful, almost a mirror of the vine-covered hills behind him. He tried to rub the sense of misgiving from his head, but the feeling wouldn't ease. There was something hidden in all this, something that would make everything that had happened become clear.

He prayed for enlightenment, but none came.

In the bailey just below he saw Peter practicing his swordsmanship on a battered dummy. The straw man had been slashed from all sides but it still stood, despite Peter's fierce blows. The forcefulness of the blows told of Peter's feelings. Hermann wished there was something he could do to alleviate the boy's grief.

Farther away he saw a small band of travelers. Three men and a woman. He could tell by their clothing that they were the ones who had found Walter. He wondered where they were headed and why, but only idly. As he watched, another man appeared from the riverbank. The sun glinted on something metal in his hand and Hermann felt a sudden fear that they were about to be assailed while he was too far away to do anything but watch.

Instead the four greeted the man as an old friend and, after a moment of talk, they all started off again.

Hermann's sense of disquiet grew. There was something wrong about the last man. He didn't seem to fit with the others. He stood too straight, held his head too high. This wasn't someone used to taking orders and trying to be invisible. The others were peasants. This one was free. Hermann tried to define what bothered him about this. As they passed from his sight he finally realized why the stance of the man upset him so. He didn't move like a free man who is a master and has one above him. No, this was a person who owed nothing to anyone. He had no place in the order of the world. There was no one above to govern him and no one beneath him to care for. This man was dangerous.

The wine came. Hermann picked up his goblet and when he looked back, the party was gone. He shivered, then laughed at himself for his fancy. Who could conclude so much just from the movement of a man? It was nonsense. He had let his disquiet affect his reason. He took a long gulp from the goblet. Wine would restore his balance.

Through the window he could hear Peter's grunts as he dismantled the dummy.

Walter was able to get around almost as usual within a week. The humiliation of riding on a mule seemed to speed his healing. After a day he decided that he much preferred staying with them than taking hospitality from the monks.

"Monks don't make enough noise," he confided to Catherine.

"That's never a problem here." She laughed.

"But it's a good noise," he told her seriously. "Even when you're fighting I can hear the love underneath."

"Saint Eustace's brazen bull, Walter! Just when I think I know you, you say something that makes me cry." Catherine wiped her nose on her sleeve, wondering if perhaps she might be pregnant again. Perhaps it was just her fear for Agnes that made simple things so significant.

What if one day dear, sweet Margaret despised her as much as Agnes did? How could Catherine be sure it wouldn't happen? She had assumed nothing could destroy the bond between her and her sister. But something had. If that could be broken, who else might grow to loathe her? Her thoughts started drifting into perilous depths.

"Don't even imagine it." The voices of her childhood rarely in-
truded on her life, but Catherine was grateful now. *"What could happen to you and Edgar that you haven't endured together already?"*

Before Catherine could answer, the voices went on.

*"Nothing. So don't indulge yourself in melancholia. There's work to
be done."*

"Catherine? Are you talking to yourself?" Walter was caught
between amusement and concern.

"Sorry," she said. "Just a silent prayer of sorts."

"Try not to do it outside of church," he advised. "Is that Hubert
at the door?"

Catherine went to look.

"No, just someone passing by. Father's been spending a lot of
time talking with the merchants of Trier. I'd think he'd have learned
all they knew about Lord Gerhardt by now."

"It takes time to winnow truth from gossip," Walter said.

"We only have until the end of summer," Catherine reminded
him. "And we've found nothing that would help Agnes so far."

The next sound at the door was Hubert. His face was so grey
that Catherine's first thought was that something had happened to
Agnes.

"No, your sister is unharmed, as far as I know," Hubert said when
she asked. "I've heard more about this monk, Radulf, who is preaching against the Jews in Germany. They say he's left Lotharingia and
is coming to Köln. He's supposed to have another monk with him
to translate the exhortations. Both of them want the Jews destroyed."

"I thought Astrolabe was sent to warn Abbot Bernard about
him," Catherine said.

"The abbot has sent letters telling people not to listen to this
man," Hubert said. "But he's still spreading his poison. More people
gather to hear a rabble-rouser than ever attend a Mass. Sermons read
on Sunday won't stop Radulf."

"What about at Troyes?" Walter asked. "Is Solomon in danger?"

"I've no news of him," Hubert answered. "But I have faith that
Count Thibault will allow no such persecution in his land. We've
told you how quick his son was to stop those trying to drive the Jews
from the fair."

"All the same, I'm glad we decided to bring the children with us," Catherine said. "Even though they've been a nuisance." She had raised her voice as she saw James peeking around the door. But her open arms told him that she wasn't serious. He ran to her and then hugged Hubert. As Catherine watched, she was grateful, too, that James and Edana were with them. It was one more bond to keep her father from sliding back into the faith of his ancestors.

"You don't think there will be trouble here, do you?" she added.

"The *parnas* of the community thinks not," Hubert said. "The burghers here don't have the animosity against the Jews that they do in the bigger cities. Perhaps there aren't enough here to threaten them. And the slaughter here in 1096 appalled everyone. I don't think there are many who would want it repeated."

"Good. Then we won't worry about it for now. You look tired, Father. Will you have some wine and food?" Catherine tried to divert him from his memories.

"No, Mina fed me, thank you," he answered. "Where's Edgar?"

"Brother Berengar came by and offered to show him some repair work being done on one of the Roman buildings." Catherine smiled. "I expect he won't return before dark; he took his wax tablet and stylus."

Hubert shook his head. "I don't see how you can be so indulgent, daughter. It's one thing that your husband makes toys for the children or baubles for the nuns, but at least he works out of the sight of our friends. And it makes him feel useful, even with his injury."

"Father," Catherine warned.

"But you really have to stop him when he goes about where masons and carpenters are working and makes suggestions to improve building methods," Hubert persisted. "It's not only undignified for a man of his rank, it could also get him a crack on the head worse than Walter's. Craftsmen don't appreciate men who poke into their trade secrets."

"Are you finished?" Catherine said. "Edgar knows all these things but there's something in him that comes alive when he can watch *engignors* at work. If he wants to join their guild and they'll have him, I will be as proud as if he'd been given a castellany."

Hubert turned to Walter for support. "You see what happens when to let your daughter marry for love? Her common sense flies out the door."

"I have a fascination with machines, myself," Walter said. "I don't blame Edgar for his interest. But I don't think you should worry. After all, whoever heard of a one-handed master mason?"

"Papa!" James cried, looking over Hubert's shoulder.

Hubert spun about. Had Edgar heard?

Edgar greeted them all as usual, but Catherine saw the hurt. He had indeed heard them. Her thoughts toward Walter and her father were not charitable.

"Catherine." Edgar took James from his grandfather and then leaned over to kiss her. "I have news for you. Whether it's good or not is for you to decide."

"Edgar, don't be mysterious," Catherine said. "Is that the reason you've returned before dark?"

Edgar ignored the taunt. "A messenger was on his way to us but spotted Berengar with me. Lord Hermann has decided to honor your request and allow you to visit Agnes."

"Just Catherine?" Hubert was indignant.

"It seems so," Edgar answered. "Berengar says that he'll come for you just after Prime. Well, aren't you pleased?"

The last question was because of the consternation on Catherine's face. She looked up at Edgar.

"I don't know," she said. "I've wanted to see her for so long but now I'm afraid. Lord Hermann may have given me permission to come, but will Agnes let me in?"

Thirteen

Trier. Monday, 7 ides of July (July 9), 1146; Trisha B-v, the
day of lamentation for the destruction of the Temple. Feast of
Saint Agilulf, bishop of Köln circa 770, martyred during general civil unrest.

עֶלְיוֹן, נַחֵם אִם לֹא נֶחָמָה,
פְּנֵה נָ א וְרַחֵם אֶת לֹא־רֻחָמָה;
צוֹרְרִים אוֹמְרִים: „לֹא תֶחֱזִי נֶחָמָה‟;—
אֲנִי־שָׁלוֹם וְכִי אֲדַבֵּר חֵמָּה לַמִּלְחָמָה.

O, Most High, console thy people that are disconsolate: Turn
to her that is not pitied and be merciful. My enemies say,
"No comfort shalt thou ever see."—I am all peace: but when
I speak, they are for war.

—Joseph ben Isaac ibn Abitor
Hymn on Psalm 120

$\mathcal{H}$ermann sent Berengar and an armed escort for Catherine. He wanted no repetition of what had happened to Walter. Margaret begged to be allowed to come along.

"Not this time, *bele suer*," Catherine told her. "For all I know I may not be there long enough to wash my hands. It will be better if you stay with Edgar and Father."

"But Edgar spends all his time watching the church repairs," Margaret protested. "James and Edana don't mind playing there but I'm so bored. Please!"

"Father, can she go with you?" Catherine asked.

"Not today, Catherine," Hubert said. "It's the fast of Av and I'm going to spend it with Mina and her family, fasting. Margaret wouldn't enjoy it."

"Father!"

Catherine was furious. She pulled him out into the back garden of the lodging and spoke softly but with great intensity.

"This has got to stop, Father," she said. "You are a baptized Christian. How can you risk your immortal soul, not to mention the lives of your family like this?"

"Perhaps it's my soul I'm considering, daughter," Hubert answered, equally angry.

Catherine exhaled in exasperation. "*Merderie!* That's what this is. I love you. I love Solomon and Johanna and Eliazar. I like many of the other Jews we know, but I don't want you to be one of them. They're obdurate in their belief despite all the proof of centuries. They won't even pay outward respect to the true Faith. They live on the edge of doom. You're a baptized Christian. How can you attach yourself to a despised and outcast race?"

Hubert drew away from her.

"It seems to me, Catherine, that all of those things were once said of Christians," he said.

"But . . . but that's different!" Catherine sputtered.

Hubert grew icily calm. "Why? Because you won? I'm going to spend the day in mourning as seems more and more appropriate. Take Margaret with you. If your sister tells you any way in which I can help her, I will do it at once. You don't have to remind me of my duty. It's the cross I carry."

He walked away, leaving her gasping as if drowning.

"Papa," she whispered.

She was still staring after him when Edgar came out in search of her.

"*Carissima!* What's wrong?" he said.

Catherine clung to him.

"We're losing him, Edgar," she wept. "He looked at me as if I were an enemy. Oh, Edgar, Agnes hates me because I wouldn't abandon Father and now he hates me because I don't want him to abandon Christ. I can't endure this!"

"My dearest." He pushed a sticky curl off her face. "Your father was never truly Christian although he behaves more like one than many I know. You know what Master Abelard said about conversion. As a matter of fact, what all the doctors of the Church said."

"Yes, I know, that belief must lie in the heart, not in actions alone." Catherine held him more tightly. "But I thought his heart was with us."

"Maybe, but I don't think his spirit is," Edgar said. "And we can't force him. Nevertheless, I think he has a better chance of Heaven than my father ever will."

"Thank you." Catherine gave him a salty kiss. "Perhaps it's arrogant of me to assume. Papa has given up much for all of us. Now, I don't suppose you could find something to do today that Margaret would enjoy, too?"

Edgar smiled. "Yes, of course. Actually, I suspect that she wanted to go with you on the chance of seeing the young lord again."

Catherine gave him a look of horror.

"*Carissime,* I'm not prepared to deal with that as well," she said. "Please, for now let's concentrate on returning home safely with my sister and my father. If you think we should start looking for a husband for Margaret, it can wait until then."

Edgar laughed outright. "Very well, now, go wash your face and prepare for the challenge of getting sense out of your stubborn sister *nolens volens.*"

A short time later, impeccable of dress but highly rumpled of spirit, Catherine found herself in the great hall of the castle. Berengar introduced her again to Gerhardt's family. She presented Maria with a gift of silver and onyx earrings that Edgar had made, although she didn't mention that. She was offered cakes and wine, which she choked down as good manners demanded. Finally she found herself standing before the door to Agnes's room.

Hermann lifted the bar and opened the door. She stepped in and Berengar followed.

"I've been told stay with you and note what you say," he said in Latin. "To be sure you don't plan her escape. Please don't speak French too quickly."

Catherine had expected that, but she feared that a stranger in the room would make it impossible to reach Agnes.

Agnes must have been told she was coming. She had dressed herself in her best clothes and looped her braids into an intricate pattern. She was sitting in the shadow by the window. Catherine couldn't make out her face.

"Agnes, are you all right? They haven't hurt you, have they?" she asked. "I brought you some strawberries. We picked them this morning."

"I have not been mistreated," Agnes answered steadily, ignoring the gift. "Except for the false accusation against me and the denial of my freedom."

Catherine took a step closer. She felt as if she were approaching something wild that might bolt if she made a sudden move.

"We won't leave here until you've been exonerated and freed. Father has promised to give all he has in your defense," she told Agnes.

"I don't wish him to pay for a crime I did not commit," Agnes voice rose.

Catherine stepped back.

"Then you have to help us, dear." Her voice shook. She swallowed. "We've been here for weeks and can't find anyone else who might have done this. No one will even tell us exactly what happened."

. "That's because I was alone with him," Agnes told her. "Nobody else knows."

Catherine came closer again, gesturing to Berengar to stay in the corner where he had seated himself. She knelt before Agnes's chair and reached her arms up to her.

"Please, let us help you," she whispered. "Confide in me as you used to. I want so much to release you from this nightmare."

She waited for the rebuff accompanied by an outpouring of scorn.

Agnes only sighed.

"There's nothing you can do, Catherine," she said finally. "I don't know why Gerhardt died, either. I understand completely why they accuse me. No one else could have put poison in his food without killing me, too."

"That can't be," Catherine insisted. Inside she was rejoicing that Agnes had relented and was confiding in her. "Do you mean that you ate from the same plate, drank from the same cup and stayed together every moment?"

"We were only married three weeks," Agnes retorted. "Isn't that how you and Edgar behaved?"

Catherine felt herself blushing.

"Actually, things were rather confused just after we were married," she said.

"That doesn't surprise me." Agnes's voice turned sour again. "Gerhardt and I were never apart."

"I'm glad that you had some happiness, then, before the tragedy," Catherine said with sincerity.

Agnes closed her eyes and sighed. "Does that man have to be here?" she asked, referring to Berengar.

"Lord Hermann insisted," Catherine said. "But his French is rudimentary. And I think he's dozing now."

They both looked over to where the monk sat with his hood up and his chin down, breathing slowly.

Catherine leaned against Agnes. "Tell me what happened," she said again, gently. "Maria has told everyone that she heard you crying on the wedding night and as for those maids of yours—!They would have it that you're a wanton and a virgin both. Did Gerhardt hurt you?"

She waited so long for the answer that she nearly fell asleep, herself.

"No," Agnes said at last. "Not in the way you think. I was prepared for pain. I'm not an innocent. No, what he did was worse. He rejected me. He refused to even get in the bed."

Catherine looked up in astonishment. "How can that be? You're perfect. When you walk into a room, all the men start readjusting their belts."

"Elegant as always, Catherine." But there was a hint of amusement now. "I believe that Gerhardt's physical reaction to me was something like that. When he came in after I had been left in the bed, I lifted the blankets for him to join me and he took one look at me and groaned. Then he backed away, mumbling something that I couldn't understand. But he made it clear that he wouldn't get in with me, although his body made it clear that he wanted to."

"But why not?" Catherine asked.

"It took some time for me to find out, since we didn't feel like calling for an interpreter," Agnes said. "When I covered myself he regained some composure. He then managed to explain that he had taken a vow of chastity after his wife died and begged me to agree to a spiritual marriage."

"Oh, Agnes!"

"Don't you laugh, Catherine," Agnes warned.

"I'm not even thinking of it," she said. "How could he do that to you? He might have mentioned his vow before the wedding."

"Why did he even contract the marriage in the first place?" Agnes's hurt and anger were obvious. "What I think is that his family didn't know about his vow and, for some reason, he wouldn't tell them. He was using me, Catherine. I was part of a deception and I don't know why. But that wasn't enough for me to kill him. I could have had the marriage annulled since it was never consummated."

"Why didn't you tell your maids?" Catherine asked.

"I was ashamed," Agnes said. "They love gossip, as you know, and they didn't like me. And I hoped that I could change his mind."

"You'd entice a man to break a vow like that?" Catherine kept her voice down and glanced at the corner. Berengar hadn't moved.

"He made a vow to me, too," Agnes reminded her. "He had to break one of them."

"Saint Melania convinced her husband to have a spiritual marriage," Catherine mused. "And any number of other couples have died virgins: Saints Amator and Martha, Sigolnea and Gislulf, Injuriosus and—"

"Thank you, Catherine," Agnes interrupted. "But if I had wished to be celibate, I would have entered a convent."

"Yes, of course. Sorry."

"I was considering explaining the situation to Walter when he returned," Agnes continued. "Although that would have been almost as embarrassing. But then, suddenly, Gerhardt died."

She thought for a moment. "You know, I don't believe anyone poisoned him. I think he was ill and trying to hide it from his family."

Catherine grasped at this eagerly. "What makes you say that? Did he appear ill?"

"Not exactly, except at the end, of course," Agnes said. "And I didn't know what he was like before. You'd suppose his family would have noticed if his behavior had changed."

"In what way?" Catherine pressed.

"Well, he was always moving about," she said. "I thought it was excitement, or an attempt to contain his lustful thoughts. But sometimes he would rub his head, as if it ached and his hands were cold, even when he'd been running. He was thirsty all the time. He kept a pitcher of water or beer at hand always and emptied it four or five times a day."

"That does sound like an illness," Catherine said. "I know this is painful, dear, but what about the night Gerhardt died? Did he seem worse in the hours before?"

"No more than usual," she said. "He was trying to teach me German words. But now and then he would stop and stare over my shoulder, as if he saw a ghost . . . Oh, Catherine, you don't think first wife was haunting us, do you?"

"No, I don't," Catherine said. "Go on."

"I'm trying to remember." Agnes pressed her fingers to her head.

"We prepared to sleep. He had a mat on the floor in front of the door. I presume he didn't want anyone to know we didn't share the bed. We knelt together and said our prayers, but he kept stumbling over the words. He seemed exhausted and confused. I blew out the lamp."

"And then?"

Agnes drew away as if even the memory could hurt her.

"Far into the night I was awakened by his screams. He was having some sort of fit, thrashing about and yelling. I called for help as I ran to him. I tried to keep him from hurting himself. Aren't you supposed to put something in their mouths? I was feeling about for a stick when he began to gasp for air. I thought he'd swallowed his tongue. All the while I was screaming. It seemed days before anyone came. By then he was almost dead."

Catherine went over this slowly. "Can you remember what he was saying at the end?"

"No. He said my name once. Then it was just gibberish. Oh, yes. Sometimes he would shriek 'min Got.' That means he was asking God to save him. I've been learning the language, you see."

"Could he have been accusing you of poisoning?"

Agnes seemed surprised. "I . . . I don't know," she hesitated. "No, if he had been, then there would have been no doubt and I'd be dead or in chains by now."

Catherine's head had begun to ache, too. There was something she should be asking.

"Who arrived at the room first?"

"They all came in at once," Agnes answered. "Hermann first, I think. He broke in with some servants who brought light. Then Folmar and Maria. She tried to keep Peter out but he wouldn't listen."

"Oh, poor boy!" Catherine exclaimed. "Now, this may be important, did someone say then that he had been poisoned? Who accused you first?"

"I don't know, Catherine," Agnes said. "It was horrible. Gerhardt on the floor, thrashing among the rushes, and there were people everywhere. I was afraid they'd start a fire. Everyone was shouting at me and I couldn't understand. Hell could be no worse."

"Oh Agnes, I'm so sorry." Catherine took Agnes's arms and slid her down until they were both on the floor. She held her sister and rocked her just as she would have Edana. "This should never have happened to you. You're the good one; the dutiful child."

"So was Job," Agnes snuffled.

"I never really understood that book," Catherine said. "But life did turn out well for him in the end and it will for you, too. You've given me enough to work with. I'll find how who did this and how. Or I'll find a way to prove Gerhardt died naturally. But I promise, promise that we won't ever leave you here alone."

Agnes suddenly realized that the monk was awake and watching them. She pulled away from Catherine and straightened her head scarf. Catherine had forgotten all about him. She got up and went over to his corner.

"I know you didn't understand all of that," she said in Latin. "But my sister made no confession. What she did tell me has created a lot of questions. Will you help me ask them?"

Berengar let his cowl fall back. He smiled at her. She realized that he had been awake all along.

"I saw nothing that would make me believe that child could do murder," he said. "Yes. I will help."

Catherine was halfway back to town before it occurred to her that neither she nor Agnes had once mentioned their father.

In Trier, Hubert made his way slowly to the Judengasse. At first he was so angry at Catherine that he could have struck her. Then, as he walked off some of his fury, he realized that she had only spoken the truth as she had learned it, a truth self-evident to most of the people around her.

That didn't make it any less bitter.

What could he tell her, that he would be a good Christian for her sake? He'd already tried that and all he could manage was an outward image. The pain of having to do that much had always been like a dull knife cutting into his gut. But in recent years the knife had grown sharper and the pain could no longer be ignored.

As he approached Mina's door, he was relieved that this wasn't a day of rejoicing. His grief would be unfeigned, although the destruction of the Temple was not such a loss to him as the tearing apart of his family.

Mina greeted him quietly. "The men are all at the house of prayer," she said. "My oldest son has gone there, to represent the family until Simon returns. I'm telling the other children stories. Would you like to join us or the men?"

"You, please," Hubert said. "I never learned the prayers and my ability to read Hebrew is only good enough for simple things. I am ashamed of this. I wasn't much older than Asher when I was adopted. Almost everything I know was learned after I was grown."

"We won't mock you for it," Mina led him in. "Asher hasn't started proper school, yet. His father will take him to the teacher's home for the first day when he returns from England."

Asher overheard this. "But when will that be? Abba said he'd be back by today," he complained.

"He hoped to be," Mina answered. "But you know how many things can delay one."

"I certainly do," Hubert agreed. "Buyers who can't decide, sellers who don't appear when they said, goods that are not what was promised, all these things cost days. And add to that bad weather, detours because of bad roads or sickness in the towns. I could tell you so many tales of woe!"

"But you always made it home," Mina said.

"Oh yes, of course," Hubert added hastily. "All I had to do was think of my children waiting for me and I packed up my horse, no matter the weather, and stayed on the road until I saw the spires of Paris."

"And your Abba will, too, Asher," Mina finished. "Now, you and Rebecca may go and and play . . . but quietly."

"I would offer you something," she added to Hubert when the children had gone. "But not today. There is a bit of information I can share, though."

She seemed eager and Hubert felt a dawning of hope for Agnes. "Of course, something that will help?" he asked.

"Perhaps," she said, seating herself by the window where she could keep an eye on Asher and his sister. "According to a Christian woman I know, Gerhardt was in the habit of going to Köln every month or so. He said it was to arrange for the shipping of his wine, but really, no one needs to do that every month! And Maria's husband, Folmar, does most of the shipping, anyway."

"So why did he really go?" Hubert asked.

"That's the odd thing; no one is quite sure," Mina answered. "At first it was believed that he had a concubine there, perhaps one of our women, whom he would be ashamed to bring home."

"That's most unlikely!" Hubert said.

Mina gave him a look of derision. "Surely you don't think it never happens? There is a man in town, we call him Shem. He lives with his father, Moshe. His mother was a Christian girl from a village downriver. Her family disowned her, of course, when she went to live with Moshe, but she never became one of us. So of course, Shem isn't either. And yet he still insists he's a Jew."

"So he willingly attaches himself to a 'despised race,' even when they don't want him," Hubert turned this over in his mind.

"What did you say?"

Hubert looked up. "Nothing. So now you don't think it was a woman that drew Gerhardt to Köln?"

"Not according to my friend." Mina dropped her voice to a whisper. "She says her brother saw him coming out of the home of a man who just three years ago was tried for heresy."

"That doesn't agree with the things I've heard about him," Hubert said. "He was supposed to be exceedingly pious."

She shrugged. "I've heard that these heretics are bad even for Christians. They don't accept the Torah at all, and only some parts of the books of the crucified one. They have strange rites where they perform acts only done in Sodom and Gemorrah."

Hubert nodded. "I have heard of these things in the past few years, but I thought them only idle gossip. Are you certain of your information?"

"I'm certain of where he was seen," Mina said. "As for the rest, it's only hearsay. For all I know, the man no longer lives there and it's now a convent. But it's something for you to look into, don't you think?"

"Yes, I do," Hubert rose. "I'll go myself. Thank you, Mina."

By unspoken agreement, Catherine and Hubert said nothing of their argument that morning. Both prefered to spill out all they had learned.

"From what Agnes told me, it's possible that Gerhardt's death

was from illness, not poison," Catherine said. "We have to find out
if he'd been behaving strangely or acting as if he were in pain before
Agnes arrived in Trier."

"And I'm leaving as soon as possible for Köln to investigate
Gerhardt's actions there," Hubert added. "We may yet find someone
who wished him dead."

Edgar and Margaret listened politely. In the middle of Hubert's
talk Edgar noticed that Edana had grabbed a table leg and was leaning back with a reddening face. He picked her up with a practiced
motion and deposited her on a handy chamber pot.

"Stay there until you finish," he ordered her. "Now, Catherine,
you haven't asked what we did today."

Margaret was grinning. "You aren't the only ones who can get
information, you know."

"But how?" Catherine asked. "Who could you talk to?"

"We didn't have to talk," Margaret said proudly. "We just
watched."

She meant to tease them for leaving her behind but Hubert had
spent too hard a day.

"Please, child, tell us," he begged.

Margaret glanced at Edgar who was still monitering Edana. He
gestured for her to continue.

"Well," she began, "we were resting under the trees by the cathedral. James and I were counting the different pilgrims. Eighteen
on crutches, five children carried, three women heavily veiled,
eleven lepers with a keeper . . ."

"I'm sure that was very good for teaching James to count," Hubert said. "But then what happened?"

Margaret took pity on him. "Among all the pilgrims we saw
someone familiar. It was Lord Hermann."

"So?" Catherine wasn't impressed. "Why shouldn't he be at the
cathedral?"

"In a hooded cloak in the middle of summer?" Margaret rebutted.
"And sneaking in a side door? He was on some secret business, I'm
sure of it."

"But why should he want to enter the cathedral secretly?" Hubert asked, looking toward Edgar.

"We could think of no reason that was honest," Edgar replied.

"But there is all this unrest between the archbishop and the burghers. What if Hermann has changed sides?"

"I don't know," Catherine said. "Edana, stay there until Papa says you can get up! Lord Hermann seems so willing to let us prove Agnes innocent. If he were doing something underhanded, wouldn't he want to make sure the blame was firmly on her?"

"If he knows she didn't kill his brother then just keeping her confined at the castle might be enough to draw attention from himself," Edgar suggested. "His conscience might be strong enough to prevent him from turning her over to the town or the archbishop."

"He doesn't strike me as being capable of such subtle thought," Catherine said. "I've observed him closely. Sometimes not knowing what people are saying makes it easier to see what they really mean."

Just then, Hubert realized that there was someone missing.

"Where's Walter?" he asked.

Edgar grinned. "He has volunteered to be our spy and is at this moment sitting in the tavern across from the cathedral, suffering through flasks of wine and tedious ribaldry just to gather information for us. Yes; if you promise you're finished, you may get up, Edana. Is there anything to wipe her bottom with?"

"Here." Catherine gave him some straw from the floor. "I can see you're jealous of Walter's job. I only hope no one realizes what he's doing. After all, the whole town knows he's with us."

"But he's also a lord and a pilgrim," Edgar said. "And he's very large, even among Germans. He also radiates goodness, haven't you noticed? People trust him."

"That's true," Catherine conceded. "In that case, I ought to be putting together a remedy for the effects of drink. Do we have any almonds?"

"Catherine." Hubert had noticed that Catherine was avoiding delicate subjects, but he had to know. "How was Agnes? Did she look well? You said nothing about her health."

"She's fine, Father," Catherine said curtly. Something of the anger she had felt that morning came through. Then she paused, considering. "She's in excellent health. And yet, if she's right in that she and Gerhardt ate and drank the same things from the same dishes, she shouldn't be, should she? At least she should have been ill if Gerhardt was being given poison, don't you think?"

"Isn't that part of the reason she's under suspicion?" Hubert asked.

"Yes, but no one seems to have wondered if Gerhardt might have been ill before he died," Catherine said. "Or even considered that he might have received poison by another means."

"Do you think anyone at the castle will tell us?" Edgar asked.

"No, but they might tell Berengar." They all turned to her. Catherine was pleased at the reaction to her surprise. "He's willing to join us in finding the truth."

"Really!" Hubert said, raising his eyebrows. "That monk must not be as dried up as he looks."

"I believe he was impressed by her piety," Catherine said straight-faced.

"Whatever the reason, that is good news," Edgar said. "I was beginning to lose hope, but now there may be a chance. Of course, it would help Agnes's cause if someone could convince that ass Jehan to pack up his tent and return to France."

"Saint Brendon's burning house!" Catherine exclamied. "I'd forgotten all about him. He didn't even come to see Walter while he was mending from his attack. Are you sure he's still here?"

"Oh yes," said Edgar, "We saw him today, too. He stalked through town like Death looking for a sinner, bought some cheese and bread at the market and then stalked back out again. I didn't speak to him, but I wish someone would make it clear to him that he isn't doing Agnes any good."

"I doubt he'll listen to anyone but Agnes, herself," Catherine said. "Walter told me he'd tried to get him to leave right at the beginning of all this."

"For now, let's just hope he does nothing more than lurk by the castle gates," Hubert said. "We can't force him to do anything. We're not his masters."

Catherine and Edgar agreed with this, but reluctantly. They didn't feel safe knowing that Jehan was in the vicinity and brooding.

"So, when will you leave for Köln?" Edgar asked.

"I can get a boat by Sunday afternoon," Hubert answered. "I know a few people there and Solomon knows many more. The use of his name will open doors."

Catherine didn't mean to start the quarrel again, but she couldn't help the snake of worry that slithered across her mind.

"Didn't we hear that this monk Radulf was on his way to Köln?" she asked.

"Only simpletons will pay him any mind," Hubert said.

"But if you were faced with a mob of simpletons, Father?" Catherine looked at Hubert earnestly. "Would you remember us and save yourself?"

"Daughter, I won't speculate on such things," Hubert said firmly. "I have all the seals and warrants of a merchant of Paris. If anyone assaults me, it will be for my money, not my faith."

With that Catherine had to be content.

Much later, Walter returned with cold soup and beer for everyone. He was pleased with the amount of information they had gained that day, although he could add little to it.

"I can't believe how much Gerhardt was admired among the townspeople," he told them. "No one will breathe a word against him."

"Perhaps they'll not be so protective in Köln," Hubert said.

Walter's eyebrows drew together in thought. "I should go with you," he said. "I can speak with more people."

"No, Walter," Hubert answered. "I'll find someone to interpret for me. I'll feel much better if you're here, keeping an eye on my family. If I find out anything important, I'll return at once. If not, it may be a couple of weeks before you see me."

Catherine made no comment on his decision. In her heart she knew that Hubert was going to do just what he said, find out everything he could about Gerhardt's business in Köln. But a voice in her mind kept reminding her of how large the Jewish community was there, and she couldn't help fearing that Hubert might lose himself in it or, even worse, find his true home.

Fourteen

Trier. Thursday, 8 kalends August (July 25), 1146; 25 Ab, 4906. The feast of Saint James, apostle, name saint of Catherine's son.

Tunc es elle qui mendaces facies prophetas et evacuebis omnes thesauruos pietatis et misericordiae Jesu Christ?

Are you the one who makes liars of the prophets and empties the store houses of the piety and mercy of Jesus Christ?

—Bernard of Clairvaux
Letter 365, on the monk, Radulf

*I*f the reason for their visit hadn't been so dire, Catherine would have enjoyed spending the summer in Trier. Even with the bustle associated with the archbishop's court and the wine trade, the pace was slower than in Paris and the people more inclined to find excuses to stay out in the sunshine. She even liked the smells of the town: flowers, the scent of the river and through it all the tang of grapes in all their manifestations.

"I just don't understand why I can't learn the language," she complained to Edgar, after a frustrating attempt to buy replacement herbs for her medicine box. "I had the same problem with English. All I ever can remember are a few words. Latin is so easy for me but it's helpful only in debates with scholars. I can't use it when I want to go shopping."

"Margaret seems to have picked up quite a bit of German," Edgar said. "Even James jabbers away with the local children. It doesn't sound like anything to me, but they all seem to comprehend. Perhaps we're too old to twist our tongues in new ways."

"I don't think twenty-six is ancient," Catherine retorted. "Of course at thirty the mind is certainly starting to decay."

"Oh, really?" He reached out and grabbed her, causing her to fall onto his lap. "Anything else you feel is eroding with age?"

"What I can feel right now is in excellent form." She wiggled to be sure and then kissed him. "When do you expect the children will be back with Walter?"

"All too soon," he said sadly. "But I'd be happy to have you make an inspection later to be sure none of my parts are showing signs of decrepitude."

"I promise to be very thorough."

Catherine rested her head on his shoulder. She closed her eyes. People thought it odd that after seven years she still found her greatest comfort in his arms. Catherine thought it impossible that she could find it anywhere else. Edgar was the balance that regulated her life. Without him she knew she'd soon slip far into melancholy or choler. Some people used herbs or relics but for Catherine his presence was all the talisman she needed.

That was why she had refused to let him despair when his hand had been cut off, and why she couldn't bear going anywhere far from the refuge he gave her.

"What are you thinking?" He tilted her face to his.

"Something sacrilegious," she teased.

Edgar considered what it might be. It would be a shame not to find out.

"You know," he said. "It might be some time before the others return, after all."

Walter had discovered a new talent: he made a wonderful uncle. Everything he did seem to appeal to the children. It was like having one's own sycophants constantly in attendance, but his were sincere in their adulation.

Today he had decided to load everyone on the mule and take them wading in a little creek he had found that emptied into the Moselle. He was still lamenting the loss of his horse and the older two had been drilled to keep a constant watch for it.

The day was warm and Walter got into the spirit by splashing with the little ones wearing only his tunic and rolled-up *brais*. James and Edana were worn out after a few hours and by midafternoon they were both curled up asleep against Walter's comforting bulk, lulled by his rhythmic snores.

Margaret had played, too, but wasn't tired. She had brought a bag and planned a search near the creek for plants that could be used, either for food or for Catherine's store of remedies. The medicine box was easily depleted by all the scrapes and upset stomachs that the household was subject to.

She was happily up to her knees in a patch of peppermint and willowherb when she had the shivery feeling that someone was watching her. Slowly she looked around. There on the other side of the creek was Peter, the boy from the castle. She gave him a timid smile.

Peter turned bright red and then gave her a little wave.

"Waz tuost dû?" he called to her.

She held up the plants. *"Heiltranc!"* she called back. She *thought* that was the word for medicine.

"Can I help?" he mimed picking the plants.

Margaret nodded. Peter waded across the stream. She showed him which plants she needed. Picking a leaf from the peppermint, she held it under his nose. He sniffed and then caught her hand as the leaf tickled him. Margaret started like a rabbit and pulled away.

"Ez ist mir leit," Peter said. "I didn't mean to frighten you. Here, I'll get some from this patch, shall I?"

Margaret only understood part of what he said, but his expression made the rest clear. She smiled an acceptance of his apology and returned to gathering the herbs.

Peter bent to his work but watched her out of the corner of his eye. He liked the way her red braids swung, sometimes dipping into the water when she fought with a resisting root. Her body curved nicely, too, but she didn't seem aware of it. The girls his age around the castle all treated him with a certain deference now that he was the lord, at least in name. It confused him, as did the obvious advances of some of the older ones. This was the kind of thing his father had been good about explaining. Peter didn't feel comfortable talking with Uncle Hermann about it.

But Margaret wasn't like the local girls. She was—Peter hunted in his mind for the right word—she was foreign, even mysterious. She was also very pretty, and the slight air of fearfulness about her made him feel very grown up and protective.

The afternoon passed with both of them working their way farther up the bank, not saying much as Margaret's vocabulary was still limited. As last the bag was full and Margaret sat down under a tree to sort and tie the herbs. Peter sat beside her wanting to help but feeling suddenly clumsy.

Margaret was busy braiding the peppermint to dry and sorting out the other things she and Peter had found. She popped one of the mint leaves in her mouth, savoring the bite. The she offered one to Peter. He took it and ate it. Then he looked around for something to give her.

He spied a horseradish plant and went over to tug it out of the soil. Not as delicate a gift as mint, but very useful. He cut a bit from the root and handed it to her.

Margaret had been busy with the braiding and had not paid attention to what Peter was doing. She took the slice of root absently and was about to bite into when she recognized the plant.

"Peter! *Nein!*" She knocked the piece he had just cut for himself from his hand. "It's poison!"

She didn't know the word in German. "It's not radish; it's wolf's bane. One bite can kill you!"

She made a face as if she were gagging and choking, the stuck her tongue out and rolled her eyes back.

"*Himmeltrüt!*" Peter cried and the color drained from his face.

"Oh, Peter, I'm sorry." Margaret brushed the herbs aside and put her hands on his shoulders. "It was so thoughtless of me. How could I do that after the way your father died! Please forgive me!"

He didn't understand the words, but the meaning was clear. He put his hand on her cheek.

"I understand," he said. "You were trying to warn me. Thank you."

Margaret felt the warmth of his hand and smelled the mint-laced scent of his breath as they moved closer to each other.

At this interesting moment, Walter appeared, splashing upstream with Edana in his arms and James at his side.

"What's this?" he shouted. "Peter, *wes wil du beginnen?*"

Margaret fell back and tipped over the herbs. Peter got up hastily.

"I was helping Margaret," he said quickly.

"We found peppermint!" Margaret held up the plants.

"So I see." Walter was reconsidering his enjoyment of uncledom. "Margaret, would you take the little ones and put their shoes back on? Peter, I need to speak to you."

With a nervous glance from Walter to Peter, Margaret took the children's hands and guided them back to where the shoes lay in a pile by the stream. Peter looked up at Walter.

"We weren't doing anything wrong," he stated.

"I'm glad to hear it," Walter said. "Because Margaret isn't some goosegirl for you to practice seduction on. Besides being the daughter of a lord in Scotland, Catherine told me that she's also the grand-daughter of Thibault of Champagne."

"The count!" Peter was amazed. "I didn't know. She didn't mention it. That's terrible! That means no one would ever consider an alliance between us. He's almost as powerful as the emperor."

"There's plenty of time to plan a betrothal, young man," Walter said. "Both of you are too young for such things now. And by the time you're sixteen or seventeen, there may be someone else who seems more suitable for you."

Peter looked so dejected that Walter had a hard time keeping himself from laughing. Then he remembered his Alys. He had loved her from the time he was Peter's age and had gone on loving her despite her marriage to another. He would love her until he died. Who was he to poke fun at the boy's infatuation?

"I suppose there will be many men who'll want her," Peter said wistfully. "She'll have a large dowry."

"Perhaps not." Walter decided to throw him a bit of hope. "Margaret is legitimate, but her mother wasn't. And now that her uncle is lord of Wedderlie, he may not be eager to give her much as a marriage portion. Of course, that might lessen her in the eyes of your family."

Peter's eyes lit. He was at the age where such obstacles only made the prize greater.

"Now," Walter added. "I want you to promise not to speak to her of such things. Not until you're older and certainly not until the death of your father has been resolved."

Peter nodded, serious again. For a while he had forgotten that he was now the lord, even though Uncle Hermann was doing most of the work for him. Walter's words laid the burden back.

"Have you found anything?" he asked. "I don't want to have to see my stepmother punished if she did nothing wrong. But I don't know how long we can go on with this uncertainty."

"Yes, I know," Walter admitted. "We have some clues that lead away from Agnes. Her father has gone to Köln to seek more information. Peter, what we discover might put your father in a bad light.

I have no proof, or even a guess on what it could be, but you should be prepared."

"My father was an honest man." Peter lifted his head proudly. "He was kind and brave. However it might look, I don't believe he did anything shameful. You'd have to lie to bring such an accusation against him."

"Hubert won't create a false tale," Walter said. "Not even to save his daughter. He's an honorable man."

"Just remember," Peter said. "Your proof must be undeniable before my uncle and I will release Agnes. Someone must pay for my father's death."

Walter saw in his face the toll the past weeks had extracted from the boy. He wished he could offer some sort of comfort.

"Walter!" Margaret called. "I just heard the bells for Vespers. Shouldn't we be getting back?"

"Coming!" Walter called back. "Now, Peter, it's time that you went home, as well."

Peter sadly picked up his shoes and started to put them on. "Walter?" he asked as the man was leaving. "May I see Margaret again before she goes back to France?"

"If her brother permits it, I don't see why not," Walter answered. With that Peter had to be content.

It had been several years since Hubert had been in Köln and he didn't remember the streets as well as he'd hoped. The Jewish population here was much larger than Paris and spread through several neighborhoods. As his stumbling questions were met with incomprehension, he cursed his own pride for not taking Walter with him.

Finally he found someone who spoke French and could direct him to the synagogue. The man gave him a look of deep suspicion that should have put Hubert more on his guard. His preoccupation was so great that he simply thanked his informant and hurried to reach his friends before night fell.

As he passed through the streets, trying to keep the directions straight, it appeared to him that a number of people were going the same way. He wondered if there were a local festival. Everyone seemed in high spirits.

At last his turn took him away from the flow. He went down a narrow walkway and into a small courtyard surrounded by houses. Hubert relaxed. This place he knew. The house on the left had baskets of flowers hanging from the balcony. Without hesitation, he knocked on the door.

There was a sound from inside, but no one came. Hubert knocked more loudly. Finally, he called in Hebrew.

"Hezekiah! Are you in there? It's Chaim ben Solomon, from Paris."

There was a rush of footsteps inside and the rasp of a bar being lifted. The door opened only far enough to let him in.

"Hezekiah, what is it?" Hubert asked as his old friend pulled him in.

"What a time you've picked to visit!" Hezekiah motioned for Hubert to follow him into the main part of the house. "Don't you know that the devil is here in Köln? He looks like a man, but he barks like a hound from Sheol. He calls himself Radulf and he's inciting the Edomites against us."

"Radulf! Here?" Hubert exclaimed. "I thought he'd been stopped by the abbot of Clairvaux."

They had come into the hall where the leaders of the community were gathered. Hubert recognized a few of them, but there were many young men who were strangers. They all wore the same face of apprehension.

"A blessing on this house," Hubert said. "I apologize for interrupting your meeting. I've come from Trier on a family matter."

"Hubert is one who was forced under the filthy water when he was a child," Hezikiah explained to the group. "But he's still one of us in spirit. We may speak freely before him."

There was some grumbling, but eventually some men moved down on their bench to make room for him.

"Let us finish this first," Hezekiah said. "And then you and I will eat and you can tell me what brings you here."

Hubert sat and listened. He couldn't follow when they switched to German but what he heard was enough to frighten him.

"Many of you are too young to remember when the followers of the crucified one came to Köln before," an old man was saying.

"That doesn't mean we didn't grow up hearing about it, Joseph," another interrupted. "None of us is indifferent to the problem."

"The question is, what is our best course of action?" Hezekiah said. "We have friends who will hide us in their homes but I, for one, don't want to have to put them at risk."

"Also, if it comes down to giving us up to the mob or having their own homes destroyed, how many Christians will have the courage to protect us?" the younger man asked.

"Exactly what I was thinking," Joseph said. "We've tried prayer and the giving of bribes, but I don't want to have my family exposed to the whim of the bishops or the greed of the lords. I say we negotiate for a fortress where we can gather and prepare our own defense."

"All of us together?" Hezekiah was doubtful. "It's dangerous to draw the attention of the soldiers to one spot. If we disperse to many villages then there's a better chance that some will survive, should it come to that."

"No, I agree with Joseph." Another of the younger men, Judah, spoke. "In 4856 the bishop sent us to seven of his villages to hide. Only one village was spared. If we had all been together, all might have been saved."

"Or all might have died," a old man said. "My wife and I were in that protected village. I grieve still for the others but I'm glad we survived."

"I'm tired of depending on the good will of the Christians," Judah answered. "I would rather die in the Sanctificaion of the Holy Name than live like a rabbit, shivering in fear, ready to bolt back into my hole at the slightest noise."

"And so would I," Joseph rose. "It may be that our fears will never take shape, even with the barker monk preaching our destruction. But I would rather be prepared than face the loss of life and the desecration of the Torah that we endured before."

Others stood as well, and for a few minutes everyone spoke at once, each trying to be heard above the others. When Hezekiah managed to restore order, however, it was clear that a consensus had been reached.

"Very well," Hezekiah said. "We shall decide how much we can afford to give Archbishop Arnold for the use of one of his fortresses. If we can convince him to agree, we'll have to start preparations to move there at once."

"Exactly," Judah said. "Preparations. There's no need to go unless we can see there's danger."

"No! You mustn't wait. Go now!"

All eyes turned to Hubert.

They had switched back to Hebrew and he had understood that final part. He quailed a bit under their outraged glare, but stood firm.

"No," he said more quietly. "By the time you see the danger, then it will be too late. Believe me. In Rouen we thought we were safe. But the soldiers came without warning and when they left, dozens were dead, including my mother and sisters."

"Blessed be their memory," Joseph added. "My parents chose death, as well, and I would have died with them had I not been at Ramerupt studying. This man is right. It's better to lose a little through overwatchfulness than to lose everything through complacency."

Hubert sank back. His heart was beating slowly again and his fingers were cold. He tried to breathe deeply and calm himself. Fifty years had passed and still the memory haunted him. Would he never find peace?

The others continued discussing the situation, but Hubert paid them no more attention. Eventually the men rose to leave. As they did, Hubert held up his hands for attention.

"Please, as long as you are all here, I'd like to ask about something different," he said. "It's of no consequence to the community but of great importance to me. Do any of you know a Lord Gerhardt, from near Trier? He has a vineyard."

Judah stepped forward. "Yes, I've bought from him. Always a fair man. I thought he had died recently."

"Yes." Hubert licked his lips. "There's been some question about how it happened and I need to find out about the man's activities in Köln. Can you help me?"

"Of course," Judah told him. "But not tonight. My wife probably thinks I've gone to the tavern on the way home. I promised I'd be back long ago."

They arranged to meet the next morning. Hezekiah bid his guests good night and then called up the stairs to his daughter to come down and see to Hubert.

"Thank you, old friend," Hubert said. "I can see you're curious about why I want to investigate the death of a German lord. I will explain everything in the morning."

"There's no need for you to explain at all." Hezekiah smiled. "I know you must have a good reason and therefore, I'll do what I can to help."

Hubert slept that night on a soft featherbed. For the first time in weeks, he had no bad dreams.

Peter was quite upset by his encounter with Walter. It wasn't that he had intended any harm to Margaret or her honor. He hadn't been thinking at all, really. But now he was. Too many things had been thrust on him too quickly. He had hardly been given time to grieve. Instead he was sitting at his father's place at the table with everyone watching him, waiting for him to make a mistake. Or perhaps waiting to see if his food was poisoned, too.

He wanted it all to be over. And it wouldn't be until Agnes was out of the castle. She had to be freed or she had to be tried. He couldn't stand wondering any longer. After all if, as he hoped, Agnes had nothing to to with his father's death, then someone else did. Someone he cared about, perhaps. Someone he believed cared about him. But what if they didn't? What if whoever did this wanted him dead as well?

Peter walked more quickly between the rows of vines now ripening in the rich sunlight. He wasn't going to let anyone murder him. He was going to grow up and find a way to marry Margaret. And they would have lots of sons. His father's vision of the land wouldn't die with him.

He found his uncle Folmar in the stables, saddling his horse.

"Where are you going, Uncle?" he asked.

Folmar jumped. "Peter! Don't creep up on me! I thought you were going to Saint Marien to see Brother Berengar."

Peter's mouth dropped open. He'd forgotten completely. He'd asked Brother Berengar to teach him French and the monk had promised to see him at Tierce for a lesson. The meeting with Margaret had driven it from his mind.

"I'll go tomorrow," he said. "Something came up."

Folmar continued adjusting the stirrup. "I wish your aunt would stop using my gear when she rides. I have to change it all back every time."

Peter tried again. "Are you going far?"

"Just into Trier," Folmar answered. "Hermann wants me to see to some things."

"May I come with you? I can be ready in a few minutes," Peter asked.

Herman gave one last tug on the leather. "No, this is just business. And, as it's getting late, I'll likely have to spend the night there. Anyway, it's not the sort of thing you need to worry about."

Peter was becoming tired of being treated like a child.

"Everything that has to do with my fief is my business," he said. "Father would have wanted me to know all the sides of my duty to it. I'm coming with you. Wait while I get my riding gear."

Folmar could only stand and fume.

When he brought Margaret and the little ones back, Walter took Catherine aside and told her what had happened.

"I don't believe that the boy had any dishonorable intent," he said. "But at that age they haven't learned how to control such urges."

"Some never do," Catherine said grimly. "Thank you for warning me. I'll let Edgar know."

"Will you talk to Margaret?" Walter asked.

"I don't know," Catherine said. "Perhaps in a general way, about keeping herself free of scandal. I don't want to shame her. You say she did nothing improper?"

"Neither of them did, really," Walter said. "Of course, if I had arrived a few moments later . . ."

Catherine gave a deep sigh. She was just as glad her father wasn't there. He'd find her discomfiture highly amusing.

The next morning, Edgar was sitting under a tree watching the builders at work on the cathedral. People had become used to seeing him there with his children and were slowly changing their opinion of the family of this foreign woman. The maimed man seemed harmless and the children well-behaved. Perhaps, the talk at the fountain went, perhaps this French girl isn't a sorceress after all but just a murderer. And, since everyone knew that she hadn't been married long enough for a widow's portion, people began to speculate as to what the noble Lord Gerhardt could have done to cause her to want him dead.

Much of this had been relayed to Edgar by the man who had stopped the boys throwing rocks. His name was Egilbert and he had decided to adopt the strangers.

"Amazing how quickly minds change," he commented, handing a cup of local wine to Edgar. "I've even heard some say that the poor woman should be released into your care and sent home with only her nose slit."

"I don't think my wife or her father will accept that," Edgar answered. "And I'm sure Agnes won't. She's ready to stay in that room until there's no doubt of her innocence."

Egilbert took a gulp from his cup. "Well, unless she's ready to undergo the ordeal, I don't see how that can happen. Poison is a tricky thing. Anyone could have dropped a potion in his meat sauce."

"He didn't eat meat," Edgar said. "Or fish or cheese. Nothing but beans, bread, herbs and wine, Agnes says. Some sort of penance or something."

"Really?" Egilbert considered this. "Well maybe he wasn't poisoned at all, then. Maybe he just farted his brains out."

He thought this joke was so good that he repeated it in German for the benefit of his friends.

All at once the laughter stopped, except for one man who was wiping his eyes. When he looked up he saw the cause for the sudden quiet.

Peter had just ridden into the square. He felt the stares and lifted his head higher. Then he dismounted, handed the reins to a servant and went into the cathedral.

"Poor lad," someone said.

There were mutters of agreement. Edgar felt the wind begin to change.

They needed to discover the truth behind Gerhardt's death soon. He wondered if Hubert had found out anything in Köln.

∞

Peter could feel them all watching as he entered the cathedral. He fought the urge to run. The noise of the workmen faded as he shut the door behind him and the perpetual coolness of the stones made the air around him still and peaceful. He made his way along the ambulatory and then crossed to the nave where he knelt in front of the altar.

He began to recite *Aves* but his mind wasn't on God. When Folmar had been so mysterious about his visit to town, Peter had assumed, hopefully, that his uncle was going to a brothel and didn't want him to know. But, when they arrived, all that Folmar had done was consult with a man at the wine market and then tell the cook at the town house that they would be eating there that night.

After he had gone to bed Peter had listened for the sound of footsteps. Sometime after midnight he was rewarded with a creak and a click that said the front gate had been opened. But when he went down to follow his uncle, he heard voices coming from the hall and realized that Folmar had been letting someone in.

Cautiously, he tiptoed down the stairs and stood in the shadows by the door. The voices were soft and he nearly stopped breathing in the effort to make out words. One thing he noticed immediatly was that the guest was a man.

He heard the glug as Folmar poured wine for his visitor.

"Thank you," the man said. "It's been a long ride from Köln, and the road was dusty. We need rain soon."

"The grapes like a dry summer," Folmar answered. "It was wet enough at Easter."

Peter tried not to yawn. He'd stayed awake half the night for talk of the weather? The guest continued, his voice taking on a different tone.

"Even though the *perfectus* is lost we must continue with our plans," he said. "Right now the people are attacking the Jews. With all the attention on them, and with the armies of pilgrims passing through, we'll be able to convert many to our way. We need your help, Folmar. Now that Gerhardt is dead, the link is gone."

"Yes, Gerhardt is dead," Folmar answered. "And so is your messenger. What if Gerhardt died because of something your man spilled before his throat was cut? The archbishop may know all about us and only be waiting to spring his trap."

"Not after all this time," the stranger said. "Your brother was a martyr, but only because of the passion of his wife. Obviously, the woman was enraged by his saintliness and decided to kill him so she could be free to marry a man who would indulge her filthy lusts."

Peter just managed to keep from a cry of surprise. What could they mean? He wished the stranger would be more specific about the lusts.

"I wish I were as sure as you," Folmar said.

The voices were coming closer. Peter edged farther into the dark corner.

"If your faith were perfect, you would be," the guest told him. "This is no time for uncertainty. We are on the brink of the millennium and only those who have purified themselves will be among the saved."

"Yes, I know." Folmar said. "Thank you for coming and bringing the news. I'll do what I can."

"No, Brother," the man said. "Do what you must."

To Peter's relief Uncle Folmar didn't go upstairs immediatly after letting his guest out. Instead he went back to the hall. There was the sound of more liquid being poured. Hoping that Folmar would drink his wine downstairs, Peter hurried back up to his alcove, drawing the curtain closed behind him.

He thought he wouldn't be able to sleep after what he had heard. His nonentity of an uncle was involved in some dangerous plot. That was amazing enough. But how could his father have been part of it, as well? Something was wrong here. It was up to him to find out what. The problem went round and round in his head until, only a few moments later, he was asleep.

The first thing in the morning Peter had left his uncle and taken his worries to the only one he felt sure he could trust.

He only hoped God would tell him clearly what he should do.

Fifteen

A street corner in Köln. Tuesday, 7 ides of August
(August 7), 1146; 27 Av, 4906. Feast of Saint Victorix, Roman soldier, then bishop of Rouen, who protected virgins and
widows from the influence of heresy.

ונצעק אל

אלהינו ונאמר אהה ה אלהים הן עתה לא עברו חמשים יי שנה בשנח
היובל אשר נשפך דמינו על ייחוד שלך חנכמד ביום הרג רב. הלעולמים
וישמע ה את

We cried out to our God, saying, "Alas Lord, God, not even
fifty years have passed, as the number of a jubilee, since our
blood was shed on the day of massacre in witness to the
Unity of Your Revered name. Will you forsake us eternally,
O Lord?"

—Ephraim of Bonn
Sefer Zekirah

*T*he thin man in the dingy grey robe could hardly be seen for the crowd around him, but his voice pierced through to every corner of the square.

"Why do we send the best of our knights, who are the finest fruit of our orchards, all the way to the Holy Land to fight the infidel, while we allow the infidel in our midst to grow rich? The Jews laugh at our piety as they take in our coins and give us less than a tenth the value of the treasures we're forced to pawn. Shall we continue to allow this blasphemy?"

His audience roared a negative.

"That monk does have an air of authority about him," Lanval told his wife, Denise, as they made their way past the gathering. "Look how he's able to draw together so many people with his words."

Denise wasn't so impressed. She watched Radulf for a while, noting the passion with which he exhorted the populace to forego killing Saracens long enough to first take revenge on the Jews in their midst. She wondered what they had done to him to cause such animosity.

"He has an air of madness." She sniffed finally. "His words are nothing to me. What do I care about the conversion of the Jews to a religion already so corrupt? I shouldn't like to be forced to undergo baptism. I only wish I hadn't been given it the first time."

"Denise!" Lanval looked to see if anyone had heard her. "Not here!"

"Husband, if not here, then where? When?" she answered. "We came all this way to find others like us. I grant you that it's gratifying that there are so many with us in this city now. I'm awed by the holiness of our *perfecti*, especially the bishop. But we still hide in cellars and meet in secret. Why don't we have the courage of the first Christians, to proclaim our faith openly and die for it, if we must?"

That had been bothering Lanval as well, but he didn't want to admit it. "Astolfo says that the *perfecti* will know when the time is right. We must wait until then."

They watched the preacher for a while longer. Denise noted that not everyone was listening with rapt attention. There were those who edged around the crowd with an expression of disgust, or fear. Others stood for a while and then laughed at Radulf before returning to their business. But there were still many who nodded grim agreement to every word. What would they do when the words stopped?

Denise had been watching the faces. Anger made them ugly. Suddenly, she realized that, in the midst of them, there was one she knew.

"What's Andreas doing there?" she asked her husband.

"I don't know," he answered. "Perhaps trying to gauge the danger to us."

"I don't see how that can be, when almost no one knows we exist," she argued. "We should be up there preaching just as this Radulf is."

Lanval disagreed. "I think that our leaders are right," he said. "There's no reason to proselytize openly yet. If these people run out of Jews to torment, they may start on us. It frightens me."

"Lanval," Denise said. "Sometimes I doubt that your faith is complete."

"I know, my love," he said. "Sometimes I do, too."

Hubert had found out more than he needed to know about Lord Gerhardt. Unfortunately all of it was approbation.

"I'm sorry; he was a good man," Hezekiah said. "Always honest and respectful in his dealings with us. He didn't play dice or visit the brothels. At least no one ever caught him at either. The people who live in his house are sickly looking, but it's to his credit, too, that he would take them in."

"What people?" Hubert asked. "What house?"

"Just a place near the quay," Hezekiah told him. "The sort a man would buy who was tired of staying at inns when he came to town. There are ten or twelve people who stay there. Some may be servants; they dress very plainly. I don't know what they are to him Not family, I'm sure. They aren't lepers, at least. The burghers wouldn't allow it, even if Gerhardt were holy enough to risk associating with the unclean."

"Interesting," Hubert said. "Can you direct me there? I'd like to pay them a visit. I wonder if this house belongs to his son now, or if he donated it to these people."

"You shouldn't face them alone," Hezekiah warned. "I'll have my friend Matthias go with you. He lives across the square from them, but he's traveled much in France so you'll have no trouble speaking to him. And, if anything were to happen, you'd want a citizen of Köln with you."

"*Todah robah*, old friend," Hubert said. "Please send word to this Matthias that I would like to meet him as soon as possible. I need to return to Trier soon. I've been too long away and had no messages from my family."

"Simon will be going in a few days," Hezekiah said. "He's waiting for a boat that can sail his English wool and hunting dogs upriver. He'd be glad of your company."

"Simon has returned safely?" Hubert's face lit. "Mina will be so relieved. She tried not to show it, for the children's sake, but she's been worried."

Matthias sent back that he would be happy to meet with Hubert. Hezekiah confided that they'd all been curious about the lodgers in Gerhardt's house but no one had had a reason to confront them while the lord was alive.

So, the next morning Hubert was introduced to a strapping young man with brown hair, light eyes and a chin that could chisel stone. Matthias greeted Hubert enthusiastically.

"There's been gossip about these people for months," he told them. "But one doesn't like to interfere when they are doing one no harm. There are too many others that one has to guard against."

"It's a sad truth about our trade," Hubert agreed. "From brigands on the road to the ones in our own guild, one must always be ready for attack. I wouldn't ask you to help me in this but I must know who these people are."

"Oh, I don't mind," Matthias said. "I've had my suspicions, lately. There seem to be more of them staying there in the past weeks and the new ones much poorer than the first. I wonder if it isn't one of those places that takes in runaway serfs."

"*Stadt luft macht frei,*" Hubert said. "It's almost the only German I know."

"Yes, they'll be free if they can stay here a year and a day and if they can support themselves," Matthias said. "But we don't need the streets filled with foreign beggars and this lot doesn't look strong enough for hard work."

They had reached the gate by this point and were about to knock.

"Remember," Hubert told Matthias, "I've come from Rouen by boat and only just learned of Gerhardt's death. But don't tell them I'm a merchant. Perhaps they'll think I have something to do with alms-giving and let slip who they are."

"I know what to say," Matthias told him. You don't need to worry. Just stay close and look wealthy."

The gate was opened by a young man. He was pale as a recluse who never saw the sun. He seemed unsure about what to do with the two well-dressed men before him.

Matthias didn't give him time to think.

"We've come to see your master," he ordered the man. "Take us to him at once."

He entered the courtyard before the door could be shut in his face.

"Who are you?" The young man held onto the door handle. "What do you want with us?"

"To see the leader of your group, as I told you," Matthias answered. "This gentleman has come all the way from Normandy to visit. Where is your hospitality?"

"Don't confuse the poor lad."

Hubert looked over the young man's shoulder. At the doorway stood a woman of about his age, certainly not more than midfifties, wearing a simple blue *bliaut* over a white *chainse*. She wore no jewelry, but her presence was enough to convey a sense of dignity and status.

"Lady," Matthias removed his hat and bowed. "We have come only to consult with the master of this house. Can you help us?"

The woman seemed amused. "This house has no master," she said. "But I am mistress here. If you have a question, I'm afraid there's no one else to answer."

Matthias explained to Hubert.

"Is this a religious house?" he asked, confused.

"Of course," she answered. "Lord Gerhardt established us only a few months ago. Didn't you know that?"

Hubert tried to cover his ignorance. "I didn't realize that it had been formally instituted. Are you followers of Robert of Arbrissel, then, that an abbess governs both men and women?"

"We have our own Rule," the woman said severely. "May I offer you refreshment while you explain the purpose of your visit?

They accepted and were led into the house. Hubert looked around curiously. The walls were completely bare, with not even a cross or a bright cloth hanging. All the windows were open to entice a breeze through. The effect was oddly soothing, but strange.

They were given water scented with rose petals and small honey cakes. The woman who served them seemed familiar to Hubert.

"Didn't we meet on the road outside Trier?" he asked.

Denise nearly dropped the tray. She looked first at the woman and then nodded.

"You were kind to stop your journey to help my friend," Hubert continued. "We wanted to show our gratitude, but you had gone on."

"No thanks were necessary," Denise answered. "No earthly reward matters to us."

"A noble sentiment," Matthias said. "Not enough of our so-called religious adhere to that belief in these corrupt times."

Denise's eyes lit. "Oh, no, there are many who feel as I do!"

"And," the woman broke in, "we shall be happy to tell you of them, if you'd care to hear. But I'm sure you didn't come here to convert, since you didn't even know of our order."

Matthias inclined his head. "I fear that I have not been given the temperament for the monastic life. However, my friend is most interested in Lord Gerhardt's beliefs and why he founded this house for you."

The woman raised her eyebrows as she studied Hubert.

"Lord Gerhardt is dead," she said. "Only he could say what his beliefs were. He did express to me his intention to retire to this house when the time was right."

"Did he feel that would be soon?" Matthias asked at Hubert's prompting.

"Let us say that I was most surprised to learn of his marriage," the woman told them. "I was under the impression that he was waiting only until he felt his son old enough to assume the responsibilities of his position before he retired from the world."

Hubert wanted to know more, but the woman was not forthcoming with information, not even, he realized, her name. All he could do was thank her for her hospitality and ask if he might visit again.

"All who come in the spirit of charity are most welcome," the woman told him as she signaled for Denise to take them to the door.

When they were back out on the street, Hubert thanked Matthias for his help.

"Did you learn what you wanted to?" Matthias asked him.

"Not really," Hubert said. "These new religious houses are everywhere, lately. It could be just what it claims."

"Or that woman could be using Lord Gerhardt's piety for her own ends," Matthias said. "The place certainly didn't have the feel of a monastic house."

"Yes, it did," Hubert disagreed. "Any number of these small convents are very sparse as to furnishings.

"That's not what I meant," Matthias said. "The bells rang None while were were there and yet I heard no chanting of the hour. The abbess, if that was her true rank, didn't even seem aware of the time. I know of no religious house that doesn't observe the Hours."

"That's true." Hubert nodded. "It is unusual. Can you think of anyone who might know more about these people?"

"No, we've all wondered," Matthias answered. "It didn't seem anything worth troubling the archbishop about, but now that I consider it, he might be very interested. A place like that should be under someone's supervision. I'll speak to some of my more highly placed friends and have him approached on the matter."

"Still, I doubt it will cast much light on why Lord Gerhardt died," Hubert said. "Even if he were involved in some wickedness with them, or if he discovered an evil about them that he threatened to expose, how could anyone from here manage to poison his food?"

Matthias had no answer for that. He offered to walk with Hubert back to Hezekiah's home, perhaps first finding something more substantial to drink than rose water. Hubert agreed with alacrity.

The tavern they stopped at had a number of benches and tables placed out in the open, across from the marketplace. It was full of people this hot afternoon but they were able to squeeze in next to some merchants that Matthias knew.

While the men exhanged news in their own tongue, Hubert idly watched the animals being brought in to sell that day. It wasn't until a man came by with a string of horses that he came to attention. There was one among them that was obviously out of place. That big grey had never pulled a wagon or a plow in his life.

Hubert stood and pointed.

"That's Walter's!" he shouted. "You there! Where did you get that horse?"

The men didn't understand the words, but the gestures were clear. They all stared at Hubert.

"Matthias, I know that horse," Hubert said. "It was stolen several days ago from a friend of mine, a knight named Walter of Grancy. Please, ask that man how he came by it."

Matthias hesitated. "Are you sure, Hubert?" he asked. "That's Meinwerk from Aachen. He's well known here as an honest trader."

"Honest he may be," Hubert said, "but Walter has a scar on his temple from the one who ambushed him and stole that horse. Look at it. Is that the usual quality sold by this man? Find out who sold it to him."

Matthias set down his beer and went over to the horse trader, who was now looking decidedly uneasy. They spoke for a few moments while Hubert tried to contain his impatience. Finally Matthias returned, while Meinwerk waited, now holding the bridle of the grey.

"He says that a man sold it to him only yesterday, while he was on his way here," Matthias reported. "The man told Meinwerk that he was the servant of a lord who had to sell the horse to pay a gambling debt. Meinwerk was suspicious because the seller was willing to take so little, but his desire for the horse overcame his doubts."

"Go back and tell him that if he'll sell it to me for what he paid, I'll return it to the owner and there'll be no trouble for him," Hubert said.

"Forgive me, Hubert, but how can Meinwerk be sure that you aren't just trying to buy a fine horse cheaply?" Matthias asked.

Hubert was annoyed, but saw the justice of the question. "Hezekiah will vouch for me," he said. "Also, I can identify the bridle, if it's the same one Walter used. There's a silver rondel on each side with a walnut tree etched into it. That's the symbol of Walter's family."

Matthias went back and checked. Then he nodded to Meinwerk who managed to look both relieved and disappointed at the same time. Hubert came to join them.

"Tell him I'll pay for his trouble, as well," he told Matthias. "The man who owns the horse may also want to reward him for returning it. He's about to set off for the Holy Land and is feeling generous."

Meinwerk perked up at this news. Hubert arranged to pay for the animal and have it brought to a stable nearby.

"Now," he added, "can you find out if Meinwerk could identify the man who sold him the horse? What did he look like?"

When questioned, Meinwerk scratched his chin beneath his beard. "The man was on the tall side," he said. "Fair, with brown hair and not much of a beard. Oh yes, he had an accent. Lotharingian, maybe, or French. I couldn't be sure. His German was good."

"Thank you," Hubert said. "It's not likely that he'll see the man again, but if he does, Matthias, may he come to you with the information?"

"Of course," Matthias, agreed. "Now let's finish the beer before the sun boils it away."

They returned to the table, where Matthias explained to his friends what had happened.

"I think the man may still be in the area," one of them said. "Someone tried to sell me a saddle with a walnut tree symbol on it just this morning. I don't trade in such things so I sent him on his way. But I remember him well, just as Meinwerk said. If I spot him, I'll raise a cry after him."

Hubert thanked them all and went back to Hezekiah's. If he

hadn't done much to help Agnes, at least Walter would rejoice that he could once again ride as befitted his station.

At that moment, Walter felt as if he had become a beast of burden, himself. James and Edana had abandoned their father to perch on his shoulders, so broad he could balance them on either side, although the grip they had on his ears was almost painful. Catherine and Edgar walked behind him, ready to catch should either child fall. Margaret was at his side, carrying a basket of food and face cream for Agnes.

They slowed down as they came to a stoic figure, seated by his tent at the place where the road divided.

"Jehan, why don't you go home?" Walter asked. "You know that your devotion only makes it harder to prove Agnes innocent."

"I must be here if she needs me," Jehan replied without looking up. "She knows I'll do anything to save her. Unlike some, who seem to be treating her peril as a chance for a summer outing."

"That's a lie!" Catherine bent over so he had to look at her. "We're all worried about her. But there's no proof of her guilt and, if you just went away, we might get Lord Hermann to let her go in our custody!"

"And forever have the stain of murder on her." Jehan sneered. "That's like you. Do whatever least upsets your life. I've offered to exonerate her as her champion over and over. She must know that someone is willing to defend her with his life."

Catherine tried to be gentler, even though Jehan could be very annoying.

"Everyone knows that," she said. "It's very brave of you to offer to endure the pain of the ordeal for her sake. But there are always those who'll deny the proof of it."

And, she added to herself, there's always the chance that you'd fail.

He saw the doubt in her eyes and spat on the ground by her feet.

Edgar stepped forward. "How dare you insult my wife!" He shouted, raising his fist.

Jehan only laughed. "Or what? You'll pound me into the earth like a nail? I wouldn't stain my sword with the likes of you."

"Here now!" Walter put the children down and loomed over Jehan. "None of that. A man who's taken the cross shouldn't behave like this. If you want to help Agnes, then you should pray for her instead of making a fool of yourself where everyone can see. You're a soldier of Christ and should act with more charity."

"Only to those who deserve it, Walter." Jehan stood so that Walter's bulk wasn't so overwhelming. "As a soldier of Christ you should be more selective about the company you keep."

"Walter?"

He had wanted to raise his hand to the man but there was someone holding it. Margaret looked up at him.

"Don't hurt him," she pleaded. "He's so unhappy already."

Catherine felt a rush of shame. Of course Margaret didn't know all the insults and injuries Jehan had given them over the years. But that shouldn't make any difference. If they couldn't forgive their enemies then what right had they to castigate others for not behaving like Christians?

However, Catherine found that the best she could do was to hold her tongue. Edgar noticed the way her lips tightened to keep the sarcastic words from escaping. He smiled at her tenderly. Then he sighed; his heart wasn't yet ready to feel charitable toward Jehan.

Walter's fist unclenched under Margaret's gentle touch.

"Jehan," he said softly, "she's right. And there's nothing here that will bring you happiness. Go home. For Agnes's sake. Go home."

Jehan turned away from them. Catherine thought she saw tears glittering on his lashes.

"I can't do that," he said brusquely.

He bent down and went into his tent, pulling the flap down after him.

"Well, that was a cheery diversion," Edgar commented as he picked Edana up from the roadside where she had been eating flowers.

"I only hope Agnes is more appreciative of our company," Catherine said.

Agnes was becoming heartily sick of the wall hangings in her room. The blue and yellow woven pattern grated on her, especially when the sunlight struck it showing all the dust that had accumulated since

they were last taken down and washed. She knew she couldn't com-
plain of ill-treatment. Every morning the chamber pot was emptied
and a ewer of warm water brought her to wash with. Once a month
a boy came to sweep out the old rushes and replace them. She was
fed the same food the family ate. Lately she had received a clear
impression that the family was beginning to doubt that she had killed
Gerhardt. Even Maria, who had been the most fervent in her accusations, was relenting. Perhaps her father and Catherine were
helping.

So why was she still a prisoner?

The worst of it was having so much time to think. It wasn't
something she had ever felt the need to do before. She usually
had spent some time each day planning what needed to be done
and what she hoped to do, but this enforced lack of activity had
driven her to speculation in areas that she would rather not have
entered.

She said her prayers as she embroidered the cloth sent to her by
the nuns of Saint Irminen, each flower or animal a symbol of the
faith. She tried to concentrate on saints who had been unjustly in-
carcerated and miraculously freed. But against her will, her thoughts
kept going back to her father. She had spent so many years blaming
him for her mother's unhappiness. But Madeleine had known of
Hubert's Jewish parentage when they married. Perhaps it was her
own guilt that had sent her into madness.

At least her father hadn't waited until the wedding night to tell
her mother what he was. He hadn't rejected her mother or called
her terrible names just because she was happy to take up her marital
duties. If Gerhardt hadn't wanted Agnes, then why had he gone
through with the ceremony in the first place? What kind of man
would be so hypocritical?

These things went round and round in her head with no satis-
factory answers. There were days when Agnes wondered if they were
leaving her alone so much so that she would go mad, as well, and
thus save everyone the scandal of a trial.

It was in this frame of mind that she began looking forward to
Catherine's visits. Even her sister's peculiarities were preferable to
the notions lurking in her own mind.

Today she heard the dogs barking below and Walter's clear voice as he shouted over them. She wondered how many of the others had come. When the door finally opened, Catherine was there alone.

"Brother Berengar couldn't come today," she said. "So Hermann will only let us have a few moments. Edgar has been allowed into the library at Saint Maximin and I've gone through all the medical manuscripts that the nuns had and we've found no illness with symptoms like those you described."

"Well, I'm sure you tried." Agnes didn't hide her disappointment.

"But," Catherine said, "we did find cases of a nervous condition that could either arise from a seriously troubled mind or—and this is the crucial part so please stop that sewing, Agnes."

"Catherine, if I don't do this, I'll start poking you with the needle," Agnes answered. "I wish you'd stop using rhetorical devices and just tell me what you found."

"Sorry, I slip into it without thinking," Catherine said. "Very well. Gerhardt was behaving in a way that might conform to slow poisoning. If he had a small amount of poison, an extract of monkshood or wolf's bane, for instance, every day, he could have been building up enough in his body until one day, it was enough to kill him."

"Are you sure?" Agnes felt a glimmer of hope. "But what could he have been eating that no one else had?"

"Well, it might be something he particularly liked and others didn't," Catherine said. "Can you think of anything like that?"

"No, I can't remember anything," Agnes said. "No sweetmeat or delicacy. He ate very little, really. It would have been easier to poison me."

"But there must have been something," Catherine insisted.

"If there is, I don't know it," Agnes told her. "Don't you think I'd tell you? Do you think I enjoy being up here all summer with nothing to do but wonder if I'll live to see the autumn? And don't you realize that if you can't find a food that was only for Gerhardt, they might go back to assuming I had to have killed him through sourcery? For such a crime, I could be burned."

Catherine fell back on her chair. She hadn't considered that. She had only been so excited to find a poison that someone else could have administered.

She took a deep breath and set her jaw.

"Then we'll have to find out what this was put in, that's all," she said firmly.

Agnes nearly laughed. "That's all? Oh, Catherine, for once I'm almost glad of your amazing pridefulness. You really believe you can uncover the truth no matter what."

"Not alone," Catherine said. "Edgar will help me. We look at problems differently, you see, and so together we often find a solution."

Agnes's throat felt suddenly tight. "How lucky you are," she said wistfully. "Are you at all thankful for what you have?"

"Every day, Agnes," Catherine said. "And we're going to get you out of this."

There was a knock on the door, signaling that their time was up.

Agnes rose and hugged her sister. "I'm going to pray tonight for the faith to believe that you can do it," she said.

"You mustn't give in to despair, my dear," Catherine whispered. "It's only then that the devil wins."

Downstairs the rest of the family were having a fairly pleasant time, under the circumstances. They had been offered white wine, chilled in a brook that flowed near the castle, and bits of herbed meat and fruit. Margaret was surprised to find herself put next to Peter.

She smiled shyly at him. He blushed and offered her a plum from his plate.

Maria watched them with a satisfied smile. She beckoned to Walter.

"Peter told me that the child is no blood relation to Lady Agnes," she began.

"That's correct," he said. "She's Edgar's half-sister."

"And her mother was?" Maria waited.

"He name was Adalisa," Walter said. "I believe her mother's family was from north of Paris somewhere."

Maria licked her lips in anticipation. "We understand her mother's father is a man of some note."

Walter shuddered. Catherine had confided the name of Margaret's grandfather to him with the injunction to tell no one. Now he understood why.

"My information is that he is from Blois and Champagne," Walter admitted. "But Margaret is unaware of the relationship and it's up to her brother to decide when, or if, she should know."

"But Adalisa was of good family and acknowledged by her father, wasn't she?" Maria said.

Walter guessed she already knew the answers. A few questions to friends in the neighborhood would elicit all the gossip of the past thirty years. It was the same everywhere.

"I believe so," he said. "But I really know little about it."

"She's a very sweet child." Maria smiled at her. "And Peter is quite enchanted by her."

"I made it clear to Peter that in my opinion they are both too young to be thinking of an alliance." Walter tried to close the conversation.

"Oh, they are," Maria agreed. "But it's high time someone began making arrangements for them. I'm sure Lord Edgar has already started looking for a suitable husband for Margaret."

Walter knew damn well that Edgar hadn't and would be furious to know what Maria was thinking. He was grateful that Maria couldn't approach his friend without an intermediary.

But Edgar had been watching the conversation, especially the nods and smiles at Margaret and Peter. When Walter managed to extricate himself from Maria, he walked directly into another predicament.

"You told them about Adalisa's father, didn't you?" Edgar accused him. "Did you also mention that Margaret's other grandfather is spending the rest of his life atoning for murder?"

"No, but I don't think Maria would care," Walter said. "As long as he was of noble birth and the penance was conducted somewhere else."

Edgar saw the truth of that. "You shouldn't have said anything to Peter about it. It was only to be expected that he'd tell his aunt. It was that woman's scheming that brought Agnes here, remember? I have no intention of leaving Margaret under her care."

"Of course not," Walter said. "But she is right about one thing,

Edgar. The child isn't a child anymore and you have to start thinking about her future now before she decides it for herself."

Catherine had entered the hall just in time to hear the end of his statement. She came over and linked her arm in Edgar's.

"That true, *carissime*," she said. "Or Margaret may suffer my fate and be married all on her own to a man she adores."

Neither Walter nor Edgar could think of a rebuttal.

Sixteen

The home of Hezekiah, in Köln. Monday, 2 ides of September (August 12), 1146; 2 Elul, 4906. The feast of Saint Gaugeric, vulgarly called Géry or, even worse, Guric, who was born in Trier and became bishop of Cambrai.

ויהי בחרש אלול בצת חהיאאשר בא רודולף הכומר ירדפהו אל
ייהרפחו לקלוניא וְהגה ר שמעון החסית אשר מציר טריכרש שכ
מאונגלטרא אשר צמד שם כמה ימים

In the month of Elul, at the time when Radulf the priest—may God hound and smite him—arrived at Köln, Simon the Pious, of the city of Trier, returned from England where he had spent few a days.

—Ephraim of Bonn
Sefer Zekirah

I'm sorry, Simon," Hubert said. "Now that I've found some men to ride to Trier with me, I think I'll take Walter's horse back by the road, rather that risk losing him in the river."

"It's a wise decision." Simon laughed. "I confess to being glad of it. I wasn't eager to share my boat full of wool and furs with a nervous stallion. The dogs might not like it, either. In that case, you'll probably arrive before I do, so you'll stop by and let Mina know I'm on my way?"

"Of course," Hubert said. He was delighted to see that no harm had come to Simon on the journey to England. With the country still fighting a civil war, any trip there could be fatal. He asked Simon how the news of King Louis's expedition had affected the Jews in England.

"Oddly enough, that seems to be one thing King Stephen has control over," Simon answered. "There's been no talk of persecutions as far as I know. Wandering preachers who came to ecourage pilgrims to take the cross were forbidden by the king to speak against the Jews. Of course it may just be that the English have enough to worry about without bothering with us."

Hubert shook his head. "I don't know. When times are bad, people look to find a cause for their misery. Too often it seems to be us."

"Ah but in England they're all too busy blaming each other." Simon stretched out on the warm bench and closed his eyes in contentment. "Why are you worried? There hasn't been trouble here, has there?"

"Nothing major," Hubert said. "Mostly from *routiers* and layabouts, the kind always ready to create mischief. There has been a man in town for the past few weeks who's attracted large crowds with his preaching against us, but so far there's been no violence."

"Not even the gentiles want a repeat of the murders at the time of Pope Urban," Simon said, though he was too young to remember them. They were part of legend now, like Judah Maccabee, and be-yond his understanding.

"No one in authority at least," Hubert said. "But I don't like the passion of this Radulf or the way some of his listeners look as if they're dogs only waiting the right moment to be unleashed upon the hunted."

Simon gave Hubert an encouraging pat. "Köln is a city with too many strangers," he said. "We'll be back in Trier soon and among friends. The emperor has shown no interest in joining this mad army of King Louis's. Without his support, few others will go and the preaching against us should soon end."

"I hope you're right, Simon," Hubert said. "So, when are you leaving for home?"

"Tomorrow," Simon told him. "They're loading the boat now. We'll set off just after dawn. I can't wait to be home. My son is starting *cheder* as soon as I get back."

"May he grow strong in the Torah," Hubert replied.

Each man sank back into his own dreams. Simon of the family he would soon rejoin and Hubert of the world he could only watch from the edge.

In Trier Catherine was pacing back and forth across the main room of their lodgings, kicking up chaff as she went.

"*Leoffest,* could you please do that out of doors?" Edgar said. "I'm trying to put a varnish on James's toy bow and all this upheaval is leaving bits stuck to it."

Catherine stopped. "Very well," she said. But instead of going out she plunked herself down on a stool next to the work table Edgar had set up.

"This is becoming ridiculous," she complained. "No one really thinks Agnes killed Gerhardt any more. Everyone seems to want her released, but unless we can find a poison . . ."

"Or prove he was ill," Edgar added.

"Or that," she agreed. "No one will set her free. I know how angry you are that I spoke to Walter and he to Peter and so forth, but since she found out about Margaret's grandfather, Maria has been much more helpful about searching her brother's possessions for some clue as to what killed him."

"Not that it's done any good," Edgar grunted. "My dear, you're leaning into the varnish."

"Sorry." She rubbed the sticky patch on the end of her braid. "It must be something simple, something so normal no one would think of it. I know that when we find it, we'll be astonished at our blindness."

"Perhaps." Edgar didn't have Catherine's faith in their deductive ability. "Nonetheless, I want it understood that Margaret is not to be the price of Agnes's freedom."

"Of course not!" Catherine was hurt that he'd think she'd even consider such a thing. "She does seem to be very taken with Peter, though, and he's a nice boy."

"He's just turned fourteen," Edgar reminded her. "That's the year I was sent to Paris to study."

"So?"

Edgar rolled his eyes. "Boys are sent to other cities at that age not for the repute of the master but to get into trouble far enough away that their families won't be embarrassed by them."

"Really?" Catherine was amused. "Is that why your friend John came from England?"

"John sent himself, Catherine," Edgar said. "That's different. I don't want Margaret left alone with Peter, however honorable he thinks his intentions might be."

"I love it when you act the paterfamilias." Catherine kissed the bridge of his nose. "But I agree. We have enough to worry about here already."

Catherine went back to her pacing. "If only I could find what the poison was in."

Edgar gave up trying to work and hung the bow on a hook above the billowing dust.

The sun was just above the horizen when Simon finished his prayers and left for the river. This wasn't a bad time of year to be trying to go upstream on the Rhine. The rains of spring were past and the river moved slowly. With a sail and oars, he should be home in a week.

He was thinking about the children and wondering if Mina's prediction had come true and there was another baby on the way. He didn't notice the group of men who had emerged from a side street near the edge of town.

It wasn't until he was out of the town walls and on the path that led through the vineyards to the dock where the ship waited that Simon realized he was being followed. He carried no weapon and had thought he needed none in the city. He moved more quickly on the path and began looking around for a house to run to.

Not far ahead was a barn with fermentation vats around it. It was early in the year to be picking grapes but still there might be someone inside willing to help him. Simon changed his course to approach the barn.

That was when the men overtook him.

One caught him by the arm and spun him around.

"I know you." He smiled. "You're a Jew. A stinking Jew. A filthy murderer of Christ strutting along the road like you owned it when you should be crawling through dung for your sins."

"Please," Simon said. "I haven't much money but you may take all of it."

"Money!" The man spat on him. "Thirty pieces of silver, I suppose."

Simon realized he'd made a mistake. These men weren't thieves who would take a bribe for his life but fanatics, and what was worse, they reeked of sour beer. They'd probably steal all he had in the end but they wanted to have some fun with him first.

"Robbers!" he shouted. "Someone help me!"

Another man grabbed him and dragged him in among the vines. The others followed, grinning.

"No one's going to help you, *judeswîn,*" the first man gloated. "Nothing will save you but salvation."

"What do you want from me?" Simon managed to get out as he was bumped along the dirt.

"Why, come be baptized, of course," the man said. "Accept the salvation of Christ and then, being good Christians, we probably won't kill you."

All his life Simon had wondered if he'd be strong enough to stand firm if the time ever came. He never thought it would happen in a vineyard covered with mud.

"Please," he tried again. "I have a wife, small children."

"There, isn't that fine, Andreas?" the first man said. "A whole family brought to the Faith. If he accepts Christ, they'll be bound to follow."

Simon had no illusions. He suspected they were just sober enough to spare his life if he agreed to convert and equally just drunk enough to slay him if he didn't. What was it after all, a little dirty water thrown on his head? What was that when weighed against his life?

Too much.

"Never!" Simon said, glaring up at his persecutor. "I will not worship your idols or your hanged god."

That was the last sentence he could utter. They hit him, over and over. He could taste the blood in his mouth and the pain told him they had broken one of his arms.

"Hurry!" Andreas said suddenly. "Someone's coming."

Simon heard him and prayed that the Holy One had sent an angel to smite these wicked men.

The men lifted Simon and took him into the barn where they found barrels stacked and the wine press ready for the next harvest.

"No water," one man said, "But, look, we can anoint him anyway."

He rubbed his finger in the blood from Simon's mouth and smeared it on his face. "There," he said. "I baptize you in the name of the Father, Son and Holy Spirit."

Simon tried to rub the blood off onto the man's tunic, but he was too weak.

"Quick, bring him over here!" the first man said.

They dragged him over the vat and shoved his head over the side below the press, two of the men holding him there. With a grunt the leader climbed on top of the press and began turning the handle so that the pressing board screwed down into the vat. Simon gave one scream that stopped abruptly.

The men stared at the result of their work.

"Good God, Dieter," Andreas gasped. "You've ripped his head clean off! We've got to get rid of the body before we're found."

"Don't be such a coward," Dieter said. *"Gehabe dich als ein man!* It's not murder. It's 'vanquishing the infidel in our midst,' just like the preacher said."

"Right," the other man agreed. "But we can get into real trouble for ruining a wine press."

They tried to unscrew the press but it wouldn't budge. In the end they carried Simon's body back outside and dumped it in a ditch, after first removing his money pouch and his boots. Finally they went down to the river to wash off the blood.

A few minutes later the overseer of the field workers entered the barn with one of his men.

"Well, there's no one here now," he said, as the sunlight flowed into the barn. "Nothing here to steal, anyway."

"But I was sure I saw some men go in," the serf told him. "They had a bundle with them, like old clothes."

"If so, they've gone now and nothing's damaged," the overseer said. "Except . . . what in God's creation is that smell? It's like a butcher's pen."

"It's strong over here." The serf went toward the wine press. "The planks are tilted. Could those vandals have stuck a cat in there?"

He bent down and peered into the vat.

"Mother of God!" he cried, blessing himself hastily. "It's a man!"

It was several hours before Simon's body was identified. His face was battered beyond recognition. The overseer had sent for his master and they had managed to get some men to pry the crooked press loose and extricate the head. A search was made for the body, which was then brought back to the barn. It was then that it was discovered that the man was Jewish.

"Or born one at least," the overseer commented.

"Was he from Köln?" someone asked.

"Let me see him!" a voice called from the back. "I might be able to tell you."

They let the man through and he knelt and examined Simon's

clothing and what was left of his face. Finally he found a few English coins tied into his sleeve.

"Yes, it's him," he said finally. "He's just back from England. He'd hired my boat to go back to Trier. When he didn't show up this morning, I came looking for him. They told me at the place where he was staying that he'd already left."

"What shall we do with him, then?" the overseer asked.

Someone in the crowd snorted. "I say throw the body in the river with the rest of the offal."

"No, we take it to the magistrates," the master decided. "They'll have to bury him quickly in this heat. They can charge it to the Jews of Köln."

So it wasn't until that evening, when Hubert was preparing for the next day's journey, that word was brought to Hezekiah of Simon's death.

The first reaction was stunned disbelief.

"Was it thieves?" Hezekiah asked in horror.

"Probably." The official who had been sent was uncomfortable with such news.

"Probably," Hezekiah repeated.

The official hesitated. "He had been robbed but, before he died, someone had painted a cross on his forehead in blood."

"Before he died." Hezekiah was trying to grasp that fact alone.

"Yes."

Since no one said anything more, the man bowed and left.

Hezekiah didn't notice his departure. "Simon dead? But he was on his way home. This can't be."

But as the truth of it sunk in, so did the significance of the cross. Falling to his knees, Hezekiah began to sway back and forth, wailing his grief.

"Oh Lord, have pity on us, as a father his children! Do not pass judgement on us, for in your sight no man is justified! Rembember, Lord, how we stand against the children of Edom who said, 'Destroy Jerusalem.' You will rise and have mercy on Zion, for it is time to pity her! Oh, Lord, accept your martyr, Simon, the pious one!"

His lamentation brought the rest of the household to him and then, when the reason for it was known, the rest of the community.

Hubert watched them, too stunned for tears. He realized with horror that he didn't know the words of the prayers being said for Simon, although he had learned the proper ones for mourning a Christian.

"I should have been with him," he whispered.

In Trier, Catherine was becoming increasingly discouraged. When Edgar asked if she wanted to come with him and Brother Berengar to talk to some villagers she just shook her head.

"What use is it to question people?" she complained. "It's always the same. 'Gerhardt was a good man. He had no enemies. He treated his people well. He and Agnes ate from the same plate and drank from the same cup. Apart from a problem with his joints swelling and aching in bad weather, he was in fine health.' Did I forget anything?"

"Yes, that he's dead," Edgar said. "And we both know there's an answer somewhere. We just haven't asked the right questions."

"Then you go and ask them," Catherine said. "I need to get some cloth to cut Edana a new tunic. Half of what she has is too small and the other half is stained beyond wearing in public."

Edgar left her to it, hoping to find her in a better mood when he returned. He met the monk just outside the *porta nigra*, the northern gate of the town. Berengar was sweating in his black robe and Edgar felt guilty about asking him to take the long walk up toward the castle in such heat.

"Not at all," Berengar said. "It's a small price for the improvement my Latin has received since you and your wife have been here. I've learned so many new words. It will help when I go to Metz as the representative of my abbot."

"And when will that be?" Edgar asked politely.

"In the autumn, I think," Berengar said. "The archbishop is hoping that the pope will consent to come here sometime next year and give a personal judgement on the fight between him and Burgraf Heinrich."

"That's hardly a papal matter, is it?" Edgar commented.

"It is when it involves the jurisdiction of an abbey that answers to Rome," Berengar explained. "Which Saint Maximin's does.

Actually, I think Archbishop Albero wants to use the authority of the pope to bolster his own standing in the town. That's why Abbot Siger wants someone in Metz to speak for us."

"Ah, yes," Edgar said. "There doesn't seem to be a great deal of respect for your archbishop here."

"Well, he is a foreigner, after all," Berengar said. "Oh, dear, I didn't mean any insult to you."

Edgar laughed. "Don't worry, after all these years, I'm either a stranger everywhere or nowhere. Now," he added as they reached the village below the castle. "Where should we begin?"

The village was only a cluster of huts wedged between the river and the hillside. A wooden palisade separated it from the road. Edgar looked at it in puzzlement.

"Is the village often attacked?" he asked.

Berengar grimaced. "Not exactly," he explained. "Pilgrims coming to view the holy tunic seem to feel that they are entitled to whatever they can reach. So the vegetable gardens and chicken runs have been encircled. I don't blame the people here. One can only give so much in alms and still feed one's family."

"Of course." As a pilgrim Edgar had always offered to pay for his food. He didn't feel much sympathy with those who stole under the guise of piety.

They entered by the gate near the dock. Edgar noted that at least three of the buildings had symbols on them indicating that they sold wine and beer. They were much more substantial that the little stone structure marked by the cross over the door.

"There is no parish priest at the moment," Berengar explained. "Lord Gerhardt was to have found another, but he hadn't done so when he died. The cathedral sends one of the canons down to do baptisms and burials when needed."

"Why didn't Lord Gerhardt fill the vacancy at once?" Edgar asked. "Did he want to collect the tithes for himself?"

"Oh no!" Berengar was shocked. "He wasn't that sort. I don't know why. Every time someone asked him he just said that the right person hadn't appeared, yet."

"Interesting," Edgar said. "You'd have thought that he had a poor cousin or bright tenant who could take the job. But I don't suppose it was of any great import, with the canons able to take the sacraments."

They wandered between the cottages, Berengar greeting the inhabitants. Edgar stopped for several minutes to watch a smith repairing a grape cutter. An assistant pumped the bellows until the broken edges were hot enough to solder back together.

"He does good work," Edgar commented. He wished he could stride in, pick up the tongs and go to work himself. But these days he had to set up all sorts of vises to hold a project before he could begin, and his days of using large amount of glowing metal were over. A man needed both hands to manage the weight.

The fumes rising from the forge burned his lungs and his eyes, but he would have given a great deal to spend his days inhaling that acrid air.

Something about the smell set off a memory. Edgar turned to Berengar.

"You know, it seems to me," he said, "that we've been looking at Gerhardt's death from the wrong angle."

"And which angle should we find for a viewpoint?" Berengar seemed to find the idea amusing.

Edgar ignored that. "All we've done is try to find what the man was eating. It's done no good at all. But there are other ways to poison someone. Many a goldsmith has died from breathing quicksilver while trying to mill the metal."

"We have no goldsmiths here," Berengar said. "In Trier, of course, but Lord Gerhardt would have no reason to see them."

"He wouldn't have to." Edgar was becoming enamoured of the idea. "All one would need was quicksilver, trapped in some other element. Most goldsmiths would have it. Did Gerhardt receive any gold objects as a wedding present? No, not gold of course, something else for the quicksilver to be in, good wax candles, perhaps."

"We can ask his sister," Berengar said. "But how could anyone be sure such a thing would harm only Gerhardt?"

Edgar's mood deflated. He had been so certain he was going in the right direction.

"I don't know," he said. "Unless he had a private chapel where only he prayed. I suppose that is too much to hope for."

Berengar looked thoughtful. "I don't think he did, but many people are reticent about making their private devotions public."

"Of course," Edgar agreed. "That leads to hubris."

The monk gave a laugh. "Correct. I should be used to you and your wife by now, but I must admit that in my experience such learning is only found inside a monastery."

"Neither Catherine nor I would last long inside a monastery," Edgar said. "Especially a double house. We have no illusions about our ability to maintain chastity,"

"I wish others were so honest about their weaknesses before taking vows." Berengar sighed. "Now, back to Gerhardt. He may have had a private chapel with candles poisoning the air. But it seems a long chance. However, I think you may have the tail of it now. We've only sought out things the man might have eaten. What if something he touched or breathed were tainted?"

"I've heard of such things," Edgar said. "Although mostly in stories of magic and marvels. Still, it's the first new thread we've had in this skein. Where should we start looking?"

Margaret felt that she had done something wrong but wasn't sure what. It wasn't that her brother and Catherine were treating her unkindly, quite the opposite. They were as careful of her as they had been in the horrible year after her mother died. But why? At first she thought it was because she had made friends with Peter, but they insisted that wasn't anything to fret over. Edgar did say that he thought she shouldn't see him until the business with Catherine's sister was resolved, but that really had nothing to do with her, although she hoped the poor woman would be released soon. So what had changed?

She and James had gone down to the old Roman baths to play. All the broken stones and steps were a wonderful place for hide-and-find. There were other children there who joined in with them. Mindful of Catherine's orders, she always made sure James was in her sight. But he soon tired of the boredom of hiding and decided to amuse himself by climbing up a series of steps on one side of a short hill and rolling down the grass on the other. He seemed happy to continue the routine until dark.

Margaret was sitting at the crest of the hill where she could watch him on both sides when she suddenly felt herself turning red. She could think of no reason to blush until she turned her head and saw Peter a few feet away, watching her.

"Hallo," he said.

"Hallo," she answered.

He scuffed his toe in the dirt.

She rearranged her skirts.

"Hallo," he said again.

"I can't come over," she explained. "I have to mind my nephew."

"Can I come up there?" he asked.

She nodded.

Peter climbed up the steps and then rolled down the hill a few times with James, partly because he felt shy and partly because he was still young enough to think it was fun.

Finally he set James down with an avuncular pat and seated himself next to Margaret.

"Did you come into town with your uncle?" she asked.

"No, I rode by myself," he answered. "After all, I'm the master now. I should be able to do what I like."

"Of course you should," Margaret said firmly.

"I didn't sneak off, either," Peter said. "I told them I was going riding and would be back later."

Margaret was impressed and said so. "Of course, you have a horse," she added sadly.

He understood. "It's different for women."

"I know. But I go out alone in Paris and no one worries," she said, believing it to be true. "And Trier seems a nice, safe little town."

"Well, not always," Peter said. He didn't want her to think he was allowed out simply because there was no danger. "There was a courier murdered and thrown in the river below our castle just a few months ago."

"Really? Who was he?"

"We never found out," Peter admitted. "But I know a secret about it."

"What?"

For a moment Peter considered bargaining for the information but then he remembered Walter's warning. Margaret was to be treated with respect.

"Uncle Hermann gave the message the man carried to my father," Peter whispered, then waited as James careened between them.

"Did he read it?" Margaret asked. "Did you see what was on it?"

"Even more," Peter told her. "I have it. Father tried to scrape off the marks but I was able to retrace the lines."

"Why would he do that?" Margaret breathed.

Peter hesitated. He hated not to have the answer.

"I don't know," he finally admitted. "The message had no words on it, only a drawing of a man and not a very good one, at that."

"Did you ask your father about it?" Margaret said.

"No, I didn't find it until after he died," he answered sadly. "But I recognized the vellum and the place where the wax had been."

"But you should tell someone, Peter," Margaret insisted. "The same person who murdered the courier could have killed your father, too."

She had mixed in French words where she didn't know the German and it took a moment for Peter to understand.

"But how?" he wondered. "There were no strangers around before Father died."

"Well, then," Margaret said, "then they both must have been murdered by someone you know."

She didn't realize how much at that moment she sounded like Catherine.

Peter thought about that for a moment, trying to take it in.

"I never thought we were important or wicked enough for anyone to want to kill us," he said at last. "All we have is a few hectares of vines and a proud name. Who among those around us could wish us dead?"

"Not you!" Margaret was alarmed. "Perhaps your father was part of the revolt against the archbishop and he had him killed."

Peter shook his head. "Everyone knew what side my father was on. He paid tithes and service to the archbishop, but never made a secret of his dislike for the man's arrogance. Anyway, I already told you that we aren't worth the trouble. That's why Uncle Hermann is afraid that your grandfather won't let me marry you."

"My grandfather?" Margaret missed the second part. "He's a lay brother in Scotland. What has he to do with me?"

"But Walter said that your mother's father was the count of Champagne!" Peter insisted.

"Where could he have gotten that idea?" Margaret asked.

Then she remembered the day she had been taken to meet the countess and the odd looks that had passed between her and Catherine. Margaret felt suddenly sick. She stood up and then fell as James knocked her over on his round.

"Are you all right?" Peter helped her up.

"Yes, quite well." Margaret brushed off her skirts absently. "But I have to be going. James! Come with me! It's time to go!"

"No!" James shouted back and ran away.

Peter ran after him and brought him back, the child kicking and wiggling in the crook of his arm.

"Shall I carry him for you?" he asked Margaret.

"James," Margaret said, "do you want to be brought back like a baby or to walk as my escort?"

James kicked a few times more for effect then went limp.

"Walk," he said.

"Thank you, Peter," Margaret said as he set James down. "Let's go, James."

"If you come to the church in the village at the foot of the hill by the castle on Friday afternoon," Peter called after her, "I can show you the message. You can take it to your brother and his wife. Maybe they'll know what it means."

"All right," she called back. "After Tierce."

She didn't look back as she hurried James through the streets to their lodging. She was going to confront Catherine about this at once. Why had no one told her about her grandfather before? Did everyone know but her? Now that she considered it, her mother had spoken little about her family in France and nothing about her father.

It was a very odd feeling to learn that your mother was a bastard.

As they came out of a side street, they nearly collided with a man on horseback, leading another horse. Margaret and James looked up.

"Grandpapa!" James cried, lifting his arms.

Margaret hoisted him up into Hubert's arms. She glanced at the other horse and gave a shout.

"Oh, you found Walter's horse! How wonderful!"

She ran to the house and called for Catherine.

"Come quickly. Look! Your father is home and see what he brought!"

Catherine came to the door with Edana on her hip.

"Father! I'm so glad you're back," she said. "And Walter will be overjoyed when he sees the horse. Where did you find it?"

Hubert handed James down and then dismounted. He hadn't spoken. Catherine looked into his eyes and her throat constricted. She had never thought of her father as truly old until that moment.

"Father," she croaked. "What's wrong? Something about Agnes? What did you find?"

"Agnes?" he said. "Oh that. Yes, I found something but I don't understand it yet. Later. I'll tell you when I get back."

"Back? From where?" Catherine stood with a child in one arm and reins wrapped around the other, staring at her father as if they'd never met.

"Mina's," Hubert said. He closed his eyes and took a deep breath to still his faltering heart. "First, I must go to see Mina."

He left the horses standing and Catherine staring after him in fear.

Seventeen

Trier. 7 Tuesday, 13 kalends September (August 20), 1146; 9 Elul, 4906. Commemoration of the Prophet Samuel, author of the Book of Ruth.

וְטוֹב לָצֵאת וְלָבוֹא אֶל אֲבֵלִים לָךְ, מִבּוֹא בְּבֵית מִשְׁתֶּה וְגִילִים.

It is more praiseworthy to come and go to a house in mourning than to go to a house of feasting and rejoicing.

—Hai ben Sherira Gaon

$\mathcal{H}$ubert came back from his visit to Mina looking haggard and feeling shaken to the bone. Behind him the wailing rose as the news was carried from house to house. He longed to return to share in the communal grief, but feared he wouldn't be welcomed.

Catherine asked no questions when he came in, only kissed him and made him sit and drink a cup of white wine in which she'd steeped mint and borage. The way his hands trembled frightened her and she begged him to lie down for a while.

"No, I don't want to close my eyes," Hubert: replied. "Every time I do I see him, so happy to be almost home and then . . . and then his poor tortured body!"

He dropped the cup and put his face in his hands, sobbing. Catherine knelt and wrapped her arms around him. He put his head on her shoulder and cried out his misery and guilt.

"I should have been with him," he kept repeating.

"Who, Father?" Catherine asked softly.

"Simon! Poor martyred Simon!" he cried.

In fragments he told her what had happened. At first her only reaction was relief that he hadn't been there to die with his friend. Then she remembered Mina and the children, including the one yet to be born. Hubert had asked her a few weeks ago if she knew of anything that could help Mina's morning sickness, but all the remedies Catherine had were already known to the Jewish midwives. Such a shock at this time could cause the poor woman to miscarry.

"What will happen to them, Father?" she asked. "What can we do to help?"

"The community will care for them," Hubert said. "And there is nothing you can do; it was your white monk's preaching that lead to this. And to think I wasn't there to help Simon because I was returning a horse to a man who wears a cross on his chest!"

He clawed at his own chest as if to rip out the pain.

The moment he had seen Hubert's face, Edgar had hurried the children upstairs out of the way. Then he went out hunting for information. As he passed the *judengasse* the keening poured out knifesharp on his ears, made even sharper by the terror at its edge. How long before there would be others to mourn?

There were a number of people coming across the square toward the narrow street, men and women, all with set expressions. Edgar moved to block them, not certain of what he could do. He saw Egilbert, the man who spoke English, among them.

"Egilbert!" he called. "What's happening? Has a plague come to town?"

"Haven't you heard?" Egilbert answered. "Simon's been murdered on his way home."

"So where are all of you going?" Edgar wished that Walter were there to help him keep these people from doing anything violent.

"To see his family, of course," Egilbert said. "They won't eat our food so we couldn't bring the funeral meal, but at least we can give them our consolation and money to help retrieve his body. Simon may have been a Jew but he was also of Trier. He was an honest man and my friend."

Confused, Edgar let the people pass. He had heard that the parents of the townspeople of Trier had slaughtered several Jews and destroyed their holy books and objects in 1096. He wondered how only fifty years could have changed them. But all behavior in this regard was strange to Edgar, who had never seen a Jew until he came to Paris. He had never been able to associate the people he knew with the stories of the Bible, any more than he would confuse the pope today with Saint Peter or judge one on the behavior of the other.

Once he felt certain that the townspeople intended no violence, Edgar returned to the house. There he found that Catherine had given her father another cup, this with some valerian in it, and he was now resting.

"Father blames me, too," Catherine told him. "He thinks I would rejoice at this man's death. How could he? I tried to explain that I would be glad only of a true conversion, but I don't think he saw any difference. When I asked him not to spend so much time with the Jews, I was only thinking of his safety."

"Catherine, it's a chasm neither of us can cross." Edgar smoothed her hair and drew her closer. "We know this from Solomon, no matter how much we care for each other."

Catherine was motionless in his arms. At last she gave a long, shuddering breath.

"We're losing him, aren't we?" she said. "Not all the love we can give seems to be enough to make my father happy. I thought he would try to be a good Christian for the sake of his grandchildren, but I can feel him drifting farther from us every time news comes of another atrocity. What can I do?"

Edgar kissed her forehead. "I don't know, *leoffest*. Only continue loving him, I suppose."

Across the square, the lamentation went on.

Denise was, for the most part, happy with her new life in Köln. She felt that she was being allowed to live with angels. If their bishop should suddenly sprout wings and ascend to heaven, Denise would have felt it only to be expected. There was something about the house that made her feel purified. Slowly she was weaning herself from the weaknesses of the flesh and there was hope that one day she might become a *perfecta* herself. This was a true Christian society.

So the fact that she was doing the laundry at the moment didn't upset her. What she was worrying about was that she, Astolfo and Lanval might have been responsible for bringing a wolf into this innocent fold.

She realized now that she'd been blinded by Andreas's fervor and eagerness to join them. So many others had proven unable to endure the hardships. But since they had arrived in Köln she had grown more doubtful of his sincerity. He had spent more and more time away from the house. She had noticed him outside a tavern one day, drinking with some other men in a way that suggested they knew each other well. She was almost certain that he was eating meat. And now he'd vanished, leaving his second-best clothes behind.

Denise had left his tunic and *brais* until the last, and not just because they stank. She had heard about the Jewish merchant who'd been murdered and that no one was hunting very hard for the men who'd been seen running from the place where it had happened. The incident had revolted her. Denise believed in dying for her faith. She absolutely refused to kill for it.

She held up the *brais*. As she had feared, they were stiff with the brown stains of spilled blood.

"Oh, Andreas," she moaned. "What have you done? And where have you gone?"

Walter's joy at the return of his horse was diminished by Hubert's obvious sense of grief and guilt.

I'll pay you back whatever it cost to buy him," he told Hubert.

"No, thank you, Walter," he answered dully. "Give it to Mina for the children. No, wait, not with that symbol on your clothes. It would be like slapping her. Take it to the *parnas* of the community. He'll see that she gets it."

Walter went into the back garden where the rest of the family had gone to escape the heat.

"I never thought I'd feel ashamed of wearing a cross," he said. "How can this monk claim to be a follower of Abbot Bernard and preach such things? The abbot made it very clear that we go to fight the infidel because they have attacked the holy places with swords. What harm had Simon ever done anyone?"

"Something has to be done, before more people die," Catherine said.

"From what I've seen in the past few days, I don't think anything like that will happen in Trier, at least," Edgar said. "Most of the people in town seem truly shocked by what happened."

"I thought it couldn't happen in Paris," Catherine reminded him. "But we saw the mob there. It doesn't take a whole town to do such things. Only a few people full of hate and many more who are cowards."

Edgar heard the self-loathing in her voice.

"It's hard to risk everything for a faith you don't share," he argued. "Would you stand between a mob and its victims if it meant leaving your children motherless?"

Edana had just run to her with a scraped knee. Catherine kissed it and embraced her fiercely before sending her back to play. Edgar went on.

"Would you have wanted your father to choose to die defending Simon? Or for me to be killed along with him, if Solomon were attacked?"

"That's not fair!" Catherine said. "We could never leave Solomon to the mercy of rabble!"

Edgar smiled. "Of course not. But could we be as brave for strangers?"

Catherine hated to say it but he was waiting for the answer. "I don't know," she said. "I wish I could be sure but I can't. It's true that in Paris my only thought was to save the children. It's so much easier when there's no one you love that needs protection." She gave a rueful smile. "When I read about the Christian mothers who exhorted their children to face the lions bravely, I begin to think my faith isn't what it should be. Yes, you're right. I won't judge others as cowards unless I can prove I would do better."

There was a knock at the door. Edgar went to answer it.

Brother Berengar smiled at him.

"I have news," he said. "I spoke with our infirmarian, Brother Zacharias, and he knows of several concoctions that could kill a man without his eating them."

He was so cheerful about this that Edgar was forced to laugh.

"Come in," he said. "Catherine will want to hear your information, too."

Once Berengar was settled in the garden with a plate of grapes and cheese next to him, he resumed his explanation.

"Zacharias says that many medicines work by penetrating the body's other orifaces and shouldn't be eaten," he said. "And if medicines will work in this way, there are caustic substances that can also be administered in the same way to cause death."

"That's logical," Catherine said. "What sort of substance should we be looking for?"

"Well, he wasn't sure about that," Berengar said. "I almost believe that he was worried that I was planning to use one myself, the way he scrutinized me. But I finally got him to suggest that we look for something Gerhardt would use often and that was only his, such as Edgar's idea about candles. If he had hemorrhoids, there's a soft white stone that one grinds to a powder and applies. It would be simple to adulterate it with a harmful powder."

"But did he?" Catherine asked.

Berengar shrugged. "Not that I know of. That was only an example. There are things one inhales for a congestion of the nose and head also."

"The point is that Gerhardt needn't have eaten the poison that killed him," Edgar finished. "Now we have more possibilities."

Catherine wasn't so elated by this. "That might only pointed the way back to Agnes. And even when we know how, it will still be hard to discover who. If the poison was in something like a medicine, he might have received it anywhere, at any time. It wouldn't have to have been someone in the household who prepared it. In my opinion, we've only made the number of suspects greater and our likelihood of solving this that much less."

The two men looked at her in disappointment.

"We can't think that way, Catherine," Edgar said.

"Maybe not, but it would be much more useful if we could find just one enemy for this man. No one has yet had a word against him. Autumn is coming soon and we're no closer to saving Agnes than the day we arrived." Catherine's eyes filled. "I'm sorry, Edgar. Please excuse me."

She ran back into the house. Berengar looked after her in sympathy.

"This must be a very difficult time for her," he commented. "To have the life of a beloved sister hanging in the balance for so long and then to be living in a strange place, as well."

"Yes, I suppose," Edgar said absently. He suspected, despite Catherine's earlier denial, that there was another child on the way. After almost seven years, three births and too many miscarriages, he thought he knew the signs.

He drew his attention back to the monk.

"What were you saying?"

"I said that I think we should go up to the castle and find out if Lord Gerhardt was afflicted with hemorrhoids," Berengar said. "His brother would probably know."

The prospect of another long hot walk just to ask one question didn't excite Edgar.

"Perhaps we could ask when we visit Agnes again," he suggested. "I don't want to leave my family now while they're so unsettled by Simon's death. Is it likely that Hermann will come into town soon? We might contact him then."

"It's possible," Berengar said. "Gerhardt sometimes arranged to have his wine shipped with that of the archbishop. I understand that Hermann has been to the bishop's palace often recently, perhaps to discuss this. On my way back to the monastery, I'll stop at the palace and ask if he's expected any time soon."

Edgar stood to see him out. "Thank you, Berengar. I'm sorry to have brought you out in this heat for so little."

"Not at all." Berengar smiled. "A little warmth now may spare me a greater one later. And convey my sympathies to your friend's family. I heard on my way here. Wicked, wicked men!"

After he left, Edgar went up to see about Catherine. He found her with Margaret, showing her how to do a complicated embroidery knot. All trace of tears was gone.

"Did you give my apologies to Brother Berengar?" she asked. "I can't imagine what was wrong with me."

"I can," Edgar answered. "And he was not at all insulted."

Catherine looked up at him. He held her eyes, daring her to prove he was wrong. Margaret watched them, puzzled. At last, Catherine lowered her eyes and nodded.

"I didn't want to add to our problems here," she said to him. "Why does this always seem to happen when we travel?"

He stooped and took her in his arms.

"You'll be fine," he said. "If we can't get home in time, we'll stay right here until you're both well enough."

"By then I may actually have mastered this dreadful language." Catherine sniffed.

Understanding was dawning on Margaret.

"Oh, how wonderful!" she exclaimed. "I hope it's another girl."

Edgar held out his left arm to her and she took it in both her hands.

"I think we'd rather wait a while before telling Hubert," he said. "He has enough to worry about. Do you promise not to mention this until I give you permission?"

"Of course, Brother," she answered. "But I wouldn't wait too long. I remember the last time. Catherine did not enjoy her food and everyone was extremely aware of it."

"Especially on the boat back to France." Catherine grimaced. "Never again."

Edgar put his hand over her stomach. "I promise. This time, no boats."

He was already wondering where they could find a midwife who understood French. The muscles in his neck were beginning to tense. No matter how pleased he was with the news, it was also one more thing for him to worry about.

Bernard de Fontaines, abbot of Clairvaux, and arguably the most influential man in Christendom, was enjoying a rare moment of private meditation. Though he was fond of his friends and always mindful of his duties, Bernard was happiest when he could be alone with God.

He was aware of the interruption long before the knock came on his door in Metz. The argument was being carried on in whispers more piercing that shouts would have been.

Bernard arranged his face to tolerance.

"Geoffrey, Nicholas, what brings you here at the time of afternoon response?" he asked pleasantly.

The two monks avoided looking at each other. Nicholas stepped forward.

"I hate to disturb you, my lord abbot," he said.

Geoffrey gave a sound something like a snort. Nicholas paused.

"It was my doing, my lord," Geoffrey said. "This message just arrived, and considering the other news from Germany, I felt you should know at once."

Bernard was alert at once. His eyes lit. "The emperor has decided to take the cross!" he exclaimed.

"No, Lord Abbot," Nicholas said. "Joyous news like that I would have sung from the belltower of the cathedral. Geoffrey?"

Geoffrey's head slid back into his cowl like a turtle trying to avoid a blow.

"Forgive me," he said. "But I'm afraid the news is unsettling. Despite your letters, the monk Radulf has continued his exhortations for the extermination of the Jews. Last week, a mob in Köln murdered a trader of Trier. There have been other reports of destruction and beatings. A woman in Speyer had her nose and thumbs cut off because she refused to convert. They say that this Radulf has now moved on to Mainz to continue his false preaching."

The two monks waited for some reaction from the abbot. His lips tightened, as if to hold back the words that threatened to erupt. His right hand moved into a fist and then, with an effort, opened again.

"Nicholas," he said. "Prepare for us to leave at once. Geoffrey, see to it that my traveling altar and vessels are packed. Everything else can follow later. We'll stop at Trier on our way to Frankfurt. Send another letter to the bishop of Mainz warning him of this demon. He must be stopped."

The monks bowed and left.

Alone again, Bernard's thoughts were far from peaceful. He fell to his knees.

"A man has died, Lord," he wept. "Through my words, however much they had been twisted. Even worse, this soul died in darkness, before he could be convinced to come to You. The people heeded me so eagerly when I asked them to take up arms for Your sake. How could they become so deaf when I forbid them to harm the Jews? Help me. Send me the wisdom to prevent this evil from spreading."

He remained in prayer until called to Vespers.

As they went to make the preparations for departure Nicholas turned to Geoffrey. "You see what you've done?" he complained. "If you'd been willing to wait, I could have told him more gently, along with other matters. Now he's decided to set off on an uncomfortable journey with not enough time to make ready."

Geoffrey had no sympathy even though he wasn't overly fond of Jews, himself. "We were going to Frankfurt soon, anyway. If leaving earlier will save a life, or a soul, then we should be glad to do so."

Nicholas muttered something in reply. Geoffrey prayed for the day when he would be free of this insufferable man. Then he went to get ready for the journey. He didn't mind the travel, at all, if Nicholas suffered too.

Besides, he'd always wanted to see the Holy Shroud at the cathedral in Trier. He might never have another opportunity.

∞

It was Friday afternoon. Hermann and his brother-in-law were taking advantage of Maria's absence to do nothing down by the river.

"How long do you think it will take her to deliver alms to the cottagers?" Hermann asked from under his woven hat.

"Most of the afternoon, I hope," Folmar answered. "She likes to be thanked enthusiastically."

"You haven't been going with her, lately," Hermann commented.

"To be honest, I became tired of listening to the sermons she delivered with the bread," Folmar confessed. "Some women know how to preach without preaching and others don't, if you follow me."

"Of course," Hermann answered. "She is my sister."

They were silent for a while. A boat went by, headed upstream under sail. Folmar watched it from under his hat.

"Isn't it time someone decided what to do with that woman in our tower?" he asked. "The harvest is approaching, after all."

"To tell you the truth," Hermann lowered his voice, "I know what I'd like to do with her."

Folmar raised himself on one elbow and tilted his hat back.

"You astonish me," he said. "Especially considering what happened to Gerhardt. Well, if you're brave enough, she's right there and you have the key. Why don't you?"

Hermann lifted his hat from his face and turned to Folmar.

"I want to marry her first," he said.

"What? *Es ist dîn spot!*" Folmar sat up. He held his hand up and began to count. "I can think of several reasons why I'm sure you've suddenly lost all sense. Firstly, the woman was married to your brother. Secondly, she may have murdered him. Thirdly, even if the first two could be overcome, you've held her prisoner for several months now. She might not be inclined to remain here."

"I know all that." Hermann replaced his hat. "But she hasn't been harmed while in our care. Also, I don't believe that she did kill Gerhardt. Finally, I could marry her if the first marriage was never consummated."

Folmar leaned over and slid Hermann's hat to one side.

"What makes you think it wasn't?" he asked, his eyes narrowing. "Did Gerhardt tell you something?"

"Not in so many words," Hermann admitted. "But I'm almost

sure of it now. Maria finally admitted to me that the sheets in the marriage bed were unstained. If Agnes is proved innocent of murder, she might be proved innocent in other respects. We could get the archbishop to . . ."

He stopped. His fantasy hadn't considered that. Archbishop Albero wasn't likely to do favors for a minor lord who had taken the side of the townspeople against him.

Folmar lay down again. "I think your scheme has too many barriers to surmount. Why don't you just rape her and have done with it?"

"Folmar!"

The tone said that Hermann was truly angry.

"I wasn't serious," Folmar said quickly. "I know you wouldn't. But I doubt very much that you'll have her any other way. You didn't bother to mention that her family might also object to Agnes staying here with a man who has little property of his own and fewer prospects. Or that, if the sight of you should please her, she still might not want to remain in a place where she had gone through so much."

Hermann got up. "Thank you. I knew that confiding in you would destroy any hope I had."

"Life isn't a minstrel's tale, Herman." Folmar sighed. "I wouldn't be here if it were."

Brother Berengar was delighted with the progress that Peter was making with French. He realized that the boy's questions would soon go far beyond what he could teach.

"It's a shame you can't have your stepmother help you," he said.

"Do you think she would?" Peter asked.

"She might," the monk answered. "It must be dull up there all alone."

Peter jumped up and ran from the room. In a moment he was back.

"I know where Uncle Hermann keeps the key," he explained. "Shall we go up and ask her?"

Agnes heard the voices whispering at the door and felt a stab of fear that became a stab of pain as she stuck herself accidentally with her needle. When the door opened. Peter and Berengar found her sucking her finger. She didn't seem happy to see them. Peter held up a tray of bread, fruit and beans.

"Isn't it early for food?" she asked.

Berengar shrugged. Agnes indicated that Peter should put the tray on the table. She tasted a peach.

"*Guot*," she said.

"*Merci*," Peter answered shyly.

Agnes broke off a corner of the bread. She looked up. Peter and Berengar were still there.

"Well? What now?" she asked.

"We think . . . thought, *daz ist*, Peter want French to learn," Berengar explained.

"From you?" Agnes raised her eyebrows.

"We hope from you," Berengar said.

Peter smiled. Agnes set down her sewing and looked around for a cloth to wrap her finger in. The other two waited nervously. When she had finished, she looked at them.

Peter did seem a nice boy. And the days were very long.

"Very well," she said. "What have you taught him so far?"

Berengar explained. Agnes corrected and Peter tried as hard as he could to learn. The afternoon went surprisingly quickly and Agnes was secretly delighted when Peter asked if he might come back the next day.

"Peter," Berengar said at last, "I think I hear your aunt returning. We should go down and greet her."

"Oh yes." Peter picked up the wax tablet he'd been writing new words on. "I don't know if she'd approve of this. *À reviser, ma dame.*"

"Excellent." Agnes smiled.

They hurried out. Neither one of them noticed that they hadn't locked the door. But Agnes did.

Peter clattered down the stairs and arrived breathless in front of his aunt.

"What were you doing up there?" she asked suspiciously.

"You were so late, Aunt, that I thought I should take Agnes her dinner," Peter explained. "Brother Berengar went with me."

Maria noticed the monk as he entered the hall.

"That was generous of you," she told Peter. "It will save your uncle Hermann the trouble of going up when he returns."

"There's hours of light left," Peter said casually. "I think I'll go out for a while."

"How far?" Maria asked.

"Oh, just down to the village," Peter told her. "I want to see if the potter has a pitcher to replace the one I dropped last week."

It seemed reasonable, but Maria sensed an eagerness in the boy that couldn't have been caused by a desire to atone for an accident. However, she was feeling more indulgent lately with the vision of a fine dowry from Margaret's grandfather glittering in her mind.

"Very well," she agreed. "If you see either of your uncles, you might remind them that they haven't ordered the vats prepared for the new harvest, yet."

"Yes, Aunt." Peter ran up to his father's old room and rummaged in a linen casket until he found the mysterious paper. Then he splashed some water on his face and swished his hands through the basin, wiping them on the back of his tunic.

Maria was consulting with the cook when he raced back through the hall.

"Back before Vespers!" she called after him.

He barely heard her.

When he reached the village, he noticed that there was some commotion over by the well. Several men were milling about, seeming both pleased and sheepish. He knew all of them but one and considered going over to see what it was all about but was afraid that if he did, he'd miss Margaret. He didn't want her to think he'd forgotten their meeting.

The bells ringing for Vespers clanged on Hubert's ears like hammer blows. How could poor Mina bear the sound? He entered the gateway to her street and cringed as people peeked out windows and then stepped back into the shadows.

The door was open and the area resonated with the prayers of lamentation. Hubert almost went away but Mina came out of the back room and saw him standing on the threshold. She held out her hands to him and, gratefully, he entered.

He took his place among the other mourners and bowed his head. After a few moments he began to sway back and forth with the others to the rhythm of the prayers.

"*Baruch atta Adonai,*" he murmured. "Forgive me, Lord of the universe. Forgive me for my ignorance. I can't even speak to you in the language you gave us. But accept my prayer for your martyr, Simon, and for his family. Hover over them and protect them in these dark times. Let his sons, Asher and Levi, grow strong in the Torah and become filled with wisdom. Let his daughter be above rubies to her husband and may they never suffer the sorrow their mother has now."

He closed his eyes and let the words around him flow into his heart. After some time he felt a light touch on his shoulder. He looked up. Mina smiled down on him, despite her face streaked with tears and her rent veil.

"He would not have wanted you to bear guilt with your grief," she said. "The Holy One, blessed be He, has given Simon an honored place in the garden, along with your mother and sisters. We should rejoice that they are now saints."

"It's so, Hubert," one of the men agreed. "You can't spend your life saying, 'If I had done this, then that wouldn't have happened.' Simon doesn't blame you, and neither do we."

Hubert covered his face with his hands. When he dropped them, his cheeks were wet.

"Thank you, thank you all," he said. "I came to try to give Mina some comfort and I've found it for myself, instead."

He stayed with them until the stars came out. Mina lit the Sabbath candles and the *shabbas goy* appeared at the door with a torch to lead the men to their homes.

"Will you stay and eat with us?" Mina asked.

"My daughter will be worried if I don't return soon," he said. The room was still filled with family, ready to see that Mina wouldn't have to bear her grief alone. They didn't need him. Catherine, and most of all Agnes, did.

He let himself in to their lodging and was surprised to see everyone still up. Edana was dozing in her mother's lap, but James sat by the cold hearth and watched the adults with wide eyes. Walter and

Edgar were lacing up their boots, as if preparing to go out. When he entered, everyone looked up. He saw the disappointment on their faces when they realized he was alone.

"What's wrong?" he asked. "Why aren't the children in bed? Has something happened to Agnes?"

"You didn't take Margaret with you, did you?" Edgar asked, going back to struggling with his bootlacings.

"No, I was at Mina's. Why?" Hubert said, cold creeping into his stomach.

"Margaret went out sometime this afternoon and never came back." Catherine's voice broke and she hid her face in Edana's hair.

"We've asked all over town," Walter added. "Someone thought they saw her on the river road. We're riding that way now."

"Stay with Catherine," Edgar said. "One of us will return if there's news."

Hubert nodded numbly and sagged onto a stool. None of them voiced what they were all thinking. Margaret was a dutiful child. She would never run off without telling someone. Margaret was also almost a woman and more men than Peter had noticed.

For the second time that night, Hubert began to pray.

Eighteen

Trier. Early in the morning of Saturday, 9 kalends September
(August 24), 1146; 13 Elul, 4906. Feast of Saint Eptadus of
Autun, who ransomed Arian captives of King Clovis and sent
them home free and unconverted; *Parashat Ki Teze*.

Olimbrius et autre gent
qui o lui erent a torment
Quand il voient de sa char tendre
De totes pars le sanc espandre,
Lor ex et lor chieres covroient
Car esgarder ne le pooient.

When Olimbrius and the other people
Who were with him at the torture
Saw how her tender flesh
was covered all over with blood
They covered their eyes and faces,
For they could not bear to look.

—Wace
Life of Saint Margaret of Antioch

*T*hey're hiding something," Walter told Edgar. "And they're frightened."

"I know." In the light of the full moon, Edgar's face was grey from worry and lack of sleep. "Something happened to her after she reached this village. Something bad enough that no one will tell us what it was."

Walter didn't answer. From the way the men's eyes had darted when he questioned them, refusing to look at him directly, he feared the worst. There was no point in his telling Edgar this. Edgar's mind already saw the horrors that might have happened.

"What next?" he asked instead.

"Hermann is lord of this village," Edgar said. "If he can't get these men to talk then I'll ask him to have their homes taken apart, log and stone, until there's no place left small enough to hide her."

Walter mounted his horse and Edgar the mule and they both set out for the castle. Behind them a group of villagers gathered. As soon as Edgar and Walter were out of sight, in silent agreement, the group headed for the church. The moon cast long shadows from behind so that it seemed as if there were phantoms walking in front of them.

"Are you sure the girl was Jewish?" one man said. "What if it's the same one?"

"I saw her with the Jews in Provins," Andreas answered. "And again in the town here. The old man who lives with them stayed in a Jewish house when he was in Köln. These people are only pretending to be like us, the better to destroy us. You did the right thing."

"Walter of Grancy is no Jew," the man said, doubt creeping into his voice.

"Ah, but he's been taken in by them, ensorcelled," Andreas whispered. "Just the way your poor lord was by that woman. The merchant's daughter, they say, but he's dark and she's fair as you are. Who ever heard of that?"

"Well, there was Johann from Pfalzel," another spoke up. "His mother was from the south, but he was blond like his father."

"Of course," Andreas said. "Children are in their father's image. Everyone knows that. But I'll wager this one was born dark like her sister and wove spells to change her looks so that she could ensnare your lord. And the red-haired girl did the same."

"How do you know what the sister looks like?" the man asked. "I thought you only passed through here once before."

"Isn't that your wife calling you?" Andreas said. "I told you, I saw them in Provins, and then again here, when I stopped on my pilgrimage to venerate the Holy Shroud."

"Even if they are all Jews and possessed by the devil and we did well to destroy this girl," a third man broke in, "we still have to get rid of the body before those at the castle find out. If you're right, then they've all been magicked as well and won't reward us for killing her."

They had reached the church door by now. The bar was still in place.

"We'll throw her in the river," Andreas told them. "If she's ever found, no one will know where she went in. Now, hurry, before those men bring down help."

The bar was lifted and the men crowded into the little church. One took out his flint and struck it until the lamp by the door was lit. They all looked toward the altar where they had left the girl arranged like an offering that afternoon.

It was empty.

All but Andreas crossed themselves.

"Who's been in here? Tell me," he demanded.

There was a mumbled argument. Then one man spoke for them all.

"None of us," he said. "We all went back to finish the drinks we were in the middle of when you pointed her out to us."

Andreas ignored the reproach. "One of you came back and removed the body."

"No, then we all went back home to wash off the smell of blood," the man insisted.

"And the shame," a voice murmured.

"Someone came back for her," Andreas insisted. "You heard that the Jews will pay well to have the bodies of their baptized dead returned so they can wash off the sacrament."

"They will?" the argumentative man said. "I didn't know that."

"Andreas, no one among us wanted anything more to do with this," the spokesman said. "We all had chores to finish. No one was about until those men came and called us from our families to help in their search."

"I suppose Satan flew by to claim his own," Andreas sneered.

There was some agreement to this, but the naysayer shook his head firmly.

"Everyone knows the devil can't enter a church."

"Are you sure?" someone asked. "I thought he just couldn't stay for the elevation of the host."

"That's demons," the other corrected him. "Satan is so wicked that the holiness inside the building would break him into slivers."

Andreas lost patience.

"Look, you left the body here and barred the door," he said. "It's not here now, so someone came and got it. We have to find it."

"Why?" came a voice. Andreas could tell whose.

"Because . . ." Then he thought. Why indeed? No one in the village would confess if there were punishment in the offing and everyone would if there were ransom money. The girl's body could stay wherever they had hidden it for now. After all, he had bigger things to do.

"Very well," he said. "Someone has taken care of the problem for us. Now, go home. You've done a good day's work, ridding the world of another one of them."

They dispersed quickly but, as they went, Andreas caught one querulous comment.

"I thought we were only going to baptize her. What was the point of killing her, too?"

Andreas shook his head. He had thought this preaching would

be profitable work and less dangerous than the company of heretics, but if these and the men in Köln were the kind of people he had to rely on, it might be safer to go back to slitting throats on dark pathways.

To Agnes, it seemed forever before the bells tolled for Compline and the castle settled into silence. All evening she had been sure that someone would come and find the door unlocked. Then, as dusk came, it was hard not to leave too soon and run the risk of being discovered. She had schooled herself to calmness for so long that it wasn't until there was a chance of freedom that she realized how desperately she wanted it.

She kept herself awake during the dark hours by trying to think where she would go. Not to her family. That's the first place they would look. Not to Jehan, that would be the second place. Also, she told herself, if she appeared and begged him to ride off with her, she would probably have to marry him and that was too high a price for her liberty.

In the end, she decided to wrap up the bread, cheese and fruit left in her room and head south, following the river until she heard French again. After that, she would have to trust to the Virgin and the saints to protect her.

The door creaked as she pulled it open. Agnes was sure there would be a burst of activity as everyone leaped out to capture her.

There was only the sound of a dog far across the fields, howling at the moon.

The passageway was lit by a single torch left at the top of the staircase. Slowly she felt her way down the steps and into the main hall. Here the moonlight was bright enough to make her way around the sleeping forms of the attendants. She knew the main gate would be shut and barred but she also remembered a small door at the back that led into an herb garden and from there it was only necessary to find a break in the withy fence. Then she would be safe from discovery amidst the burgeoning vines.

She left the hall and reached the anteroom where buckets and drying racks were kept. The little door was only latched. She reached out to open it.

At that moment there came a clamor at the gate that nearly

caused her to faint. Someone was pounding and calling, demanding entrance. Now the noises she had dreaded were echoing throughout the castle. For a moment, she was tempted to open the door and run, but she would be seen in the moonlight from any window. Instead, she crawled beneath the drying racks that were laden with herbs, and hid in a corner. If only no one thought to check on her in her room, she might still get away when the commotion was over.

At the gate Edgar and Walter waited impatiently. At last they heard a shutter open and a voice called down.

"Saint Lazarus's stinking corpse! What do you want at this hour?"

"It's Walter of Grancy, and I want to be let in and then I want you to fetch your master. It's urgent."

The shutter slapped shut.

"Do you think he'll get Hermann?" Edgar asked.

"We've woken the whole castle," Walter said. "I imagine Hermann will be down at once. I would be in his place."

After a few moments, the gate was lifted and Walter and Edgar rode into the courtyard. Hermann was standing at the door to the keep in his bare feet, wearing a short tunic that he had thrown on but not taken time to belt.

"Walter!" he yelled. "Are you drunk? What are you doing here in the middle of the night?"

Walter and Edgar dismounted and hurried to him.

"I want to see your nephew, Peter," Edgar said, his face grim.

"Peter? Why?"

Walter edged between Hermann and Edgar. His hand was heavy on Edgar's shoulder.

"The Lady Margaret is missing," he explained. "She was last seen coming in this direction."

"She isn't here," Hermann said. "We haven't seen her."

"Perhaps you haven't," Walter said. "But we know how taken the boy is with her. It's not like Margaret to vanish. She's a shy creature who wouldn't go off alone without telling anyone unless she thought she wouldn't be alone for long. Peter was our first guess."

Hermann closed his eyes. "Yes, it's just the sort of stupid thing they would do at that age. Ulrich! Go see if Lord Peter is in his bed.

If he is, then bring . . . no, he *is* the master here, ask him to come down."

He turned back to Walter and Edgar.

"I remember that Peter did go out for some time this afternoon," he said. "And he was unusually rude during dinner. I thought that it was only the strain of his new position in the household."

Walter translated for Edgar.

The soldier soon appeared followed by Peter wrapped in a sheet and with his hair tousled by sleep.

"What is it?" he asked. "Did Margaret send you?"

Walter explained. Halfway through Peter let out a groan.

"It's my fault!" he said. "I asked her to meet me in the village. She didn't come and I thought she'd decided not to see me. I should have asked someone. I should have looked for her! Guards! I want every man on this estate out with torches hunting for her at once!"

The soldier glanced at Hermann but before he could answer Peter shouted at him.

"Don't look to my uncle! I am master here! Gather the men to start the search."

The man left at once.

Peter stood in the door way, stunned at the response to his assumption of authority. Then his lower lip began to tremble.

"They will find her, won't they, Uncle?" he asked.

"Of course," Hermann answered. He was glad that the boy hadn't asked if they would find her alive.

At that moment Maria and Folmar arrived, rumpled but dressed.

"What is the meaning of this?" Maria said.

"Margaret is lost," Peter told her. He was still trying to keep back tears.

The whole story had to be explained again.

Folmar listened with growing concern. "Peter, was there a stranger among the villagers when you were there this afternoon?"

"Yes, a tall, lean man, with a face like gnarled wood," Peter answered. "I watched them a long time while I was waiting. He seemed to be the center of the conversations."

"What is it?" Edgar asked.

"I'm not sure," Walter answered. "Peter says there was someone in the village today, a stranger."

"Margaret would never have let herself be lured away by some-one she didn't know," Edgar stated.

"She might if he said he had a message for her," Walter sug-gested.

"No, not even then," Edgar was sure. "She knows that dodge. I think we should go back to the village. If she made it that far, someone must have seen her."

"I agree," Walter said and translated for the others. "Hermann, Peter, will you come with us? Perhaps they'll tell you what they're afraid to admit to us."

"Yes, of course," Hermann said and Peter nodded. "Let us get dressed. I'll have some food sent down to you."

Edgar flopped onto a bench in the hall. He lifted his left arm to rub his eyes and looked again in surprise at the space where his hand had been. Would he ever get used to it? He switched to the right. If Margaret were found whole and well he would never again com-plain about what he had lost.

"Please, God, keep her safe," he begged, all other prayers for-gotten.

It was only a few moments before Peter and Hermann returned. Maria had gone to the kitchen and gathered up a bag of dried ven-ison, cheese and new carrots for them to eat on the way.

"Save some for the child, when you find her," she said. "I shall pray for her constantly."

Walter thanked her.

"Where are my riding boots?" Hermann asked suddenly.

"In the drying room," Maria told him. "They were covered in mud. I'll send Hulda for them."

"No, I'll go myself," Hermann said. "No sense in wasting time. Have the horses ready. I'll meet you all in the courtyard in a mo-ment."

Edgar wearily sat up and prepared to ride again. He glared at Peter who was sitting in his own misery nearby.

Peter looked up at him. His eyes plead for some reassurance, but Edgar was too frightened and far too angry to give him any. He got up, pulled on his riding glove with his teeth, and strode out.

Peter turned to Walter.

"He thinks she's dead, doesn't he?"

Walter had exhausted his sympathy as well.

"Yes," he said. "Don't you?"

Herman grabbed an oil lamp as he left for the drying room. It gave less light than a torch but he was mindful of all the things in there that could easily burn. As he entered, he set it on a shelf and began rummaging around the floor for his boots.

"There's one, damn it," he muttered. "Now where's the other?"

He got down on his hands and knees and felt under the drying racks. His fingers touched something and he grabbed at it.

"Ee! Eeep!" Something squeaked.

Hermann pulled his hand back at once and then reached for it again. It was definitely a boot and there was also a foot in it.

"Come out of there now!" he commanded.

There was a rustle and a blond head appeared from beneath the herbs. Agnes stood up and dusted herself off, her expression a mixture of defiance and fear.

"How did you get here?" Hermann asked.

The meaning was clear if the words weren't.

"I can't stay locked up any more," Agnes said. "I didn't kill your brother. I don't know why he died. Let me go, please!"

She knelt before him, her hands raised and clasped. "Ich wil iuch biten flêhelîch, mîn Herr," she said carefully. "I beg you, my lord."

Hermann stood with one boot in his hand, totally at a loss. "Saint Jerome's naked visions!" he breathed. "You are so beautiful."

He dropped the boot and raised her to her feet.

"Agnes, I don't know what to do," he said, still holding her arms. "You can't go out there; it's dangerous. But I don't want to drag you back to your room in front of your friends. Please, stay here until I return. Will you? Do you understand anything I'm saying?."

Her face showed only puzzlement. But she didn't try to move away from him. He could feel her breath in small puffs against his neck.

"Hermann?" she said.

"Please don't go," he answered.

His hands moved up to her shoulders and slid around her back. Still she didn't struggle. Her breasts beneath the thin summer shift were outlined in the flickering light.

Agnes gazed up at him with wonder.

"Hermann," she said.

Then he lost his mind completely and kissed her. The intensity of her response startled them both.

"My boots," he said when he could speak again. "I have to find them. Edgar is waiting for me."

He picked up the one and started looking for the other. Agnes watched him, then dove back under the herb racks and brought out the other boot. She handed it to him.

"Thank you," he said. "Agnes?"

Slowly, she smiled. "Hermann?"

He yanked the boots on, then took her hands in his.

"Don't go," he said again. "Wait for me here."

She studied his face, considering. Then she moved her hands to over his heart.

"Here," she repeated.

"Hermann!" Maria's call was piercing. "What's keeping you?"

"Coming!" he called back. "I couldn't find my boots."

"You should have sent one of the servants," Maria told him as he emerged into the night. "They always know where things are."

Early the next morning, Catherine was roused from her fitful sleep by a knock. She hurried to the door, her heart pounding.

"Mina!" she said when she saw the visitor. "What is it? Father! Come quickly!"

The woman was standing nervously in the sunlight and ducked in as soon as Catherine opened the door far enough.

Hubert came down the stairs, still dressed from the night before.

"Mina! You're in mourning," he exclaimed. "What are you doing out?"

"I had to tell you," she said. "I heard about the little girl being missing. I'm so sorry,"

"Thank you," Hubert said. "But . . ."

"Late last night word came to us that a young Jewish girl had been captured in a village north of here," Mina said. "Some men in a tavern saw her and dragged her into a church, where they baptized her, beat her and left her for dead."

"Oh dear God in heaven!" Hubert gasped.

Catherine saw the look and ran to them, her heart in her throat. Mina patted her hand and went on talking to Hubert. Catherine stood in an agony of fear. When Mina finished, Hubert thanked her again. She gave Catherine a gentle kiss for comfort and left.

"Tell me, Father," Catherine said when the door had closed. "It's Margaret, isn't it? What's happened?"

"Mina says that some monsters from a nearby village are said to have attacked a Jewish girl to force her into baptism, but there are none missing from the community here," he said. "She's afraid from the description that it may have been Margaret."

Catherine swayed. She felt that all the humors of her body had suddenly rearranged themselves. The room wavered in front of her. Hubert caught her just as she fell.

"Oh, my dear, try to keep up hope," he said. "It may not have been she. A servant from the town on an errand, perhaps. Not Margaret! She would have proved that she was a Christian."

Catherine's head slowly cleared. She heard the end of what her father was saying.

"You know what mobs are like," she said. "They may not have given her the chance. She doesn't have much German. Oh, my Margaret! Father, go find Edgar. Tell him to look in the village church for her. And then come back as soon as you can, before I go mad from dread."

In a hut on the edge of the village, an old woman sat on the dirt floor, next to the straw that was her bed. Outside, despite the heat, a fire blazed, heating water in a large cauldron so the woman could wash the sheets and table linen of the lords and richer peasants. On the bed lay Margaret.

She wasn't completely conscious, yet. All she was aware of was pain and terror.

"Mama!" she called. "Mama!"

The old woman wiped the child's face with a damp rag.

"There, there, *süzelin*," she crooned. "We'll find your mama as soon as you're better. Those horrible men. You'll get to Heaven sooner than their sort, for all you're an infidel Jewess. Don't worry, *trutgeselin*, I won't let them find you. Vinta will take care of you. You're safe with me."

Edgar wiped his face with his sleeve. He was exhausted and his temper was being held in check only by the knowledge that he had to remain steady for Margaret's sake.

"Ask him again what they did with her after they dragged her to the font," he said to Walter.

The four of them were seated in the church with a somewhat battered man kneeling before them.

Hermann glanced at Walter as he repeated the question.

"Rolf can't tell us more than he knows," he said. "But he shall tell all of that. Isn't that right, Rolf?"

Rolf was acutely aware of the soldiers standing behind him and of Walter's bulk in front. But none of them frightened him as much as the thought of what he had done to endanger his soul.

"When she made the sign of the cross, we thought she was mocking us," he said again. "Andreas said that she needed to be taught a lesson and then given God's grace to be sure she remembered it. Once we were inside the church we only hit her with our fists and feet. We wouldn't draw a weapon before the altar."

Edgar winced at the memory of the altar candles shining on his father's sword before the blow fell through his wrist. At the same time Peter shuddered at the thought of Margaret being mauled by these men.

The peasant noticed both movements and added, "No one raped her. We weren't after that. We were acting simply for the good of her soul. Forgive me, Lords. I only went with the others. I didn't strike her, myself. I didn't know she was a Christian."

Edgar stood. Rolf cringed before him, waiting for the blow. Instead Edgar walked past him.

"Get this thing out of my sight," he said.

Walter followed him out. He found Edgar emptying his stomach into a pigsty.

"We brought Margaret with us because I thought it wasn't safe enough in Troyes." He gulped. "I should have left her in Scotland where she was known. This never would have happened." A new thought struck him. "Oh, Walter, how can we tell Solomon she's dead? You know she means almost as much to him as she does to me."

"Don't lose hope, yet," Walter pleaded. "Everyone we've spoken to says the body was gone and no one admits to taking it. Perhaps she was only knocked senseless and has recovered. She may be wandering the roads now, trying to get home."

Edgar wasn't comforted. "If so," he said, "then why hasn't anyone seen her? The roads are crowded with people coming in for the grape harvest."

Hubert found them a few minutes later with the news that Mina had brought him.

"We already know," Walter said. "I'm afraid that we're almost cetain it was Margaret. But there is a chance she's still alive."

Hermann and Peter came out of the church then, followed by the guards with Rolf.

"I can punish him," Peter told Edgar. "But Uncle Hermann says that then I'd have to do the same to most of the men in town. I'll fine them and have the priest set the town as a whole an extra penance. But the most important thing is to have their help in getting Margaret back."

"That's very wise of you, my lord," Walter told him. "It's exactly what I would have done had this happened on my land. You've shown wonderful restraint."

Peter was old enough to sense the mocking underneath the words. "I know," he said. "This wouldn't have happened if I hadn't asked her to come see me. I deserve a penance, too."

"The person we should be after is this Andreas. It seems that it was he who convinced them all to bother the girl in the first place," Hermann added. "He pointed her out as a Jew and then suggested that they could also be *milites Christi* if they forced her to accept the faith. He should be found before he leads other credulous fools to violence. That's one man I'd be happy to hang at the crossroads."

"The villagers didn't have to listen to him," Edgar said. "Would you be so forgiving of them if the man had suggested that they burn your fields and they followed him in that?"

"I don't know," Hermann answered. "But I'd still want to hang the instigator."

"Margaret is all I care about," Edgar said. "My revenge can wait."

"Edgar, may I ride the mule back?" Hubert asked. "I left Catherine alone and she's ragged with worry."

"She doesn't know about this, does she?" Edgar asked.

Hubert nodded.

"Yes, take the mule and hurry," Edgar said. "Tell her there's still hope. Make her rest. I don't want her to lose another baby."

"Jesus's blood!" Hubert exclaimed. "Pregnant again. You two do pick the worst times. Don't fret. I'll see that she doesn't try to join the search herself. After all, she has two children to care for."

As he rode off Walter turned to Edgar.

"Should I congratulate you?" he asked.

"Only after it's born alive," he answered. "And then only if Margaret is back with us. Now, how should we organize this search?"

Vinta came out of her hut into the dawn. She sniffed the air. Another fine day. God willing, the weather would hold until the grapes were picked. The poor child was sleeping now, but the pain of the bruises was making her toss and that might hurt the ribs those horrible men had broken. Vinta knew where there was a stand of willow by the river. Willow bark soaked in hot water and wrapped in a cloth would ease her. Rolf's wife could spare one of her fine linens from the washing. If she protested then Vinta would tell her just which of the girl's injuries had come from the toes of her husband's boots.

She took a small knife and made her way down to the waterside. There were a lot of people there, both men and women, going up and down the bank, hunting for something. Vinta could guess what. But she wasn't about to reveal the girl's hiding place. Those *bæsewihte* wouldn't have the chance to finish what they had started.

She took some strips of bark from a sapling, grunting a reply to the people who passed, ignoring their questions. No one paid her any mind. It was just old Vinta, no husband, no children, a bit dull but harmless. There'd been some scandal about her, years ago, but no one remembered what. Now she was just a toothless crone still strong enough to wash their sheets and with a talent for concocting little remedies to help them hide their sins.

She hated them all.

When she returned to the hut, the child was awake but feverish. Her words were a jumble of German and something else that Vinta didn't know. She tried to pay attention to them in case they were

Hebrew incantations. Eveyone knew Hebrew words were powerful magic. She went out and put the willow bark in the cauldron.

"There now," she told Margaret when she came back. "A few hours and I'll make the poultice. It will pull all the pain from your limbs and bring down the fever. Then we'll see about getting you home, unless you have no home, and then, my precious, I swear you'll always have one with me."

Hubert had worded the message to Catherine carefully, leaving much more room for confidence in Margaret's safety than he actually had.

"Edgar says you're to rest and try not to become agitated," he finished.

"You know I can't do either," Catherine said. "But I'll steep some camomile in wine and then see if I can find a chicken to make soup with. Edgar and Walter will need feeding when they return, and broth will be useful if Margaret is unwell."

Hubert let her bustle, knowing how her helplessness galled her. He took it upon himself to amuse his grandchildren, although it was hard to put them off when they asked why Margaret wasn't home yet.

It was nearly dark when Walter brought Edgar back, so tired that Walter had to keep an arm about his friend to prevent his falling off the horse.

"We didn't find her," Walter told them. "Nor any sign of a new grave. Strangely, I'm beginning to believe she might have survived. If only we can find her soon. Edgar and I have to get some sleep, but we'll start searching again at dawn. It's a warm, dry night. She may just be hiding somewhere, afraid that those men will come back for her."

"They hurt her badly, didn't they?" Catherine asked quietly.

Walter couldn't lie. "From the description, I'm afraid they did."

Catherine didn't say anything more. One look at Edgar told her that he had imagined every horrible possibility many times over. She tried to keep from thinking of her little sister-in-law lying unconsious in the woods with wolves and other wild animals prowling.

The next day was Sunday, and Catherine went to Mass at the cathedral after Edgar and Walter had left to resume the search. She was amazed at the number of people who nodded to her or pressed small gifts on her. One woman had a daughter with her much the same age as Margaret. She gave Catherine a cross made of beads, then put a protective arm around the girl as they walked homeward.

She laid the tokens on the table when she got back.

"I don't understand it, Father," she said. "Edgar says that many of the men who attacked Margaret are now helping to hunt for her. And the townspeople used to throw rotten vegetables at us. How can the same people be so cruel and also so caring?"

"You're asking me?" he replied. "You're old enough now to know that I have no answers, especially when I try to comprehend the human soul. I don't even know the secret corners of my own."

They settled down for another day of waiting, although Catherine flew to the window every time they heard hoofbeats. About midafternoon there was the distinctive clopping on the cobblestones and then the noise stopped in front of their house.

"Father!" Catherine called. "It's Solomon!"

She threw the door open and flung herself into his arms.

"I came as soon as I heard," he told her. "I didn't realize you would be so upset."

"What do you mean?" she asked. "How could I not be upset? But I don't see how you got here so quickly. She's only been missing two days."

"Missing?" Solomon said. "Who's missing? I came when I learned about Simon's murder and to tell Uncle Hubert what's been happening in Troyes."

Nineteen

Trier. Sunday evening, 8 kalends September (August 25), 1146; 14 Elul, 4906. The fourteenth Sunday after Pentecost and the feast of Saint Hundegunde, who tricked her fiancé into a pilgrimage to Rome before the marriage and there became a nun, instead.

Com ut of an hurne hihendliche towart hire un unwiht of helle an dracon liche . . .
Thet milde meiden Margaret grap thet grisliche thing . . . hef him up + duste him dunriht to ther eorthe ant sette hir riht-fot on his ruhe swire.

Out of a corner, rushing toward her, came a creature from hell in the shape of a dragon . . .
That mild maiden Margaret seized the grisly thing, lifted him up and dashed him down to the earth and set her right foot on his rough neck.

—Old English life of
Saint Margaret of Antioch

I have to go look for her," Solomon said at once.

"No, please stay with us." Catherine took his hands. "Edgar and Walter will be back when it gets dark and half of Trier is looking for her, also. They don't need you and I do."

"You should stay, Solomon. You've just ridden hard for nearly a week," Hubert added. "You're worn out and in need of a bath. They may have already found her by now and you wouldn't want to greet poor Margaret smelling like a dead horse."

Solomon reluctantly admitted that he could do with a wash and a few hours' sleep.

"I'll take you to the bathhouse," Hubert said. "We can get a private tub with curtains for a few *münzen* extra. While Catherine is getting the food, tell me what's wrong in Troyes. Are Eliazar and Johanna safe?"

"They were well when I left them." Solomon said. "Within the city all is peaceful, but there was an attack on the Rabbenu Tam at his home in Ramerupt not long ago."

"What happened?" Hubert leaned forward. "Did he survive?"

"Yes, but he's moved into Troyes for now," Solomon said. "A group of the cross bearers broke into his home while he was alone, studying. The tore up all his books, ripping the Torah to shreds in front of him and then dragged him into the field next to the house. First they tried to convince him to convert, but he countered every one of their arguments so they beat him, cutting him five times on the head, for the five wounds of their savior, they said."

"How did he escape them?" Hubert was horrified.

"A knight from a neighboring manor rode by and Jacob called

out to him," Solomon continued. "The knight knew him and came to see what was going on. The Rabbenu offered him a warhorse if he would disperse his aggressors. The knight agreed and drove them off."

"Was anyone else harmed?"

"No," Solomon said. "The *mesfée* who tormented him said they had picked him because he was the wisest and most learned of the Jews and the leader of all those in Champagne."

Hubert raised his eyebrows. "Did Rabbenu Tam tell you that? Well, he's been saying it about himself long enough. Still, I would never have wished his boastfulness to come back at him in such a bitter manner. There's been nothing else, though?"

"Count Thibault keeps tight control on his lands," Solomon said. "Most of his vassals know that any persecutions would be punished."

"May the Almighty One keep it so," Hubert said.

Solomon took the cup Catherine held out to him and drank it without noticing what it was.

"Now, take me to the baths," he said. "Then let me sleep, but only for a little. If there's nothing I can do for Margaret, then I should go see Mina and give her my condolences. But, if Margaret's not found soon, I'm going looking myself and I won't return without her."

Hearing his last statement as she came in with the tray, Catherine smiled for first time in days.

"I believe you will," she said. "Oh, Solomon, I'm so glad you've come. Whatever happens, at least now the family can bear it together."

When Hermann returned to the castle he went first to the drying room where he found Agnes curled fast asleep in the corner where he had left her. He tried to wake her gently but his touch was enough to make her cry out in fear.

"Shshsh." He put his finger to his lips.

It was a moment before her eyes focused, then she smiled at him sleepily and with so much trust that he longed to carry her up to his bed right then. Instead, he held out her tunic that she had been using as a blanket.

"Put this on again," he said. "I'll have to take you back upstairs, but I promise, no more locked doors."

He wished she could understand everything he said. But instead she seemed to know all he wanted to say.

"You won't let them hurt me." She put her hand in his.

As they went up the staircase they met Maria, coming down.

"What's she doing out?" she asked suspiciously.

"I came back from the village and thought that Agnes might like a walk in the garden," Hermann said. It didn't sound likely, but it was the best he could manage. "I heard her moving about in her room and knew she was still awake."

Fortunately, Maria wasn't concerned enough to question this.

"Did you find Margaret?" she asked.

"No, and Peter won't come home until someone does," Hermann aswered. "He sent me back to rest and see that the preparations for the grape harvest aren't delayed."

He gave a rueful smile.

"Can you believe it? He told me what to do. Not rudely but with firmness. Gerhardt would be so proud of him."

"Yes," Maria agreed, staring pointedly at Agnes. "Your dead, unavenged brother would be pleased with his son. What would he think of you with this *kebse?*"

Agnes withered under that look. She had no trouble imagining the words that went with it. Hermann drew himself up and glared at his sister.

"I am sure Gerhardt would know that I am doing everything I can to protect his holdings," he said. "And, until another answer can be found, I have kept the suspect imprisoned."

"Really?" Maria said. "From here it appears to be the other way around."

She continued down to the hall where she met Folmar.

"I can't believe it," she complained. "Only months since our brother died and Hermann's courting his murderer."

Folmar sighed. "Maria, can't you even consider the thought that Gerhardt might have died from illness or by accident? Agnes gains nothing by his death. Her family would long ago have paid to free her if she hadn't been so insistant on having her innocence proved. Hermann doesn't think she did it and neither do I."

"If not her, then who?" Maria turned on him. "No sickness causes such sudden convulsions, and if it were an accident then why haven't we found the cause? You men have been enchanted by a pretty face and form. If it had been my decision she would be locked up in a convent now, doing bitter penance for her sin. Or she would have been tried by ordeal and the truth established."

"Yes, my dear, I know," Folmar said sadly. "But it wasn't your decision and that didn't happen. In the meantime we've learned to know her along with her family, who are even better born than we. Now it seems that the one being punished is that lovely child, who has done nothing at all."

Maria closed her eyes and put a hand to her forehead. "Folmar, this can't continue much longer. I don't sleep well; I can't eat. We'll never be able to put Gerhardt to rest until we know why he died."

Her husband reached for her and then drew back. "Yes, Maria," he said. "I've come to that realization, too. His death must be explained."

Solomon had intended to bring Mina some solace, but it was she who wound up comforting him.

"I'm sorry," he said, wiping his eyes. "I grieve so for you and Simon. I'll miss him the rest of my life. But finding out that Margaret was persecuted and may have been killed because she was seen with us! It's more than I can bear. Mina, I swore to her mother at the moment of her death that I would always take care of Margaret. I couldn't save Adalisa and now I've failed to protect her daughter. I wasn't even there to die with Simon."

"So who are you mourning for, Solomon?" Mina asked. "Them, or yourself?"

Solomon stared at her. Mina was gaunt from sorrow and her eyes lost in dark shadows. But her sadness was for his pain more than her own.

"I'm angry at myself," he said. "For my own cowardice. I hate the way we have to live. I despise the people I travel among. It sickens me to trade with men who would be happy to see me dead and to know that sweet, gentle innocents are being brutalized and slaughtered. Yet I'm able to do nothing to prevent it!"

He laid his head on the table and sobbed, pounding with his fist.

Mina waited for his outburst to subside. Then she stroked his dark curls softly.

"I see," she said. "Poor Solomon. You loathe yourself because you aren't the Almighty and you can't mend the world. What a dreadful thing to find out. You're only a man, after all."

Solomon opened one eye. She gave him an understanding smile although her face was wet with tears.

"I do hate to believe that, Mina." He smiled ruefully. "I've always wanted to be something better. But, I fear you're right. With the meager capacity of my imperfect state, is there anything I can do for you and the children?"

"As a matter of fact, there is," she said. "Simon was to have taken Asher to his first day at *cheder*. I think they both would like it if you would take his place."

Solomon stood and bent to kiss her on both cheeks.

"I would be honored," he said.

Vinta was growing worried. The willowbark poultice had brought the fever down and eased her restlessness but the girl still wasn't lucid. Vinta tried to speak with her but she only stared at her with empty eyes or turned her head away. There wasn't a spark of comprehension. Could the beating have affected her mind?

Now that she was awake, the child had to eat, but Vinta couldn't get her to take an interest in it.

"Now, *friedel*," she begged. "I've heard your people think they're too good for Christian food, but I don't have any of the things you eat. Try this. I made it especially for you, nice gruel with even a bit of honey."

She put the cup to the girl's mouth but it only spilled out and down her chin. Vinta clucked to herself.

She had more luck with whey, tipped between the girl's lips through a hollow reed. But it wasn't enough to sustain life.

Vinta sighed and ran her hands through her thin hair.

"I can't let you die, girl," she announced. "Then those bastards won't be denounced. We can't let them live unpunished. I'm going to wrap you up here and leave a cup on the floor here in case you decide to drink. I'll be back as soon as I can but I have to go find your kin. Maybe they'll know how to heal you. I've done all I can."

She put on a ragged scarf, picked up her walking stick and set out on the road for Trier.

Inside Margaret lay silent, staring at nothing.

Catherine couldn't bear the waiting. She paced around the garden as if on guard duty. Hubert was getting dizzy just watching her.

"I'll take care of the little ones," he said finally, "if you want to go with Solomon and join the search. Your distress is worse for you than the activity would be."

Catherine stopped. "Thank you, Father. You should know that I would have gone long ago if there were only myself to think of. Right now, I don't want James and Edana out of my sight. As much as I want to be doing something to help, I can't leave them, not even with you. I don't want them torn from their family as you were."

She started circling again, somewhat hampered by Edana's clinging to her skirts and James running around her on some mission of his own. Hubert regarded her with amazement. What had happened to his headstrong daughter? Marriage and motherhood seemed to have given her a prudence he would never have expected.

Catherine's stability was only in her devotion to her children. Even though her body insisted on staying with them, her mind roved freely and now, to avoid fretting about Margaret, it was working fiercely on pulling together all the loose bits of information they had about Gerhardt.

There were pieces missing, she knew. But not as many as there had been, and a picture was slowly forming. She ticked off on her fingers the facts they had.

Gerhardt had taken a vow of chastity.

He ate no meat, nor cheese nor eggs. But unlike most ascetics, he did drink wine. Perhaps because it was his own, but perhaps because he hadn't been forbidden it.

He gave alms, but directly to the poor instead of through his family monastery.

Finally, there was the house that he had bought in Köln and given to a group that called themselves the "poor of Christ" who were governed by a woman.

Alone these things meant nothing. Many penitents went to extremes in their fasting. The roads were full of *"pauperes Christi,"*

some seeking Heaven, some just hoping for a better life. But all
together, it reminded Catherine of something she had heard of before. It was a new heresy, or a very old one, depending on whom
one talked with. It had begun in the east somewhere and rumors of
its spread had circulated for the past few years. Its adherents rejected
all things of the corporeal world and believed that Jesus had been a
bodiless spirit who took the form of a man. They also thought the
hierarchy of the Church corrupt and answered only to their own
priests and bishops, some of whom were women.

Actually, from what she had heard, Catherine was inclined to
approve of much of their teaching. There was a great deal of it that
appeared to return to the days of the apostles when all lived simply
with no thought of wealth.

But to deny the sacraments, especially baptism of infants, was
too much. It gave Catherine great solace to know that their stillborn
child was safely in Heaven.

However, the question was not her own beliefs but those of
Gerhardt. Had he accepted the teachings of these people? If he had,
it might well be a reason for someone to want him dead—many
people, now that she thought of it.

But this was all speculation. They had no proof that Gerhardt
was a heretic and even less that anyone else knew of it. If only she
could find one more piece.

"Mama! James hit me!" Edana splintered her concentration with
wailing and Catherine was forced to return to maternal duty.

Vinta hobbled down the side of the road, ever watchful for horsemen
or carts that might delight in driving her into the thistles along the
verge. She noticed the man coming from the town long before he
saw her.

He had nearly passed her when she called out to him. "Ho, there,
man! Stop a moment."

Solomon turned and regarded her. He saw a bent hag with scrag-
gly hair and only a few teeth, her face a mass of wrinkles. If he had
met her before, it was in a nightmare.

Still, Johanna had raised him to be polite. He bowed and greeted
her.

"What may I do for you?" he asked.

"I don't know yet," she answered, peering at him. "You're dark enough for one and have their sort of beard, but it's hard to be sure. You a Jew?"

Solomon blinked. "Why do you ask?"

"I've got something for you, if you are," she answered.

"And what would that be?" Solomon asked, preparing himself to jump back if she went after him with her stick.

Vinta shook her head. "I can't tell you unless I'm sure."

"What would you have me do, old woman?" He began to find the situation amusing. "Drop my *bruchen* for you here in the road."

Vinta considered it. She hadn't seen a nice big *ocker* in years, but she knew he'd take her request the wrong way. There wasn't time for dallying.

"I've found something that belongs to your people," she said. "It's in my cottage. Come with me and I'll give it to you. That is, if you promise to give it back to those who had it first."

"Back to your cottage?" he asked, starting to move away. "I'm sorry, but I really have to be going. Maybe I could come by with my friends later."

At this Vinta made a feeble swing at him with her stick. "You're all the same, Jew or Christian! There'd have been a time when you'd have crawled through briars for a visit to my cottage, you scum. I try to do some good and all I get is scorn. Never mind. Go swill beer with your friends. I'll limp into Trier and find her family myself."

"Wait!" Solomon took her arm. "Forgive me, good woman. I'm hunting for a lost child, a girl. She may be badly hurt. Do you know where she is?"

"Maybe." Vinta looked him up and down. "What is she to you? There are those who'd do like to do worse to her, I fear. Perhaps keep her from naming those who treated her so."

"What is she to me?" The answer hit Solomon with the force of a landslide. "She's the whole world, the sun, moon and stars as well as all that remains of a woman I loved dearly. Please, take me to her. I implore you, kind lady."

Vinta gave him her arm.

"Now that's the way I like to be spoken to."

∞

Hermann felt as if he'd been dropped into a raging river. He tried to tell himself that Agnes was only using him to free herself. How could she care about him after he had kept her prisoner so long? They couldn't even speak to each other properly. And all the while his thoughts were trying to make some sense out of what had happened between them, his body had to keep up with Edgar, Walter and Peter as they went through every house, hut, barn, mill, kitchen, grainstore and dovecote in their frantic hunt for Margaret.

"I don't think the villagers are hiding her," he told them after they had all become covered in bird droppings while disloging a number of chickens to examine the space behind the nests. "Everyone wants to help, even those who were a part of it. Anything to keep you from destroying their winter stores."

Edgar spat out something disgusting and reached for the water bag.

"If she was as badly hurt as they say, she can't have gone far," he said. "Unless someone carried her. So, either she's hidden in the village or one of your people isn't telling all he knows. Now, where do we look next?"

Walter leaned on a garden fence that creaked under him.

"Edgar, we've taken the place apart," he said. "We were more thorough than the tithemen. She isn't here."

"She has to be, Walter. I won't leave without her."

"Edgar, think of the boy, here," Walter said. "He hasn't eaten or slept in nearly two days. He blames himself."

"Good," Edgar said. "I blame him, too."

Peter didn't need the translation for that. He sat disconsolate on the ground wondering if anyone would mind if he hired on as horseboy to Walter and went to get himself killed at Edessa. It seemed the only way to atone.

He watched without interest as old Vinta came across the fields and between the vines, occasionally whacking something out of the way with her cane. She'd been on the fringe of the village as long as he or most anyone else could remember. There was a story about her. Some scandal almost as ancient as she was, but he had never known what. He wondered where she was going in such a hurry.

Walter was watching her, too.

"Who's that woman?" he asked. "I don't remember going to her home."

"She's just a laundress for the church and the castle," Hermann said. "I don't think her house has a place to hide anything."

"She's coming this way," Edgar said. "We might as well question her."

Vinta didn't give them a chance to ask any questions. She went straight to Peter and bowed.

"You'll be the young lord," she said. "You look just like your grandfather."

Peter nodded.

"I don't know that I should have left him with her," she continued. "He said he was family to her, but I've no proof of that. I mean, he wouldn't even show me his *ocker.*"

"He wouldn't?" Peter said. He looked at Walter for guidance.

"No, so how could I be sure?" Vinta went on. "But he seemed to know her and was very gentle. He sent me to find her brother, somebody called Edgar, I think. Strange name."

"Edgar!" Peter and Walter said together.

"We've found her!" Peter yelled and burst into tears.

Edgar turned to Walter, not daring to hope.

"It must be Margaret," Walter said. "But I don't know who the man could be."

"Hubert?" Edgar guessed as he ran after Peter, who was off in the direction of Vinta's hut.

"Does it matter?" Walter called back. "We'll take care of him when we get there."

But the thought of her being spirited away again by a stranger made them run all the faster.

Hermann watched them sprint off and decided that someone should return to tell Agnes the good news. He appointed himself.

Solomon had sent Vinta away only partially from a desire to inform Edgar. He didn't want the old woman there if Margaret woke and didn't know him. She'd been like this once before and he'd been able to waken her from the nightmare, but a second time might be too much to ask. He knelt over her and stroked her cheek, a finger circling the bruise under her eye with the cut at the center. There was another cut on her temple and her nose was swollen, if not broken. He was afraid to find out what else had been done to her.

"Margaret, *cossete*, my dear, can you hear me?" he said softly. "Oh, Adalisa, I hope you don't know how badly I've failed to watch over your daughter. Margaret?"

She didn't wake, but rolled to her side. As she did, her hand fell upon his and her fingers curled around his thumb, holding on tightly. Solomon didn't move. When Edgar arrived at the hut he found them so, Solomon twisted at a most uncomfortable angle to keep from causing her to lose her grip on him.

Now that Margaret was found, Edgar suggested that Peter go home and sleep. There was nothing he could do at the moment. When he had reluctantly left, Edgar then ran ahead to tell Catherine and Hubert while Walter brought Margaret cradled in front of him on the horse with Solomon walking alongside to see that she wasn't jostled.

Vinta watched them go. They had hardly thanked her. That was the way of men, as she knew all too well. She knelt by the pallet and gathered up the blankets to wash.

Peter felt neither hunger nor fatigue as he raced up the hill to spread the word. He waved and shouted it to all he saw, and more than one man crossed himself and vowed to light a candle to the saints in gratitude that he didn't have a murder on his soul.

Maria saw him from the gate and guessed his news. She quickly ordered a bath for him and food prepared.

She met him at the door and was rewarded by a filthy hug.

"I don't have time for a whole bath, Aunt," Peter said as he snatched up a hunk of bread. "Have someone saddle a horse for me. I'm going to the house in Trier so I can be nearby if she needs anything."

He took the steps two and three at a time, slamming against the stone wall as he went round the curve. He went straight to his room and took out his best tunic, pants and shirt, with hose to match the tunic. Then he ruined them all by stuffing them into a bag. After that he rummaged around in a box that his father had kept by his bed.

"Ah, there it is," he said at last. "This will be good."

He put the stone jar in the bag, as well, and pulled the strings. He took another bite of the bread and started back down.

"Send a barrel of last year's wine from Saint Agatha's field after me," he told Maria. "You and Uncle Folmar can come with it, if you like."

His horse had been hastily saddled. Peter checked the girth and then mounted and galloped off.

"What was that?" Folmar said as he came up behind his wife.

"Our nephew," she replied. "I can't how believe this girl has changed him."

"It's only his first infatuation," Folmar said. "The feeling will soon pass."

Maria looked him up and down.

"I'm sure it will," she said sadly.

The dust kicked up by Peter's horse as he made the turn into the main road fell gently onto the figure of a solitary man sitting cross-legged in front of his tent. The cross on his tunic was grimy, but he kept the one on his shield bright. It proclaimed to all that he was neither beggar nor brigand but a soldier of Christ doing his work.

By now most of the local people had become accustomed to seeing Jehan there. Opinion about him varied. Some brought him offerings of food or small coins. Others mocked his devotion and hurled insults or road apples at him. Familiarity had lessened the earlier belief that he was an accomplice in Gerhardt's death. Now he was just another oddity of the community.

He had whiled the time by practicing his swordsmanship on a makeshift dummy, hung from a branch. The village children found this eternally entertaining and there were usually three or four of them watching from a safe distance. He told himself that he had to be prepared for the moment when Agnes saw reason and allowed him to champion her in combat or even let him under go the ordeal in her name.

The weeks passed, though, and no summons came from her. She didn't even send a message. No one would allow him to see her, and Jehan was beginning to suspect that he had made a fool of himself for a woman who was just as cruel to him in her way as her sister, Catherine, had been. Agnes didn't care for him. She never would.

Even if she should change, he had nothing to offer her except a readiness to die on her behalf. He wondered if she would regret it if he starved to death waiting for her here, but he was too much a soldier to succumb to anything so ignoble.

It was in this state of gloom that Andreas found him.

Jehan was staring mournfully at the hills beyond the river when his view was blocked by a tall, lean man with a weather-beaten face. He waited incuriously for the traveler to pass.

Instead the man crouched down, turning his head this way and that, as if to have the benefit of several angles before making a decision.

"What is it?" Jehan snapped. "I have no alms for you."

Andreas grinned. "Ah, but I'm not asking for help; I'm offering it. You look like a man with a problem."

"Nothing the likes of you can aid." Jehan stood and made to return to his tent.

"Don't be so sure, friend," Andreas said more loudly. "You suffer from a common affliction, the scorn of a lady. It bites sharper than a tipped flail, doesn't it?"

Jehan didn't turn around. "That's none of your business," he growled. "Get away from me."

Andreas took a step toward him. "But if this scorn could be turned to love, even adoration, what would a man give for that?"

Despite himself, Jehan was intrigued.

"A man might give a great deal, if it worked," he answered.

Andreas smiled in satisfaction. He opened a bag hung around his neck and pulled out a crumpled piece of parchment. He held it up just out of Jehan's reach.

"Yes see this?" he asked. "Can you read it?"

"I can make out French," Jehan said. "That's not it."

"Of course not," Andreas said. "This is an ancient charm written in the language of the prophets. What do you think took Bathsheba from the arms of her husband and into King David's bed?"

"Money?" Jehan guessed.

Andreas lifted his eyes to Heaven. Not another one.

"No," he answered. "Money can't buy a virtuous woman."

"Then maybe she wasn't . . ." Jehan said.

"No, it was this very incantation!" Andreas wasn't about to get into another unprofitable debate. "Words of power that cast a lasting spell to make any woman your adoring concubine . . . or even wife, if you prefer," he added as Jehan opened his mouth again.

"What good is it to me if I can't read it?" Jehan asked.

"You don't need to," Andreas answered. "You eat it. First you soak it for three days in the blood of a heifer. Then you mix it with red wine. After that you rub the letters off the parchment so that they dissolve in the liquid. Then, on the night of the new moon, before there are more than three stars in the sky, you line a cup with oak leaves and drink it, all the while thinking of the face of your beloved. The next morning she will wake with a desperate desire for you."

Jehan scratched his chin. "It sounds reasonable," he said. "But the new moon is over a week away. If it doesn't work, you'll be long gone with my payment."

Andreas hadn't expected this much sense from him. He decided to take a chance. He drew himself up and placed his right hand on the hilt of Jehan's sword.

"I swear to you by the cross that you wear and by the blood of Our Lord, that this charm will bring you all you desire from your lady," he said.

"Very well," Jehan said. "I'll take it."

The price was high, a fine pair of leather gloves, but Jehan would have given much more to at last win Agnes's devotion.

It was only after Andreas had vanished down the road and Jehan sat examining the parchment that he realized there was something familiar about it, especially the French words only partially scraped out on the reverse side.

He jumped up angrily, preparing to go after the swindler and retrieve his gloves, preferably with the man's hands still in them. Then a thought occurred to him. If this were what he thought, it was certainly a sign from God. How else could a complete stranger bring him the one thing that might convince Agnes to give him her body, if not her heart?

Catherine sat on one side of the bed and Solomon on the other. They had watched all through the night but Margaret's condition hadn't changed.

"What more can we do?" she asked. "Her poor body is beginning to heal, but her spirit has fled."

"I hoped that when she heard my voice, she'd wake at once." Solomon bit his lip. "That was prideful of me, wasn't it?"

"There must be a way to get her back." Catherine sighed. "Brother Berengar says that he'll ask the infirmarian to come by and examine her."

Edgar woke and came to watch with them.

"We must send someone up to the old woman's hut with a gift," he suddenly realized. "She thought Margaret was a Jewess but saved her life anyway. That was very kind of her, and very brave."

"I'll try to find out what she needs most," Catherine said. "And bring it to her, myself."

Hubert came in just after dawn. "The boy Peter is here," he said. "He wants to see Margaret. Will you let him? The lad seems so miserable."

"I don't suppose it will harm her," Catherine said. Solomon nodded agreement.

Hubert left and returned a moment later, followed by Peter. The boy gasped when he saw Margaret's battered face.

"Will there be scars?" he asked.

"On the inside, certainly," Solomon answered. "We don't know about her face."

Peter hesitated, then unknotted his sleeve and took out the clay jar.

"I thought this might help her," he stammered. "Father said it eased the pain in his hands and shoulders. He used it every night."

Catherine reached out for the jar. She untied the twine holding the lid on and sniffed it.

"What's in it?" she asked. "Where did it come from?"

"Father got it from a friend who had the making of it from the convent at Mount Saint Rupert," Peter answered. "The abbess there is known for her wisdom and skill with medicine."

Solomon translated and Catherine sniffed again. "Yes, I've heard of her. Mother Heloise corresponds with her from time to time. This seems to be the same compound that they used for Sister Bertrada's suffering."

She dipped a finger in the salve and licked it. She made a face and wiped her tongue on her sleeve.

"It's all I could think of, and I so want to help," Peter pleaded.

"It might ease her pain." Solomon took the jar and started to rub some into the angry cut on Margaret's cheek.

"This tastes like . . . Solomon, stop!" Catherine cried as she knocked the jar from his hands. "Peter, where did this salve come from. Who made it? How long did your father have it? Solomon, ask him!"

Solomon did. "What is it, Catherine?"

"There's something in there that I don't believe was put in at Mount Saint Rupert," she answered. "Solomon, I think I know how Gerhardt was poisoned. Now we just need to find out who did it."

Twenty

Monday morning, 7 kalends September (August 26), 1146; 15 Elul, 4906. Feast of Saint Roc-Amador, the earliest Christian hermit in France, arriving before the death of Saint John. Getting there first allowed him the cave with the best view.

Homo, qui mollem carnem habet et de superfluis potionibus de gutta, id est gich, in aliquo membro suo fatigatur, petrosilinum accipiat et quater tantum de rutha et in patella de oleo olivae frixet, vel si oleum non habuerit, cum hicano sepo infriaxi faciat, et herbas istas calidas loco, ubi dolet, imponat et panno desuper liget.

A man with tender flesh and troubled in any limb by excess flux of gout, that is "gich," should take parsley and four times that amount of rue and roast it in a dish of olive oil. And if he has no oil, he should have it roasted in goat grease He should put the herbs warmed in this way on the place it hurts and tie it up with a bandage.

Hildegarde of Bingen,
*Liber compositae medicinae de
aegritudinum causis, signis
atque curis. liber v*

*P*eter was mortified that Catherine believed his offering to be tainted.

"But Father used it for years," he insisted. "It always eased the pain."

"There wasn't wolf's bane in it originally, I'm sure, Peter," Catherine said. "But there is now. I know the taste of it. When I was around your age I helped in the infirmary at the Paraclete. Sister Melisande taught me the difference between horseradish and wolf's bane. Many people have eaten it accidentally and become very ill. They don't often die because the taste is vile and they recognize it at once. But the oddest thing about this poison, she said, was that it could be potent if one only touched it, although it would take longer to kill a person that way."

"Wolf's bane?" Peter said. "There's some growing by the stream just south of the castle. Margaret stopped me from eating it."

The memory and the sight of her still form on the bed were enough to cause his eyes to fill again.

"Peter, all we can do for Margaret now is wait and pray," Catherine said. "But now that we have this we might be able to find the person behind your father's death. Now, do you have any idea when this jar was made up for him?"

Peter tried to remember. "After Easter, I know, because he was complaining that it was almost gone then. He had thought there was more."

"Did he have to send to this convent each time or did someone here know how to make it?" she asked.

"Oh, anyone could do it," Peter said. "It's just parsley and rue roasted in goat tallow. You heat them in a little pot and put the preparation on a cloth while it's still hot as a poultice. But father didn't always have the patience to wait and so he just rubbed it on, especially when it was warm out. You know, he did say that the latest batch was the best, yet. It made his skin tingle and he felt the warmth through to his bones."

"It would, at the beginning. Did anyone else in the family have this problem with swollen joints?" Catherine asked. "Hermann, Maria?"

"No, just Father. He said my grandfather had been troubled by it, too."

"Who knew where the jar was kept?"

"Oh, everyone, I suppose." Peter shrugged. "It was in a box in his room, along with the cloth for the poultice."

Catherine sighed. That didn't narrow down the possibilities much. Even Agnes could have ground up wolf's bane and mixed it in with the tallow. So, even though she now knew how and had an idea of why, the who still eluded her and until they found that, Agnes would never be free.

In the meantime, there was the question of this man who had incited the villagers to attack Margaret. Catherine could feel no forgiveness for those who had listened to him but was willing to leave them to Peter and the abbot of Saint Maximin. However, the kind of monster who would enjoy stirring people up to viciously harm an innocent girl, that was a man who should be destroyed. Vengeance may belong to the Lord, but Catherine wanted to be there to cheer when He collected from Andreas.

At the moment Andreas was not far away, blissfully unaware of the hatred directed toward him. He had also yet to learn the magnitude of his mistake in thinking Margaret Jewish. The men he had fallen in with in Köln had been eager to punish the infidel at home rather than go all the way to Edessa. The men in the village near Trier were angrier about the bad harvests and the continual fighting between the archbishop and Graf Heinrich. It was harder to get them interested in saving a soul for Christ. And in the end the girl had nothing valuable on her, after all.

Andreas sat up and stretched. It was time for him to be heading somewhere else. South, perhaps, into Burgundy. He had only joined up with the heretics because of his belief that they had wild orgies as part of their rites. A man at a tavern in Provins had told him that these were like the Manichees that Augustine wrote about. They would have a service and at the end, when the candles were blown out, each man would grab the woman nearest him and they would couple as many times and in as many ways as they wanted.

Instead he found that they didn't believe in sex at all, even in marriage. Their food was terrible. Moreover, everyone was expected to share all they had with the others, except their women, of course. Andreas had left in disgust. If he'd wanted that kind of life, he'd have sold himself to a monastery as a lay brother. At least he'd be guaranteed care in his old age. These people were likely not ever to reach their dotage. No one had told him until he arrived in Köln that just three years ago, some of this same sect had been burned at the stake.

Now it seemed like a good idea to distance himself from them. And what better way to do it than by denouncing that one up at the castle? It was the rich heretics who were the most dangerous. They could bribe officials to protect their people, just the way the lousy Jews did. Andreas sneered just thinking about it. No one had ever paid to save him from anything and he had the scars on his back to prove it.

Andreas rolled up his pack, secreting the gloves he had received from Jehan deep in the middle. First he would go to the bishop's palace, where the archdeacon had promised him a reward for his information and then he would slip out the south gate and try to get as far away as he could by nightfall.

Peter was deep into speculation about who had contaminated his father's salve and what he should do about it. He didn't notice Andreas coming across the marketplace until he nearly bumped into him.

"Out of my way, lad," Andreas pushed him aside.

"How dare you, peasant!" Peter pushed him back. "And I'm not a lad; I'm a lord. It's your place to make way for me."

Andreas looked at Peter's worn clothes and dusty boots and realized that they were finer than anything he ever hoped to own. Swallowing his bile, he stepped aside.

"Forgive me, my lord," he said.

Peter got a good look at his face then and leaped for him. *"Du mortraete!"* he screamed. "Murderer! Help! Edgar! Walter! Come quickly! It's him!"

Andreas spun in Peter's grasp and twisted the boy's arm painfully so that he had to let go. The man then loped off toward the palace. He didn't know what the boy thought he had done but it was better to deal with it from the safety of the archdeacon's office where he could present his information in trade for protection.

"After him!" Peter shouted at the townspeople who had gathered at his cries. "He tried to murder Margaret."

Andreas could feel the chase but knew better than to take the time to look. He flung himself at the cathedral door knocking over a cripple begging in the porchway. He then ran down the east aisle and past the altar screen into the choir.

"Hoi! You're not allowed in here." One of the canons stopped working to chase him out.

"Get the archdeacon for me!" Andreas ordered. "Now. I have information about a conspiracy against the archbishop. Heretics have infiltrated the nobility. The archdeacon knows me. Tell him Andreas has returned."

The crowd had poured into the cathedral now. Their angry voices were not muted in reverence. The canon thought quickly.

"Come with me," he said and led Andreas out through the choir to a narrow door. It opened into a small room hung with robes and vestments.

"Wait here," he told Andreas. He left, locking the door behind him.

Andreas had never been so relieved to be shut in. He fumbled among the robes, searching for one long enough for him. None had cowls, he was sorry to discover. There must be something in the room he could use to hide his face. He continued his search.

In the cathedral, the people had gathered in the nave and were calling for the fugitive to be turned over to them.

"Why should he take refuge here when he denied it to that poor girl?" someone said.

There was a chorus of agreement. Finally one of the canons came out, flanked by guards.

"Please disperse," he said nervously. "The man you seek is at the moment under the protection of the archbishop. We shall see that he is tried according to custom and, if he is guilty, he shall be punished. Now, I've been asked to remind you of where you are. Go home, or even better, stay and pray with me."

He knelt on the stone floor. After a momentary shuffle, most of the townspeople knelt as well. Peter said a quick pater noster and then slipped out. He had to find Walter. The lord of Grancy would be able to treat with the archbishop if anyone could. He would see to it that Margaret was avenged.

Inside, Andreas was aware that the clamor had ceased. He took a deep breath and relaxed. When he told them who had owned the heretic's home in Köln and who the owner was now, he would be granted any reward he demanded. High on his list was a fast horse.

Agnes had convinced herself that Hermann regretted his moment of insanity in the night. She wasn't at all sure how she felt about it. Then he came into her room and she knew from the way her stomach jolted and her face flushed that she was well and truly lost.

"Something's wrong!" she said when she saw his expression.

"The archbishop's soldiers are coming up the hill," he said, pantomiming it for her. "I don't understand it. Peter wouldn't have sent them. What happened to you was our decision."

He held her tightly and then kissed her.

"I won't let them take you," he swore. "O mînes herzen trût, come with me, quickly.

He took her hand and hurried her down the stairs and through the hall. Agnes understood little of what was happening, only that they were being attacked and she needed to flee.

"Hermann!" Maria came after him. "Where are you going with that woman? Didn't you see the soldiers? They've come for her at last, no doubt. Folmar! Stop Hermann at once. He's lost his reason."

They were in the courtyard when the soldiers arrived. Hermann was just about to mount his horse and pull Agnes up behind him.

"What are you doing here?" he demanded. "Who sent you? This woman is my prisoner and I'm not releasing her."

The captain came up to Hermann and signaled the others to surround him. Agnes clung to him, white with terror.

"We're not here for the woman, my lord," the captain said. "By orders of the archdeacon. we're to bring you back to Trier to answer charges of heresy."

Hermann blinked. "What?"

"Heresy, my lord. You have been accused of supporting a group that denies the body of Christ and refuses to answer to any earthly power."

"But that's insane!" Folmar shrieked. "Hermann would never—"

"Then he can answer before the archbishop," the captain cut him off. "My orders are to bring him back to do so."

Hermann shook his head. "A Cathar, they think I'm a bloody Cathar!"

He took off his sword and handed it to the captain. "I can prove on my body that I am a true and orthodox Christian. This is a vile slander. Folmar," he shouted over his shoulder as they took him away, "take care of Agnes."

Agnes watched in bewilderment. Were they punishing Hermann for his kindness to her? She wanted to call out to him in German, so he would be sure to understand. But, under the circumstances, *"Ich liebe dich"* seemed an imprudent thing to say. And Agnes, unlike Catherine, had a large share of natural discretion.

Instead she turned to Folmar, who was standing in slack-jawed shock.

"Get Brother Berengar," she said, pronouncing the name slowly and carefully. "I want to talk to him."

Jehan had seen the guards pass with Hermann in their midst. Then the guards from the castle rode by, Folmar in the lead. He didn't care what had caused this exodus. The only thing he realized was that this might be his only chance.

He took down his tent and packed it up, along with his cooking pot and blankets. He cut down the dummy he'd slashed to shreds. Then he checked the area for anything else he wanted to take along. Win or lose, he wasn't coming back.

In the castle it seemed to Agnes as if the world had been turned upside down and shaken. This was as bad as the night Gerhardt had died. She went up to her room again, not because anyone forced her. Everyone seemed to have forgotten all about her. It was just the only place she could be sure she was out of the way of the people running around like ants whose nest has just been scattered.

She occupied herself by rearranging the bed and tables, refolding all her clothing and, when all else failed, sweeping the dust and rushes on the floor from one side of the room to the other. Finally, the door opened.

"Oh Brother Berengar, you've got to tell me—" she began.

Then she saw who it was.

"Jehan! How did you get in here?" she gasped.

"In all the confusion, no one even noticed me," he said. "I've come to rescue you."

"Oh no, you haven't," Agnes said. "I'm not going anywhere until I know what's happen to Hermann."

Jehan looked as if he'd run through a curtain and straight into a stone wall.

"Agnes, this is our chance!" he said. "Come with me and I'll see that you get safely back to your grandfather."

"Jehan, I won't go anywhere with you," she said. "I've told you over and over but you refuse to believe me. Not even to save my life."

Jehan's expression turned abruptly from beseeching to angry.

"Very well," he said. "But I've given too much of my life to you to leave with no reward. You have a choice. Either you come with me or I give this to the archbishop."

He showed her the parchment. Agnes reached for it, but he stepped back.

"You can see it from where you are," he said. "One side has a message from your grandfather that I delivered to Hubert. The other has magic Hebrew words on it. I know how they came to be there and so do you."

"Nonsense," Agnes said, but her face gave her away.

"I thought so." Jehan smiled. "Your choice is simple, Agnes. You won't even have to think about it. Your father's safety in exchange for freedom and life with me. Or at least a few good nights. I can assure you, you'll enjoy it. I'll make your German husband seem like a eunuch."

Agnes managed to regain her composure. She almost laughed

when Jehan compared himself to Gerhardt. Thank the saints he didn't know the truth. She prayed he never would.

"You're despicable," she said quietly. "I'm sure my father has a simple explanation for this, but even if he doesn't, why do you think I would debase myself for his sake, when I cut myself off from him years ago?"

Jehan was horrified. "But he's your father!"

"My filial duty is not strong enough to give up my virtue for it." Agnes turned away from him and went to the window by her embroidery frame. "Now leave, Jehan. Take your scrap of parchment and your disgusting offer and never come near me again."

"You *bordeleuse!*" he whispered as he came toward her.

Agnes opened her mouth to scream. At the same time, her hand went out for her curved thread scissors. She held them by her side, ready to strike up at his most vulnerable area.

Jehan was saved by the arrival of Brother Berengar. The monk took in the situation at once and advanced on Jehan in utter indignation.

"Take that cross off at once!" he ordered. "You're not fit to wear it! Did he harm you, my dear?"

Agnes hid the scissors in the folds of her *chainse.*

"I'm fine," she answered shakily. "Jehan was just saying goodbye, weren't you?"

Jehan's lips tightened, but he nodded.

"I'll see him out," Berengar said and took his arm.

When they had gone, Agnes sat down with a thump. She was numb with the enormity of what she'd just done. Not only had she left Hubert open to charges of apostasy, she had made an enemy of the one person who had stood by her through all the turmoil of her recent life.

Then Brother Berengar returned and the only thing that mattered was finding out what had happened to Hermann.

It had taken some time to convince Peter that he couldn't raise an army and burn Andreas out of the cathedral. Part of the reason it was so difficult to dissuade him was that those arguing with him privately thought it a wonderful idea.

"The man is nothing more than a murderer," Catherine said. "The archdeacon has no right to protect him."

"Catherine?" Edgar said. "Is that you speaking? Would you have us be as barbarous as he? What if Peter is mistaken in his identification?"

"Do you think he is?" Catherine challenged him.

"No, I don't." Edgar admitted. "I find myself hoping that he will be released so that I can see that his death is slow and that every time he screams, he knows why and for what."

"May God forgive me, Edgar." Catherine laid her face over his heart. "I would help you do it. Oh, why won't Margaret wake!"

Hubert and Walter had taken Peter back to his own house. They returned with a collection of the rumors whipping through town.

"I don't believe what's going on out there." Walter balanced himself on a small stool. "The world must be about to end. All the demons of hell have been let loose and they're dancing in the steets."

James had been busy in the corner building a castle from wooden blocks for Edana to knock down. Now he looked up at Walter.

"I don't want the world to end," he said. "I don't want demons!"

He started crying and Edana joined him. Edgar and Catherine hurried to comfort them. Walter tried to apologize.

"Never mind, Walter," Edgar said. "We haven't taught James about metaphor, yet."

"Oh," Walter said. "Let me know when you do, I'd like to learn about it, myself."

He poured himself some beer and gestured for Hubert to explain with less exageration.

"They've just brought Lord Hermann into town in chains and taken him to the archbishop's palace. Some say he murdered his brother and tried to kill Peter, as well, to gain the land. Others think he betrayed the archbishop and the city to Graf Heinrich. I even heard some wild tale that he was the leader of a band of heretics who wanted to destroy the church. This Andreas seems to be mixed in with it somewhere, but no one is sure how. Where's Solomon?"

"He went to Mina's," Catherine said. "To see if any of her friends knows of something that could help Margaret. He also said something about arranging for Asher's first day of school."

Hubert sighed. "At least for once the townspeople aren't rioting against the Jews. I suppose he's in no danger."

Catherine had succeeded in calming Edana who was crying on the principle that if James was upset something must be wrong. She rocked the child back and forth as she went over the report Hubert had given.

"I don't think Hermann's a heretic," she said at last.

"That was the most preposterous of the rumors," Walter said. "I don't think he did anything he's accused of. Perhaps conspiring to get the bishop to end the war, but everyone in town wants that."

"Heresy isn't that impossible," Catherine said slowly. "But I don't think Hermann is the heretic. Father, you said Gerhardt had given his house as a home for some 'pauperes Christi.' From Agnes's information, I'm sure he was one of them, himself. Perhaps he intended at some point to abandon his family for them. If Hermann knew about it, he might well want to stop his brother before they were all caught in the scandal."

Edgar shook his head. "I just can't imagine Hermann committing murder. Especially in such a roundabout way. How could he know that Gerhardt would die before selling all his property?"

"That's true," Catherine admitted. "Depending on how often Gerhardt used the salve, it could take days or weeks for the poison to work. It might only make him sick if he applied it infrequently enough."

"But also, we're the only ones who know how Gerhardt was killed," Walter said. "Hermann's arrest was after Andreas went to the archdeacon. How could he have known about the salve? What else could his information have been?"

"I don't care," Hubert said. "If it frees Agnes so that we can leave, that's all that matters."

"And what of Andreas's crimes?" Edgar asked.

Hubert slumped in his chair. "That's not for me to decide. I grieve with you for your sister, Edgar. But I also grieve for Simon and my mother and sisters and for the vicious attack on Rabbenu Tam. And I know that no one will ever be called to account for those deeds, not in this world. I've worn myself out with sorrow and guilt and have no strength left for revenge."

"Then I'm glad I do," Edgar said.

∞

Peter was inside sleeping when his uncle was brought through the marketplace to the bishop's palace, so he knew nothing of it until his other uncle shook him roughly awake.

"I've brought the guards," Folmar told him. "But I don't know if we have enough people to rescue him."

"Unh?" Peter said.

"Hermann's been taken for heresy," Folmar said. "We have to save him before he's questioned."

Peter was awake at once. "But why? Uncle Hermann can easily prove he's no heretic. It must be a mistake."

"Oh, it is, Peter," Folmor said with feeling. "But it was your father who made it and now the rest of us will have to pay unless we can keep Hermann from talking."

"I don't understand," Peter pulled on his tunic, picked his *bruchen* up off the floor and followed Folmar down to the hall where the guards were gathered. "What did my father do?"

"The idiot received the *consolomentum* and then went and got himself married," Folmar said.

Peter sat on a bench to put the pants on.

"I don't know what you're talking about," he said. "Are you drunk?"

"I only wish I were." Folmar went into the courtyard and peered over the wooden fence. "There are people collecting in the square. Some of them have sickles and pitchforks. I even see a couple of swords. Who do those burghers think they they are, with nobles' weapons?"

"What are they doing?" Peter asked.

"Preparing to riot," Folmar said. "Come on. It's too dangerous now to try to save Hermann. We have to get back to the castle, pack up and escape."

"Uncle!" Peter grabbed him with both arms and held him there. He was surprised at his own strength. "I'm not going anywhere. Our family doesn't run away. Now tell me what you know about my father."

Folmar did, though not everything.

∞

Between Maria's fury and Berengar's broken translation, Agnes finally understood why Hermann had been taken.

"I should have known," she said. "It's my fate. If not infidels, it's heretics. So that's why Gerhardt wouldn't come to bed with me. And Hermann is one, also? I can't believe it."

"Neither can I," Maria said. Her face was grim. "But I think I know who is. The cowardly bastard. Come with me, Agnes. Yes, of course you, too, Brother. How else can I talk to her? We're going to put an end to this now."

"Will Hermann be all right?" Agnes asked Berengar as she snatched up a scarf and veil.

"If the Lady Maria has any say in it, he'll be home by Vespers," Berengar answered.

Agnes wondered if she really wanted a second opportunity to have this woman for a sister-in-law.

Walter and Edgar went out to see what the citizens intended to do. Edgar saw his friend, Egilbert, among them.

"You seem to always appear when there's trouble," he said.

Egilbert grinned. "I find town life boring compared to the excitement of sea travel and trade. When something happens to liven things up, I always investigate it."

"And what is it now?" Edgar asked.

"A quandary," Egilbert said. "My friends can't agree on why this local lord has been taken. If he's against the bishop, they'll fight for him. If he's a heretic, they'll burn down his house. You see the problem."

"Not an uncommon one, I fear," Edgar commented. "Do you think they'll decide soon?"

"Not unless someone comes out and makes a pronouncement," Egilbert said. "If one sat on the benches outside the Green Grape, one would probably still be able to see what was going on and join in before it was over."

"I think this one will," Edgar said. "Coming with us, Walter?"

Walter was talking earnestly with a man carrying a pruning hook. He shook his head. "Save me a spot. I'll be along soon."

Egilbert and Edgar got cups of wine and settled on the bench to observe. Owing to the heat, a number of other people had had the same idea and the benches in the shade were full.

"This Andreas fellow," Edgar said, "he isn't local, is he?"

"I've never seen him before," Egilbert said. "A man I know told me he had a Flemish accent. I'll wager he's a heretic, himself. You know how they are in Flanders. The weavers are almost a sect unto themselves."

Edgar wasn't about to get drawn into a discussion of the tight grip the Flemish had on the cloth market and their propensity for lay piety. "Does anyone know when he first appeared here?"

Egilbert thought. "About the same time you did, it seems to me. I first saw him about the time I saved you from those boys."

"So he wasn't around when Lord Gerhardt died?" Edgar was disappointed. He wanted to put the blame for every evil on the man.

"Not that I know of," Egilbert said. "But I can ask around."

He shouted the question at those sitting nearby. They stopped in their conversations a moment, answered something that Edgar could tell was negative and went back to their drinking.

"So, he doesn't know the situation in Trier well," Edgar said. "Therefore, it's unlikely he could have proof that would brand Lord Hermann a heretic or anything else. I think that he just made the accusation because he'd been recognized from the village and wanted the protection of the archdeacon long enough to escape us."

Egilbert sadly agreed. "That will soon put an end to the fun. I'll have some more wine to make up for it."

"And one for me," Edgar said.

While he was waiting, Edgar scanned the square, observing the many different classes of people, from foreign traders to local officials to peasants in town to sell the surplus from their gardens. He wasn't paying close attention to anyone when he caught sight of something that made him sit up and rub his eyes. When he looked again they were gone.

"Egilbert, did you see that?" he asked as his friend gave him the cup. "I could have sworn that I just saw a group of white monks going into the Jewish quarter."

Egilbert took the cup back and sniffed it.

"I think you need to get out of the sun, Edgar," he said. "There are no white monks around here and even if there were, they wouldn't be hunting for lodging among the Jews."

Solomon and Mina were sitting at her table going over the ceremony for Asher's introduction to the Torah when the *parnas* of the community came to the door.

"Mina," he said excitedly. "You won't believe this, but Abbot Bernard of Clairvaux is in my home. He has asked if he might see you."

"Me!" Mina went pale. "What would such a man want with me?"

"I can't be certain," the *parnas* told her. "But I have the feeling that he wants to ask your forgiveness."

Twenty-one

Evening of the same day.

וישמצ הי את
נאקתינו ויפן אלינו וירחמנו ברוב רחמיו והסדיו יישלח אחרי וה חכליעל
כומר אחר הגוך גדול ירכ לכל הכוסרים יודע רחם ומבין ושמו בירנט
חאכר מקלירכלש העיר אשר בצרפת

The Lord heard our pain, and he turned to us and had mercy
upon us. In his great mercy and grace, He sent an honest
priest, one revered and respected by all the clergy in France,
named Abbot Bernard of Clairvaux.

—Ephraim of Bonn
Sefer Zekirah

*D*o I have to see him?" Mina was trembling.

The *parnas* wasn't sure. "It wasn't a command, I don't think," he said. "But he might not take it well if you refuse. Solomon, you know the French Edomites better than I do. What do you think?"

"I think Mina shouldn't have to see anyone she doesn't want to," Solomon stated. "Why should she forgive this man? I heard him preach at Vézelay. It was his words that stirred the people up against us. Simon might be alive if not for him."

The *parnas* licked his lips. He was the richest man in the community and hence the one chosen to act as spokeman for all in dealing with gentiles. Often this put him in an uncomfortable position. Right now he felt as if he were sitting on a spear tip.

"I believe the abbot knows that," he said. "He seems to be trying to atone. We've had word that he's been preaching throughout Lotharingia against this barking monk, Radulf. He's on his way to Frankfurt now, to force the monk to return to his monastery."

"And how much are we paying him for that?" Solomon asked.

"Nothing that I know of," the *parnas* answered. "There's been no call for tithes to bribe him with, at least."

"I don't believe it," Solomon insisted. "No Christian leader has ever apologized to us. There's been no protection without payment. And they've never given us anything freely except scorn."

"Solomon, you don't have to tell me that," the man said sharply. "My grandfather was beat to death by the mob in 1096. All we ever got as apology was an edict saying that we could return to the faith if we had been forced to undergo their baptism. The emperor certainly didn't come to console my mother. Mina, I won't force you, but I think you should meet this man."

Mina looked to Solomon. He lifted his hands.

"It's not my decision," he said. "But, if you go, I'll accompany you and tell you what he says."

"Very well," she said. "Let me change and get my veil."

She didn't take long. A few moments later they arrived at the house where Bernard waited with his secretary, Geoffrey and a few others of his order. He stood when they came in. He saw a slight woman clad in widow's purple, her face veiled. The bulge below her waist startled him. He hadn't known she was pregnant.

Mina came forward and took the seat the secretary vacated for her. The abbot sat facing her. She said nothing. He wasn't what she had expected.

What Mina saw was a gaunt man in his fifties. His robes were simple, not like those of the archbishop and the cathedral canons. She didn't understand how he could be considered the most powerful man in Christian lands. She lifted the veil to see him better.

And was caught in his eyes. Mina's own eyes opened wide in astonishment. His eyes were dark and in them burned a passion so intense she could almost feel it scorching her. She knew then that whatever this passion was unleashed upon, there could be no defense against it.

She shuddered under his gaze.

Bernard lowered his glance.

"Tell her, please, that I know nothing I say can repair the wound in her heart," he said and waited for Solomon to repeat the words. "All I can do is beg her forgiveness for what has been done in my name and promise that I will do everything in my power to see that no other women suffer as she has."

Mina was silent for a long time after Solomon finished.

"I believe," she said at last. "I believe you are a decent man even though an idolator. I accept that you truly regret what has been done to my husband and our people. When I think of my orphaned children and of the one who will never see his father's face, it's hard to find forgiveness."

Solomon translated every word, despite the gestures of the *parnas* to soften it.

The abbot bowed his head. "I understand. It was much to ask of you."

Mina extended her hand. "It's hard," she finished. "But I do. The Almighty One, blessed be He, forgave his people when they turned from him in the desert. May your people also one day find their way back to Him. Until then, I bear you no ill will."

The monk, Geoffrey, gave an indignant snort, but the abbot lifted a hand to silence him.

"Thank you," he said. "I have asked to speak to the people of the town before I go. I'll tell them of your generosity of spirit."

He signaled to the other monks.

"We have imposed on these people long enough." He bowed his head to them all and led the others out.

"Mina!" the *parnas* expostulated. "Couldn't you have been a little more conciliatory?"

Mina got up. "No," she said. "That was the best I could do. Good night."

The news that the abbot of Clairvaux was in town spread through the crowd and other concerns were, for the moment, forgotten. The people dispersed to put on finer clothes in which to greet Bernard.

"They say he's a living saint," one woman told her neighbor. "I wonder if his blessing could cure my son's blindness."

"Not everyone thinks he's all that holy," the neighbor answered. "But you've tried everything else. Bring the boy with you. A blessing couldn't hurt."

When Catherine learned about the abbot's presence, her reaction was that of the neighbor.

"He does have a power for persuasion," she said. "And it may well come from God. But he's guided too much by others and by his own feelings. He doesn't think logically. And it's hard to forget how he tormented Master Abelard."

"I know, Catherine." Solomon fidgeted uncomfortably. "I always thought that his vaunted humility was just another form of pride, but he was sincere in his regret for Simon's death. I'm sure of it."

"I'm sure he was," Catherine said. "What worries me is that he'll hear about Hermann's arrest and his abhorrence for heretics will cause him to ignore the facts and encourage the archdeacon to have Hermann punished."

Edgar disagreed. "The abbot spent several months a few years ago exhorting heretics in Provence to return to the faith. It might be to Hermann's advantage that he knows them so well. A few questions would convince Bernard that Hermann is no heretic."

"You seem to know a great deal about this belief," Solomon told them.

Catherine shook her head. "Not enough. There are so many ascetic bands wandering about these days. Most of them are harmless. This one simply seems more organized than the others. Like many they're determined to remove themselves comepletly from the authority of the Church hierarchy, but this group has also set up its own orders. They seem to want to create another regime, outside of our laws and customs."

"Ah, rather like the Jews," Solomon said.

Catherine gave him a sharp look, fully aware of his sarcasm.

"Very much," Edgar said quickly before she could answer. "But you don't proselytize or refuse to pay taxes. They do."

"Which one is worse?" Solomon asked.

"The first leads to the second." Edgar grinned. "That means the kings and bishops both want them destroyed, if for different reasons."

"So, do we want to ask the abbot to take a hand in our problem, or not?" Solomon asked.

Catherine and Edgar looked at each other.

"Perhaps we should discuss it with Peter, first," Catherine suggested. "His family will be affected as much as ours."

Solomon declined to join them. "I'll stay with Margaret," he said. "Uncle Hubert will see to your progeny."

They left him sitting by the bed, holding her hand.

They collected Walter, and explained their conclusions to him. He insisted on being included.

"I've been in this from the beginning," he said. "I don't want to miss the finish."

When they reached the house, they found Maria there already.

"Where is your husband?" Walter said. "We have some questions for him."

"And a good day to you, as well," Maria answered without rising to greet them. "I imagine I can tell you most of what you wish to know. Brother Berengar! Would you ask Agnes and Peter to come down?"

"Agnes?" Catherine was startled.

"I have been forced to abandon my belief that she was responsible for my brother's death," Maria said. "There was no reason to give her a free room any longer."

Agnes entered the room and Catherine rushed to her, hesitating a fraction as she drew close. Then Agnes held out her arms and Catherine went to them. Nothing was said as both were crying too hard to speak.

"Well, it seems that we've accomplished what we came for," Edgar said sadly. "Agnes is free and undamaged. But Margaret is imprisoned in a broken mind and body, and she was far more innocent. What sort of justice is that?"

Walter put an arm across his shoulders.

"I felt the same when the man who killed my Alys went free," he said. "I never found the answer, either."

He turned back to Maria. Peter had now joined them.

"Your husband?" Walter repeated.

"Upstairs," she answered. "He says he's dying. He may be correct."

Walter didn't know what to make of her calm statement.

"Peter, what does she mean?" he asked.

"My uncle says he has swallowed the remains of the wolf's bane he used to kill my father. He told me he'd prefer to die quickly before he breaks his oath, whatever that means." Peter said. "I can't believe it. Father and he were friends."

"Are you sure he ate this poison?" Walter asked.

"Absolutely," Maria answered. "I saw him do it. I thought he was seasoning his bread. He gagged on it but forced it down. The coward."

Walter explained to the others. Catherine wiped her teary face with her sleeve and came over to the table.

"Is Folmar conscious?" she asked. "Should we send for a priest?"

"Catherine, he has to do more than confess to a priest," Agnes said. "He must admit that Hermann knew nothing of it. Otherwise they'll still say Hermann was a heretic, too."

"Agnes?" Catherine heard the panic in her voice. "Don't tell me you . . . he's a landless man, you know. You said you'd never . . ."

"Don't throw my words in my face, Catherine," Agnes said angrily. "I don't care if he has nothing more than a cloak and set of spurs. Mock me all you want but save him."

"I'm not mocking, dearest," Catherine said. "We'll find a way."

"Peter," Walter asked. "Is Folmar rational now? Would he talk to us? Do you think he'll exonerate your uncle Hermann?

"I . . . I don't know," Peter said. "He may be coherent, but after he came and told me what he'd done, he fell to his knees and began reciting paternosters over and over. He only stopped when he asked me to send for the *perfecta*, whatever that is."

Walter queried the others.

"I don't know what he means," Catherine said. "But there's someone here who might. Walter, you've met Abbot Bernard and you're wearing the cross he gave you. Do you think you could convince him to come to us?"

"Tell him a man's soul hangs in the balance," Edgar said.

"I'll try," Walter said. "Where is he staying?"

"With the canons of Saint Florin," Peter said. "I'll take you there."

A shadow passed across Margaret's face. Solomon looked out the window. Clouds were gathering for the first time in weeks. The air stirred the wilting roses in the garden. There would be rain before nightfall.

These thoughts rested on the surface of his mind. Everything else in him was concentrated on bringing Margaret back. He ran his fingers through what was left of her beautiful red hair. Part of it had been cut to stitch up the gash on her temple and the rest shorn to keep it from sapping her strength. The left side of her face was swollen, with purple and yellow bruises covering most of it. Both eyes had blackened when her nose had been hit.

"What kind of God lets this happen?" Solomon murmured. "What possible purpose could there be in letting good men die and a radiant child be battered like this? What lesson can there be in it?"

It wasn't the first time Solomon had asked such questions. He had seen so much injustice in his life that the need to make sense of it occupied most of his sober moments.

He gently stroked the undamaged side of Margaret's face; noticing with wonder how much more defined it was than he remembered. The child was disappearing and a woman about to emerge.

If she lived.

"In a proper world," he continued, "you would have been my daughter. You and your mother and I would have lived on a hillside far from any town. We'd have had goats and chickens and I'd never have traded farther away than the next farm. The harvest would always have been abundant and the grapes always sweet. In a proper world there would be no Edomite, Ishmaelite or Jew, but only men, women and children who care for each other, as much I care for you. Oh, Margaret, I wish so much that instead of waking again to this place, we could both wake into a proper world!"

Margaret gave a deep sighing breath and turned onto her side. Solomon's hand stayed cupped beneath her cheek.

Her eyes very slowly opened. She saw his face. Her eyes closed again and, with a lopsided smile, she fell into a natural sleep.

Solomon sat motionless, his mouth hanging open. A miracle had occurred between one breath and the next. Although not a proper world, this one suddenly seemed tolerable once again.

Everyone except his wife was up in the room where Folmar lay waiting for the first pangs that indicated his death was at hand. Maria had elected to stay and wait for Walter and Peter to return.

"At the moment I'm feeling neither wifely nor charitable," she stated. "I'd rather hasten my husband's demise than ease his suffering."

"I must admit I agree with her," Edgar whispered to Catherine. "The man is a heretic and a fratricide. He doesn't deserve to have a deathwatch."

"Well, I want to be there in case he explains why he killed his own brother," Catherine answered. "I thought it was because Folmar had discovered that Gerhardt was going to alienate the property and give it to the heretics, but now it seems that Folmar is a heretic, too, so that doesn't make sense."

Lying in a large curtained bed, Folmar appeared to be in no pain as yet. He was pale, though, and fearful. Brother Berengar bent over him, asking again if he would like the last rites. Folmar shook his head and continued his praying.

"Berengar, make him confess," Agnes insisted. "He has to admit that Hermann knew nothing of what he did."

The monk threw up his hands in exasperation.

"We've asked him several times, my lady," he said. "But all he does is repeat the Our Father and occasionally call for the *perfecta*."

Folmar made out that one word. He lifted his head.

"Did you find her?" he asked. "Is she coming? I must have the *consolamentum* before I die."

"How can he let himself die with murder on his soul?" Catherine said. "Even heretics must know that's a sin."

Berengar tried again. "At least repent of the death you caused," he implored.

"It was an accident," Folmar whined. "He wasn't supposed to die. I only wanted to save him from damnation. Once he'd agreed to marry, I knew he couldn't stay chaste. The salve was just supposed to make him too weak to copulate."

Catherine let out a sigh of satisfaction and started for the door. Agnes rounded on her.

"Just because your puzzle is complete, that doesn't mean it's over," she said. "You and Edgar can't leave now."

"Agnes, we had no such intention," Edgar said. "If you had a good look at your sister, you'd see that she's about to vomit. Would you like her to do it here?"

"Not again!" Agnes bit her tongue to keep from finishing her thought.

She stood aside and Catherine rushed out.

"See what you have to look forward to?" Edgar said. "Are you sure you want to stay here and marry?"

"I intend to manage my pregnancies much better than Catherine," Agnes answered confidently. "For one thing, I won't be spending them away from my home."

A few moments later Catherine returned, looking decidedly worse for wear than Folmar. She leaned over the bed to see him better.

"How long ago did he eat the poison?" she asked Berengar. "Shouldn't he be writhing by now, or something?"

Her stare disconcerted Folmar, who shrank into the bolsters to avoid it.

"It was about Tierce, Maria said," the monk answered. "I'm not trained in this sort of thing. I don't know how quickly poison acts."

"If he swallowed a lot on bread, I'd think he'd be at least getting twinges." Catherine was more and more suspicious. "Is there anything left in the container?"

"I'll see," Berengar left.

He returned shortly with a wooden box containing a thin layer of white powder. He gave it to Catherine, who sniffed and then tasted it.

"Catherine, don't!" Edgar and Agnes exclaimed together.

"Don't worry." Catherine threw down the box in disgust. "This is just ground horseradish root. The worst it will do is make one spend a bad night in the privy. Berengar, make him get up."

Edgar didn't wait but threw back the blanket and rolled Folmar onto the floor.

"What are you doing?" he yelled. "I'm a dying man."

Catherine held up the box. "Not from this, you're not."

Folmar took the box and tasted it. "But that's impossible," he told Brother Berengar. "Yesterday there was wolf's bane in this. I put it there, myself."

"I think you can thank your nephew for that," Berengar answered, enlightenment hitting him. "Peter came to me yesterday with a root to ask if it was safe to eat. I do know the difference between the plants and I assured him that it was. My guess is that he found your store and replaced it."

Folmar's expression was almost laughable.

"Oh no! I have to escape somehow," he wailed, trying to stand in his unbelted robe. "You can't take me to the authorities. They'll torture me to betray the others. I'll never endure it. I have to get out of here!"

He stumbled from the room with Edgar right behind him. As they reached the staircase, Edgar caught at Folmar's robe with his good hand. The material ripped as Folmar teetered and then went crashing down onto the stone floor below.

Edgar reached out his left arm to hold him but realized too late that he had nothing to grip with. He could only watch as the man tumbled.

Maria came out of the solar and stared down at the groaning shape of her husband. Then she looked a question at Berengar.

"He wasn't poisoned after all," the monk told her. "He wasn't going to die."

Maria regarded Folmar again, prodding him with her foot. He shrieked.

"Will he die now?" she asked.

Catherine knelt beside him. "His back is broken. Yes, I think he will."

Maria exhaled slowly.

"Good."

Hubert sat under an awning hastily rolled out in front of the tavern and watched his grandchildren playing in the warm rain. He adored them both, especially Edana, who so resembled his mother. He kept telling himself that being there to see them grow up was worth the constant tension of having to live in two worlds. But he felt that slowing of his heart more often lately and wondered how much time there was left. One day he feared the beats would grow farther and farther apart until they stopped altogether.

The wind had picked up and he was herding the children back to the house when his way was blocked by a man on horseback. Hubert knew both the horse and the man.

"So you've finally regained your senses, Jehan," he said. "It took you long enough. Well, good luck in Edessa. May you win honor and fame and a castle in the Holy Land."

He took each child by the hand and started to walk around, but Jehan dismounted and clapped a firm hand on his shoulder.

"I'm not going to Edessa, yet," he hissed. "First I'm going to finish what I started in Paris. You wrote this, didn't you?"

He thrust the parchment in front of Hubert.

"Ridiculous," Hubert said, trying to pull away from him.

"Don't lie. I know it's yours," Jehan said. "And I know enough more to ruin you. No man will marry Agnes when they learn what you are."

"You can't prove anything," Hubert said calmly. "You've made a fool of yourself here and no one will believe anything you say about us."

"This time they will, *Chaim*," Jehan said. "They call you that. I've heard them. Did you think I was deaf and blind, all those years you used me to guard your property and carry your messages? You may have managed to convince Bishop Stephen once of your piety, but this time I have enough to prove you're really a Jew, pretending to be one of us, spitting on the cross and defiling the sacrament like they all do. And your daughters knew of it and helped you hide your shame. Now all of you will be exposed. You'll be executed for your apostasy and your family will be impoverished."

"You're mad," Hubert said, but his voice shook.

Jehan smiled. "I may be, but I'm not wrong about this. Hebrew incantations written in your own hand will convince the bishop along with your continued association with members of the Jewish community."

"Incantations?" Hubert realized that Jehan didn't know what was written on the parchment. "Jehan, those aren't magical words; it's just the measurements for a candle holder. The only thing they'll summon up is a silversmith."

"I don't believe you," Jehan said, uncertainly. "It doesn't matter anyway. The fact that you can read them is enough."

"No it isn't, Jehan, and you know it." Hubert knew he had the upper hand now. "The bishop may listen to you, but Abbot Suger won't, and Count Thibault will support me as well. Spreading these lies will only reflect badly on you. Would you like Abbot Suger to have a word about you to King Louis? He might not want a known troublemaker among his knights."

Jehan wavered. He knew from bitter experience how much power this man had. His eyes strayed to James and Edana, who were happily splashing in the muddy puddles. Hubert followed his thoughts.

"Don't even think it," he said. "If any harm comes to my grand-children there will be no place in the world you can hide, in or out of Christendom. If you're right in your accusations, then you know that the Jews have a trading network that reaches into lands that never saw a priest. And they won't kill you, I promise. They'll see that you're captured, castrated and sold to the most vicious slave-owner in Bagdad. Believe me."

His heart was pounding slowly and his hands were icy. He prayed that he wouldn't lose consciousness again in front of the little ones.

The knife at his throat was almost welcome. It cleared his mind. But the cut didn't come.

"Do you know what it is to hate?" Jehan's mouth was close to his ear. "Do you know what it's like to see everything you've ever wanted or loved torn from you?"

"Yes," Hubert said simply.

"No you don't." The knife pressed harder against his neck. "You can't begin to. You think you've stopped me, but I will be avenged if it takes the rest of my life."

The knife slid along the side of Hubert's neck, leaving a thin trail of blood. With a strangled cry of fury, Jehan mounted his horse and rode away. Hubert watched him until he was lost among the narrow streets. It was only then that he dared to breathe again.

He went back to the tavern and called for another cup of wine. He sat thinking for a long time, with the laughter of his grandchildren filling his ears.

By the time Walter and Peter returned, Folmar had been carried to a pallet hastily made up in the hall. His moans were lower now as he grew weaker.

Catherine saw the grey robe first. She hadn't realized that the mission had been successful. She bowed her head as Abbot Bernard knelt on the floor on the other side of the pallet from her.

"Thank you for coming, my lord abbot," she said. "This man has fallen into heresy, and although he's dying, he refuses to recant and accept the viaticum. Please try to reach him. He has done terrible things, but I believe he's more foolish than wicked. I don't want him damned forever."

Bernard took Folmar's hand. It hung limply in his. He then touched the man's forehead. Folmar opened his eyes.

"I'm here to save your soul," Bernard said. "Do you understand."

There was a slight shake. "No, I must have the *consolamentum*. If I don't, I'm doomed to be reborn into this evil flesh."

Bernard rocked back on his feet. "Oh, dear, a Cathar. This will be difficult. Leave me and Brother Berengar alone with him, please.

And send to the cathedral for the holy oils, in case I succeed, so that I may give him the last rites."

Catherine did as she was told.

Agnes stopped her in the doorway.

"Will Folmar exonerate Hermann?"

"I don't know," Catherine said. "He's very weak and Abbot Bernard is mostly concerned with bringing him back to the faith before it's too late. But he's already admitted to poisoning Gerhardt. I'm sure that with his confession and Hermann's testimony of orthodoxy we can confound this Andreas so that his accusation will have no weight with the archdeacon."

Agnes rubbed the knot at the back of her neck. "I only wish it were over. Once Hermann is free then I have to prove my marriage to Gerhardt was never consummated and get an annulment. I don't want to wait any longer than necessary."

Catherine thought about reminding her that in the next room a man was dying. Surely that was of greater import than Agnes's legal entanglements. She drew breath to speak and then changed her mind. It wasn't more important to Agnes. Folmar had been the cause of all her troubles. It was only right that he pay. But knowing that justice was being served didn't make Catherine any happier.

When Peter came back with one of the canons bringing the accoutrements for the last rites, she was surprised to notice that he was wet. She hadn't noticed the rain begin.

Agnes went to the canon at once for news of Hermann.

"The archdeacon examined him this afternoon," the priest told her. "Hermann answered every point thoroughly. His case was also helped by the discovery that his accuser had fled, taking with him a silver candlestick and salt cellar."

Agnes was too happy too speak. She scandalized the canon by hugging him and then caught up to Peter and danced him around the room, which completed the canon's outrage. He found a seat as far away from her as possible and settled himself to wait.

It was nearly dark before any sound came from the room other than an occasional moan. The servants were lighting the lamps when Abbot Bernard came out, worn but exultant.

"Come with me," he told the canon. "The man has made a full

confession and wishes to die in a state of grace. *Deo gratia.* But hurry. He won't last much longer."

Catherine was almost asleep with her head on Edgar's lap. He roused her and helped her to stand.

"It's all over, *carissima*," he said. "I think it's time for us to go home."

Epilogue

Trier, Monday, 5 ides of September (September 9), 1146; 1 Elul, 4907. Rosh Hashonah, the first day of the new year.

Omnes quidem homines, dum parvuli sunt . . . constat eorum hominum fidem vel consuetudinem sequi, cum quibus conservantur et eorum maxime, quos amplius diligunt. Postquam vero adulti sunt, ut iam proprio regi possint arbitrio, non alieno, sed proprio committo iudico debent.

All people, when they are children . . . follow the faith and customs of those who care for them and especially of those whom they love more dearly. But after they are adults and are able to decide for themselves, they ought to be committed to their own judgement, not that of others.

—Peter Abelard,
Dialogue of the Christian,
the Philospher and the Jew.

*M*argaret sat up in her bed, cushioned on all sides. The swelling in her face had gone down and the bruises were starting to fade. Brother Zacharias had ordered her to remain in bed for several more weeks to allow the damage to the rest of her body to heal. Her ribs were sore and there was some pain in her back that caused the infirmarian to cluck with worry.

"I hope you plan to stay here at least until the feast of the Nativity," he said. He looked at Catherine's stomach. "Perhaps even a few months after that."

Edgar assured him that they had no intention of going home before next summer at the earliest.

"Excellent," Brother Zacharias said. "I'll be back later with a salve to help the cuts heal."

He didn't understand why everyone in the room was suddenly afflicted with a fit of coughing.

That night, after Margaret and the children were asleep, Hubert decided it was time to tell Catherine and Edgar of his plans. He knew they would object, but he had to try to make them understand.

"I won't be staying with you through the winter," he began. "Walter is letting me go with him back to Paris."

"Oh, good," Catherine said. "Would you have Samonie pack my furs and woolens to bring back with you? And ask her if she can spare Willa to take care of James and Edana during my confinement."

"I shall," Hubert said. "But I'm not returning here from Paris. I'm going south."

"South? But why?" Catherine asked. "I thought Solomon and Eliazar did the trading there now."

Hubert bolstered up his courage. He had to tell them the truth.

"Catherine, I'm not coming back," he said. "I've sent a request to be admitted to the community at Arles. I need to go where no one knows me as a Christian."

Catherine didn't understand him at first. When she did, she looked as if he had struck her.

"Oh, Father!" she breathed. "Don't do this. Please, I beg you!"

She fell to her knees in front of him and took his knees. Gently Hubert pushed her away.

"I must, my dear child," he said. "I can't live like this any longer. I love you all so much it's like a brand burning in my soul, but I am a Jew, no matter how much I try to pretend I'm not. Sooner or later, this would have come out, to your misery."

"If you'd only try." Catherine was weeping now.

Edgar put his arm around her.

"He has tried, *leoffest*," he said. "We can't force him to believe because he loves us any more than the rest of the Jews can be forced to believe through fear. Remember the abbot's sermon."

Catherine did. It had been inspiring and powerful. More than one listener had been moved to tears. Bernard's sermon had assured that no more persecutions would take place, at least in Trier. But it was easier to accept that God would choose the time for the conversion of the Jews when one of them wasn't her father.

Hubert continued. "I'm fifty-six, Catherine. I want to study the Torah as my father did. It will be ten years before I know enough to begin. I can't wait any longer. I know how this hurts you. But it would give me great solace if I could depart with your blessing."

"But what about the property in Paris?" Catherine tried. "What about your contract with Saint Denis?"

"That's one of the reasons I'm going to Paris first," Hubert said. "I intend to give you and Edgar the Paris house and all it contains. Guillaume has his castellany and it appears that Agnes will stay in Germany, so it should be yours. As for the contract, I think we should wait until Solomon is here to discuss that."

"Tomorrow, then," Edgar said. "It's late; we all should sleep on this before any more decisions are made."

"But Edgar!" Catherine exclaimed.

"In the morning," Edgar answered. "You can see how exhausted your father is."

They went to bed then, but no one slept.

When Solomon came in the next morning, Catherine accosted him at once.

"Did you know of this plan of my father's?" she greeted him.

"He mentioned something about Arles," Solomon admitted.

"Why didn't you tell me?" she wailed.

"Because I knew exactly how you'd take on," he said, grabbing a hunk of bread before she yanked the tray out of his reach. "Just as you are now."

"He wants us to tell everyone he's dead!" she said. "That means he won't be able to visit. We'll never see him again."

"Perhaps," Solomon said. "Or perhaps you'll come to Arles one day."

Catherine wasn't ready to be comforted. She sulked over her beer and barley gruel until Hubert and Edgar came down.

"Solomon!" Hubert smiled. "I've been discussing with Edgar the idea of him taking over my half of the business. What do you think of it?"

"I don't know." Solomon gave Edgar a wicked look. "He's coming to it a bit late, isn't he? You had me on the road when I was ten."

Edgar raised his eyebrows. "I imagine I can pick up enough to get started," he said. "But I haven't agreed to it, yet. I spent ten years studying the quadrivium and part of the trivium. Spending the rest of my life buying and selling seems a waste after all that."

"Edgar," Catherine said. "You were born a nobleman. You shouldn't demean yourself like this, not even for me."

"That's right," Solomon agreed. "Think what your father would say if he learned that you had become a common city merchant."

Edgar did. As he imagined his father slowly turning purple with chagrin he began to smile.

"Very well, Solomon," he said. "Consider me your new partner."

Afterword

Catherine, Edgar, Solomon and their families are all imaginary characters. However, the time they lived in and the events that affected them are real. The second crusade was led by Louis VII, who left France in May of 1147. There are a number of chronicles of the events of this expedition. By the way, they weren't called crusades at the time. The term was generally *pilgrimage*.

The preaching of the monk, Radulf, and the subsequent attacks on the Jews are also well substantiated in both Christian and Jewish sources. I invented a family for Simon of Trier, but the mode of his death is from Ephraim of Bonn, who was thirteen at the time. I doubt I could have made something like that up. Also from Ephraim is the story of the Jewish girl left for dead and rescued by a Christian laundress. I have adapted the story for my purpose because I was so impressed by the courage that the unnamed woman showed in saving the girl.

Bernard of Clairvaux, who moves in and out of Catherine and Edgar's lives, was certainly a real man who had a tremendous impact on Western Europe at this time. He preached the crusade but, more important to me, he also took responsibility for the persecution of the Jews that followed and really did travel throughout Lotharingia and Germany in an effort to stop it. Bernard was well aware of the power of words. While there is no record of him being at Trier at the time I mentioned, it was on his way to Worms where he was at the beginning of November. He did visit Trier the following year.

Nicholas and Geoffrey, Bernard's secretaries, were also real people. Nicholas will one day get his comeuppance. Geoffrey will one day become abbot of Clairvaux.

At this time, there were many popular religious movements in Europe. Some died out of their own accord, some were labeled heretical and others were incorporated peacefully into the mainstream of Christian belief. The Cathars are one of the best known. From the beginning they set themselves apart from orthodoxy and, in the next century, the crusaders were sent to destroy them.

Archbishop Albero and Heinrich of Luxembourg and Namur

were at odds with each other from about 1140 on, which caused much misery to the inhabitants of the area. I thought they would figure in this book more, but I realized that, like most of us, Catherine and Edgar are not the movers and shakers, but the moved and shaken. Therefore, the deeds of the rulers of a place are only noted as they influence my characters' lives.

Finally, anyone wishing to know more about the period and the specific sources for this book is welcome to send me a stamped, self-addressed envelope, care of the publisher. Currently, the bibliography for the first four books is on my Web site.

Once again, I thank all the readers who have followed Catherine and Edgar through the last five books. I hope that this journey is also diverting.

—Sharan